The Quisling Legacy

Rob Harris

authorHOUSE®

AuthorHouse™ UK Ltd.
500 Avebury Boulevard
Central Milton Keynes, MK9 2BE
www.authorhouse.co.uk
Phone: 08001974150

First published by AuthorHouse 10/21/2009

ISBN: 978-1-4490-2885-5 (sc)

This book is printed on acid-free paper.

Quisling – *noun /'kwɪz.lɪŋ/* a person who helps the enemy army that has taken control of his or her country; a **traitor.**

PROLOGUE

*Extract From the Private Logbook of Leutnant Günther Bauer
Commander of S-Boot 397.*

Berlin 17th April 1945

23.00 hours

My visit to the Reich Chancellery this evening took longer than anticipated, so I have only a limited time to record these few notes before we set sail.

Considering the grim atmosphere prevailing throughout the whole of the Chancellery building and for that matter the whole of Berlin, all Germany even, the Fuhrer was in quite unexpectedly high spirits. He even laughed and joked with his Staff Chiefs and only turned to a more sombre mood after requesting that all excepting myself should leave the immense room that is modestly referred to as the Fuhrer's office.

With little preamble the Fuhrer issued clear and concise instructions, informing me that I was to carry out a mission of which he termed, perhaps the most important of the whole war. An unexpected and heavy burden placed on my shoulders.

He handed me a package ordering that I carry it to Norway and deliver safely into the possession of Minister President Vidkun Quisling and only him.

The Fuhrer's parting remark to me was that the whole future of the Thousand Year Reich would depend on the success of my mission. I was to guard the package with my life.

My crew of S-Boot 397 are all on board and we sail for the port of Namsos in the North of Norway within the hour.

I only pray that I can live up to the expectations of my
Fuhrer. The honour is indeed great.

CHAPTER 1

Shrieking like a banshee, the gale force wind compressed the bright orange survival suit almost flat against Doug McCann's compact body as he worked his way cautiously down the exposed steel ladders of the rig. He struggled to maintain his balance as the huge vessel heaved and rolled beneath his feet. The relentless bombardment of the ocean waves, lashing over the hull pontoons way below him, generated massive vibrations throughout the whole of the gigantic steel structure.

It was already mid April, but the wind blowing from the north east was as cold and as cutting as ever, out there in the middle of the North Sea. The icy blast seemed to threaten it could even cut through to the very core of a man's soul. But, it was not the weather that McCann needed to fear. There was a far deadlier spectre awaiting him and his crew.

Swinging around the bottom of the ladder and coming perilously close to the rail and the promise of a seventy metre straight drop to the grey, angry sea below, McCann continued on to his destination - the drill deck - just one more level down.

Doug McCann was a stocky, tough and confident man. Despite the limitations of his build he was naturally required to be both tough and confident, because he held the most senior position on the drilling rig *Highlander*. Not an easy job. A lot rested on Doug McCann's compact, square shoulders. Officially, he was the Barge Master, although he was rarely addressed on the rig by any other title than Boss or Chief. As familiar as even such titles might have appeared to an outsider, there was always just the correct amount of respect tagged on to it - so it never bothered him. Controlled familiarity, he chose to describe it.

Regardless of the grim weather and numerous other pressing matters on his mind, Doug McCann was in fact, in a very buoyant mood. For once he would be the bearer of glad tidings, and nowadays, any good news at all was a rare commodity on a drilling rig operating in the North Sea, or anywhere else on the high seas of the world for that matter. Times were desperately bad in this business.

Finally stepping safely down onto the drill deck, McCann was greeted by a totally different kind of blast. This time he was hit by a direct and relentless explosion of sound. One even louder than the unceasing, howling gale. It was the normal clamour of oil rig activity. The rig doing its job.

Undaunted, Doug pulled himself erect, and looking around the busy work area, immediately spotted his quarry standing amid the action taking place ahead of him in the centre of the drill deck. The unmistakeable, six foot four, muscular frame of Jack Curtis, the rig's brawny American, Senior Tool-pusher, stood out like a sturdy ship's main mast.

Jack Curtis, standing with his legs set well apart, stabilising his broad frame against the erratic rolling of the rig, was fully occupied in organising his six-man gang as they operated the machinery and equipment employed in heaving up the five metre lengths of steel drill string from the depths of the ocean. Only a few hours before, these very same sections of pipe had finally served their working purpose, guiding the first, newly discovered flow of crude oil up from the vast oil field lying in the depths of the ocean far below the rig.

For the *Highlander* drilling rig and its crew, the main task had finally been completed. They had successfully achieved what they had been contracted to do. Drill for, and find oil. Job done. As soon as the last section of the drill pipe cleared the seabed, some 70 metres below, the *Highlander's* divers would go down to temporarily cap the new well. Making ready for the installation of the production platform that would soon be towed to the site and then, with its massive steel legs submerged and settled into place on the bottom, the task of retrieving and processing the new oil would commence. Then the black gold, as it once was called, in more romantic times, would be pumped on its way to the insatiable users on the shore, some 300 hundred kilometres to the west.

Jack Curtis was critically studying the scene before him. He watched intently as each solid pipe section was hoisted up and hosed down, spraying the drilling platform with a mixture of oil, mud and sand, before being finally pulled away for stacking in the racks located on the side of the deck. Ready for use on the next job. The rattle of chain and whine of motors was deafening, but at least it was the clangour of action - of progress - of work underway - much needed work and far preferable to the whine of the gale howling incessantly around them.

Doug hesitated for a second as he studied, with more than a little admiration, the big man going about his work, and waited for him to relax for a second and take a few paces back from the job. What Doug had to say was important but so was the lifting of the drill string. The sooner that was accomplished the sooner they could be on their way.

Totally unaware of Doug's presence on the drill deck, Jack Curtis continued overseeing the operation going on in front of him, and not without some pride, observed the strenuous efforts of his dedicated, hard working crew. Every single man on the team, Jack knew and treated almost like a brother. That's the way it was in this tough business. One looked out for the boys and more generally than not they looked out for you. It was a work ethic that had followed him through most of his adult life.

Studying the growing pile of steel pipes, Jack wondered when those vital sections would be needed again. They all knew it was the end of a contract and nobody had the slightest idea when or even if another one was going to come along. Times were really bad. Jack was dreading the announcement that he would soon probably have to deliver to the guys - accompanied no doubt by their signing off documents. End of contract. End of job. Start of? Well, no good answer to that question.

'Okay lads, just four more strings to pull and that's it, we're done,' Jack called out, competing with the clash of steel against steel and the persistent whine of the wind tormenting around the deck.

Doug worked his way to where Jack stood and touched him lightly on the arm.

'Nearly finished then, Jack?' Doug shouted, cupping a hand to his mouth to shield against the din.

Swinging around, the Big Yank, as he was affectionately known by all on the rig, registered his surprise at discovering the Barge Master standing at his side.

What was the Boss doing down on the drill deck in person at this time of day? Trouble of some description, Jack assumed.

'Oh. Hi Chief,' Jack yelled back above the noise. 'Yeh, just about done. Another few strings,' he said waving proudly at the rising pile of steel tubes being stacked in the frame at the side of the deck. 'So what brings the Barge Master down here? Not quite the weather for an afternoon stroll. You slumming or something?' Jack questioned, a broad grin spreading over his rugged features which easily cancelled out any note of disrespect in his voice.

'Oh no Jack, make no mistake, this is your domain. You look after things down here and I take care of things up there,' Doug said raising an arm upward, indicating the Rig Control Room towering way above them. 'And occasionally the twain shall meet.'

Not exactly the truth, because Doug McCann was responsible for every single item on the rig. Anything from a wing nut to a hundred and ten kilo tool-pusher.

'So to what exactly do we owe this honour then?' Jack asked again, but by now, he had recognised the glint in Doug McCann's eye and the smile creasing the little man's rugged face. Jack's instincts kicked in immediately. The Boss was going to brighten the day. Jack knew it for certain!

'I thought you might be interested to know, I just received a signal from the top, the head office in Aberdeen. Good news. As soon as we tie things up here, we're on our way to a new location. North of 64 degrees. Virgin oil Jack and a brand new two year contract with none other than Unicorp Oil.'

'That's tremendous news, Doug.' Jack made no attempt to disguise his elation. In fact, he barely restrained himself from encasing the Barge Master in a huge bear hug.

'North of Latitude 64 eh?' Jack raised his voice above the noise. A more serious, questioning tone this time. 'So the Norwegian Authorities are letting us go up there at last? Backing off on the environmental restrictions.'

'Looks like it. No longer out of bounds. Oil is money, Jack and money talks.'

'As soon as we get these last strings up, I'll inform the lads,' Jack said. 'There's going to be a lot of smiling faces today. No dole queues waiting for these guys this time. You've just got yourself a bunch of very happy men.'

'So, Mr Senior Tool-pusher,' Doug proclaimed in a voice of mock authority, 'when all these bits are up and washed and secured, please advise the Control Room, and we shall get those anchors lifted off the sea bed and be on our way. Just waiting on you now, Jack.'

By mid afternoon the wind had dropped to force four, a gentle breeze by North Sea standards. The waves moderating and the white horses diminished to just lightly tipped foam rollers. On the other hand the temperature was going nowhere, the needle still hovering around 4 degrees C and the unrelenting wind ensuring that it was still going to feel more like zero.

Doug McCann decided that it was safe to lift the anchors from the sea bed and just hold the rig in position using the eight four thousand horsepower, propeller thrusters. The state of the art, satellite controlled, dynamic positioning system - DP for short - would do the rest. All rested now on Big Jack and his team, finishing off, three decks below.

Jack relayed the all clear at just after three o'clock when the PA system crackled into life.

'All done and stowed on the drill deck.' Jack's broad American accent, mingling with just a hint of recently acquired Scottish brogue, emitted joyfully from the speakers and echoed around the rig for all to hear, 'So lift them up, get them out and roll them on…Rawhide… Yeehaaa.'

Doug lifted his own hand microphone and keyed the send button.

'Take it easy cowboy we're on our way.'

The fun was over - time to move the *Highlander* out.

'Stand-by main motors,' Doug ordered, waiting just a second for the affirmative acknowledgement from his Senior Engineer, Mike Holden sat at his usual position in front of the machinery control panel, just a few feet away.

'All systems ready,' Mike confirmed.

Doug gave the order. 'Full ahead all. Course 015.'

Time of departure - 15.24 hours.

Time remaining for *Highlander* and her crew - 23 hours.

CHAPTER 2

The news that *Highlander* was in trouble on the new field location travelled like wild fire to the company head office of Highland Drilling Limited in Aberdeen. The hard facts landing with a resounding thump on the desk of Phil Williams, the base Office Manager, barely three hours after *Highlander* had arrived at her new co-ordinates.

Right in the centre of a drilling sector designated Block Number 6042, was the place where *Highlander* had run into trouble. A position on the map where the bleak North Sea ends and the even bleaker Norwegian Sea begins, and continues its way in ice-cold resolution up into the hostile waters of the Arctic Ocean.

Couldn't have happened at a worse time, in a worse place, thought Phil Williams, and wasting no time at all, had radioed the Rig directly. Only to be presented with the full, dismal details from a very concerned Doug McCann. The news was bad, really bad. The last thing the company needed at this particular point in time. Not that it would have been greeted with open arms at any other time for that matter.

Phil hardly needed to remind himself that things had been running pretty much low key at the Aberdeen Head Office for some time now. Everything in the industry was on a downer, with what appeared to be no end in sight. Then a glimmer of hope had risen on the horizon, from a business point of view that is. At last, things had started to look up for the company that owned and operated twelve mobile semi-submersible, deep sea, offshore drilling rigs, in a theatre of operation that spanned practically the whole world. Concern of threatened lay-offs, asset selling and even talk of receivership had hung over the company for the past eighteen months.

Many of their fleet of floating drilling rigs were just laid-up in shallow waters around the globe. Doing nothing and earning nothing as the price of a barrel of oil scraped along the bottom of the international energy market. Put simply, it was costing more to get the stuff out from under the depths of the sea, than it did to sell it on to the less thirsty consumer market.

Then, thankfully, signs of a slight change for the better.

Marginal stability in the Middle East - if one discounted the war in Iraq, the conflict between Israel and Palestine and the fight against global terrorism and warming - had started to push the price of oil back up to a feasible commercial level.

In this rejuvenated, economic environment however, rig operators like Highland Drilling were still being forced to chase and fight for the few viable commercial contracts becoming available. But, slim though they were, the opportunities were definitely there, and the Highland Drilling Company was doing its fair share of the hard chasing, and at last, appeared to be starting to get lucky. Or so it seemed until this latest news from *Highlander*.

Phil Williams scanned the sheet with the notes he had made during his grim conversation with Doug McCann on the satellite connection, that morning.

The implications were just unthinkable. The outcome could be disastrous and this was not the least of Phil's worries. The fact that this news had still to be relayed to the Offshore Operations Manager, Jim Bowen, in his office down the corridor, had to be taken into account.

Phil was well aware that sixty year old Bowen was a devotee of the old school. The one from where many of his generation seemed to take morbid delight in persistently reminding everyone and anyone, particularly their junior associates that they had graduated from. The school of 'hard knocks' - with honours mind you. Then, as Bowen put it, had fought their way up from rags to tailored stitches, crawling over broken glass and living off their wits and the ability to suffer fools long enough to find a good excuse to sack 'em. Whoever those poor unfortunate fools might currently happen to be.

Clutching in one hand the original, official single page print-out received from the *Highlander* and in the other, his own scribbled notes, Phil headed for Bowen's office along the corridor, trying to ignore the additional fact that his boss was also a member of the fraternity that subscribed wholeheartedly to the philosophy, where appropriate, of shooting the messenger.

'Shit, Phil – what the hell's going on out there?'

Bowen had read the message from *Highlander* and was, to put it mildly, seething. His face had turned a deeper shade of red than usual as he fired the question like a personal missile at his junior manager. The implications to his own professional wellbeing, suddenly very much uppermost in his mind. Trouble like this could easily wreck what was left of Bowen's own career. Bowen wasn't alone in realising that in the cold light of day; he was long past his sell by date and just when things seemed to be improving this shit had to be hurled at his particular fan.

'What does this mean – an obstruction?' Bowen rasped, angrily stabbing a smoke yellowed finger at the document lying on the desk top in front of him. 'Have you spoken to them out there?'

'Just got off the radio phone. I contacted them as soon as I received the alert. Doug McCann explained the situation to me,' Phil was nervously building up to relate the whole sad story to his unhappy boss.

'I didn't ask if you had a nice chat with them, I asked you what the bloody obstruction is.'

'It's a wreck, a ship. Before they could even get the anchors out on the station, the rig's divers went down to carry out the usual preliminary bottom survey. Didn't take them long to discover a sunken ship of some sort right beneath them. Directly on the primary drill line in fact.'

'God almighty,' Bowen left no doubt of the seriousness of the situation – for all of them – those on the rig and on the shore. 'So, can it be moved, this derelict heap of shit?'

'Doug McCann says it's a big mass of metal but he thinks it may be possible to shift it.'

'So what's everybody waiting for? Shift the god damned thing for Christ's sake.'

'Apparently, it's not going to be so easy.' Things were not getting any easier for Phil Williams either; a layer of sweat already coated his face and a single bead had succeeded in making a tortuous trail down as far as his shirt collar.

'Tell me,' demanded Bowen.

'The Norwegian Maritime Directorate wants to investigate the matter.'

'Bloody investigate? I thought we'd already got the all clear from the Norwegian Authorities to test drill up on that location.'

'Apparently they had no knowledge of any obstruction anywhere in that area. Certainly no navigational hazard of any significance had been posted. Charts are all clear.'

'So how do they propose to fix it?'

'They want to survey the site and then arrange for a floating heavy lift vessel to come in and remove the wreck.'

'Well they'd better pull their fingers out. If we don't start drilling within forty-eight hours our contract with Unicorp Oil is out the fucking window. And somebody is going to pay for this - dearly!'

CHAPTER 3

It was already getting light at 4am in the port of Stavanger on the west coast of Norway, when a Volvo swung into the deserted car park outside the offices of the Norwegian Maritime Authority.

The driver was Nils Olsen, a senior official of the organisation that operated out of the building and totally controlled all marine activity in the seas around the seemingly endless 22,000 kilometre long coastline of Norway.

What brought Nils Olsen to the offices at this ungodly hour, had very much to do with what was currently taking place out in those same deep waters, and the disastrous consequences that seemed destined to result.

Olsen left the car, forgetting to lock it and walked hurriedly to the main office entrance where, with trembling fingers, he punched in his security pass code and entered the building.

Two minutes later he was at his desk on the vacated third floor. Pushing aside a pile of documents to gain access to the telephone, and with fingers still shaking, he hit the keys and waited. The usual clicking sounds of the transmission took a few seconds before contact was made, and he heard the ringing at the other end, and then somebody picked up.

'Ja?' the voice was German - the accent rasping and heavy with interrupted sleep.

'Otto, it's me Nils. There's trouble...' Olsen spoke in English the formal language agreed to be used by the group.

'It is most foolish of you to make contact like this, Olsen, outside the approved procedures.'

Ignoring the rebuke, and despite the rapid pounding of his heart inside his chest and the uncontrolled gasps for air, Olsen carried on. It sounded to the German at the other end as if Olsen was recovering from the effects of a hundred-metre dash.

'I know this is not the agreed procedure but it is important.' Another intake of breath then he blurted it out. 'A rig has gone up to drill in block 6204.'

The line remained silent.

'Otto, did you hear what I said?'

Further seconds passed before Otto Klensch replied.

'Ja, ja. I hear you, but I just do not know how this can possibly be? It was our clear understanding that the Norwegian Oil Directorate and the Maritime Authority would veto all requests to drill for oil above the 62nd Parallel. All that, protect the environment nonsense that nevertheless served our purpose perfectly. It was you Nils who was supposed to be in a position to ensure that this scenario could never happen. Not before we had finished up there anyway.'

'I know, Otto,' the phone in Olsen's damp palm shook uncontrollably. 'And I am afraid that's not all.'

'Tell me.'

'They've found the ship. They were positioned to drill right above it. Their divers discovered her, Otto.'

'Mein Gott! Divers? Divers were down there? You fool Olsen. You must terminate this operation at once.'

'It's too late Otto. It is out of my hands.'

Another long silence dragged by before Otto Klensch growled one last time into the phone.

'Well Nils, it's not out of my hands.'

Nils Olsen flinched as he heard the receiver at the other end, clatter back into its cradle.

CHAPTER 4

At Block 6204 in the Norwegian Sea, daybreak brought a temporary respite in the weather. The wind dropped, and even the sun deemed to spread a little of its light and warmth over the grey expanse of ocean.

Conditions would have been ideal for drilling. No such luck for Doug McCann and his crew though.

Before they could even secure the rig by letting out the eight massive anchors, they had to be assured that the wreck lying in the mud some 70 metres beneath them on the seabed, although of no immediate threat, would soon be moved out of their way.

Consequently, the whole Rig was strangely silent, apart from the dull rumble of the diesel generators deep below decks and the normal sounds of the crew moving around inside the accommodation block. Stark contrast indeed to the usual racket generated by the combined everyday activities of a drilling rig running in full operation.

The silence boded well for nobody.

High up in the Control Room however, things appeared to be going on much as normal. The guys in the vessel's nerve centre still had the crucial task of maintaining the stability and positioning of the Rig. Holding the massive floating structure in position with the powerful propulsion motors coupled to the huge five bladed bronze propellers.

It was now a waiting game.

On to this scene Jack Curtis lumbered. The big fellow was, unusually for him, unoccupied. At this early stage in any contract, Jack and his team of Roughnecks would have already sunk a dozen or more lengths of drill string, deep into the seabed. Signalling the preliminary phase of the quest for oil. But despite the overshadowing problem and having to put everything on hold, Jack was in quite high spirits. In addition to the new contract, the big man had a more personal reason for feeling good.

'Morning all,' he greeted Doug and his Control Room brigade. 'Nice day for a vacation on a five star island in the Norwegian Sea.'

'Very funny, Jack,' snapped Engineer Mike Holden from his control panel position. Mike was just as busy as always. He carried the full responsibility for the smooth running of all the machinery on the rig, whether they were in the process of drilling or not. 'You might be on holiday, Jack,' the Engineer continued, a slight hint of humour taking the edge out of his initial response. Like most of the crew, he got on well with the big Yank. 'But some of us have still got work to do.'

'Oh, poor you,' Jack replied, landing a friendly pat on the Engineer's shoulder, as he passed by, heading across the deck to where Doug McCann was peering out through the wide front screen windows.

'How's it going, Chief?'

'Not so good Jack. We've got a fair old obstruction under us.' Doug spoke without taking his eyes off the desolate expanse of grey sea outside, extending away into the light mist and beyond to the distant horizon. 'I can't see you starting any drilling until we get the damn thing shifted. And the worst of it is they're going berserk back at HQ in Aberdeen.'

'I'll bet they are,' Jack agreed grimly. 'So what's the plan?'

Doug turned from the window to face his Senior Toolpusher.

'The Norwegian Authorities are sending us some assistance. A Diving Support Vessel, with heavy lift capability. A really big bastard by all accounts. She's called the *Sea Hawk*."

'Sounds good. So what's this big bastard going to do when she gets up here?' Jack queried.

'Apparently, the plan is to break the wreck up into small manageable pieces and then lift the bits out of our way.'

'And how do they propose to acquire these small manageable pieces?'Jack enquired again, this time a certain note of scepticism creeping into his voice.

'Big bang theory.'

'You mean blow the thing up? Jesus, what about us?'

'It would appear that we will be expected to pull off location, a safe distance.'

'I suppose they know what they're doing,' Jack muttered, still not totally convinced. Jack Curtis knew a thing or two about explosives. 'How long is all this supposed to take, anyway? I was hoping to get a few strings down before I go on leave. I'm off on Wednesday you know. As long as the weather stays calm enough for the chopper to fly out here and back, that is. Pete Simmons is on roster. He's coming out to relieve me. This is one trip home that I am afraid I just can't miss, Chief.'

Doug raised his eyebrows in surprise, for an instant. Then a broad grin of understanding wrinkled across his features. He remembered precisely what the big fellow was referring to.

'Oh yes, I'd almost forgotten. You're about to become a new Daddy. How is Jean? When's the big day?'

'It's not a wedding, Chief. The parents don't actually fix the date in these cases, you know.' Jack issued a friendly reprimand. 'Any time now. She's fine though. Moves around a bit like a barge in full ballast but no, everything's going good. We just want it to hurry up and happen.'

'I am sure you do, Jack. If there's anything I can do to help...'

'Actually, I would like to get in a radio telephone call to the mainland. See how Jeanie's doing.'

'No problem at all, Jack. Any time you're ready. You can make the call from up here.' Doug gestured to the radio communications panel across the control space.

Before Jack could express his thanks, he was interrupted by the voice of one of the junior Marine Officers calling across the bridge deck.

'Offshore Supply Boat approaching, Boss.'

Forgetting Jack for the moment, Doug turned back to the window and raised his binoculars.

'God that was quick work. I wasn't expecting them for another couple of hours.'

The time - 11.30 hours.

Time remaining for *Highlander* - 3 hours.

CHAPTER 5

The vessel cutting at full speed through the cold grey waters of the Norwegian Sea, heading towards the rig *Highlander* was sleek and fast. But in fact, the *Panther*, as the name painted on her bow proclaimed, did not look very much like the sort of heavy lift ship that Doug McCann had been expecting to come to *Highlander's* assistance.

Initially, he even doubted that the sophisticated craft, with virtually the whole superstructure painted black - a most unusual combination - and the streamlined, almost artistic lines, could possibly be the vessel sent to deal with the removal of a sunken wreck? But anyway she was steering straight for *Highlander* and her intention was soon confirmed as Doug's radio crackled into life.

'Diving Support Vessel, *Panther* to Drilling Rig Highlander – over'

Doug lifted his hand set.

'This is Highlander. Welcome *Panther*, we have been expecting a Diving Support vessel but we thought it was going to be the *Sea Hawk*.'

Over on the Bridge of the approaching *Panther*, the First Officer had been thrown into something of a dilemma. He looked questioningly across at his Captain who quickly reached to relieve him of the microphone and the responsibility of having to reply to the unexpected query from the rig.

'This is the Captain of the *Panther*. Yes Sir, the Sea Hawk was unable to clear her previous contract in time. So a slight change of plan. Don't worry we can do the job.'

Doug's response came back immediately.

'Of course Captain, no offence intended.'

'None taken, Sir. But we need to get our divers down to the wreck as soon as possible. I would also appreciate if you could pull off station at least two kilometres.'

Again a quick response from Highlander.

'Affirmative *Panther*. We are on DP at present, anchors still up. We can move immediately. Two klicks, though? Rather a long way?'

Panther's Captain made an effort to stem the irritation in his voice.

'We intend to employ very high explosives, Sir. As you know, underwater pressure waves can be quite severe. Don't want to damage your hull in any way.'

'Understood *Panther*.' Doug's reply crackled back across the airwaves.

'Just one last request, Sir.' *Panther's* Captain was not finished. 'When you have completed re-locating, I would appreciate it if my divers could come aboard *Highlander* before we commence operations. We need to study your proposed anchor spread and charts of the area and I think it would be a good idea to assemble your people together in a suitable location for briefing?'

'No problem, Captain.'

'Thank you *Highlander*. We'll get started then. Over and out.' *Panther's* Captain terminated the conversation and thrust the microphone back into the hands of his First Officer. 'So let's get on with it, shall we? Give them the go-ahead down there.'

Back on Highlander, Doug McCann was also getting things moving.

'Right, you heard the man. We need to pull off station.'

Engineer Mike Holden tapped a sequence of commands into his engine control computer, and immediately the steady throb of the propulsion motors began to vibrate through the steel structure of the rig.

'All ahead slow,' Doug McCann commanded.

Time - 13.30 hours.
Time remaining - One hour.

CHAPTER 6

It took *Highlander* less than half an hour to pull off the original location and take up her new position, just over two kilometres distance from where they had discovered the wreck.

As soon as she was in place, Doug radioed the *Panther* and gave them the all clear to proceed.

Within less than five minutes of his signal, Doug spotted two large, high speed, inflatable craft heading towards his rig. Each carrying four men, all kitted-out with the latest, sophisticated diving gear. They looked as if they knew what they were about, but Doug was surprised at the number of divers bunched together in each boat.

'Looks like they are sending an invasion force,' Doug muttered to himself, and then turned to issue an order to a member of his Control Room team.

'Rodgers, can you get down there and make a visual on the pontoons and ladders. Make sure they are all clear for our visitors to come aboard. We don't want any of our friends to unintentionally tumble off into the drink. Then stick around until they reach the main deck and show them up to the Heli-Room.'

There was no need for Doug to explain to those around him that the visitors were going to have to climb nearly 40 meters from the pontoons up to the main deck of the rig. And Doug McCann literally didn't want any slip-ups.

Way below, the divers had arrived on the scene and cutting the powerful outboard engines, quickly secured their boats to the rig's starboard pontoon. All but one man scrambled out of the boats and up onto the flat steel top.

The loner was about to execute his own separate and quite specific orders.

Fixing his breathing mouthpiece firmly in place, the diver grabbed a heavy sling bag and slipped smoothly into the water and disappeared beneath the dark waves.

The others in the team commenced their climb up the winding steel ladders to the rig's main deck.

With all the activity going on around him, nobody in the Control Room was paying much attention to Big Jack Curtis. He was tucked well out of the way, partially hidden from view, at the side of one of the large control panels. He had the ship-to-shore radio telephone receiver pressed firmly to his ear as he communicated with his wife Jean on the other end of the line, in Aberdeen.

'As long as you feel OK, Jeanie, that's the most important. I'll be home on Thursday if you can just manage till then… Yes; I know you always manage but…'

Seven hundred and fifty kilometres to the South West, Jean Curtis mildly rebuked her husband.

'Jack will you stop going on like an old woman? I'm supposed to play that role in this family.'

'Sorry, Darling. It's just I do worry about you when I'm away.'

In the background, Jack could hear Doug McCann rallying his crew.

'They're here lads,' Doug advised everyone, watching the team of divers appear one behind the other up through the access opening onto the main deck. He wondered why the whole team had to make the journey en masse, so to speak. Just to look at some charts and give a safety briefing.

Doug shrugged and raised the microphone to his lips again.

'Attention everybody. This is the Barge Master. As you all know we are unable to commence drilling due to an obstruction on the sea bed. The thing is directly on our drilling line…'

Back in Aberdeen, Jean Curtis could hear Doug's voice echoing over the PA system in the background.

'What's that, Jack? What's going on there?'

'It's alright, Jeannie. Just the Boss talking to the crew over the Public Address system.' Jack played it down. The last thing he wanted was to get Jeannie all het up. 'We've got a wreck or something on the sea bed just below us. We can't start drilling until they've cleared it out of the way.'

'Wreck?' a note of concern crept into Jean's voice.

'Nothing to worry about. We've got a big Diving Support vessel called the *Panther* alongside. Come to sort the problem out for us.'

'So we require all hands...' Doug continued with his instructions to the Crew over the public address system, '...all hands requested to assemble in the Helicopter Transfer Room for an update on the situation, and a run-through of safety procedures. This exercise will only take a few minutes. So everybody please report immediately. That's it.'

From every corner of the Rig, men ceased what they were doing and headed up to the Heli-Room. The space dedicated as a transit waiting area. Some of the lads had christened it *the Happy-Sad Lounge*. It was here crewmembers gathered to await the arrival of the helicopters that would rapidly whisk them back to the mainland and their waiting families and friends, for the proverbial well-earned break. Unfortunately, things were countered by the not quite so enthusiastic, incoming personnel, going through the arrival drill – hence the dual name. The room was also employed for instruction and lecture sessions on safety procedures. It was spacious enough and ideal to accommodate a large number of bodies for briefings, just like this.

Down on the main deck, Rodgers greeted the Divers as they scrambled up the last few steps of the ladder, and trooped through the hatchway onto the main deck. It was quite a hike from the pontoons to this level, but even humping heavy rucksacks, the visitors displayed no signs of physical discomfort. Rodgers beckoned, and wondering why these guys hadn't left their back packs down below, led the way up to the Heli-Room.

In the Bridge Control Room, Doug McCann rallied his team.

'Okay guys, everybody to the Heli-Room except Davies. You hold the fort here, son. This shouldn't take long. You too, Jack, chop-chop.'

Jack Curtis was still occupied talking to his wife.

'Give me just two seconds, Chief.'

'Okay, Jack but wrap it up quickly, please.' Doug ordered, at the same time herding the other guys ahead of him, out through the Control Room door.

In Aberdeen, Jean was still trying to make out what was happening out there on her husband's rig.

'What is going on, Jack? I can tell there's something wrong?' she begged, a clear note of concern in her voice, now.

'No, Jeanie - really nothing to worry about. They're calling for a drill, that's all. I've got to make tracks in a minute. Now if there is anything you need, just get it - your Mother will help you.'

There you go again Jack. Trying to teach your Granny to suck eggs,' Jeannie reprimanded.

'Hey, that's a new one. You Brits have got some quaint expressions, you know.'

One level down, the Heli-Room was filling up. Practically full to capacity with the noisy Rig Crew members, all closely packed into the space.

Doug and his boys arrived just as the *Panther* divers lumbered up from the main deck. Each man looking quite out of place, kitted in full diving gear. Everything except flippers that is. Obviously not the most practical form of footwear for climbing up 40 metres of open, steel stairway.

The guy at the head of the group held out his hand. It struck Doug as rather odd that he hadn't even bothered to remove his waterproof gloves. These divers obviously intended to waste as little time as necessary up here on the rig.

The diver introduced himself.

'Smit, Lead Diver, *Panther*, Sir,' the greeting was curt and impersonal.

Doug thought he detected a slight foreign accent, but couldn't place the exact origin.

'Doug McCann. I am the Barge Master.'

'May we get started, Sir?' The Lead Diver was polite but decidedly uninterested in extending the niceties.

Doug pointed to a small raised lectern stand on the far side of the Heli-Room - the usual position from which to deliver information and instructions to an assembled audience.

The Lead Diver moved across to the stand as his men stationed themselves in various positions around the edge of the room. He raised a hand and the room quickly fell silent. The sooner this was over, the rig crew could get back to what they had been doing, and let this gang get on with their job.

'Gentlemen, I promise you this will take no more than a few seconds,' the Lead Diver said, speaking so quietly that those men at the back craned forward to listen. One voice in the crowd even called out, 'Speak up a bit, mate.'

Ignoring the request, the Lead Diver leaned over to reach for the rucksack that he had placed on the floor at his feet. He calmly extracted a machine pistol, raised it and commenced firing into the mass of unsuspecting men in front of him. On cue and simultaneously he was joined by each of his men, who had also retrieved their weapons, and started to spray death to every corner of the room. Nobody stood a chance.

'What the...' was all Doug McCann could utter before stepping forward into a hail of bullets directed at him from one of the divers covering that sector of the room. Doug McCann died on the floor of the Heli-Room alongside his crew. None of them ever really knowing what had happened or why. It was all over in seconds.

The sound of the firing reached the Bridge Control Room.

'What the hell is that?' Jack Curtis shouted, instinctively covering the phone mouthpiece with his big palm, blocking the noise from reaching his wife's ears.

'Get yourself down there, Davies and see what's going on,' Jack shouted at the young man who'd been left in charge. Then into the telephone, 'Hold on a minute Jeannie…there's some commotion going on here.'

Davies never made it to the door. One of the *Panther* divers appeared, levelled a machine pistol and fired a short but lethal burst into the young man's chest.

Jack instinctively pulled back searching for cover behind the control cabinet he had been propped against.

'My God, Jeanie,' he blurted into the phone, 'there's a madman in here with a bloody gun.'

Those were Jack Curtis's last words. The killer diver came into view around the corner of the console and fired at the Big Yank. Jack fell instantly to the deck, letting the phone slip from his grasp, leaving it to swing uselessly on its cable. Jack Curtis no longer heard the shrieks of his wife coming from the earpiece.

Stepping over Jack's body, the killer grabbed the handset and ripped the cable from the cabinet, letting it drop to the deck where it lay, as still and lifeless as the big man lying sprawled alongside it.

More than seven hundred kilometres away, Jeannie continued shouting into the dead phone. 'Jack, Jack what's going on? What's happened? Are you alright Jack?' But the line was dead and so was her husband.

Time - 14.00 hours. Time left - Zero

CHAPTER 7

The *Panther* Execution Team had finished their gruesome task in the Heli-Room. A couple of them moved through the bloodied bodies, prodding here and there with the muzzles of their guns, looking for signs of life. Nobody moved. They were all dead.

The Lead Diver keyed his radio.

'Is everybody clear?'

One by one the responses came in from around the rig.

'Two all clear.'

'Three, clear.'

Impatiently the Lead Diver keyed again.

'One, do you copy?'

Some forty metres below Diver Number One was heaving himself out of the water, up onto the rig pontoon. Reaching for his hand set, he spoke into the mouth piece.

'One. All charges set.'

'OK,' with a nod of satisfaction the Lead Diver gave the order for his men to depart the scene. 'Let's go.'

Ten minutes later, approaching the *Panther*, the Lead Diver in the first boat waved a signal to the ship's Bridge.

A few seconds after that, a massive series of explosions took place in the depths of the sea below *Highlander*. Travelling shock waves rattled at the *Panther's* steel hull as huge plumes of water shot metres up into the air, and within a few more seconds, the Rig began to list and settle slowly into the sea.

Satisfied with the result, the *Panther's* Captain issued one final order. 'Engines Full Ahead. We are finished here.'

CHAPTER 8

If somebody didn't act pretty soon, the little bastard was going to die!

I was well aware that that somebody would inevitably have to be me. But I didn't have to convince myself it would be more out of duty than compassion.

This young kid, I call him a kid although he was twenty years of age, had turned out to be nothing but a pain since he'd joined the course. His name was Edwards, Mark Edwards and he had got himself into this current predicament while taking part in a safety training course I was running for him and seven other young men, all around his age and all bent on qualifying to work professionally offshore.

Arriving just a few days earlier, the group had been placed in my hands.

My job?

To put them through a crash safety course. These guys had to know this stuff if they were going to survive out there working on the rigs and ships, very often under perilous conditions, and in some of the most hostile oceans and seas of the world.

For me, this was a part time exercise. My full time occupation being dedicated to the Offshore Department of the Health and Safety Executive - Marine Division, based in Aberdeen. But it wasn't unusual for me to be now and then seconded to one of Aberdeen's Safety Training establishments. Thankfully, a career in the Special Boat Service, although cut prematurely short, for reasons I preferred not to talk about, provided me with the necessary qualifications and experience to work for the HSE, and at the same time, provide training to personnel wanting to make a career in the marine and offshore industries.

So that's what I did. It was a living. One of the good things about it all was, for me that is, there were no weapons of any kind involved.

Anyway, the current training programme, although getting off to a fine start, had now deteriorated into what only could be termed, a class A disaster. Putting it bluntly, one of my trainees along with a professional diver was about to drown in five meters of cold, salt water. Despite the implementation of all reasonable safety practices and procedures, I now had something of a desperate situation on my hands.

Mark Edwards was trapped in the hull of an upturned, mock-up helicopter. If he had carried out the instructions he'd been given, he would be out and safely on the surface by now, and so would Dave Steel my good friend and support diver, who was wedged unconscious in the escape exit of the submerged helicopter.

Thirty minutes earlier Mark Edwards, together with seven other team mates had stepped into the indoor training tank. In this somewhat claustrophobic, steel box enclosure, a huge pool had been constructed. Designed to take a hundred thousand gallons of ice cold sea water, it was the venue for men and women where, to coin a phrase, they would be thrown in the deep end. Very deep, and not to mention, very cold. Simulation being the key word.

On arrival at the 'Big Tank', as it was more commonly known in the business, the group of trainees had been in high spirits. Especially the loud mouthed Mark Edwards. It irritated me to witness the loutish behaviour of this character. He really held a high opinion of himself; while at the same time exhibiting a total disregard for any form of authority. This kid always insisted in addressing me as Steve, as if we had been long time buddies. I don't stand on too much ceremony, but a certain level of respect between student and tutor usually establishes a good working relationship. All the other members of the group addressed me as Mr Craig, a couple of them even using Sir now and then.

Edwards was quite short, about five four - maybe one of the key reasons he needed to act the big shot. Dark haired, good looking, and he knew it. What was not immediately apparent was that, despite his loud mouthed bravado, he was, underneath it all, a total coward. Oh, he was smart enough alright, in fact you could say he was above average intelligence. He probably could rattle off his own IQ to the nearest unit and there was no doubt, in the classroom he excelled. Mark Edwards's written stuff put him top of the class and he knew that too. On paper he was the best but in action he turned out to be the worst - as the preceding twenty minutes had already proved.

I spotted the change in Edwards a few seconds after I'd outlined the nature of the test the group was about to undergo.

'That contraption at the other end of the pool,' I'd explained to the eight young men in the class, each now fitted out in a bulky, Hi-Vis Orange coloured, waterproofed suit, 'is a full scale mock up of a Sikorsky 76 Helicopter. As used to shuttle crews out and back to Rigs around the world.' They all turned to look. 'In fact,' I continued, 'this one was once the real thing - we've just taken a few redundant bits off.'

It was plain for them to see, there were no longer rotor blades or a tail section of any kind attached.

'We have just added a few bits and pieces. Mainly the gantry mechanism that's designed to turn the whole thing upside-down.'

It was at this point, and for the first time, I caught the panic stricken look on Mark Edwards's face. He was standing with the others, up to his waist in cold seawater in the shallow end of the big pool. What I observed was sheer terror. Suddenly it had dawned on the mouthy kid that this was the point in the proceedings where the theory ended and the practical began. I watched his expression as I continued to outline what was required for the exercise, and frankly I held little sympathy for him.

'As a team, you will swim the length of the bath to the Helicopter,' I explained. My eyes still focused on Mark Edwards. 'You are expected to continue to work as a team and assist each other to get yourselves up and into the passenger cabin, take up your seats and secure your belts. Last man in closes the main door.'

If they thought that was it, they were mistaken.

'You will get 10 seconds after that door closes,' I continued. 'Then we are going to rotate the helicopter 180 degrees and lower it until it is fully submerged upside down in the water. All you guys have to do is to get out.'

No one thought that it was a laughing matter anymore. Least of all Mark Edwards. But, as punishing as it might turn out to be, this was anything but a punishment. It was a vital, first hand demonstration of the reality that any or all of them could be faced with out in the real world, in the real sea, on a real job and at any time.

'Alright, take it easy,' I said, preparing them for some words of consolation. 'We do not intend to leave you completely on your own down there.'

The combined sigh of relief from the group was actually quite audible; even before they knew what I was about to say. I guess they felt that any small consolation whatsoever was sure to be a bonus.

I continued.

'You will notice, standing up there by the Helicopter, a gentleman kitted out in full diving gear, including breathing apparatus,' I said, and waited while they all turned to see the person I was referring to. 'Gentleman, that is Mr David Steel, you can call him Dave. Dave is going to watch over you. Anybody needing a bit of help will get it - from Dave.'

'Is there a time constraint on this exercise, Sir?' It was a thickset lad, one of the slower members of the group, named Billy Williams, asking the question.

I said. 'Yes, Williams. Get out before you drown.' Some of the others thought that quite funny and chuckled but I wasn't pulling any punches. If they did ever find themselves in a similar situation, they certainly would not have the luxury of preparing for the event in advance, like this.

'Right, let's get this show on the road.' I held my arm aloft, nodded to Dave who slipped easily into the water and swam to a position close to the Helicopter. Then I gave the order for the test to commence.

'Exercise starts now,' I called out, at the same time pressing the timer button on the stop watch.

In unison, the group turned and struck out up the tank towards the waiting Helicopter test rig.

At a small, elevated control position overlooking the scene, another of my colleagues, engineer Tom Wilson stood patiently waiting. When the time came, he would operate the mechanism designed to rotate the Helicopter housing.

The first part of the exercise went off reasonably well. I was even pleasantly surprised to note the determination of Edwards. There was little sign of the earlier panic as he hauled himself up and into the Helicopter cabin, when it was his turn. Although his face still remained as white as a ghost. Maybe he was just feeling the cold. But still, I noticed he couldn't resist the temptation to elbow one of his colleagues, a slight fellow named Lockley, out of his path as he pushed to get inside the cabin. It crossed my mind, he probably was going to grab a pole position, near the escape door and I was right. The first come first served principle, came into play.

With the last man in and the door secured, I clicked my stopwatch again, to automatically record the time of the first phase, and then restarted it as the second phase commenced. Simultaneously, I waved the go ahead to Tom and watched as he manipulated the levers on the panel in front of him. There was a high whine as the electric winch motors kicked into life, and instantaneously, the Helicopter housing began, first to rotate, and then started to lower into the water.

Through the windows of the chopper I could see the grim faces of some of the group. Just one stood out of course - Mark Edwards's. I noticed his face had taken on a sort of zombie like grimace, and his eyes stared unseeing into space as the unit began to disappear from view. For a fleeting second, I almost felt sorry for him.

From that point on, things began to go wrong. First indication of a problem was when the lights in the hall flickered a couple of times, to the accompaniment of an ominous buzzing sound from the main switchbox mounted up high on the wall. Then, in an instant, all power failed completely, leaving the space illuminated only by the dull rays coming through the roof skylights. In itself, no big deal. There was sufficient light to carry out the exercise.

'All the power is off. It's the motors, they sometimes overload the damn fuse breakers,' Tom shouted from his platform. 'I won't be able to lift the rig until I fix it.'

'Doesn't matter,' I called back as the first guy broke the surface above the upturned Helicopter. 'We just need to get them all out. Shouldn't need any power for that. They're already on their way up.'

One by one the trainees began to surface. Each of them appearing in turn. Heads popping above water, with looks on most faces, of something between relief and victory. But not one wasted any time in striking out for the safety of the poolside.

I was expecting to see Edwards coming up fairly early. After all, he had secured a convenient seat near the escape door. I took it for granted that he would want to be out of there as soon as possible. Not until the fifth lad came up did I begin to have reservations. When number six appeared I definitely knew there was something horribly wrong. The next one up, the last but one, was not Edwards either, but the cumbersome Billy Williams and the look of panic on his face confirmed my worst fears.

'It's Edwards!' Williams shouted, treading water and gasping for air. 'He can't seem to move down there. He's paralysed or something! He won't budge from his seat. I tried to pull him...' Williams shook his head.

Dave, unaware what was going on until that moment, didn't hang on another second. He dropped under the water immediately. I looked at the stopwatch - nearly two minutes had elapsed since we lowered the helicopter. I knew we had to work quickly. What I didn't know, was what the hell was taking place at that very moment, deep in the pool and inside that framework of the mocked up helicopter.

Dave had reached the paralysed Edwards and had tried to grab hold of the petrified lad. Intending to physically hoist him out of the confined space. Then it appears that Edwards had just gone totally berserk. Kicking and punching, he attempted to ward off Dave. In an irrational but desperate effort to release himself from Dave's hold, Edwards had ripped the mouthpiece out of the diver's mouth. In trying to retrieve his life line, Dave's head had violently impacted the edge of the helicopter escape opening. Stunned, Dave Steel had blacked out.

At that point, up on the surface, I was faced with the question. Who's going to save the little bastard Edwards from drowning? But now there were two people needing assistance. Dave should have brought Edwards up by now.

The stopwatch registered two minutes and 15 seconds, and counting. I looked up questioningly at Tom, who was now perched on a stepladder, delving the internals of the switchbox. My expression asked if he could get the power back on in time to lift the rig. He just shook his head. So, there was no choice. I had to go in, immediately.

Apart from kicking off my shoes I wasted no more time in stripping off any of my gear, and dived, fully clothed, into the pool. I hit the surface, and for a second was almost paralysed as the freezing water engulfed me. The sudden shock almost causing me to pass out. But thanks to some intensive training that had been driven into me, time and time again, not so many years back, I managed to gain control of my body. I gulped in as much air as I could without hyperventilating, and dived below the surface of the water.

Of course, lacking the illumination from the large spots positioned above the pool, the depths were dim and murky. The small amount of light filtering down from the roof skylights above the pool did little to help lighten things up. I pulled deeper towards the helicopter and reached the exit door, only to find Dave Steel's bulky frame jammed in the opening. He was still unconscious, his air pipe dangling uselessly down the front of his suit. Grabbing the mouthpiece I took a quick lungful of air myself and then thrust it back between Dave's slack lips. Almost instinctively, his mouth closed around the rubber and he took in a huge charge of air. He came to his senses, but I could see he was still suffering from the effects of the blow to his head. Pulling him out of the doorway, I pushed forward and sent him, unresisting, on his way to the surface.

Forcing myself to ignore the pain beginning to building up in my own lungs, I swung my arms about in the vicinity where I knew Edwards had been sitting. Sure enough he was there. I didn't know if he was still alive or not. I unbuckled his seat belt and dragged his limp body to the door and virtually kicked him through it. Using my feet to push him, I produced the required leverage with my arms holding onto the cabin metal framework. Once through the opening and clear of the helicopter shell, there was sufficient buoyancy, in his suit to take Edwards upwards. I followed, and broke the surface just ahead of him, and yanked him up until his head was clear of the water.

There were more than enough hands to pull us both from the tank. Dave, by now fully recovered and divested of his cumbersome diving equipment, quickly attended to Edwards and started the resuscitation procedure. Just after a few thrusts on his chest, Edwards coughed up a load of salt water and began to move. He was going to be just fine.

An hour or so later, I was in the Changing Room towelling my hair dry. The trainees were noisily getting showered and dressed around me. The main topic of conversation was, of course, the previous events.

'Well done, Mr Craig, Sir,' Billy Williams called across to me.

That set the others off clapping and whistling and shouting words of praise. Actually I felt quite good about it all. I was more than satisfied that my actions had prevented a tragic accident taking place. There was little doubt that, if I had not gone in when I did, both Dave and Edwards would probably not have made it out alive.

The noise abated and the room fell silent as Edwards himself returned from the shower room. He still maintained the arrogant swagger as he tucked his towel around his waist and walked towards me.

'I just want to say thanks for your help Steve. I probably would have managed on my own if that diver guy hadn't knocked himself out and blocked the exit. Still…'

I was spared the response and the decision of whether or not to punch the guy. But, for the worst possible reason.

'Hey guys, there's been an accident!' Lockley was shouting as he burst into the changing room. He'd gone out a few minutes earlier to buy some cigarettes. 'A Drilling Rig called *Highlander* has blown up in the North Sea. It's on the news!'

CHAPTER 9

By the time I reached the Administration Office of the Aberdeen Safety Training School, up on the second floor of the adjacent building to the test tank, a gang of office staff was already clustered around the TV set. All staring in morbid fascination at the pictures flashing across the screen. Devastating scenes of what was left of *Highlander*. I could just make out a section of the accommodation housing and the drill platform with its latticed stack, protruding up at an angle out of the relatively calm surface of the sea. The gruesome shots and the clinical running commentary sent a chill running through my spine.

'The *Highlander* Drilling Rig is still just afloat.'

The well modulated and low keyed voice of the commentator, only seemed to add more horror to an already horrific series of pictures being relayed back from the cockpit of a helicopter circling above the stricken rig.

'But we have just been informed,' the commentator continued, 'that it can only be a matter of minutes before *Highlander* sinks completely.'

My blood turned cold as I moved in closer to the set. Like everyone else present, shocked at what I could make out from the pictures being displayed on the screen. The camera zoomed in, and I could see more detail of the Rig. She was tilted over at an extreme angle. It was clear she would not remain afloat for more than a few more minutes. It was also obvious that she had sustained severe underwater damage. I could picture the tons of water spilling into the huge ballast and fuel tanks inside the pontoons and the support columns.

'The actual cause of the explosion is a total mystery at the present time.' The voice of the commentator went on, as the aerial camera continued to pan across the scene.

'A spokesperson for The Rig Operators, Highland Drilling, informed us that *Highlander* had only recently arrived on the new field location, and had not commenced drilling. Thus ruling out the possibility of an accidental ignition of oil or gas from an active subsea well.'

Gasps circulated around the room as we all watched *Highlander's* drill tower slowly and finally slip beneath the waves, leaving only a scattering of foamy sludge and flotsam mingled with a spreading black oil slick.

The TV commentary continued.

'Whatever the cause, the explosion on board the rig must have been colossal, and as far as we know, at this point in time, not a single member of the crew managed to get off the rig before it sank. This is a terrible tragedy.'

I wasn't the only one to wonder what the hell the commentator was talking about. We all knew the crew would have had plenty of time to evacuate. What was he talking about? Then it struck me like a hammer blow. Not a single lifeboat, life raft, dinghy or lifebuoy could be seen afloat over the entire area. The sea where *Highlander* had gone down was totally empty. Not a soul in the water. In fact if it wasn't for the flotsam drifting on the sea surface, and the spreading oil slick, no one would ever believe there had been any craft there at all. The implication had somehow not been realised by the TV reporter, who carried on in his well modulated voice, doing his best to describe the scene and trying to relay the sketchy information he had been given by God knows who.

The commentary continued as the aerial camera changed direction and homed in on a large Offshore Support Vessel circling the area.

'A Supply Boat, the *Sea Hawk* that arrived on the scene a short while ago, apparently discovered the *Highlander* in distress and raised the alarm. We understand that no actual Mayday or any other signal for help was sent from the rig.'

'This is bullshit!' I couldn't contain myself. 'What the hell do they mean nobody got off? No call for help. They had plenty of time to evacuate the whole crew. The damage was mainly below the waterline, we could all see that. So where was everybody? That main deck was empty. Lifeboats and rafts all in place! Nobody had made any attempt to get off!'

Leaving us all the more confused and frustrated, the TV transmission cut back to the studio, where a well known anchor man took over and attempted to sum up the situation.

'Steve.'

I turned to see John Hughes the Training Centre Manager, standing in the doorway to his room, waving me over.

Inside his office John Hughes was as shocked as any of us.

'I am sorry Steve. Jack Curtis, your friend, was out there on Highlander.'

'And a few other guys I knew. But Jack was special, we were in the Gulf together. What the hell's happened out there, John?'

'I really don't know,' John Hughes said grimly. 'But, I got a call a few minutes ago from Broadhurst at the HSE. They would like you over there right away. You are going to be needed Steve.'

'Yeah, right,' I said, still somewhat dazed.

'Steve, you OK?'

'Yes, I'm alright John but there is something I've got to do!'

I headed for the door, then turned back for a second.

'John, can you explain to Broadhurst at HSE? Tell him I'll get over there as soon as I can. There's somebody I've got to visit first.'

CHAPTER 10

There were two cars parked in the small driveway of the home of Jack and Jean Curtis. I parked behind the one that had a sticker in the window identifying it as a doctor's. Stepping out of the car I could see a group of friendly neighbours standing a short distance away viewing the house; some shaking their heads sadly. The terrible news had travelled fast. The radio, television and media had been pumping out the horrific details almost non-stop. The whole country was in a state of shock, but no one had yet to answer the questions, who and why?

I walked up the short driveway and rang the front doorbell of Jack's house.

The attractive lady, in her late fifties, who came to the front door, with tears still glistening in her eyes, managed to give me a weak smile.

'Steve. Thank you for coming.' Jean's mother Mary put her arms around me and we hugged.

'I am so sorry, Mary. How is Jeannie?'

'Not good, I'm afraid. The Doctor is with her now. In the sitting room.'

'Can I see her?'

Mary nodded and walked ahead of me into the room where Jack's wife Jean, known to most of us as Jeannie, sat on a small sofa. The Doctor, a tall, grey haired man with a stethoscope hanging around his neck, stooped over Jeannie, taking her blood pressure.

Jack's pretty, dark haired and very pregnant wife remained motionless and dazed and staring into space, as the doctor carried out his examination.

The effect of the devastating news on her was clear to see. What else would one expect under such circumstances? But it was Jeannie's vacant gaze that was more disconcerting to me. Jeannie was out of it completely.

The Doctor removed the arm band and turned towards Mary and me, shaking his head.

'Her blood pressure is very high. We need to get her into hospital as soon as possible. I have already called for an ambulance. Should be here any minute.'

I nodded towards Jeannie on the sofa and raised a questioning eyebrow at the Doctor.

'May I? I am a very close friend.'

'Of course,' he said, 'But please remember, she's very distressed.'

I settled beside Jeannie and took her hand.

'Jeannie, I am so sorry. We are here for you, you know.'

Still in a daze she lifted her head to look at me and frowned, as if she didn't recognise me. Her gaze seemed to pass right through me. Then she spoke in a low, toneless voice.

'It was the *Panther*. The *Panther* did it.'

Puzzled, I looked up at Mary and the Doctor questioningly.

They both shrugged and the Doctor, shaking his head, said quietly and gently, 'She's in deep shock.'

'She's been like this since the last news bulletin,' Mary whispered quietly close to my ear.

'What is the latest on it?' I whispered back

Mary reached down to take my hand, and with a finger pressed briefly over her lips drew me up and over to the doorway. The Doctor moved again to take my place at Jeannie's side.

'They say it was a terrorist attack.' Mary continued to speak in low tones.

'Terrorists? But how? Why?'

'I don't know, Steve,' Mary failed to stifle a sob. 'Bodies have started to come up. They say they've been shot. All of them.'

Before I could say anything, the siren of the approaching ambulance pierced the air.

Mary and I stood back as the ambulance crew, a young couple, man and women in green overalls, efficiently transferred Jeannie onto a wheeled stretcher. The Doctor gave them some medical instructions as they started to wheel her out.

Passing us, both Mary and I were taken by surprise as Jeannie reached out a hand towards her Mother and me, and said in a surprisingly firm voice.

'It was the *Panther*.'

CHAPTER 11

Arthur Broadhurst, the Senior Executive Officer of the Marine and Offshore Division of the HSE, moved across the room and took up a position in front of a whiteboard already covered with a dozen various aerial photographic shots of the stricken *Highlander*. Each shot had already been daubed with a variety of handwritten comments, arrows and red circles.

Holding up his hand for silence, Broadhurst started to address the gathering.

'It's still too early to say exactly what happened on the *Highlander*. The only thing we know for sure, is that not a single person onboard survived, and the rig is on the bottom in seventy odd meters of water.'

The fifteen or so people in the room, men and women, listened to Broadhurst's words in silence. Most of the gathering still occupied their own normal duty desks, while others, hurriedly drafted in especially for this assignment, had taken up whatever free space was available.

'From the manner in which those on board died, we can rule out operational error or equipment malfunction. This was definitely no marine accident,' Broadhurst continued, and as far as those around him were concerned, had just stated the obvious.

Heads just nodded in polite agreement

Broadhurst continued.

'It is patently obvious that this was some kind of an act of terror, although up to now, no group or faction has claimed responsibility. But it's my guess this has got something to do with the current oil crisis.'

'Which particular oil crisis would that be, Sir? There's a half dozen going on around the world as we speak.' The young man, sitting at a desk near the front, got a laugh he had not deliberately solicited.

'It's not funny, ladies and gentlemen but Simpson has got a point. These terrorists could have originated from anywhere in the world, supporting any one of a dozen crackpot causes.'

'Do you think their aim was to stop production from that field, Sir?' Another member of the group, at the back of the room, questioned.

'A bit premature if they did. The Highlander had not even started to drill.' A young female officer's voice cut in. 'There may not have even been any oil down there at all. In any case, it would have made more sense if they had waited until the well was in production or, more explainable, if they had targeted an operational platform.'

Broadhurst shook his head.

'I think that this is all immaterial. This was clearly a demonstration hit on a soft target. They wanted to show us how easily it could be done. Get in, strike and get out.'

'Then why didn't they just sink her over the well?' A voice from the back asked the question.

All heads turned to observe the man who had just entered the room and voiced the question. Everybody there at once recognised the dark haired Steve Craig standing broad and a little over six feet tall in the doorway behind them.

'Ah, Steve - glad you could make it.' Broadhurst proclaimed.

Ignoring the hint of sarcasm in Broadhurst's greeting, Steve Craig moved into the room and took up a prominent position near the front of the group. He was obviously determined to get his point across.

'Why go to all that time and trouble to make her change position?' Craig persisted. 'We know *Highlander* shifted her location some two kilometres. Clearly verified by our own Satnav monitoring read-out here.'

'Just hold it there, Steve,' Broadhurst interrupted. 'We know *Highlander* had to pull off because she had an obstruction on the sea bed, directly below her. That's what the *Sea Hawk* was deployed to do - shift it.'

'But the Sea Hawk hadn't arrived. So who gave *Highlander* instructions to pull so far off station, and why?'

Everybody in the room could see that Steve Craig was not going to be fobbed off so easily.

'I don't know, Steve. But don't you forget these people are fanatics they do irrational things all the time.'

'Well perhaps you can explain to me then, just how irrational were they in this case?' Steve was in full battle mode now. 'They knew *Highlander's* exact position and that she was on location alone. No support vessel in attendance. They also were aware that the nearest help was more than two to three hours away. And where did they get the information and the exact timing of the *Sea Hawk's* arrival on the scene?'

'They could have used an air strike,' Somebody called out from the depths of the room. 'A plane or helicopter maybe.'

'And what? Bombed her? Fired torpedoes at her? If that was the case, who shot every single one of the crew or do you think they were all lined up on the main deck standing there just waiting like sitting ducks?'

'Take it easy Steve.' Arthur Broadhurst felt he was losing control of his meeting.

'You are asking me to take it easy?' Steve Craig retorted angrily. 'I would like you to know, that I have just come from the home of Jack Curtis. Along with forty odd other men, that guy was murdered today out there and his wife is about to give birth while in a state of severe shock. Don't tell me to take it easy. There are too many questions to be answered!'

'And that's exactly what we intend to do. Our intention will be to answer all those questions and a lot more.'

Nobody had noticed the arrival of the three men who had quietly entered the office. The room fell silent as everybody turned to observe the newcomers, one of whom had just spoken. He was the one wearing the uniform of a very senior police officer, and stood flanked by what looked like two of the types you would expect to be guarding the President of the United States, not a British copper, regardless of his rank.

Broadhurst was the only person not displaying any signs of surprise. In fact, he had immediately identified the speaker, and now raised a hand to wave him forward.

'Ah, Commander Bruce. I have been expecting you. Please.'

The Police Commander alone moved forward, his men preferring to take up what appeared to be more strategic positions, one on either side of the room, close to the exit doors.

At that point Steve Craig was more interested in the two heavies rather than the Commander. He realised that these guys were not just your every day policeman. Steve had been long enough in the business to recognise two strong-arm men. So what were they and their big boss doing here?

Broadhurst vigorously shook Commander Bruce by the hand before formally introducing him to the assembled group.

'Gentlemen, ladies. May I introduce Commander Bruce of the International Security Division. The Commander will be heading up the whole investigation. Commander,' Broadhurst said guiding the policeman to a pole position in front of the group.

Ignoring the ripple of surprise running around the room, Broadhurst stepped to one side offering the floor to the policeman.

Bruce was a tall, ruggedly handsome man. He looked as fit as he probably had done when he was on the beat - Lord knows how many years ago that may have been. He had not lost the characteristic roll of a Plod, but there was no mistaking the air of full command and experience when he marched forward and took up position directly in front of the gathering. Completely overshadowing, in presence and authority, the short and somewhat overweight Broadhurst.

'I'll get straight down to business,' Bruce said, offering no preamble. 'You are all probably thinking, what is this copper doing standing in front of a room full of HSE officers, if the ISD is already set up and running with the case.'

The people in the room exchanged knowing looks. A few nodding in agreement with the sentiments just expressed.

'Well it is quite simple,' Commander Bruce continued. 'This is the first time ever that an offshore rig has come under terrorist attack in European waters.' He paused, letting the point sink in. 'To handle this quickly and efficiently we need the expertise, knowledge and most of all the familiarity with the intricacies going on out in the North Sea that only you people of the HSE possess in any real dimension.'

Bruce knew he had them, as he registered the expressions on the faces of the people filling the room around him. Looks changing from suspicion and disbelief to the more satisfied expressions of appreciation.

'However,' Bruce continued, wasting no more time with the pleasantries, 'as much as we respect your individual abilities, there are three people in this room whom we consider to be, shall we say, too close to the case.'

These last words once again puzzled most of the gathering.

'I realise quite well,' Bruce continued, 'that a number of you here will probably have had some familiarity with the victims of this terrible act. But, those who have lost relatives or close friends out there, will be excused all further duties on this case.

A ripple of sympathetic accord travelled around the room.

'And what if those persons choose to contribute?' It was Steve Craig putting the question, obviously concerned where this was all leading. Commander Bruce turned to engage him.

'Mr Craig isn't it?' Bruce made it sound as if they were old acquaintances. 'I understand totally how you feel, but it is the way we would like to handle this matter. Therefore, to you and Messrs. Coulthard and Murray, may I extend my deepest sympathy and ask you to concentrate on the personal and private matters that will surely require your full attention in the coming days. I have spoken with Mr Broadhurst and all three of you are relieved of duty, for the time being.'

'May I correct you, Commander?' Steve interrupted. 'I am not a relative of anyone of those who lost their lives on *Highlander*.'

'Come now, Mr Craig.' Bruce shook his head knowingly. 'Your relationship with Mr Jack Curtis and his wife Jean, I know for a fact, is as close as any blood tie. And from what I understand Mrs. Jean Curtis could well do with your help and support at this particular time.'

'You seem to know a lot about me, Commander.' Steve snapped.

'It is my duty to know as much as possible about the people who may work for me.'

Steve had no intention of giving up the floor that easily.

'Then what about our contributions to this case?' He waved his arm to include Jim Coulthard and Ian Murray sat somewhere in the room behind him. Each of the two men had lost a brother out there. 'You said yourself, you are here to utilise our expertise.' Steve persisted.

But, Bruce had no intention of being dissuaded either.

'Relevant information or suggestions from any of you will be taken into serious consideration, I promise. Please write down anything you believe to be of value to the investigation and pass it to Mr. Broadhurst, who will ensure it is effectively dealt with, through the proper channels.'

'Commander, Sir.' Steve was finding it increasingly difficult to control his frustration. 'I really must ask you to reconsider.'

Bruce cut him off sharply. 'Mr Craig, I think I have made myself perfectly clear on this matter. It is not ISD policy to employ people on a case who may have biased views and could be influenced by personal grievances. Now, if you don't mind we have a great deal of work to be getting on with. My deepest condolences to you and both Mr Coulthard and Mr Murray.'

Without any comment, Coulthard and Murray rose to their feet, gathered some bits and pieces from their desks and headed for the door. A few seconds later Steve Craig followed them. He did not look back but could hear the voice of the Commander addressing the group.

'Right, people. We are treating this incident as a terrorist act, carried out by a group of militants, presently unidentified.'

CHAPTER 12

I was pretty angry as I drove out to the Aberdeen Infirmary, and more than a little sceptical of the sudden desire of the ISD to tie-in with the HSE on the case. There was something about Commander Bruce that just didn't sit so comfortably with me. Perhaps I was just annoyed about being thrown off the investigation. Although he seemed to have learned a hell of a lot about me and my friendship with Jack and Jeannie, and in a very short time. Of course I did not have any real reason to suppose he wouldn't carry out a thorough investigation into all this, but still, something doubtful nagged away at the back of my mind.

On exiting the HSE Offices, my mobile had rung with the first bars of *The Star Spangled Banner*. A silly ring tone that I had let Jack Curtis download on it, in a moment of weakness, or perhaps to be more precise, in a moment of in-sobriety. Not that I had anything against the American national anthem. It just served as another reminder of how close Jack and I had been. Those six months undercover in the desert with the Big Yank, and his later unconditional support when things had turned really bad for me, would take forever to forget. It was a real bonus when Jack decided to stay in the UK after the Iraq thing. In fact, it was I who'd encouraged him to take the job on the *Highlander*. It was the least I could do for him. He had made the difference at my court martial. But now, I regretted ever having introduced Jack to the offshore industry and the *Highlander*.

The call was from an excited Mary, telling me that Jeannie had given birth to a healthy baby boy. She quoted me the weight and the time and some other connected information, but like a lot men with other things on their minds, I guess I forgot the details just a few seconds after switching the phone off. And, this time, I certainly did have other things on my mind, as I headed for the hospital.

Mary was just on her way out of the building when I arrived. As usual, she greeted me warmly with a tight hug.

'Thank you so much for coming, Steve. She seems to be handling it very well. The baby is beautiful. He's helping her to deal with this more than I ever imagined.'

'Is it alright for me to see her?' I asked.

'Of course it is, Steve. I told her you were on your way. She wants to see you.' Mary touched my arm affectionately. 'Look, Steve I've got to go and pick up some clothes for the wee thing. It's all happened so quickly. I will be back in an hour or so. You, just go on up. 3rd Floor, Elgin Ward, Room 18.' She pointed in the general direction and headed for the exit.

'Oh, Mary.'

She turned at my call.

'His name? The wee laddie – what's his name?'

Mary just smiled at me.

'What do you think?'

It took me just a few minutes to stop at a small florist's boutique in the foyer, and with a bunch of mixed flowers clasped in my hand, I headed up to the maternity ward.

'Jack would have been so proud of him,' Jeannie said.

I was relieved to see that Jack's wife was almost back to her old self as she turned young Jack in her arms to show me his tiny, wrinkled face. As Mary had said, I could see the little chap was going to help Jeannie get through this thing.

'I must say he does look very much like his Dad. After a few pints that is.' I tried to make light of it and was rewarded by a peal of Jeannie's infectious laughter.

Then, shifting the baby into a more comfortable position in her arms, she became serious again. Her eyes starting to glisten.

'Why did this have to happen, Steve? Why Jack? Why now? Why like this, so pointless?'

'I don't know,' I said. I had no satisfactory answer to any of Jeanie's questions. 'It seems to have been another senseless terrorist attack. Who really ever knows what motivates these people to carry out this sort of thing?'

'Do they know who did it?' Jeannie enquired hopefully, drawing the baby closer to her as if the answer might place him in some sort of danger.

'Not yet. Nobody has claimed responsibility. Which I find rather strange. Some lunatic faction or other usually wastes little time in getting its name printed on the front pages. But, at the moment there is absolutely nothing to go on.'

'What about the ship? The support vessel? What information did they get from her?'

'The *Sea Hawk* you mean? She arrived too late I'm afraid. It was all over when she got there.'

'No, Steve. I don't mean the *Sea Hawk*,' Jeanie said coolly – looking me straight in the eyes. 'I mean the *Panther*.'

CHAPTER 13

'We have received no notification of any surface vessels of any significant size whatsoever in the immediate area of *Highlander*, before or after the attack. In fact the nearest ship was the *Sea Hawk* and she was over three hours away.'

It didn't surprise me to discover that Commander Bruce had staked claim to Broadhurst's office at the HSE. He was now sat in front of me, occupying Broadhurst's desk, arms folded, back straight. I also noticed that the top of the desk had been practically swept clean of the usual, nondescript piles of documents that Broadhurst usually had stacked upon it. Now, it reminded me of the polished, clinical expanse of a Bank Manager's desk on the day you go in to ask for a loan.

The Commander had wasted little time in establishing his domain at the HSE.

'Jean Curtis is adamant that her husband told her that *Highlander* had a ship standing by called the *Panther*.'

'With all due respect Mr Craig…' Without the slightest trace of due or any other kind of respect, Bruce had discarded the familiar tone of our earlier conversation. '… Mrs Curtis has been under extreme and most understandable stress. Giving birth to a baby in the aftermath of the horrific death of her husband, I admire her courage and sympathise. However, she must be deeply traumatised by the whole dreadful affair, and no doubt somewhat confused.'

'She was on the ship to shore phone, talking to her husband, at the exact moment of the attack. The very instant that somebody shot Jack

Curtis dead. She heard it all happen.' I had no intention of pulling my punches. 'God dammit, man. There must have been some ship there, or do you think the rig crew took it upon themselves to stage a mutiny, with everybody killing everybody else? The *Highlander* was not the bloody *Marie Celeste* for God's *sake*.'

'Take it easy, Steve' Arthur Broadhurst cut in. Hovering nearby, he had escaped my attention until that moment. 'That's not what the Commander is inferring.'

'It's alright Arthur.' Bruce raised a pacifying hand. 'I understand Mr Craig's concern.' Getting to his feet, Bruce turned his back on me and moved to gaze out the office window. Nobody spoke, and that irked me. After a seemingly endless duration, the Commander turned to confront me once more.

'Steve,' he said. So we were back on first name terms, or at least he was. He was definitely beginning to irritate the hell out of me. 'Steve, I am going to let you in on some information we have just received.' Now what? 'Our sources in Norway advise that a submarine may have been operating in the area.'

'And you believe that?'

'Why shouldn't we?'

'Because it's bullshit! That's why! When did terrorists start attacking with submarines?'

'It's not too hard to believe. The Nine Eleven terrorists didn't provide their own aircraft.'

'OK. So, who has reported a submarine stolen, then?'

'Steve, you are being very unreasonable. I know your intentions are honourable.'

'Honourable! I don't give a damn about honour. I'm not courting your daughter. I just want to know what really happened to *Highlander* out there. This is basic information. Any competent investigator would be following up the possibility of another ship called *Panther* being in the area. Why are you not getting on with it?'

'Just take it easy, Steve.' Broadhurst moved forward again and, for a moment I almost thought he was going to take a swing at me. Lucky for him he didn't.

'Please, Arthur,' Bruce intervened again, quite unruffled. 'Of course we will check out what you say. However, I must emphasise that at the moment we are following what information has been forwarded to us by the Norwegian Authorities. So I would appreciate it if you just let us get on with the job. I am sure you can find something more useful to do.'

'Oh, rest assured, Commander, I can certainly find something more useful to do.'

I turned and headed for the door.

'Just one thing more, Mr Craig.'

Looking back, I saw that the arrogant bastard actually had a smile on his face.

'Please don't go and do anything foolish. We don't want a repeat of the Gulf incident.'

I was out of there.

CHAPTER 14

British Airways flight BA078 touched down smoothly at Sola Airport, Stavanger, Norway just after ten o'clock the following morning, and I was through immigration and into a taxi on my way to the city fifteen minutes later. I was travelling light – just a small cabin size case with the basic essentials.

It was a clear, bright day, with still just a hint of chill in the early Scandinavian spring air. A combination of dry, mild, western winds and the warming effect of the Gulf stream, produces a much milder climate than would otherwise be expected in a country this far north.

But there was something about Stavanger. I liked the place and had visited it on a number of occasions. A Norwegian city port that played the mirror role of Aberdeen, on the opposite side of the North Sea. It's an attractive, compact and classical city port. Lot of history and charm. Far worse places than Stavanger to start digging in, I thought.

The Maritime Directorate Office is located in the heart of the city. We were there in 20 minutes. I paid off the taxi and entered the building through large, glass, swing doors.

The entrance foyer was quite spacious. I headed across the stone tiled floor towards the two lady receptionists sat behind a sweeping, polished mahogany counter. The older of the two, a woman I guessed to be in her mid forties, was turned with her back to me, speaking to somebody on the telephone.

Staring up at me from her seat behind the counter, with a huge welcoming smile and large blue eyes, was the other receptionist, a very pretty, blond girl - the classic young, fair skinned Norwegian beauty. In the UK she would have been a model not an office girl.

'God dag,' she happily greeted me in Norwegian. 'Kan jeg helpe deg?'

One doesn't spend any length of time associated with activities in the oil sectors of the North Sea without rubbing shoulders with numerous Norwegians. So, I'd picked up a little of the language. Enough anyway, to understand what her simple greeting and question of my requirement was. So I made a polite effort to respond in the same tongue.

'God Dag,' I returned her greeting and then identified myself. 'Jeg heter Steven Craig.'

'Oh, you are English,' she stated, her smile broadening as she politely cut me down to size. I guess my accent was a dead giveaway, but I think she appreciated the effort.

'And how may I help you today Mr Craig?' her English pronunciation was perfect.

'My name is Steven Craig,' I introduced myself a second time and flashed my ID. 'I am with the British Health and Safety Executive. I would like to speak to the Officer dealing with the *Highlander* Drilling Rig incident.'

'Oh yes, Sir,' her smile appeared to be a fixture, 'I think that would be Herr Olsen, Nils Olsen. Quite a few Olsens in Norway, you know. Common name, just like Smith in England.'

'Thank you, Astrid. I will deal with this Gentleman.' It was the other woman cutting in sharply. She had finished her phone call, and now turned her attention to me. Quite clearly, verbally elbowing the young girl off the scene.

'Good day, Mr Craig,' she greeted coldly, in stark contrast to young Astrid's enthusiastic and friendly reception, a few moments earlier. 'We have been expecting you.'

'Expecting me?' I had trouble disguising my surprise.

'Yes. The Senior Officer, Mr Jorgensen will be down in just a moment. Perhaps you would like to take a seat?' She nodded coldly in the direction of a leather sofa and a couple of arm chairs on the far side of the foyer.

'I prefer to stand, thank you.' I said, still smarting from the reception I had just received from Miss Godzilla. Smiling at young Astrid, I moved away from the reception counter.

So Commander Bruce had beaten me to it. He'd apparently had no problem anticipating what I was up to. Clever bastard. Well, maybe not so clever. Still, lesson learned.

'Mr. Craig,' the voice of a tall, sandy haired man in a grey suit and a striped tie, echoed across the foyer as he rapidly descended a marbled flight of stairs and walked to towards me hand extended in greeting. I shook it.

'Mr Craig, my name is Jorgensen. Commander Bruce informed me that you would probably be paying us a visit.' He sounded quite casual about it. 'I am deeply sorry for your loss on the *Highlander*.'

Sympathetic words, but it appeared Herr Jorgensen had no intention of extending his courtesy any further by, for example, inviting me into the building beyond the bottom step of the stairs in the entrance hall.

'I would like to speak to the people involved in routing the *Highlander* and contracting the *Sea Hawk*.'

'That would be me,' Jorgensen stated - just the slightest hint of unrest in his voice, I thought.

'What about Nils Olsen?'

I was actually surprised myself by Jorgensen's reaction to that question. His complexion took on a distinct and almost deathly pallor.

'Uh…I am afraid Mr Olsen took this whole matter rather badly. Actually it has affected all of us involved. He has taken a little time off from work. Gone away for a spell.'

'Away?'

'Yes.' Jorgensen offered no further explanation, and then said, 'Look Mr Craig, I can assure you we really are giving this matter our full attention.'

'Can I at least take a look at the routing and activity plan for the *Highlander* and the supporting vessels involved?'

'There was only one supporting vessel, and that was the *Sea Hawk*.' He made a point of emphasising the statement.

'Well then, can I get some information on the present location of the *Highlander* and details of the wreck that was preventing her drilling on the location?'

What little was left of the colour in the Norwegian's face drained out completely as he gave the anticipated response to my request.

'I am sorry, but we have been advised by the UK International Security Division that this matter is highly classified. I don't think I am going to be able to be of any further assistance to you, Mr Craig.'

'What about a ship called the *Panther* then?' I thought it might be worth a try.

'Mr Craig, I think you should leave. Now.'

CHAPTER 15

'He just left the building.'

The Watcher spoke into his cell phone while observing Steve Craig climbing into a taxi seconds after exiting the Norwegian Maritime Directorate office. 'He's taking a cab, and he doesn't look to be a happy man.'

'Never mind that, just follow him,' a man's voice at the other end of the line, ordered coldly. 'And make sure you don't let him out of your sight.'

The Watcher closed his phone cover and started the car. He followed the Stavanger taxi, carrying his target, as it made its way from the Directorate building along Verksgata.

Well in advance of the rush hour traffic, the route into the city centre was pretty clear. The taxi headed south skirting the Breivatnet Lake, then cut across Olavsgate before climbing the hill up to Løkkeveien and eventually pulling up outside the Radisson SAS Royal Hotel.

The Watcher waited until Steve Craig had paid off the taxi and entered the hotel carrying just a single piece of lightweight hand luggage.

'Just a flying visit then, is it Mr Craig?' the Watcher muttered to himself.

The Watcher's phone rang.

'Yes?' He said. He knew it was his contact ringing back.

'Craig didn't get anything from Jorgensen. So he probably will not waste any time in heading home.'

'Not exactly the case, I am afraid. He's just about to check-in to the Radisson.'

'Why would he want a hotel?' The man's voice on the other end sounded more irritated than curious.

'Perhaps he's got some other harebrained plan. Could he have picked up any other information back there?'

'No idea but I think you'd better stick close to him for a while. And whatever you do don't underestimate him. His killing days may not be over.'

CHAPTER 16

I was still pretty mad that Bruce had got to Jorgensen before I'd had a chance to question him properly. But I had managed to obtain something, thanks to the accommodating Miss Astrid at the front desk. Albeit just a morsel, but something to run with. The young receptionist had innocently provided me with the name of the official undoubtedly in the middle of all this - one Nils Olsen. I didn't much go for Jorgensen's story that this Olsen guy was away on leave. If he was still in Stavanger I was going to find him.

'Just the one night, Mr Craig?'

Another attractive girl checked me in at the Radisson SAS Royal Hotel. There is a lot to be said for these Nordic beauties and if I'd had more time - well? But at that moment there were other priorities looming.

'It's room 323 on the 3rd Floor.' Flashing a devastating smile, she handed me the key card. 'Lifts over there to the left. Is there anything else you may need?'

There could well have been, but as I said, some other time perhaps. I declined the offer and headed for the lifts.

Once in the hotel room, I bolted the door. No disturbance required at this time. Dropping my bag on the floor, I made straight for the phone and grabbed a pencil and pad lying conveniently nearby, before lifting the receiver and dialling. It took only a second to get through.

'Hi. This *is* the Norwegian Maritime Directorate right?' I enquired putting on my best American accent. Jack would have been proud of me.

'That's correct, Sir. How may I help you?'

I was in luck. It sounded like Astrid. Then for a moment I was tempted to slam the receiver back down on its cradle. The dreaded thought of hearing her puzzled voice enquiring, what the hell was the friendly guy she'd met earlier doing, talking to her in a funny drawling voice, gave me serious second thoughts. But she didn't.

'That's great,' I continued. 'Look my name is Captain John Smith.' God, how corny was that one? I was certainly beginning to push my luck. Now I almost expected her to reply 'Yes and I am Pocahontas.'

'Good afternoon, Captain Smith. Whom would you like to speak with?'

'I am commanding the Heavy Lift Ship *Draco*,' I lied with some conviction. 'Do you think I could speak to Herr Olsen, Herr Nils Olsen?'

'I am afraid Mr Olsen is not in the office at the present time.'

'Oh. When will he return?'

She said she didn't know and I thought I'd had it, but gave it one last try. I'd come to the conclusion that the girl was totally unaware of all the intrigue going on around this case. I might just be lucky enough to salvage something from her.

'Look, this is really important,' I went on. 'He was involved in setting up a pretty big contract for my company. I really need to talk to him personally. Do you have a contact telephone number or anything like that for him?'

'We don't usually give out personal information.' There was a note of uncertainty in her voice.

'Please, Marm,' I laid it on as thick as I could, and crossed my fingers. 'This is an extremely important contract for my company.'

Silence for a moment, then 'I do have his home telephone number in Stavanger.'

'That will do just fine.' I said, hardly believing my luck. I guessed her Godzilla partner must have been well out of earshot, otherwise I would never have got this far.

I scribbled down the number, thanked her and hung up.

I wasted little time in extracting the Stavanger and Surrounding Area telephone catalogue from the bottom drawer of the bedside cabinet. Like most tomes of its kind, it weighed a ton, and consisted of over a thousand pages.

I thumbed through the alphabetical index until I found the name Olsen.

God!

Well what did I expect? There were hundreds of them. Like Smith in England, Astrid had said, and the girl wasn't wrong. Still, I just had to get on with it. So, I started searching for the name that matched the telephone number Astrid had given me.

I started scanning the lists.

'Bingo!'

It took less time than I'd anticipated. According to the book, one Nils J Olsen resided at 16 Øvre Gata, Stavanger 4022.

It was about a fifteen minute brisk walk from the Radisson Hotel to Øvre Gata. I decided against taking a cab. I didn't want to unduly announce my arrival. The way things were going, I had visions of Nils Olsen scurrying out the rear exit to avoid interrogation.

Øvre Gata was a quiet, tree-lined street, located just north of the city centre. It commanded a magnificent view over Stavanger harbour and I could see the North Sea filling the skyline away in the distance.

House No.16 was about half way along. It was a classic example of Scandinavian urban architecture. The cellar floor extended up above ground level and was built as a solid wall foundation, mainly of concrete. Above this, the two or three floors comprising the actual living rooms were timber framed and then finished off in wooden cladding. Not only a practical all weather design, but quite attractive as well.

My expectations fell as I opened a squeaking, wrought iron gate and stepped onto the paved pathway leading up to the front of the house. The whole place was in complete darkness, a sure sign there was nobody at home. Unlike Britain and most other parts of Europe, I knew that Norwegians, almost without exception, choose to light up their homes, very often in quite a spectacular style, as soon as the light of day begins to fade. Curtains are rarely drawn at night so there's always a display of candles and lamps glowing warmly outwards from most of the rooms of any house. In contrast, Olsen's place was as dark as sin. I couldn't make out a single glimmer of light anywhere.

Mounting the steps to the front door, I decided at least to give it a try. But, before my hand could get to the doorbell, a voice behind halted my action.

'Han er ikke hjemme.'

I turned to see who was telling me in Norwegian, that Nils Olsen was not at home.

Standing on the footpath behind me, was a short, thickset man with close cropped greying hair. One of those tantalising, indeterminate age characters. He could have been fifty, sixty or even older.

Observing him standing down on the path with both hands tucked casually into the pockets of his baggy trousers, I guessed he must be one of the neighbours. He wore no topcoat, and as the evening air was already starting to chill, I assumed, he must live quite close by.

Dispensing with any efforts to converse using my limited command of Norwegian, I said, 'Oh, hi. Do you know when he will be back?' And was immediately appalled that what actual came out was disturbingly similar to the phoney American accent I had deployed on receptionist Astrid, only an hour or so ago.

The man didn't seem to notice, or care.

'I am Olsen's neighbour,' he said jerking his thumb over his shoulder, indicating the house next door. 'Name's Lindefjell. You American?' He didn't wait for a reply. 'We've had 'em all today.'

'Had them all? What do you mean?'

'Two guys this morning. The first one was Norwegian. The second guy was a foreigner. Well, I know you're a foreigner so to speak but this guy sounded like a German.'

'What did he want?'

'Same as you. To find out where Olsen was.'

'Did you tell him?'

'No. He wanted to talk German. I can't stand to hear it - bad memories.'

'So you don't know where Olsen is?'

'I didn't say that.'

Why did I get the feeling that this guy was playing cat and mouse with me?

'So where is he?' I ventured.

'Vacation.'

'Any place special?'

'Same place he always goes, I expect.'

It looked as if I was going to have to drag the information out of this character, piece by piece.

'Which is?'

'Why should I tell you all this? The German guy didn't get a thing out of me.'

'Look,' I said, dropping the phoney accent. I knew I was going to have to level with him sometime. 'The truth is I lost someone very close to me on the *Highlander*. The Rig that got blown up offshore. I'm just looking for some answers. Oh, and I am not an American, I'm British.'

'That's no big surprise. The accent was lousy. I spent a lot of time in the UK you know, in my younger days. Did I catch a hint of Scots?'

'OK, I surrender. Now are you going to tell me where I can find Nils Olsen?'

'What do you want with him?'

'To find out what really happened out there.'

'And do you think he will tell you?'

'I won't know until I ask him. So are you going to tell me where he is?'

'Sure.'

CHAPTER 17

The Watcher remained a few paces behind, tracking the route of his target along the railway platform. He waited until Steve Craig climbed the few steps up and disappeared into one of the coaches, then took out his phone, dialled the usual number and reported in.

'He's at the train station. Checked out of the hotel about half an hour ago,' the Watcher reported into the phone. 'He obviously obtained some information from the old guy he spoke to last night, up at Olsen's place. Now he's bought a ticket and has just boarded the 12.45 train to Voss.'

'What about this old man you said Craig talked to?'

'Gone. No sign of him. I asked around, but nobody seemed to know him or even recognised the description I gave.'

'Voss?' The voice on the other end sounded intrigued. 'That's a ski resort, but I doubt he is going up there to ski. Not for the fun of it anyway. Stick with him and remember what I told you.'

A few minutes later the Watcher displayed his rail ticket to the Guard, and boarded the train. He worked his way through the carriage, searching for a position where he could best observe Steve Craig, who had found a seat, and was settled in reading a newspaper. The Watcher located a convenient place a few rows back.

A shrill whistle, followed by the final clunking of the carriage doors sliding shut, announced the imminent departure. The train started to move, and then, hardly before it had gained any momentum at all, another longer and more intense whistle blast brought things to a shuddering halt.

A few inquisitive passengers peered out of the windows, wondering what was going on. Then a disturbance of some sort broke out somewhere in the direction of the rear carriages. The sound of raised voices and a coach door sliding shut, drifted along the carriage to where the Watcher sat with face turned. Shielding from Steve Craig, who, like most of the passengers, was wondering what was causing the commotion back there, and had turned in his seat to view back down through the carriage central corridor.

Whatever the interruption, it was over in a few seconds, and Steve returned to his newspaper as the train got under way again. Everybody settled down once more.

Behind both Steve and the Watcher, the man responsible for holding up the train, slid the ID card he had shown to the Station Guard, back into his wallet. It had served its purpose very well. He was safely onboard the train to Voss.

A few moments later, the latecomer found himself a seat from where he could comfortably observe both Steve Craig and the Watcher.

CHAPTER 18

With the train now speeding on a three hour journey towards Voss, where hopefully I would find Nils Olsen, and get some answers, I was able to sit back and reflect on the events of the past few days.

The pain of losing my best friend Jack, and the anguish of watching his widow Jeannie bravely holding his newborn son, had been replaced by a deep anger. An anger that was not going to be so easily tamed. But the events of the past twenty four hours were now uppermost in my mind.

What I hoped was, that the old guy Lindefjell, who claimed to be Olsen's neighbour, had provided me with the correct information. I was pretty sure he had. For two reasons, each of which, oddly enough, also exposed Herr Lindefjell as an impostor. Firstly, he was no neighbour, unless, contrary to the general custom in Norway, he chose to leave his home in complete darkness at night, while just stepping outside for a few minutes. Like Olsen's place, the house next door, that Lindefjell had claimed as being his property, had not displayed a single glimmer of light of any kind burning inside or outside. And, the second reason; he wanted me to find Olsen otherwise he could have just played dumb and denied any knowledge of the man's whereabouts. Or simply, not have shown himself to me in the first place. Whatever his motive, he wanted to make sure I got to Olsen. Of course he could be one of Jorgensen's men. But why send me on a wild goose chase up north to Voss when he could just as easily have sent me packing back home, with nothing of any value, and none the wiser? What's more, I was certain I had not seen the last of Herr Lindefjell.

The journey to Voss was, despite my restless spirit, quite a stunning experience. It was mid-May, and although the calendar of the seasons this far north generally tends to lag behind that of the milder regions further south, the weather was warm and the sun shone down from a cloudless sky. Even as the train started its ascent up onto the Hardangervidda plateau, the first layers of snow began to appear, some of it already starting to melt as the sunshine persisted. The combination of this sort of weather, with the upper reaches still covered in deep snow, meant that it was still a skier's paradise, and would continue to be so for some weeks yet to come.

The train was soon heading higher up on to the plateau, and began to rise above what was termed the *trær grensen* - the tree line, beyond which only a few sparse shrubs manage to survive the tough climate.

While contemplating the magnificence of the scenery rolling past outside the carriage window, I found I was able to relax and soon found myself drifting off into a deep and for once, dreamless sleep.

I awoke a couple of hours later to find the train pulling into the snow covered, ski resort of Voss. Following the crowd I left the train, carrying my small holdall, and headed towards a taxi rank just outside the station. The driver was out of his cab in a shot, and reaching out to relieve me of my bag, greeted me with a friendly smile.

'Velkommen til Voss.'

'Thank you,' I replied, still deciding not to get involved with the language thing. 'Do you think you could take me to Fleischer's Hotel?'

At once, the smile on the man's face broadened.

'I could,' he chuckled 'but as the hotel is only fifty meters from where you are standing, it would probably take you longer to get in and out of the taxi than it would for you to walk just up there.' He pointed to a classic building, looking more like a stately home than a hotel, located a stone's throw up hill from where we stood.

'Fleischer's,' he proclaimed proudly, as if the place belonged to him personally. 'So, maybe another time,' he added handing me a contact card. 'My name is Simon. Never know when you might need a reliable transport.'

'Thank you, Simon,' I said taking the card. 'I'll keep that in mind.' I was not just being polite. Because I was already contemplating using Simon's services in the very near future and not for myself.

I thanked him again and set off to walk the short distance to the hotel, well aware that the man, who had been following me around for the last twenty four hours, was still on my tale. I didn't know who had sent him, but I had a pretty good idea who might have wanted to keep a close eye on my movements. So be it. I decided to play the game out a little while longer. But it would soon be time to ditch this character. I couldn't take a chance on him interfering and possibly preventing me from making contact with Nils Olsen or, for that matter, me even leading this guy to Olsen.

I was welcomed and checked into the stately Fleischer's hotel by yet another, tall, attractive, Nordic blonde. These girls seemed to be following me around almost as diligently as the guy on my tail? Speaking of whom, I well expected to soon make an appearance.

There was an envelope, addressed to me, waiting at the reservation counter. Courtesy of the Radisson Hotel travel desk in Stavanger. It contained a map of the area and instructions telling me how to get to, or at least as near as possible to, Olsen's *hytte* - the name the Norwegians give to the small wooden cottages dotted in their thousands around the whole rural areas and mountain regions of Norway. From the map I could see that Nils Olsen's place was located on the slopes above Voss, but a little further north, and apparently, well off the beaten track. According to Lindefjell, Olsen spent a great deal of recreational time up in his mountain retreat. Mostly skiing, I presumed, and probably mountain walking in the summer months. Apart from enjoying the beauty and tranquillity, there would not have been a great choice of many other activities in which to participate. On the surface, Olsen came across as your regular, respectable *Mr Ordinary Norwegian* type. I still wondered how and why he had got himself tied up in all this. What part did he play, and what did he know about a ship called the *Panther*? Key questions. The answers to which, I was, hopefully, coming closer to finding out.

CHAPTER 19

The area north of the Voss ski slopes is another world entirely. The treeless terrain runs uninterrupted for hundreds of kilometres across the Hardangervidda, the highest mountain plateau in northern Europe. It's a beautiful but desolate place. I was on my way across it.

I'd managed to get kitted out with skis. The langlauf cross country type. There was no way I was going to risk trying to negotiate the plateau on slalom skis - the fast downhill blades, that racers use to get from zero to sixty in five seconds. I knew that most of the terrain ahead of me would be undulating - as much uphill slog as downhill glide, and no chair lifts en-route to help me along - not where I was heading.

It took nearly two hours hard skiing through the spectacular but tough, mountainous terrain, before I reached a knoll above a shallow valley. At the bottom of the valley I could see a solitary wooden *hytte*. According to the map, Nils Olsen's hideaway cottage in the mountains.

Deciding to get on with it, I skied down the hill directly towards the place. An array of gear outside and a number of fresh foot tracks leading up to the door, confirmed that it was currently in use. And by the different size imprints in the snow I guessed that Olsen also had visitors. Well, at least one.

I released the bindings and stepped out of my skis.

Operating the door knocker, a quaint homemade device made from a combination of deer antler and hammered metal fittings, I leaned forward to listen for any signs of life.

There was no sound from inside, so I moved to peer in through a side window. It was hard to make anything out in the dim lit interior but I was sure there was nobody inside the place. Moving around to the side, I continued checking through the windows. Nothing. Then, towards the rear of the place, I saw a set of ski tracks. Two sets of tracks in fact. They looked very fresh. So friend Nils was off skiing and he *did* have company.

I retraced my steps to get my skis, and within a couple minutes, I was following the trail down the hill.

As I made my way across the crisp layer of snow, I wondered how the guy who had been tailing me was getting on.

CHAPTER 20

The Watcher had been sat in the front passenger seat for over an hour, peering ahead through the windscreen at the dark shape of the Voss taxi they were trailing. The same taxi that had picked up Steve Craig outside Fleischer's hotel. It had finally come to rest and was now, after a fifty kilometre drive along snow packed country roads, parked alongside a row of shops in a small village. The name of the place, posted on the road sign on the approach road, was Fjellberg.

The Watcher was beginning to feel confident they were closing in on Olsen. He waited patiently for Steve Craig to get out of the taxi.

Another five minutes passed but nothing happened.

'Is that it, Sir?' his Norwegian driver enquired. Car and driver had been on standby in Fleischer's car park, for the Watcher, since his arrival in Voss. He'd called it up as soon as he'd overheard Craig ordering a local cab at the hotel reception.

'Just wait.' There was no disguising the irritation in the Watcher's voice.

The driver said bluntly, 'Doesn't look as if anybody's going to get out.'

He was right. The taxi just sat there at the side of the road.

Then it finally struck the Watcher.

'Shit!' he snarled, and was out of the car in a second and walking swiftly along the slushy pavement towards the parked taxi. Feigning a passing interest as he neared the stationary vehicle, the Watcher took a quick glance into the cab. The driver was sat at the wheel alone, reading a newspaper. No one else was or had been in the taxi, as a passenger, since leaving Voss.

'Shit, shit, shit,' the Watcher hissed through clenched teeth. 'The bastard.'

Fifteen minutes later, the Watcher was on his way back to Voss. This time, sat in the back of the car, with his cell phone pressed against his ear.

'I told you, he's smarter than you think,' the voice at the other end stated calmly. 'Anyway, we are not out of the running yet. Still a chance. Time for you to demonstrate your ski skills.'

'Oh,' was the only thing the Watcher, still smarting from the wild goose chase, could think of to say.

'Yes, we are in luck,' the voice continued. 'Jorgensen, at the Maritime Authority has dug up the location of Olsen's retreat up in those mountains. Don't ask me how. I am faxing the details and a map to your hotel as we speak. Get back there as fast as you can, and then go find Steve Craig and the elusive Herr Nils Olsen.'

An hour later, the Watcher was on his way, heading up onto the Hardangervidda plateau.

Thirty kilometres to the north, another man, who had also been showing more than a passing interest in both Steve Craig and the Watcher, stood on skis, looking down the Hardangervidda through high-powered binoculars. He'd been tracking both men since Stavanger, and was particularly impressed by the way Steve had sent the Watcher off on the road to nowhere. He had not been far away, when he observed Craig climbing into a cab at the Fleischer's Hotel main entrance. And then, a half a minute later, watched him jump out again, after the taxi had swung down the hotel driveway to the main road and stopped again. The taxi driver, who Craig seemed to have previously established some sort of relationship with, had obviously been well primed, and of course well paid, to set up the diversion. Craig had been safely screened behind a row of trees by the time the guy following appeared on the scene, in another car. This character was a professional and he obviously had back-up in the area. But he came nowhere near Steve Craig's level.

The man was impressed. Three years out of the SBS, and Steve Craig appeared to have lost none of his skills. The guy following him however, presented a whole new set of questions. Who had sent him? And, for what purpose? Still as long as he stayed out of it for the time being, the man was happy. That little problem could be dealt with later - he hoped. He was much more concerned with Steve Craig's current progress.

Through the binoculars, he could see Craig in the distance, following Olsen's tracks. He also noticed the trail was running down hill and would soon reach the *tre grensen,* below which the trees would start to thicken up again. Still, he could always follow the trail in the snow, and didn't think Craig would have to go far before catching up with Olsen.

The man was in no hurry. Everything was going according to plan.

CHAPTER 21

The trees started to thicken up around me, and the ski tracks ahead had taken up a single file formation on the narrowing path. Olsen still had company. That was until the route opened out into what appeared to be a mini mountain crossroads. At that point, the pair, for whatever reason, had decided to part company. I could see a set of separate parallel ski tracks had broken away, trailing off to the right, and heading on an angled course, back up the mountain.

The deeper impression in the snow continued on down. Whoever had veered off was the lighter of the two. Could be a female or a kid maybe. I decided to follow on down the slope, where I guessed Olsen must be heading.

I was right. Within a hundred metres I spotted the man I guessed to be Nils Olsen. He stood, resting on his ski poles in another small clearing. He looked older than I'd expected – a man in his late fifties. I noticed he had taken off his gloves and was studying what looked like a stopwatch in his hand. Every now and then he glanced from the watch up into the woods where another, more narrow trail snaked its way upward and disappeared into the mesh of trees.

I skied on down towards Olsen.

I was about twenty metres away from him when he heard my approach and swung around, a look of desperation forming on his face. He looked frantically about him, as if searching for some route out of there – a place to run or hide, but I came to a skidding halt in front of him, blocking his path before he had time to act.

'Herr Olsen? You are Nils Olsen?' I enquired, lifting my goggles and pulling off my ski-cap at the same time, trying to display a friendly, unthreatening expression.

'Who are you? What are you doing up here? What do you want?' The man really was terrified.

I tried to calm him.

'Don't be alarmed Herr Olsen. My name is Craig. I just want to ask you a few questions about the *Highlander* Rig.'

'Oh, my God,' he whispered, a note of terror still contorting his voice.

'No, please,' I urged again holding up a calming hand. 'You have nothing to fear from me. I lost a close friend on the rig. I just need to know what happened out there, that's all.'

'I can't tell you anything. You have to leave me alone. I know nothing. I came up here to get away from all that. How did you find me?'

It was obvious to me now that this man was in the thick of all this. He knew the whole story, and I was going to get it out of him. Whatever it took. I decided to stick with the *good cop* approach, for the time being.

'Did you authorise a Support Vessel called the *Panther* to clear *Highlander's* sub-sea obstruction?'

'God help me please! I swear I had no idea what they planned. I never would have agreed to it.' Olsen dropped his head in shame.

'Just tell me who *they* are. I can help you, I promise.'

'You can't help. They are far too powerful. These people are everywhere. They've started it all over again. The master race.'

'You mean Germans, fascists, neo-Nazis?' I wasn't exactly expecting that.

'They don't call themselves by that name these days. And they are not just Germans. They are all over Europe. Here in Norway too. Many of them.'

'How are you involved?'

Ignoring the question, he shook his head and muttered, 'I only wish my shame could die with me.'

I was about to place my next question to Olsen, but all I could do was watch in horror, as the side of Olsen's chest burst open, and simultaneously, the sound of a gunshot echoed from the hill behind me. Olsen collapsed into the snow at my feet.

I could see he was still alive, and as my instincts cut in, I quickly grasped his ski jacket and heaved him out of the line of fire, as another shot rang out and the snow at my side flew up in a plume of white powder. Still wearing, and impeded by my skis, I nevertheless managed to drag Olsen to the temporary cover of a large fir tree. I was tempted to leave him and get out of there as quickly as I could. Whoever it was had taken the second shot at me.

Just about to move off, I saw Olsen's eyes blink open.

'I warned you. They are too strong,' he gasped, a trickle of blood starting to run from the corner of his mouth. 'Much smarter this time… better organised. They have support and access to immense funds… a new leader. They will get everything they need from the ship at Aldvik.' With his last gasp, Olsen uttered just one final word. 'Torvald,' and died in the snow beside me.

'Very touching, Mr Craig.'

I was more than surprised to look up and see the character who had been trailing me since Stavanger, standing there. He was pointing a Sig Pro hand gun at me. So this guy was not after me, he wanted Olsen. He was a hit man, and a quick learner too. He had certainly made good time getting here; considering I had sent him quite a distance up country.

I started to rise to my feet.

'Easy,' he ordered, gesturing with the muzzle of the gun for me to raise my arms.

I lifted my hands and said, 'So this is the new order? A harmless old man and fifty innocent oil workers murdered. Great way to start your… what you going to call it this time? The Fourth Reich, no doubt.'

'Mr Craig, you have become a serious irritation to us', he said, levelling the gun at my chest.

He had no time to do or say anymore. Another shot rang out, and I could do nothing except just stare as the side of his head burst open and he fell to the ground. I turned to look up the snow track from where the shot had been fired and saw a skier - a young woman - holding a rifle.

Instinctively, I moved to retrieve the assassin's gun from the snow. It looked very much like I was going to need it. The possibility of me being twice lucky in a few minutes, seemed a non-starter. You never usually received more than one chance under close fire, and you couldn't get much closer to the fire than this.

'I do not think you should do that.' The woman shouted down to me as I got a grip on the gun. The rifle to her shoulder was pointing straight at me, and I had no reason to doubt her marksmanship. I obeyed her warning, calculating that if she'd intended to shoot me, she would have done so by now. Don't force the situation – that's what they used to tell us.

Still holding the rifle, she glided effortlessly down the slope towards me and the two bodies sprawled in the blood stained snow at my feet. Totally ignoring the man she had just shot, and still levelling the rifle at me, she looked across at the motionless body of Olsen.

'Move away from him,' she commanded fiercely. I didn't need much coaxing to back off.

She knelt down beside Olsen's body, and tenderly touched his neck, hoping, I knew, to feel a pulse. But there was no doubt, in my mind, that he was dead.

'Papa, oh Papa,' She said sadly stroking Olsen's face with a pale hand. She had removed her gloves, and I could see her long thin pianist like fingers running lightly across his features.

'Hvorfor? Hvorfor nå?' She was asking why? Why now? I watched silently as a single teardrop ran down her smooth, finely curved cheek.

'So who are you?' she turned and addressed me sharply. The period of mourning obviously short lived, for the time being anyway. The rifle was still aimed at my chest.

'You are English aren't you? I heard you talking to him,' she snarled the last sentence nodding towards the other body.

'Scottish actually,' I told her.

'Well what business did you have with my Father?'

'Miss Olsen, my name is Craig. I work for the British Health and Safety Executive.'

So far she was unimpressed and tilted her head to one side in a cynical fashion. Waiting for me to explain, further.

I continued.

'I am investigating the *Highlander* Rig case.'

Still no reaction.

'Look,' I said finally, 'Do you think you could stop pointing that thing at me? I assume you did not prevent the guy over there shooting me, so you could do it yourself.'

'It's just fine as it is,' she said coldly. 'You say you are with the HSE.' That sort of caught me by surprise. She mentioned the HSE with a familiarity as if she had dealings with that organisation on a regular basis. 'If that is true, why are you up here operating on your own?'

'It's complicated.' I said.

'Then un-complicate it for me,' she commanded, in almost perfect English, with just the smallest hint of an accent.

'I am not strictly authorised to work on this case.'

'Why is that?'

'A very dear friend of mine was killed on the *Highlander* Rig. The powers above think that I am too compromised - too close to the subject, as they put it. But I want some answers.'

'And in your investigations you discovered that my Father was somehow involved?'

'Yes.'

'Who is he?' she asked, nodding back to the body of the man she had just shot dead.

I told her, 'I don't know, but he seemed to know me well enough. He's been following me since my arrival in Norway. Pity he's dead, I may have got a few answers out of him.'

'Providing he hadn't shot you first.'

The tone in her response disturbed me.

'Miss Olsen,' I said, taking a bit of a risk, 'you know, you seem to be handling this all very calmly. The death of your father like this must surely be a shock to you.'

'Mr Craig,' she cut me off sharply. 'I don't know why I should have to explain to you, but my father has been living with this for a long time. I never really understood what he was mixed up in, but I was aware it was something illegal and very dangerous. In the past weeks, after the attack on the oil rig, he told me he felt his life was in great danger. In a way he prepared me and himself for this.' She pointed sadly to Olsen's lifeless body lying in the snow.

'What now?' I asked.

She gave me a puzzled look. 'Why, the police of course. I've just killed a man. We need to get them up here. Do you have a cell phone on you?'

'No, afraid not.' I shook my head. 'I decided I did not want to be disturbed by anybody on this particular trip.'

'Very convenient.'

'What about you?' I asked. 'Have you got one?'

'My father and I never carry the things. They are a nuisance at the best of times.'

I decided not to try to compare our individual reasons for not bothering to bring a mobile phone up a mountain.

'He might have one,' I suggested, pointing to the dead body of the killer lying in the snow.

Making sure she kept the rifle trained on me, she moved across and began to search through the dead man's pockets. Failing to find anything on the one side, she stood, and slipping out of one ski binding, pushed the body over with her foot. In another second, she had found and removed his mobile phone.

'It's crushed,' she said but still keyed in some numbers and held it to her ear. The result was obviously negative. She threw the phone angrily into the snow. Crushed and damaged and probably out of signal range anyway, the phone was obviously useless.

'So what now?' I put the question again.

'The nearest town is Helmsvik. It is quite a detour down the mountain we need to get started. You first, Mr Craig.' She waved the rifle motioning me to move off down the track. I slipped back into my skis, replaced my cap and glasses and retrieved the poles from the snow at my feet, and was about to move off.

'Hold it for just one second,' she said quietly, and still keeping me in her line of sight, moved to kneel beside her father. I watched her straighten his body and lay his arms by his sides, before lowering her head for a few seconds.

Then she was on her feet, fixing her foot back in the free ski binding, and indicating for me to lead the descent down the slope.

'What about his gun?' I asked pointing to the Sig Pro lying half buried in the snow.'

'Just leave it. The police can deal with it when they get up here.'

I didn't argue. I just turned and took off.

CHAPTER 22

Up on the Hardangervidda high ground, the man with the binoculars had witnessed much of what had gone on below. Now he could see Steve Craig and the girl setting off down the mountain. He guessed she must be Olsen's daughter. Her name was Karen, and from his sources he knew she regularly joined her father up there. They did a lot of skiing together. Apparently the girl was into winter sports. Olympic stuff by all accounts.

The magnified view through the glasses had provided him with the equivalent of a ringside seat. He'd watched without emotion, most of the display of slaughter that had taken place below, a few minutes previously. The sound of the shots fired reaching him seconds after the bodies of the two men had fallen into the snow. He had made no attempt to prevent it, but hoped that Steve Craig may have got something from Olsen before he died. If not it was going to be back to square one.

Replacing his binoculars in a case at his side he adjusted his backpack and set off down the slope.

At the scene of the double shooting, he made a cursory examination of the two bodies lying in the snow. Olsen of course, was easily identifiable, but he had no idea who the other guy was - or had been. No doubt his people would uncover the man's identity, and find out what he had been up to.

Before moving off, he made a phone call from his mobile. Speaking Norwegian, he told the contact at the other end, to advise the local police to get themselves up on to the Hardangervidda, about twenty kilometres due east of Helmsvik, and investigate the killing of two men. That should keep the local law occupied for a while and out of his hair.

CHAPTER 23

Half way down the mountain, I swerved to a halt and looked back up at the girl following in my tracks. She was still pointing the rifle at me, although something of the earlier menace had disappeared.

'So what's with the rifle? Not that many people take a gun skiing.'

'You must surely have heard of Orienteering, Mr Craig.'

'Ah! Yes,' I realised immediately what she meant. 'Winter Biathlon - cross country skiing, navigation and rifle target shooting, all rolled into one,' I said. 'So you are into all that?'

'Why else would I be skiing with a rifle? I was up here with my father, training. He is… was very supportive. In fact he was convinced I would qualify this year for the Winter Olympics.'

'At least you proved your prowess in the shooting element. Lucky for me.'

'Also very lucky for you I had this particular rifle with me.'

For a second I didn't quite understand what she was driving at.

'It's a hunting rifle, Mr. Craig,' she explained. 'Not a sports rifle. This is a .244 calibre Holland and Holland Magnum, not the regular .22 used in orienteering. The extra 24 thousandths of an inch makes quite a difference you know. This one can kill a deer at a hundred and fifty meters.'

I felt foolish. Despite my aversion to firearms nowadays, I knew enough about them to have realised that a small calibre gun had not been used to kill the guy back up there. I still could not figure out, however, how this girl was managing to remain so calm and composed, considering she had just witnessed the cold blooded murder of her father, and had then shot dead the killer. Not your everyday, run of the mill activity. Some delayed shock perhaps or an unusually strong constitution.

'So why the more powerful weapon?' I questioned.

'Simple really, my .22 is in for repair. This is my father's hunting rifle, he loaned it to me to practice.' She smiled for the first time since our meeting. 'As I said, lucky for you. Now don't you think we should be moving on?'

I stood my ground.

'Look, you must realise, I had nothing to do with your father's death,' I said. 'I only wanted information. The circumstances of the *Highlander* disaster and the nature of the ongoing investigation are extremely suspect. And, the explanations by those carrying out the investigation are just too cut and dried for my liking.'

'The media claims it was a terrorist attack.'

'I think it may have been, but not for the usual reasons.'

'So what reasons would you think are unusual?'

'That's what I wanted to find out from your father.'

'And did you? Find out anything from my father?'

'He was trying to tell me something.'

She lowered the rifle and slung it over her shoulder. I guessed I was no longer perceived as a real threat to her.

'What did he say?' she asked, and then decided not to pursue that line of questioning. 'Never mind, save it for the police.' She paused and gazed thoughtfully down the track ahead of us. 'And it looks like we are both going to have quite a bit of explaining to do. Especially me. Who goes orienteering in the mountains and ends up killing somebody, and not by accident either? And, when you bring up the story of a hunt for terrorists - well.' She raised one eyebrow.

'You're right.' I could see her point. 'Frankly it doesn't look as if that course of action will prove to be of much advantage to either of us.'

'You sound as if you think there may be an alternative, Mr Craig. So what do you propose?'

I thought about it for a moment, and then said, 'Your father was trying to tell me something, Miss Olsen. It appears he got himself involved with some extreme right wing group - neo-Nazis. He mentioned something about a ship in a place called Aldvik. Wherever that is.'

'It's a port - up north. So what are you saying?'

'I am saying, do we have to call in the police at this stage?'

'We could get ourselves into a lot more trouble if we don't. And please remember I'm the one who just shot and killed a man.'

'You saved my life.'

'I don't know,' she said, shaking her head. She wasn't convinced.

With a plan forming in my mind, I tried again.

'The police are bound to hold us while they investigate. And if the Norwegian police don't file some charges against me, the British authorities most certainly will. Which all means that the people responsible for this, are going to have time to disappear back into the woodwork.'

'Mr Craig, do I understand you to mean, go it alone? That is the expression is it not?' Did I catch a hint of humour and the slightest of smiles?

'Not exactly Miss Olsen, I had hoped you might like to join me.' Then, returning to a more serious note, I asked, 'Did anybody know you were up here skiing with your father?'

She shook her head. 'Not to my knowledge. As you must be aware by now, my father was not very keen to advertise where he had gone to get away from his nightmare.'

'Good. Then there is nothing to tie us with the bloody events back up there on the mountain.' The moment those words left my lips I regretted the phrasing, and watched what was left of the smile disappear from her face. 'I am sorry... your father. That was thoughtless of me.'

'No you are right,' she said firmly, 'I want to know, as much as you, who is behind this, and how they can be stopped and brought to justice. What do you suggest?'

'As you said, we go it alone. Get ourselves up to this place Aldvik and see if we can find out what is going on. How would we get there?'

'Only one way really; the coastal ferry. Come on, it's getting late. We need to find a stopover for the night.'

'Just one more thing,' I said, 'I'm Steve. You?'

She hesitated for a second then answered, 'Karen.'

'Well, Karen, like it or not we are in this together. When the truth is revealed, you will be commended for saving my life, and the timely disposal of a murderous fanatic.'

'I hope you are right, Mr Craig,' she said with a wry smile.

'Steve.'

'Yes, of course, Steve. Shall we go?'

CHAPTER 24

At the HSE in Aberdeen, Commander Bruce stood in Broadhurst's Office, gazing out the window. He was not at all happy. Things were definitely not going according to plan.

Deliberately trying to avoid disturbing the Commander, Broadhurst stood at a filing cabinet quietly sifting through some folders. A tap on the door caused Bruce to escape from his deep contemplation, and he turned to see the broad figure of his man Faulkner entering the office.

'Faulkner, what's happening?'

Faulkner motioned his head to one side, indicating the need to speak with his boss in private.

'John,' Bruce spoke politely to Broadhurst, 'would you mind leaving us for a few minutes. Personal matter.'

Broadhurst knew it was nothing of the kind but interrupted his search through the cabinet, and gathering up a few sheets of paper, departed.

'Well?' Bruce asked as the door closed.

'No sign of him. The Norwegians were unable to pick up his track after he left the mountain. But he wasn't alone.'

'Oh?'

'There were two sets of ski tracks leading from the crime scene. He had company.'

'An accomplice? What's he up to?'

'Could be Olsen's daughter. Apparently she skied up there with her father quite often. The girl was training for some Olympic event. She's disappeared. The police are checking around the area. Neither of them went back to Olsen's cottage. They must be holed up somewhere else.'

'Why would the girl tie up with the man who'd just murdered her father?'

'Perhaps she had no say in the matter.'

Bruce turned and walked back to look out the window across at the grey, granite buildings of Aberdeen.

'You do realise don't you Faulkner, just how dangerous a man like Craig can be?'

'Well, I heard he was in the Special Boat Service, and got himself court-martialled during the second Gulf war. Charged with deliberately killing one of his own men while in action. And, although found not guilty, decided to call it a day anyway.'

'The man he shot was one of his closest comrades. He and a guy called Lieutenant Lee Summers had been in the thick of things even before the first Gulf war. The two of them, Craig and Sommers, were on a special mission in Basra. They were joined by an American Marine. An explosives expert named Jack Curtis.'

Faulkner raised his eyebrows. 'You mean?'

'Precisely. *The* Jack Curtis who just got taken out with the others on the *Highlander*.'

'So what went wrong - on the mission in the Gulf I mean?'

'They were about to blow up a Shia rebel group, armament depot. Some Iraqi kid came on the scene - got in their way. Sommers was certain the kid was wearing an explosives vest and was about to shoot him. They say Craig pleaded with Sommers not to fire but he wasn't falling for it. So Craig took Sommers out. Said he meant just to disable his buddy, but ended up shooting him clean through the heart.'

'So how did Craig manage to get off?'

'It turned out that the Iraqi kid was clean. In fact he was one of the few pro-British locals still around. Also his father was one of the big cheeses in the area. In fact, the story was the kid had been sent to warn the three that they were running into an ambush - a camouflaged guard emplacement on their line to the target. What with the kid's testimony and his father's standing, plus Big Jack's back up, they couldn't make any charge stick. And, as the exercise was a complete success - they blew the whole place to smithereens, and shut down enemy activities in the whole area for quite some time - there were no charges effectively held against Steve Craig. He was acquitted. That unfortunately was not the end for Craig. He chose to say enough was enough, and opted out. Since then he has been working for the HSE looking after marine and offshore activities and recruit training. Doing a pretty good job, so I am informed. But you can see, where this passion to find Big Jack's executioners, comes in to play. This whole business seems to have fired up the Steve Craig of old.'

'He's certainly a man with a good excuse for a revenge mission,' Faulkner said.

'That's why I want you over there, Faulkner,' Bruce nodded. 'Take Thompson. Find Steve Craig and stop him. Do whatever it takes.'

Without another word Faulkner headed for the door.

'And Faulkner,' Bruce's voice commanded his man's attention again. 'I don't want another one of my men down.'

When Faulkner left, Bruce sat at the desk for a while deep in thought. Then he picked up the phone, dialled, waited a few seconds and then spoke.

'Jorgensen, we need to talk.'

CHAPTER 25

From the tiny, elevated window of the Pensjonat Berg, I looked out at the lights across the small town of Helmsvik. It was night time, but it wasn't really dark. The sky had taken on more of a pale grey hue. And I knew, from now on, we would see these northern nights turning lighter as spring shifted into summer, and we moved further north. I'd forgotten how different it was up in these high latitudes - in the land of the midnight sun.

Karen and I, finally settling into a sort of tentative truce, had made it, without further incident, down the mountain to the small town of Helmsvik.

We found a place to spend the night. An inconspicuous little bed and breakfast stopover or *pensjonat* as they call the homely guest houses dotted all over the place, up in those parts. We decided to play the roles of two holidaying skiers. Karen acting the caring sister to my walk on part as the hard of hearing and somewhat backward brother. Thus avoiding the requirement for any significant Norwegian speaking performance from me.

We checked in. Separate rooms of course. The brother and sister routine not extending as far as any authentic, close family scenarios. Like sharing a bedroom for example. Karen did all the talking, and managed to obtain the details of a bus service to the port of Molde, located about twenty-five kilometres further north. From there we planned to take the regular ferry up the coast to our destination - this place Aldvik.

Any illusion that we may have had, that we would be well away from the area by the time the bodies were found up on the Hardangervidda, was just that, an illusion. And it was well and truly crushed, as we discovered, while standing in the small reception area of the Pensjonat Berg. The wail of the siren could be clearly heard in the confined space as the police car raced past on the road outside.

'Second one in half an hour,' Fru Dagsland, the red faced, buxom owner of the place, a woman in her late fifties, tutted. I got the gist of the Norwegian.

'Something going on up there, they say.' She nodded indicating the mountain range above the village. 'Did you notice anything on your way down?'

Karen deliberately avoided eye contact with me.

'No,' she said. 'Nothing unusual.'

'Well I guess we will read all about it in tomorrow's local newspaper. Now, if you two young people are hungry, I do have a few bread rolls, still fresh, and some ham.'

I didn't realise just how famished I was until she mentioned the food, and was more than glad that Karen was quick to accept the offer. We sat in silence eating the ham rolls and drinking hot coffee at a wooden table in the small breakfast room.

It was getting on for midnight when Fru Dagsland reappeared, supposedly to clear away our plates, but I suspected the real reason was to bring us up to date with the goings-on up on the mountain. I was right.

'Just been chatting to my friend over at the Helmsvik hotel. Two people have been shot up there, not by accident either, so they say. Police are all over the place.' She began to gather the plates. 'So now we know. It will be the talk of the town tomorrow. Don't get many murders in these parts. Anyway you two just forget it, and get yourselves off to bed.'

Leaving it at that, she handed over our room keys and directed us up an old wooden spiral staircase, wishing us both a very good night.

I couldn't settle. My watch said 4.30 am. Our arrangement was to leave at 7.15 am, in time to catch the first bus out, to Molde. So I'd wandered over to the window to take in the view outside.

A creaking of the wooden floor boards outside my room, and then a gentle but insistent tapping on the door, drew me from the window. I opened up to find Karen standing there.

'Well,' I said in a low voice, 'this is a surprise.'

'Not in your wildest dreams,' she said, pushing past me into the room and closing the door behind her. 'Get your gear together we are leaving. Now.'

'What's the rush,' I asked, starting to shove the few bits and pieces I had into my rucksack.'

'I've just been listening to the radio. She was right, Fru Dagsland. They have discovered the bodies up there.'

'So? We knew that would happen sooner or later. That's what we expected isn't it?'

'Yes but we didn't expect them to be looking for the main suspect. One Steven Craig a British subject believed to have carried out the murders as some sort of revenge killing spree.'

'Jesus,' I gasped. 'We've got to get to them and explain.'

'If that's what you want to do,' Karen said flatly. 'But now it's not looking so good for me either. Aiding and abetting a criminal or whatever they call it.'

She was right. The whole thing was rapidly spiralling out of our control.

'I agree. We can't just give up now. At the least, they will stop me making further enquiries, at the worst; probably charge me for obstruction of justice and suspicion of murder. And I do really want to know what that mystery ship in Aldvik is all about.'

'Me too,' Karen said firmly.

'So what are we waiting for let's get out of this place.'

Five hours later, we stepped off the bus at the quay in Molde trying to look like a couple of backpackers travelling light. The skis, we'd abandon back in Helmsvik, placing them in a rack outside a ski hire shop, before we left. Not much need for them where we were going. The rifle however, had proved a bit more difficult to dispose of.

'Getting rid of a couple of pairs of skis is one thing,' Karen said, with an understandable concern in her voice. 'But the weapon used in a murder investigation, that's another matter entirely.'

I agreed with her. We solved the problem by me climbing down a steep embankment under a deserted bridge and depositing the rifle in the undergrowth. If necessary,

I would come back for it later, at a more appropriate time.

A crowd of people had already started to assemble near the ferry embarkation station on the Molde quayside, so we headed in their direction. The booking office was a small wooden hut, displaying prices, a timetable and general information about the trips available along the Norwegian coastline.

'You stay here,' Karen said, touching my arm. 'I'll get the tickets.'

She set off for the ticket kiosk. Then turning her head called back, 'And don't strike up any lasting relationships.'

'You kidding?' I replied, pleased to realise we were both lightening up a bit, despite the seriousness of the situation.

I could see there was a small queue of people in front of Karen at the kiosk, waiting to buy tickets. She would be gone for a few minutes. So, in the mean time, I just wandered around. Then I caught site of another small shop on the far side of the quay, selling light refreshments, magazines and newspapers. I headed towards it and then quickly stepped to one side, as a grey van, appearing from out of nowhere, pulled across my path and came to a halt outside the little shop. It took just a few seconds for the driver to jump out, open the rear door, and lift out a bundle of daily newspapers, which he dropped onto the ground in front of the shop. Another few seconds saw people on the dockside dodging the van as it accelerated away.

Casually strolling up to the pile of papers on the paving, I stooped to get a better look at the front page headlines. Although partly covered by a yellow securing tape, I could see enough of the sheet to send a shiver up my spine. On the front cover was a half page picture of me. The headline, in bold, black print, advised readers that the English man pictured, was wanted for a double homicide. Much of the remainder of the article in smaller print below was mostly obscured by the binding.

'Forget it.' Karen was at my side looking down at the newspaper front page. 'Just pull your hat down, keep a low profile and stay close to me.'

We moved, not too quickly, away from the shop together, Karen's arm intimately tucked in mine. We were just your everyday item, about to take a romantic boat trip.

'Could you make out anymore of that report?' I questioned.

She nodded. 'Some of it. They think you are the only one involved. Apparently you have left a very traceable track since your arrival in Norway. They knew you were asking questions about my father and acting suspiciously. They've concluded you had reason enough to kill him.'

'And the other character?'

'A passing stranger. No connection. Just a guy in the wrong place at the wrong time.'

'Well then, what about the gun he was carrying? The one he used to kill your father? The one we left up there?'

'No mention.'

'This is nothing but a set up,' I proclaimed a bit too loudly. Heads around us turned to stare at me. Karen pulled me away, and we moved further down the quay. I wasn't finished though, and said, more quietly this time, 'The only person who guessed I was coming to Norway was Bruce, the ISD guy. He must have sent the killer to dispose of your father and me.'

Karen shook her head. 'Who is this Bruce person and why would he do such a thing?'

'That's another thing I intend to find out,' I said firmly. 'Fortunately they don't know about you Karen. But it's going to be pretty difficult keeping one step ahead of them. I can assure you.'

'Not necessarily. Where we're going, nobody will recognise you.' She sounded confident. 'Not from that picture in the newspaper anyway. Provided you keep covered up as you are. And the five o'clock shadow is beginning to play its part. John public will not be looking for a guy with a beard.' For the second time that day she flashed a heart warming smile at me, a smile that changed her completely. I realised just what a stunningly attractive woman she really was. And the fact she had demonstrated that English was not her mother tongue - the 'John' instead of 'Joe public' remark, made not the slightest difference to me whatsoever.

'So you're happy to press on?' It was more of a statement from me than a question.

'Not many other options to choose from,' she replied, the smile slowly fading around her full lips. 'We can lie low on the boat for a couple of days. It's a three day trip and I have booked a cabin for us, so we can stay out of everybody's way.'

'Just one cabin?' Now it was my turn to produce the smile on my face, together with one raised eyebrow.

She didn't bite.

'It was all I could get. This is a very popular excursion for tourists, even at this time of the year. We were lucky to get any accommodation at all. It would have been almost impossible for us to book anything during the summer months, without advanced notice. And don't get any ideas. This is business, serious business.'

I could see she wasn't joking and nodded convincingly. Still I was not going to complain about having to share a cabin with a woman as attractive as this one.

'I have signed us in as Mr and Mrs Eriksen…Norwegians. Avoiding having to mess about with passports on an inland trip.'

'You appear to have thought of everything. Are you sure you haven't done this before?' I regretted it the moment the words left my lips. It was plain stupidity and thoughtless of me. It was the second time I had made such a blunder, and I knew I was sailing very close to the wind.

'What sort of a remark is that?' Karen snapped at me.

'I was joking,' I said feebly, wanting to kick myself.

'Mr Craig, you are in no position to be joking about anything,' she said coldly, her tone devoid of any of the earlier light heartedness. A second later we heard the sound of a ship's horn and looked up to see the coastal ferry approaching Molde harbour.

'Come on,' Karen said. 'We have a boat to catch.'

CHAPTER 26

'I want a boat at Molde as soon as possible. Get Andre on it immediately. Something fast and suitable for deep sea.'

The man watched Steve Craig and Karen Olsen mingling with the other passengers as they made their way up the gangway on to the coastal ferry. The name painted on the bow of the ship said *North Star*. Identifying one of a regular fleet of ships operating year round from Bergen in the south, up the coast as far north as Hammerfest – a port located well within the Arctic Circle. He wondered just how far up the coast Steve Craig and his new partner were intending to travel.

He held the line, waiting for confirmation of his order. It came back in less than a minute.

'They are on their way - Andre and Karl. They will pick you up at Molde within the hour. The boat is fast - 30 knots.'

'Good. We should be able to catch up with them at Kristiansund. It's the first port of call on the passage. Although I don't expect them to be getting off that early. If that was the case, they could have easily taken a bus to cover that short distance. I guess they must be going further up – maybe all the way.'

He closed the mobile and walked across the quay to a small coffee kiosk, from where he could keep a close eye on the ferry. He did not want them getting off before the ship sailed, without him noticing them, that is. Steve Craig was proving to be a wily character. He couldn't rule out him setting up another diversion. Craig certainly had shown no difficulty in detecting the other guy on his tail, why not have done so again?

CHAPTER 27

Onboard the North Star, Karen, doing all the talking again, had obtained the key to our accommodation, and we made our way down to Cabin number 18, located on the lower deck. The space was compact, with a sofa, small writing desk, two, tiered bunks, wardrobe and a small en suite bathroom. It was basic but comfortable.

'This is fine,' I said. 'It will do.'

Clearly staking a claim, Karen dropped her back pack onto the lower bunk and said, 'It will have to do.'

She was still smarting from my earlier thoughtless remark. 'You'd better get used to it, Mr Craig. You are going to stay in here for the next seventy two hours.'

'Don't I even get to take a peek at the famous beautiful coastline of Norway?'

'Of course you do. Through that,' she answered, pointing to the small cabin porthole. 'Meanwhile,' she continued, 'I think you'd better unpack your bag. I am going up on deck to take a look around.'

She noted my surprised look. I thought, probably she just wanted to get away on her own for a while. Her returned expression confirmed that conclusion. She left the cabin without another word.

CHAPTER 28

Up on the deck, the crew were winching in the last lengths of mooring rope. The ship was about to leave port. A blast from the horn signalled departure time, and Karen heard the gush of air coming from the funnel as the main diesel engine was started.

Most of the tourist passengers were gathered on the observation deck; taking in as much of the scenery as they could. Nobody wanting to miss a second of the voyage now it had started.

Karen slowly wandered among the crowd studying faces and body language, ready to pick out any stranger who might be interested in either her or her new companion.

The ship got underway quite quickly, and she watched the Molde quayside dropping back in the vessel's foaming wake.

Satisfied there was no immediate threat to the plan, she strolled around the deck, deep in thought. She still had reservations. She had already asked herself a number of times, if taking up with Steve Craig, had been the right choice. But there was no doubt in her mind that he would help her get to Aldvik. A woman travelling alone would be more of a target than a couple, particularly under the present circumstances.

Apart from a few stragglers, the decks had started to empty. Passengers were returning to their cabins to unpack and settle in.

Karen headed into the accommodation and worked her way back down to the cabin.

CHAPTER 29

I was still glued to the porthole when Karen returned. Even with the ship only just moving away from the shore, the scene outside was quite spectacular. From an observation point of view, the cabin was located in a perfect position, because the ferry would cruise north keeping the land on the starboard side. So I was satisfied I would at least be guaranteed a picture of this stunning coast line, for most of the voyage to Aldvik. Albeit a limited view through a small port window located very low down and only a metre or so from the water line and the sea, lapping along outside.

'We are on our way,' she said, sounding a bit happier.

'Yes, I've been getting a fish's eye view. It's beautiful out there,' I said, meeting her with some lightness in my own voice too. 'I see the pilot boat is on its way,' I commented casually.

'Pilot boat?' She sounded surprised.

'Must be. Can't you feel the ship slowing down ready to take the pilot on board?'

Karen moved to join me at the porthole.

'These ferries don't take on independent pilots. All the ships' Captains sailing on these routes up the coast are qualified to navigate the whole coastal stretch, including all the ports of call and the inner fjords. But I can see you are right, there is a small boat approaching the ship. Must be some late arriving VIP passenger with enough pull and money to, not only hold the ship and hire a launch but…unless.' She stopped speaking and turned to look questioningly at me. 'You don't suppose it's the…'

'Police?' I finished the sentence for her, with a big question mark already flashing through my own mind. 'You mean they may know we're on board? That's impossible.'

I moved closer to her at the porthole, and together we angled our heads to get a better view of the approaching launch, and I caught the lightest of fragrances from whatever perfume she was using and felt something inside me stir.

'That's not a police boat,' Karen stated positively, pulling herself away from the porthole and me. Back to reality.

'I am sure it's some late arriving passenger,' she declared with authority, but I guessed there was still some doubt in her own mind.

'And, as you just said, one with enough pull and money to pay for a private launch,' I added.

'Anyway,' Karen said, 'I think I should go back up on deck again and take a closer look. Just to be sure.'

CHAPTER 30

For the second time in fifteen minutes, Karen made her way along the upper deck and joined a few other passengers, also showing a similar interest in the new arrival. She could hear the people around her engaged in discussing a probable explanation.

'There's always one,' a man with a strong American accent sighed.

'A rich one too, by the look of it,' a Norwegian woman nearby commented in English, obviously for the American's benefit.

Then an almost heated discussion broke out between two other passengers, a man and a woman, speaking in a language she didn't recognise – mid European or something.

Karen moved away, more interested in the events taking place alongside the ship. The launch had tucked in close to the bottom of an overhanging rope ladder that had been hastily dropped down the side shell of the ship by one of the crew. The crewman now stood by, waiting to offer a helping hand to the latecomer.

A half minute passed, and then a man's head appeared above the deck level. He quickly pulled himself up, and stepped over the raised coaming and through the open rail onto the main deck. Safely onboard, the newcomer checked about him, before turning and heading towards the bridge access stair, where one of the ship's officers was heading down to meet him. Karen caught sight of the new arrival's face. She knew him. Well, that is, she recognised him. She had seen him before but couldn't recall exactly where. She should have remembered though, if not for his size alone. He was a very big man; tall, broad and muscular.

Anyway, she felt pretty sure he was no policeman and probably no immediate threat to either her or Steve Craig.

She turned and headed back to the cabin.

CHAPTER 31

I had finally relinquished my observation position at the cabin porthole when Karen returned from her second sortie up on deck.

'I don't think it's the police. Just as you said, some VIP getting the royal treatment. In fact I did recognise him. Well sort of. I mean I think I may have seen him someplace before - television perhaps.'

'That's good,' I said, and flopped down on the sofa. I suppose I was beginning to unwind a bit.

From deep within the bowels of the ship, we heard the hiss of compressed air and the rumble of the main diesel engine being restarted, and felt the vibration pulsing through the structure as once more the *North Star* got underway.

'I am going to take a shower,' Karen said decisively, rummaging through her back-pack for a few bits and pieces of toiletry, before disappearing into the small bathroom.

I settled down on the sofa. It was time to give the whole thing a good going over in my mind. Events had occurred so rapidly in the past forty-eight hours, with more than a few surprises thrown in for good measure. Not least, my association with the attractive but enigmatic woman now only a few feet away, on the other side of that door. I still had some serious reservations, whether or not we were doing the sensible thing. If we were picked up by the police now, it would only confirm that we were on the run, and as guilty as hell. On the other hand, I was certain that Commander Bruce was somehow involved in this whole business. His rapid appearance on the scene at the HSE office, and his quick dismissal of me, plus his unflagging aversion to the possibility that another ship, called *Panther,* was very much involved, all added up to something very unsavoury. And, another question - was the guy up on the Hardangervidda sent by him to get rid of both Olsen and me? Who else would want to do that? And then there was Olsen's so called neighbour, Lindefjell. Where the hell did that character fit into all this? The guy certainly seemed to want me to find Olsen. Perhaps it was he who sent the hit man? If he did, then why involve me in the first place? Why couldn't he have got to Olsen himself? And why then wait to take me out? The questions with no clear answers rattled through my brain. I could only hope that we would retrieve some of those answers in this place Karen and I were heading for - Aldvik.

Somewhere during all this brain searching I must have drifted off to sleep. No surprise really, I had not had a proper rest in seventy-two hours, apart from the nap I'd taken on the train to Voss.

For a while I must have remained in a deep undisturbed sleep, then some of the old pictures and resurrected memories were triggered, and started to flash through my brain.............

......it is hot and humid and very dark - the patrol boat moves up the delta at a slow speed - keeping the engine noise level to the minimum. Crouching up in the bow, I turn to see Jack and Lee, their painted faces displaying grim concentration. In a few minutes the three of us will be in the dinghy, paddling for the shore. The target - a weapons dump at Al Bakhir, Iraq. Lee and I are what you might term SBS veterans; we have been doing this sort of thing for quite some time. The other guy, Jack the big American Marine joined us only two days ago. Special assignment - 'just on loan so to speak' - as he put it. In a few minutes the three of us will land on the rock strewn stretch of sand. Then what happens will change my life, forever. I know what is going to happen. The dinghy hits the beach its nose sinking into the coarse wet shingle... I jump ashore...and call my two comrades to follow...

'Steve! Steve! Are you alright?'

I found myself on my feet standing or rather crouching in the cabin after leaping from the sofa. Karen stood silhouetted in the bathroom doorway, draped in a white bath towel and vigorously drying her long fair hair with a smaller one.

'I'm fine,' I said, and collapsed back onto the sofa, feeling kind of foolish.

'That was some dream you were having.' She sounded more intrigued than concerned. 'Who are Jack and Lee?'

'I'm sorry if I startled you,' I said, deliberately avoiding the answer to her question. I didn't want to go into all that. 'Yes, you're right, that's just what it was, a bad dream. Have you finished in there?' I asked, changing the subject and indicating the bathroom behind her.

'Of course. Go ahead.' She moved to one side letting me pass.

Twenty minutes and a long, hot and very refreshing shower later, I slipped back into the cabin. At first I thought Karen was asleep. She had her back to me and was curled up in the classic foetal position, the bath towel still draped around her lithe figure. I guessed she must have been too tired to bother getting dressed.

The few items of clean clothing I possessed and had luckily brought with me, were in my back-pack on the top bunk. Trying not to disturb her, I reached for the bag. It was at that point, I realised that Karen was not asleep, but just lying there - crying softly.

I left my bag where it was and bent down to her.

'Karen, you're upset,' I said. Considering our present predicament, it was a bit of a dumb thing to say. Of course she was upset.

She swung around immediately, tears streaming down her face. For a second I thought she was about to strike me for foolishly stating the obvious. But instead she threw herself into my arms.

'Oh, Steve I am so frightened,' she sobbed, pulling me closer until the scent of her body seemed to engulf both of us. 'It's all happened so quickly. I can't believe my father is dead - murdered. And me killing a man. I think it's beginning to be more than I can handle.' She drew me closer still and I couldn't avoid the view of her perfect body, more than partly revealed as the bath towel slipped down an inch or two.

I just held her, silently. The fact is I really didn't know what to say. This sudden show of emotion from the girl I was beginning to think of as the original ice maiden, had taken me by complete surprise.

'How did we get into this terrible situation?' she sobbed, modestly trying to pull the slipping towel back into place.

'It's going to be alright, Karen. I promise,' I said, trying to make my words sound convincing, even though I knew quite well, they were far from that. 'But, I do believe,' I said, drawing her closer to me, 'if we are going to put this whole thing to rest, then we must go on. We've got to get to Aldvik and find that ship.'

'I know we must, Steve,' she said, nestling closer. 'But, I don't think I could manage it alone…without you.'

Then to my great surprise and even greater pleasure, she kissed me full on the lips. Gently at first, then with a passion I did not really think she possessed. Our mouths met, then our tongues and then, still entwined in a more fierce embrace, I lowered her back onto the mattress. I could only watch mesmerised, as the towel fell completely away, and she pulled me down on top of her naked body.

I don't really know how much time had passed when I awoke, and gently moved Karen's arm from across my chest. I lifted my head in an attempt to focus across the cabin on my wristwatch that I had thrown on the sofa earlier. There was still quite a bright light coming in from outside through the cabin window, but I guessed it was already late evening. I had no idea how long we had been asleep in each other's arms, but I did remember we had made love for over an hour - how could I ever forget that? Then, I think we must have slept for a while before I was thrown into another mad session of physical ecstasy with this, the most beautiful and passionate woman I had ever known. Karen Olsen had certainly transformed, or rather melted, from ice queen to sensual siren. I never dreamed she could have turned out to be so passionate.

'That was rather sudden,' Karen said, with a lilt in her voice, as she lifted herself and turned to kiss me on the cheek.

'Shouldn't I be saying that?' I asked, turning to meet her lips full on.

It must have been another ten minutes before either of us spoke again.

Then Karen giggled like a little girl and said 'This certainly wasn't a part of our master plan.'

'I was never *that* good at planning,' I said, as I reached for her again.

'Plan or no plan,' she announced breathlessly, a few moments later, 'it was certainly very well executed, Mr Craig.'

'Couldn't be in a better place to break the ice,' I said, and was rewarded again with that captivating smile and the lightest ring of musical laughter.

Then, becoming more serious, she said, 'It was a terrible way for us to meet but I am so glad we did, Steve.'

'Me too.'

Laying back she moved easily to me, resting her face into my shoulder and letting her long golden hair fall across my chest.

'You know, Karen,' I said after a few minutes of contemplative silence, 'you know, you speak perfect English.'

'I should do, I did my finishing in England.'

'God, I must have sounded patronising just then.'

'Not at all, she said,' giving me a warm, forgiving hug. 'I have been lucky with languages. Norwegian is my mother tongue of course but I think I have mastered German pretty well and a bit of French.

'Stop! You are castrating me,' I groaned, 'but I can get by reasonably in German myself, and a touch of Norwegian.'

'Castration is not exactly what I had in mind right now,' she giggled mischievously, and pulled me over on to her.

Another hour slipped by. It was probably the pangs of hunger that interrupted things. We both needed to eat something, and pretty soon. But it was so peaceful lying beside each other, neither of us was that eager to challenge the status quo.

'Steve?' Karen said, after spending a while gazing up at the very unromantic wooden slats of the underside of the top bunk, above our heads.

'Uhhuh?' I was still drifting in paradise.

'Did my father give any details about this ship in Aldvik? Is it docked their? Does it visit regularly? How do we know what we are looking for?'

A lot of questions, to which I was able to provide very few answers. None in fact.

'I don't really know. Sorry.'

Then, as a vivid picture of the bloodied and dying Nils Olsen flashed into my mind. I sat up.

'Wait. He did say a name.'

I tried to recall the scene up on the Hardangervidda in more detail. The one that would help me remember - as grisly as it was.

'Torild I think. No Torvald. Yes, that's it Torvald. I'm sure.'

'Torvald.' Karen repeated the name slowly, searching for a link. 'Could be a contact person.'

'Or the name of the ship itself,' I suggested.

'Maybe. But he didn't mention any of the people he was involved with…the leaders…names…descriptions….contacts?'

'No, none at all. But he was deeply unhappy about their methods and what they had done. Especially what had taken place on the *Highlander*. He seemed to be even more concerned about so many Norwegians being involved.'

I noticed Karen lower her head away from my gaze. Then she spoke quietly, a deep sadness in her voice.

'It's my fault. He wanted to tell me more, but I wouldn't let him. I knew what he was doing was illegal. I begged him to stop. Then, when he said he was too deeply involved, I just shut him out. I never dreamed it would lead to all this. I was even stupid enough to think it was some sort of black market activity or money laundering, things like that - not this nightmare.'

'You can't blame yourself, Karen.' I touched her shoulder gently.

'Of course I blame myself,' she snapped, pulling herself away from me. 'If I had given him even a tiny bit of my time, as he always gave me his, then I may have helped him. Not thrown him to the wolves.'

She started crying and there was not a single thing I could do to comfort her. Slowly, I rose from the bed, and reaching for my bag on the bunk above, started to rifle through the limited contents for something suitable to wear. The moment of bliss, it appeared, had all too quickly slipped away.

Deciding it was probably a good idea to leave Karen alone for a while; I grabbed a few things from my bag and slipped into the bathroom again.

When I reappeared ten minutes later, Karen was already dressed and her smile told me everything was fine again.

'Are you hungry?' Karen asked. 'Because I'm starving,' she added quickly before I could reply. I just nodded enthusiastically, still a little unsure how fragile her emotions might still be.

'I'll go and see what I can find for us.'

I assumed Karen would be gone for at least ten to fifteen minutes. So I was surprised when the door shot open and she made a sudden re-appearance, after barely a couple of minutes had passed. She looked flushed and slightly out of breath and more than a little worried.

'What is it? Why no food?'

'No time to get any, I'm afraid. No time for anything, Steve,' she said. 'That guy, the one who came out late. He *is* a policeman.'

'But you said….'

'I know what I said but I was wrong. They are looking for you!'

'How the hell did they know we were on this ship?'

'I don't think they know for sure otherwise they would have sent more than one man. It must be a routine check of all possible routes out of the area. I managed to get some information from one of the crew. He told me they have started systematically questioning everyone on board. They are going from cabin to cabin. Fortunately for us, they've started with the passengers on the upper accommodation levels first.'

'Then I've got to get out of here right away. It's me not you they want. I need to find a place to hide,' I said, a plan already triggered in my mind.

'Where for heaven's sake?'

'A bit basic but could work,' I said. 'Up in one of the lifeboats. If this is only a general check on passengers, they won't be searching in ship's lifeboats.'

Karen shook her head.

'But what are they going to do when they can't find Mr Eriksen?'

'No problem. You tell all. Well almost all.'

'Steve, you are losing me.'

'You tell them that I forced you to accompany me. A hostage. No need to go into detail.'

'And when they ask where you are?'

'I panicked when the strange guy came out in a launch and I jumped ship.'

'You know they are bound to arrest me. Don't forget, I am responsible for one of the shootings.'

'They have no proof – no motive –no weapon and no witnesses. Karen, all you need to do, is maintain your innocence. The police will have to let you go. If they don't discover me, I'll get off the boat at Aldvik and hang around the dock until you turn up. Failing that, and when it all settles down, you go back to your father's house in Stavanger. I have the telephone number. I will contact you there.'

'Steve, this is madness.'

'Madness was once an essential ingredient in my line of work. Karen, we have no choice, if we stand any chance at all in uncovering this whole business. If we can't do it together, then one of us must go alone. Going it alone by the way, is also something I'm quite good at.'

'But...'

'Enough talking, Karen. We need to go, now.'

I slipped into my anorak and opened the cabin door.

'We'll go together,' I said, taking Karen's arm. 'Just a couple of... lovers out on deck admiring the view,' I added, looking into Karen's deep blue eyes. 'At least that definition is not totally false.'

She gripped my arm and kissed me on the lips. 'Please be careful, Steve.'

'It's going to be alright. I promise,' I said.

But then I always say things like that.

CHAPTER 32

Thankfully, there was nobody at all hanging about when we stepped out onto the aft deck from a companionway leading up from our cabin level. I guessed most of the passengers would be in the dining saloon for the evening meal.

Although quite dim, I knew that it would not get any darker than this, and the further north we sailed the lighter the nights would become, and the days, that much longer.

I put my arm around Karen, and we made our way towards a flight of steps leading up onto the starboard lifeboat deck. It was all clear up there too. The two large lifeboats sat firmly secured above us in their heavy, angled steel davits. Thankfully, I noted that the boats were of the enclosed type. Each with a reinforced fibreglass cabin, designed to protect the passengers from wind, sea and weather. Once up on the lifeboat, I would easily be able to get myself inside the boat housing, without having to disturb any sort of canvass tarpaulin cover or the like. Things had moved on since the Titanic. Also the access doors into the lifeboats are never locked.

One last look around the deck to make sure the coast was clear, and a quick, final hug with Karen, and I was on my way, shinning up the steel lifeboat davit frame. It was an easy climb - plenty of hand and foot holds to lever myself up.

I was just about to swing my leg over the lifeboat side, when I heard a cry from the deck below.

It was Karen, and she was in trouble!

'Let me go! Steve help me.'

Immediately, I released my grip on the side of the boat, and slid back down the davit. Needless to say, it was far quicker going down than climbing up, and I was able to jump the last six feet to the deck below. Regaining my balance, I looked around searching for Karen. But there was no sound other than the gentle throbbing of the engines and the rush of water rolling past the ship. It was eerily still, and I knew something bad had happened to Karen. I turned towards the ship's rail, a rush of fear taking hold of me as I pictured Karen being heaved over the side of the ship - a thousand scenarios racing through my mind. At the rail I leaned over to view the water rushing past below, for any sign of her, or a disturbance of any kind in the foaming wake of the ship. There was none.

Then a blinding light, and searing pain, cut through my brain, and all went black.

CHAPTER 33

'You'd better get the man up here quickly, Karl,' the helmsman ordered, as he pulled back on the engine throttles and felt the drag as the launch started to slow down.

'What's up Andre?' Karl queried joining his companion at the wheel.

'Looks like somebody's going for a midnight swim. Just jumped over the side of the *North Star*.'

Karl snatched a pair of binoculars from the shelf and focused through the forward window of the launch, now rapidly reducing speed through the water. Quite clearly, he could see the coastal ferry *North Star* ahead. They had been trailing her uneventfully for some hours now. The big ship continued steaming steadily on course, apparently unaware that somebody had just dropped over the side.

'Jesus! You're right,' he exclaimed. 'Who is it?'

'How the hell would I know that?' Andre replied, more than a little irritated. 'But we are about to find out. Now go and get him.'

Karl, wasting no more time, threw the binoculars back onto the shelf, turned and crossed the bridge to the stairwell leading down to the cabin space, and disappeared below decks.

Barely thirty seconds elapsed before Karl reappeared. This time followed by another man who, without a word, pushed past him and moved to the forward window. He did not require the binoculars. He could see the person in the water ahead of them quite clearly. It was difficult to say whether the man floating face up on the surface of the water was dead or alive.

'Get him up,' the man commanded. 'I'll watch the wheel.'

Andre and Karl left the wheelhouse and made their way down onto the forward port side deck area; Andre stopping only to retrieve a long handled boathook from a rack against the accommodation housing. The way had come off the launch. Now, it slowly edged closer to the body floating on the surface of the water.

'He looks a dead man,' said Karl, getting his first clear view of Steve Craig. 'Why hasn't he gone under?'

'Looks like his jacket kept him afloat,' Andre replied. 'Must have got air trapped in it. Inflated on the way down as he was falling. Acted like a parachute. Probably reduced the impact when he hit, as well. Didn't do him much good though, by the look of it. Anyway, let's cut the chat and get him on board.'

Retrieving the body from the water and on to the deck of the launch, was no easy task for the two men. The only effective piece of equipment they possessed was the hastily retrieved boat hook. Normally well equipped for most eventualities, this time they had come totally unprepared for this particular exercise. Manipulating the boathook as best they could around Steve's body several times, they eventually managed to secure a hold in the folds of his jacket, and managed to pull him up to the edge of the deck. From that position they were able to grab him and heave him aboard. Safely up on the deck, the two men laid him out on the boards.

Andre felt for a pulse and then turned to give the thumbs-up signal to the man, peering down at them through the bridge window.

'He's alive,' Andre shouted.

CHAPTER 34

…………I lead the way - Jack and Lee follow. It's dark and we don't have night vision glasses with us. There are some dim lights above the dunes ahead. They flicker like oil lamps. Now and then we observe some movement and detect the sound of voices travelling to us through the still, humid air. We are prepared to encounter any resistance from the guards at the base, but our plan is to get in and set the charges without being spotted. If it comes to a fight we will be hopelessly outnumbered. But this place has to be destroyed - at all costs. Soon we reach the outskirts of the depot. The corrugated huts are silhouetted in the wavering light from the lamps and the flames of a makeshift stove, burning in an old oil drum at the side of the dirt path. Some of the men are asleep - rolled in dirty sheets with loose clothing draped over them. The night air is not cold, but it appears as though they want to hide away from it – so they cover up.

Two guards, armed with Kalashnikovs, wander aimlessly around the huts. They exchange a few words and a joke, each time their paths cross.

Lee taps my shoulder. I turn to follow his pointing finger. He's indicating the far side of the compound. It's dark over there, nothing to light the space between the two centre huts. The piles of ammunition are laid out in sectors, but the stacking arrangement is so close together that we only need to fire one for the whole lot to go up. Lee's unspoken proposal is perfect. There will be nothing left of this place when we detonate the charges between the two huts.

I nod the okay to Lee and turn to Jack. He's happy too - he's got to be - he's the one going in to set the charges.

Everything is running to plan. But somehow I know something is going to go wrong....

There is a flash of lightening and a searing pain fires through my head. I open my eyes and all I can see is a bright strip light above me. I am lying down on my back... I must have been hit...a bullet in the head....

'Ah. I am glad to see you back with us, Mr Craig.'

I've heard that voice before, but I don't know when or where. I don't know anything. The whole place is swaying back and fore.

'Where am I?' I croak. 'The room is rocking ....'

'That's because you are on a boat, Mr Craig. Bit smaller than the last one you were on. But at least you are safe. I have no intention of throwing you back into the water.'

That familiar voice again.

'Safe?' I say, and then things slowly start to clear - first the pain in my head diminishes to just a violent throb and my blurred vision begins to clear - then, I remember..............

'Somebody hit me!' I heard myself saying as I pulled up into a sitting position on the bunk. And immediately fell back down again, as the blinding pain crashed once more through my skull.

'Take it easy, Mr Craig. You have received quite a crack to your head. Not to mention being unceremoniously thrown overboard from a ship, and then spending fifteen minutes floating in some pretty cold water.'

I was slowly coming to my senses.

This time I lifted myself more carefully into a sitting position. Then I swung my legs carefully over the edge of the bunk, my feet eventually touching the deck unsteadily.

'A nasty experience but you are going to make it.'

Herr Lindefjell walked into my line of vision.

As the pain in my head receded, I started to recall the past few hours leading up to my present state. So I had been knocked out by somebody and thrown from the coastal ferry. Somehow I had been picked up by dead Olsen's so-called neighbour, Lindefjell. Who, it appeared, just happened to be passing in his boat at the time. How convenient. But I wasn't complaining.

I scanned the space around me. I was sat on a bunk in a cabin on a boat. A motor cruiser of some dimension, and by the quality of the outfitting surrounding me, of some luxury as well. In front of me stood the man who was undoubtedly responsible for my being on the coastal ferry in the first place, and quite possibly the cause of me being hurled off it. Although, I doubt very much he would have bothered to pull me out of the drink if he had been party to that.

He looked younger to me now than he had at our first meeting in Stavanger, a few days ago. I guessed his original but not very convincing portrayal of the friendly next door neighbour had been designed to give the impression of an interfering, old man. Although that ploy had failed, the outcome of me getting to Olsen, had turned out to be most effective.

Slowly my thoughts became clearer. Then a sudden rush of panic!

'What about, Karen?' I exclaimed. 'Was she....thrown...?'

'Relax, Mr Craig,' Lindefjell said calmly, walking across the cabin and offering me a mug steaming with a hot broth of some kind in it. 'I am pleased to say that your lady companion must have been treated with a little more respect than you. I think I can safely confirm that no one else was thrown off the *North Star*. You were lucky I just happened to be sailing by.'

'Quite a coincidence, Herr Lindefjell - if that's your real name.'

'It's not actually. Total fabrication in fact,' he admitted, his craggy features breaking into something of a grin. 'Good Norwegian name though. I once had a neighbour myself with that name – nice chap, wife and two kids.'

'So what is *your* real name?' I asked, not expecting to get anything like a truthful answer.

'You can call me Oberst. Everybody calls me Oberst.'

'Oberst? That's colonel in German,' I stated.

'Absolutely correct. But it's also colonel in Norwegian.'

'So, how does a Norwegian Colonel fit into all this? And why were you following the coastal ferry?'

'Keeping a close eye on you and your new girlfriend. Lucky for you, if you don't mind me saying.'

'Karen?' I asked, reminded again of the girl I had been so close to only a few hours ago, and wondering now if she was still alive even. 'Why do you think they didn't deal with her in the same manner as me?'

'Throw her overboard you mean?' the Oberst said bluntly, before answering the question. 'It would appear that Miss Karen Olsen is of more value to them alive than dead. I am afraid the same cannot be said for you. You Mr Craig, were obviously considered to be of somewhat lesser value.'

I took a sip of the broth. It was tasty, and I was already beginning to feel better. The throbbing pain in my skull easing a bit.

'So what exactly is going on... Herr Oberst?'

'Just Oberst will do - you know the German thing I mentioned at our first meeting in Stavanger. Norwegians don't usually address any of their officers as Herr...whatever.'

'Why are you still playing cat and mouse with me?' I asked angrily. 'Is it so difficult for you just to tell me exactly what's going on?'

'All in good time, Mr Craig. Let's get you up and functioning one hundred percent, and then we will be on our way.'

'On our way where?' I asked, attempting to rise to my feet, but then weakly flopping back on the bed - my head continuing to ring from the impact of a thousand hammers. A second attempt was more successful and this time I did manage to remain upright.

'I was hoping you would tell me, exactly where *you* were heading,' the Oberst replied.

'Why should I trust you Colonel?' I said, thinking if the guy wanted to play games, so be it.

'How about because I saved your life...I haven't turned you in... I've got a boat, and I am as much interested in getting Miss Olsen safely off that ferry as you are. Oh, and I haven't got much time for the bastards responsible for all this mayhem. Including what they did to the crew of the *Highlander*.'

'Aldvik,' I said. 'We were heading for Aldvik.'

The Oberst, showing no surprise, just nodded.

Then, another thought struck me. 'You don't suppose that they may not be taking Karen to Aldvik?' I asked. 'What if they plan to get her off the ship at some other place? Aldvik may mean nothing to them'

'I should not worry yourself about that if I were you, Mr Craig. My people will cover all the stops to Aldvik. If she leaves the ship at any time, we will know about it believe me.'

'Your people?'

'We are not totally alone up here, Mr Craig.

CHAPTER 35

Otto Klensch stood at the window of his penthouse room on the top floor of the Hamburg Vier Jahreszeitan hotel, looking out across the Alster Lake.

It was a bright and clear morning, and amid the continuous flow of commercial traffic, the Alster was already dotted with the sails of small boats drifting lazily across the still water.

On his regular visits to Hamburg, Klensch stayed at this grand and famous old hotel which was probably better known internationally by its English title - The Four Seasons. He had maintained one of the penthouse suites at the hotel for many years. However, as comfortable as it was he would much rather have been at the place in Bavaria. The one that would soon become his true home - the one they had agreed to name the New Bechtesgaden Berghof; in memory of the home of the first Fuhrer of the Reich, Adolf Hitler. When the time was right, that place would become the residence of the New Aryan leaders in Germany. A similar retreat had already been established in Norway, at Aldvik.

There was a knock on the door prompting Klensch to check the time on his wrist. Right on schedule. He smiled with satisfaction. He had never known Brett to be late for anything. Klensch crossed the room and opened the door to greet his visitor.

'My dear Brett. Please come in,' Klensch said standing to one side and holding the door open for the commander of the *Panther* - Kapitän Rudolf Brett.

'Reichsleiter,' Brett said, once inside the room with the door closed firmly behind him. Accompanying his formal greeting with the slightest upward motion of the right hand as the heels of his polished black shoes made sharp contact.

Klensch returned the salute in a similar fashion, barring the heel click, and pointing to one of the two chairs placed at a round table near the window, invited Kapitän Brett to be seated. Klensch did not immediately join him, preferring to take up his original position at the window, still choosing to admire the scene outside.

'You did well, Rudolf,' Klensch said, without turning. 'They still believe it was a terrorist attack carried out by some faction in the Middle East. Although for a while I thought we were going to have a problem.'

'You mean the English man?' It was more of a statement than a question from Brett.

'He was Scotch actually,' Klensch replied. But Brett had no intention of counter-correcting the Reichsleiter, by informing him that Scotch was a whisky that was produced in Scotland, but it was the Scots who inhabited the place. 'Yes,' Klensch continued, 'Herr Craig looked as if he was going to present a problem to us. That is until his fortuitous disembarkation from the *North Star*.'

'What about the lady?' Brett enquired cautiously.

'Don't worry. She is being well looked after. Soon she will be prepared for the next phase.'

There was a light tap on the door.

'Ah!' Klensch exclaimed as he turned from the window and crossed the room to answer the knock. 'Rudolf, I have ordered some light refreshment. I trust you will join me.' It was not a request but an order.

Once the hotel waiter had laid out the platter of food, uncorked a bottle of white Alsace, and left the room, Klensch joined Brett at the table. Easing his heavy frame into the chair.

They ate the food and tasted the wine in silence for a short while, and then Brett spoke.

'May I enquire after the Fuhrer's health, Reichsleiter?' Brett asked tentatively. It was a delicate subject and he feared the worst.

Klensch lowered his glass and laid his fork carefully onto the side of his platter, and looked solemnly at Brett for a few seconds before answering.

'The Fuhrer, I regret to report, is not at all well,' he said sadly, and then in a stronger, more resolute tone continued. 'And yet, despite that and in fact because of it, there is now the utmost commitment to retrieve the contents from the ship at Aldvik and bring the whole business to its rightful conclusion.'

Brett nodded and said 'We will be ready to return to the wreck in a couple of days. The activities of the Norwegian authorities associated with the sinking of the oil rig, should soon be finalised. And it all serves our purposes rather well. The whole area within a 5 kilometre radius has been designated as a navigational hazard zone. All vessels are ordered to keep well clear of the rig and subsequently the *Torvald*.'

'Good, very good,' said Klensch, lifting another laden fork to his mouth and motioning Brett to eat up.

Brett had barely touched the food on the plate in front of him. He had really only joined Klensch in the original wine toast as a courtesy. He wanted to get on. There was still much to do.

'The *Panther* will be ready to leave for Aldvik tonight,' Brett advised his Reichsleiter. 'I have already instructed Strand to continue with the dive as soon as it is clear up there. This interruption has caused us a lot of trouble and a great deal of time has been lost.'

'Yes,' Klensch nodded. 'The *Highlander* business was totally unexpected and should have been avoidable. However, Olsen has been dealt with. He was too weak in any case. I anticipate no further interruptions.'

'What about the other Norwegian?'

'The Fuhrer trusts him implicitly. Although I have a certain reservation. However, there is no doubt about his commercial talent and his very exclusive connection to the source. We will soon find out how reliable he will prove to be.'

'When will you travel to Aldvik, Herr Reichsleiter?'

'Within the next few days. The Fuhrer insists we all attend. So please ensure everything is ready up there and make all the necessary arrangements with Strand. His contract must be terminated.'

'I understand completely, Herr Reichsleiter,' Brett replied. The Kapitan of the *Panther* understood precisely what the *necessary arrangements* were to be.

CHAPTER 36

'So Oberst. Where do you fit into all this?' I asked the man who had saved my life. He was standing next to me on the bridge of the launch. The vessel was now running at full speed and maximum power on a heading almost due north. Next stop Aldvik.

I was cleaned up, fed, watered and freshly outfitted. I suspected that the pair of trousers I was wearing had been a part of the wardrobe of the larger of the two men assisting the Oberst - the sturdy dark haired, Greek looking one they called Andre. I didn't think anything from the other guy named Karl, would have stretched to my dimensions, and the Oberst's height definitely excluded him - a little over five feet four was no match for my ten additional inches.

The Oberst turned from the forward window and the view of the North Star steaming steadily about two nautical miles ahead of us. She was also cruising at her top speed.

'Steve,' the Oberst replied, addressing me like some old friend, 'I may call you Steve?' he then added politely.

I nodded, and he went on. 'I'm employed by a European Intelligence Agency.'

'Interpol?' I supposed.

'Similar, but my group concentrates solely on anti-terrorist matters.'

'So, why me? You could have put me off the scent way back in Stavanger, when I thought you were just Olsen's inquisitive old neighbour.'

'Frankly, Steve,' the Oberst continued. That inscrutable smile appearing on his face again. 'And I hope you will not be too offended when I say it. You were a very convenient tool.'

'Thanks a lot,' I said, returning the smile. 'I have been called a few things in my time but never a tool. Not in that particular context anyway.'

'You see,' the Oberst continued. 'If I, or any of my people had gone after Nils Olsen; firstly he would have guessed who we were and clammed up immediately. Secondly, the people he was involved with, would have spotted us a mile away and realised we were on their case.'

'And instead,' I added. 'Along comes a fool of a Scotsman, chasing for answers on a purely personal basis.'

'Something along those lines,' the Oberst confirmed and then countered with, 'but you do yourself an injustice, Steve. You're no fool.'

'Thanks for that, at least,' I said, not terribly convinced. 'So, how could you be so sure I would get anything at all out of Olsen?'

'You did, didn't you?'

I couldn't argue with that. The Oberst had obviously obtained what he wanted without compromising his own position.

'Okay,' I said. 'But what about Karen Olsen?'

'Ah. Now, I must admit Miss Olsen was a surprise,' he said, shaking his head.

'Oh?'

'Yes. You see we have had Nils Olsen under surveillance for some time. Also, we were well aware that he had a daughter, but we felt there was no reason to include her in the equation.'

'Well she's certainly in the equation now,' I retorted, unable to disguise the concern in my voice.

'Quite,' the Oberst said, offering no further comment.

'And these people who are holding Karen,' I continued with my questioning. 'Those responsible for all this. Who are they? What are they? Olsen told me before he died that they were some kind of reformed Neo-Nazi group, which, I realise is a contradiction of terms.'

'They don't call themselves Nazis,' the Oberst stated. 'Even they realise that any association with that name in these times, would only be detrimental to their cause. Oh, their beliefs and ideals are based firmly on National Socialism alright, but this group prefers to be known as the Aryans or to be more precise, the New Aryans.'

'So, if you know so much about them, why haven't you rounded them all up and brought them in?'

'That, I am afraid is easier said than done,' the Oberst replied. 'You see, these people have established themselves as a legitimate, extreme right wing political organisation. Oh, don't look so surprised, Steve,' the Oberst exclaimed catching the expression on my face. 'Practically every country in the world has them – Nationalists, Far Right Wingers, plain Fascists. Even your good old democratic United Kingdom - they are all there, in one form or another. They just give themselves different titles.'

'So, why is this bunch operating undercover?'

'As the New Aryans, they are an undercover organisation. But that's not the whole story. You see, these people control almost every Right Wing organisation in the world. And, as soon as the time is right they will announce their presence, pulling all these independents into one cohesive new party – the New Aryans.'

'If that's the case and they are a legitimate, law abiding political group, why were you so interested in them - prior to the attack on Highlander that is?'

'Forgive me for not going into all the details,' the Oberst replied. Not much of an apology in his tone. 'But we believe that the New Aryans are planning something very big. We have no concrete evidence. They are extremely clever people - but we know they are behind a number of the recent terrorist attacks blamed on the Middle East factions. The sinking of the *Highlander* being just one.' The Oberst hesitated for a second; obviously deciding exactly to what extent he was going to involve me.

'For some reason,' he said finally 'the Aryans have a particular interest in Norway and I am now convinced the answer lies up in Aldvik with that ship of yours.'

'So what's the plan?' I asked, well aware that the Oberst had no intention of elaborating any further on the matter or on the background details.

'Well in the first instance we cannot continue to trail the *North Star* like this. Whoever it was on board that helped you over the side, will most certainly become very suspicious, if he spots a boat like this trailing behind all the way to Aldvik.'

The Oberst was right, and up to now, I was in full agreement with him. I waited for him to complete the details of his plan.

'I propose, we move on ahead of the ferry,' he continued. 'She's got another forty or so hours steaming and three more ports of call along the coast before she reaches Aldvik. Once we get ourselves established there, we can arrange to meet the ship when it docks, and hopefully find out who's on board with Karen, and what these people are really up to.'

CHAPTER 37

A few minutes after Brett had left the penthouse suite; Otto Klensch picked up the phone and dialled the country code for Norway, the Stavanger area code, and then a telephone number in the city. The phone at the other end was answered immediately.

'Hello.'

Klensch recognised the voice as well as the Norwegian accent.

'Olav, it's Klensch. Are you free to talk?'

'Of course.'

'There is to be a meeting in Aldvik. We will fly from Hamburg, probably on Thursday. Your presence is requested. Will you have completed all your arrangements by then?'

'I believe so but I must be in Zurich before the end of the month. Any later date than that, then you will have to relay the details directly to me there.'

'You sound very calm my friend.'

'Why should I not be? Everything is in place. All I need now is the code.'

CHAPTER 38

Having made record time up the Norwegian coast, the Oberst and I were waiting on the quay when the coastal ferry *North Star* eventually arrived in Aldvik.

The Oberst, pulling a few of the many strings he seemed to have on his bow, had provided us with suitable accommodation on the third floor of a block of flats in the centre of the town. Just a stone's throw from the harbour. He called it a safe house. Also he had managed to provide the car which we now occupied while watching the *North Star* secure her mooring lines and waited for the gangway to be lowered down onto the quayside.

I studied the activity taking place up on the decks of the ship. Paying particular attention to the group of passengers gathering around the top of the gangway, and preparing to disembark. There was no sign of Karen. Although I knew she must still be onboard somewhere. The Oberst's people had reported in regularly, confirming she had not disembarked the ship down the gangway at any of the scheduled stops on the route. Nor, I was pleased to hear, by any other method. Although how the Oberst's men could guarantee that I had no idea. I decided to stick with the optimistic view.

The passengers began to file down the gangway to the quayside. Most of them were tourists, travelling light, with little or no baggage - these were the sightseers, the tourists, the ones who would be returning to the ship later in the day, for the onward journey north.

I noticed only one individual leaving the ship carrying a suitcase, obviously having reached his final destination.

Finally, a few visiting stragglers appeared and made their way noisily down onto the quay. One man lagging behind the others, taking photo shots of practically everything in sight. His friends eventually coaxed him on to terra firmer and the group moved away from the ship at the start of their walking tour of Aldvik.

Still no sign of Karen. I began to have some doubts.

'Where is she?' I asked the Oberst, sitting beside me in the driving seat. 'Could your people have got it wrong and missed her?'

'I can assure you, she's still onboard,' the Oberst said with confidence.

'But...' I began.

'Now, this is very interesting,' the Oberst cut me off abruptly, indicating out through the car windscreen at the quay in front of us.

I turned my head to see a large black limousine driving along the dock towards the *North Star*. Not the sort of everyday vehicle one would expect to find on the roads of a small place like Aldvik. It pulled up at the bottom of the gangway, and the driver climbed out, moved to the rear door closest to the ship and opened it. Nobody got out, so I presumed somebody must be expected to get in.

'There's your friend. All safe and sound,' the Oberst said with satisfaction, referring to the person who had just come into view, up on the deck of the ship. 'And it looks as if she's got a minder,' he added, indicating the tall, broad shouldered man following closely behind Karen.

'Karen!' I could not help myself and was only held from jumping out of the car by the restraining hand of the Oberst on my arm.

'Take it easy, Steve. Let's see what they are up to.'

We watched as the minder escorted Karen down the gangway. He stayed a step behind, but was well within reach to stop her if she decided to make a run for it. There was obviously no way she would get very far with the other chauffeur guy covering the bottom of the gangway on the quay.

'She looks in good shape,' the Oberst commented.

'Yes,' I agreed. 'But who is the bull with her? Most likely the bastard who threw me off the ship.'

'You are probably right about that, but I don't recognise him,' the Oberst said as we watched the couple make their way down to the limo. At one stage, I noticed Karen stumble slightly but was quick to shrug off the helping hand offered by the big man behind her. They reached the quay, and once again Karen refused any assistance, this time from the driver, and then quickly ducking into the open doorway of the limousine.

Ensuring Karen was safely installed in the back seat of the vehicle, the minder closed the rear door and moved to take up a position beside the driver in the front. The title, 'shotgun rider', crossed my mind. By the giveaway bulge in his jacket, there was no doubt this particular minder was carrying; which led me to further speculation. What sort of influence do these people command that they can just delay ships, take and walk ashore with hostages and carry weapons with what appeared to be total impunity? Obviously very influential ones.

The limo accelerated along the quay in our direction. Both the Oberst and I turned our faces away, although we would have been unable to observe anything through the darkened windows of the big car as it picked up speed and headed off behind us. More to the point; better no one inside the limo got to take a good look at us.

'Right,' the Oberst said, starting the engine, 'let's go.'

'Hold it a minute,' I grabbed his arm. 'Don't you think it's about time we started doing something more positive to rescue Karen? Like getting the police involved for example? She's on dry land now. Surely the local law can handle things from here on in.'

Seeing Karen again, and knowing that she was still in some degree of danger, was beginning to get to me.

'Calm down, Steve,' the Oberst said, continuing to swing the car around in a tight turn on the quay. 'You could see she was unharmed. Let's find out where they are taking her. There's a good chance she may just lead us to the whole gang.' He straightened the car and we headed after the limo. 'They will not harm her while she's got information that they need.'

'What information?'

'Specifically, I can't say but if she was as close to her father as we think, then he must have confided something to her.'

'Karen told me she didn't want to discuss any of it with Olsen. She wanted nothing to do with the whole sordid affair.'

'Steve, have you considered, that maybe her father passed something on to her, that she may have decided was far too dangerous to tell you or anybody else for that matter. She could have simply been trying to protect you. And there's another thing.'

I turned to look at the Oberst, wondering what was to come. 'What other thing?'

He didn't take his eyes off the limousine leaving the dock side ahead of us, when he responded to my question.

'Steve, don't you find it rather odd that a total stranger to you, watches her father being gunned down, shoots the perpetrator to save you experiencing the same fate, and then joins ranks with you to embark on a daredevil mission to find a mysterious boat, that you say her father told you about?'

'Odd? Maybe. But like me she wants answers.'

'There's got to be more to it than that,' the Oberst kept his focus on the road ahead but shook his head. 'These people wanted to get her alone. You had to be taken out. But, Karen Olsen definitely has something they want. And they desire her to remain alive or else she would have been thrown off that ship to join you in sea. The worst thing we can do now is alert them. If we do so they will certainly scatter and in doing so, may decide not to keep the girl alive.'

'Alright, alright I give in,' I said, surrendering to the Oberst's argument. 'Let's find out exactly where they're taking her then.'

CHAPTER 39

Commander Bruce was just leaving the HSE building on his way to the car park, when his mobile rang.

'Yes, Faulkner?'

'We've got a lead, Boss. Craig was recognised boarding a coastal ferry at Molde.'

'So he did get something from Olsen. Is the girl still with him?'

'Well sort of. We checked with the Ferry Operator and discovered that a young couple answering to the descriptions of Craig and Karen Olsen, booked on as a Mr and Mrs Eriksen.'

'So where are they now?'

'You are not going to believe this, Boss.'

'Try me.'

'When the ship arrived at the destination port of Aldvik, only Mrs Eriksen got off. There was no sign of Mr Eriksen. I managed to speak to the Captain of the ship by phone and he told me she claimed her husband had changed his mind at the last minute in Molde, some big argument they'd had, and he stormed off the ship before it departed.'

'Oh, come on Faulkner. What the hell did the authorities make of that?'

'The authorities were not involved. Nobody had any reason to doubt the story. The local police didn't arrive until later with the full facts. The full report of the killings up on the Hardangervidda had not come to light before the girl departed the ship. They had no reason to hold her.'

'So she just disappeared?'

'Escorted off the ship by an unidentified man. Both of them picked up on the dockside and whisked away in a limousine.'

'What about Craig? Could he, by any chance, have been the one escorting her off the ship?'

'Not by the description given, unless he's put on about five stone and gained six inches in height.'

'Sounds all very convenient for our Mr Craig. But you can be sure he is still very much involved and running around somewhere in... What did you say the name of the place was?'

'Aldvik. A port way up north.'

'Get up there and find out what this so called Mrs Eriksen is all about, and what's happened to Craig. My guess is he won't be far away.'

CHAPTER 40

We expected the limo to head for a nearby hold-up somewhere in the town. Aldvik is not that big a place. We didn't think they would be going far. But instead, we found ourselves trailing the long, black limousine carrying Karen and her abductors, way out of the town and up on to the highway that headed in the general direction of a range of shallow mountains stretching away to the east.

The road was the main highway out of the port. Quite wide for these parts and it remained like that all the way as we climbed up to the higher ground. There was sufficient other traffic on the highway to avoid drawing attention to our tailing the limo. We continued to follow for about ten kilometres.

At the point when I was wondering exactly how far this trip was going to extend, the limo began to slow down ahead of us. We had reached a section of the highway that was forced to skirt around one of the mountain escarpments, and then continued winding its way alongside a fjord, the deep blue water of which I could see stretching inland way ahead of us.

As the terrain levelled out we started to travel alongside a handmade stone wall, obviously the boundary of an estate of some kind. Although, not the sort of boundary one would expect to find on a mountain road in the north of Norway. It looked far too modern. A short distance further on, we watched as the limo turned off the highway, into a gated driveway.

Slowing down as we passed, I could see the driver of the limo leaning out and tapping numbers into a keypad on a box fixed to a security pedestal outside the closed steel gates. Also, not the sort of gadget found in great numbers up in these parts, I guessed.

The Oberst put his foot down and picked up speed again, and drove us on for another half a kilometre up the road, before turning and heading back down the highway towards the entrance gate. A small natural lay-by at the side of the road provided a temporary parking spot away from the scrutiny of any curious party on the other side of the boundary wall.

Switching off the engine, the Oberst retrieved his mobile phone and keyed in a number.

'Andre? You need to pick up another vehicle,' he spoke in English. 'Something like a van or small truck and head up here.'

I listened as the Oberst spent the next few minutes describing our location.

'Yes, a truck,' he repeated. 'Then get some hedge trimming tools and a couple of boiler suits. You and Karl are going to do some tree pruning.' Whatever Andre replied made the Oberst laugh. 'We will wait for you, so don't waste any time.' He ended the call and switched off.

'So now I guess we wait for Andre and Karl to get up here and start cutting hedges,' I said. 'A sort of green and environmentally friendly stake out.'

'You got it,' the Oberst chuckled. Then, more seriously. 'The guys will keep an eye on things up here while we see what we can find out about this ship, the *Torvald*, back in town.'

'Can the two of them handle it?' I asked. 'I mean if things start to get, you know, tough up here.'

'Have no fear, Steve,' the Oberst produced the smile. 'The cavalry is also on its way.'

I didn't bother to delve any further. I was beginning to realise that this man had the backing of quite an extensive network, and appeared to be able to summon the required resources at will. What puzzled me however, was why, with all the available support at his disposal, he had not been able to nail these Aryan characters earlier. I guess I was just going to have to wait to find out.

'What about Karen?' I asked, still nagged by concerns for her safety, and what appeared to be the Oberst's lack of immediate concern.

Reading my mind, the Oberst said, 'Karen is quite safe for the moment, I'm sure of that. It's not in their interests to harm her. They would have done so by now, I promise you. If they move her out of this place Andre and Karl will inform us immediately, and follow wherever they take her. I am pretty certain they will not be travelling far from Aldvik. That mystery ship is going to turn up around here somewhere.'

The Oberst recognised the look of doubt on my face.

'Look, Steve,' he said, 'we have got to play it like this. If we were to barge in on that place now, there is every chance we would blow the whole thing. We don't have a single scrap of evidence of their involvement in the *Highlander* attack. Believe me, jumping the gun and going in too soon could put Karen Olsen in even greater danger.'

A half hour later, Andre and Karl turned up driving a battered white van, filled with an assortment of tools, ladders and other paraphernalia associated with cutting trees. They set up temporary camp on the verge and unloaded the van. The Oberst had a quick word with them, outlining the details of the job, and it wasn't about trees.

He returned to the car and fired the engine, and we pulled back onto the road, leaving the two guys to it.

As we drove past the closed gates, we caught a quick view of the estate on the other side. We could see a broad, straight driveway running about 150 metres into the estate. At the far end was what looked to be a pretty large and impressive mansion like building.

Big ships, big houses, and big ideas – the New Aryans seemed to do everything on a grand scale – including mass murder. I wondered just how big a fall they were going to take.

CHAPTER 41

The Cessna Turbo T206H seaplane circled once around Aldvik harbour before landing on the narrow stretch of channel leading up to the marine pier at the north end of the bay. Gliding smoothly across the surface of the still water towards the anchoring point the plane, engine just ticking over, eventually came to rest.

After cutting the engine, the pilot climbed down from the cabin, and quickly secured a mooring line to a bollard on the jetty. Then, moving to open the passenger cabin door and pulling out a set of steps he positioned it ready for the passengers to alight.

Rather ungainly, Otto Klensch was first to scramble down onto the wooden pier. Stretching his large, bulky frame, he made an elaborate show of flexing his aching limbs. The flight from Hamburg in the confined space of the passenger compartment of the aircraft had left him stiff and irritable. He was also aware that, for the same reason, the trip for the Fuhrer must have been something of a living hell. And yet he had heard not one word of complaint.

'The Fuhrer is ready, Herr Reichsleiter,' a Leutnant by the name of Horst Bucher announced from inside the plane.

Bucher was the Fuhrer's personal aide and had been for some years. Still young and handsome with a shock of the classical blond hair, he had been assigned to the position since he was twenty-one years old. More than ten years of undivided loyalty and service to the leader of the New Aryan Reich.

The sound of a vehicle engine behind him drew Klensch's attention, and he turned to witness the expected arrival of an SUV. This one designed and outfitted for a very special transportation service. Klensch waved the vehicle down the jetty and watched as it turned and reversed slowly towards him.

A third man stepped from the aircraft - another fit looking, young individual. He was Klaus Taig. Major Taig was head of the Security Division, and longed for the day when he would be permitted to openly wear his specially tailored classic, brown uniform with all the trimmings. The one presently packed neatly in his personal baggage in the cargo hold of the Cessna. It was the outfit he carried everywhere with him, in readiness for the appropriate moment. That moment now, at last, within sight.

With the SUV backed-up adjacent to the aircraft, its rear doors fully opened, Klensch gave a signal, and instantly the front of a wheelchair protruded through the door opening of the Cessna. Klaus Taig and one of the men manning the SUV moved to take hold of the frame of the wheelchair, and with the additional assistance from Leutnant Bucher inside, the men manhandled it out and down onto the jetty.

The grey haired woman sitting in the wheelchair, poised, elegant, beautiful, immaculately dressed and severely disabled, was the Fuhrer of the New Aryan Reich - her name was Annelise Raven.

In recent months, the aides and officers had become quite familiar with the routine, whenever the Fuhrer travelled, and usually had no trouble in transferring her in the wheelchair to whatever transport arrangement had been set up. This time it was from aircraft to SUV.

But on this occasion, the flight from Germany had taken more out of her than even she had anticipated. But she was beginning to come to terms with her limitations, and the terrible effects of the rapidly advancing destruction of her nervous system, and far more devastating, her rule over the New Aryans. Thank God there was a solution in sight, one that would most certainly be a crowning glory to it all. Now so close at hand.

Once again, the group of men, all equally displaying their devotion to the service of their Fuhrer, carefully manoeuvred the wheel chair up a short ramp and onto the extended lift platform. At a signal from Klensch the mechanism whirred into life and began to raise the wheelchair up to a level where it could be guided through the rear opening of the SUV. A few more minutes and the Fuhrer was safely settled within the vehicle. Klensch accompanied by Blucher and Taig also climbed in.

Inside, Klensch looked around him and questioned, 'Where is Olav?'

'Still in the plane,' Taig answered. 'He was straight on to his mobile the moment we landed.'

'Well go and get him,' Klensch ordered irritably.

'Jawhol, Herr Reichsleiter,' Taig responded and climbed out of the vehicle, and headed back to the aircraft; avoiding on his way the Pilot and one of the men from the SUV who were unloading suitcases and a number of wooden boxes containing the latest Heckler and Koch MP7 Submachine Guns.

Taig reached the open door of the Cessna and spoke sharply to the man inside, still talking on his mobile.

'Olav, you are keeping the Fuhrer waiting. Please come now.'

Taig waited as the man quickly terminated his call and then headed back to the SUV.

A second later a senior official of the Norwegian Maritime Directorate alighted from the plane and followed Taig - he was Olav Jorgensen.

CHAPTER 42

At the Oberst's safe house apartment in Aldvik, I was studying a chart of the local area, spread out across a table in the day room.

'Any luck with the map?'

The Oberst appeared from the adjacent kitchen area, drying his hands in a small towel.

'I've been trying to identify the shipping routes that would bring vessels in and out of Aldvik on a regular basis,' I answered, not interrupting my close study of the chart. 'Apart from the coastal ferries and a few traders, not many outsiders come in. Mostly it must be Aldvik registered fishing boats running to and from the North Sea. And, of course, the occasional Offshore Support vessels putting in to repair, bunker and restock.'

Then, in a flash, it struck me!

'Hang on a minute. Offshore!' I exclaimed, the real implication of what I had just said hitting home. 'What's the latitude here?' I felt the adrenalin running as I ran my finger across the chart to the edge where the latitude figures were printed.

Sensing my excitement, the Oberst moved in closer and hung over my shoulder.

'That's it!' I said. 'Sixty-four degrees. *Highlander* was about to start drilling in block 6204, one of the designated areas recently leased out for oil excavation! And only fifty nautical miles from…'

'Aldvik,' the Oberst was with me, 'and *Highlander* was about to commence drilling when she discovered an obstruction on the sea bed right below her. The *Torvald*.'

'Precisely. And then the bastards killed everybody onboard, blew her up and sank her. But not before she was made to pull clear of the location. Why make her shift position? Because they needed to have unrestricted access to carry on whatever it is they are doing on that wreck. That wreck is *The Ship at Aldvik*.'

'And now, with the area classed as a navigational hazard zone,' the Oberst added, 'they've ensured that all traffic will have to stay well clear, so they can carry on uninterrupted with the salvage operation.'

'But what are they after?' I puzzled. 'Oberst, can you find out if a ship named *Torvald* was sunk at this location? When and under what circumstances?'

'Of course,' the Oberst said crossing the room to pick up the telephone 'and when I've done that, I think it might be a good idea if we took a little sea trip.'

Within the hour we were at sea, and heading almost due west in the Oberst's launch, heading for Block 6204. The Oberst at the helm and me carrying out some pretty basic dead reckoning navigation calculations. The chart now spread out in front of me, again on a small table, conveniently located behind the boat's conning position. The course I was charting was designed to take us to the area where the *Highlander* had gone down.

It was another glorious day, the sun high overhead making its sinusoidal path across the Arctic sky. It would not set below the horizon for another seventy three days. Daylight for twenty-four hours from now on.

The land behind us remained in our sight until we were well out to sea. The view of the mountains in the background and the rocky coast line was, as usual, stunning. Under more relaxed conditions I would have wished to spend more time just appreciating that panorama alone.

'I think I can see the navigation hazard markers up ahead,' the Oberst eventually called out, cutting into my reverie.

I turned to look in the direction he was indicating, and grabbing a pair of binoculars, moved out onto the bridge wing.

'You're right. I can see the marker buoys identifying a submerged wreck'

'And obviously not the *Torvald,*' the Oberst said.

'No, the *Highlander,*' I confirmed. 'The *Torvald* must be further over.' I pointed across in a direction north of the marker buoys. 'If the authorities even knew about a wreck being down there, it was unlikely they would have classed it as a navigation hazard. Too deep to cause trouble. The chart itself certainly doesn't show any restrictions.'

I rejoined the Oberst back at the steering position.

'If you come round a few degrees to starboard we should be pretty close to the *Torvald* location.'

The Oberst swung the wheel and the launch began to swing onto a more northerly heading.

'What's this?' the Oberst questioned, nodding ahead through the front screen. 'Somebody else appears to have an interest in this area.'

Again I grabbed the glasses and headed back out onto the wing, focusing on the ship I could now see. She was holding position directly over what we believed to be the *Torvald* location.

'Fishing boat,' I said. 'Quite a big one too.' I had a clear view now.

'Coincidence?' the Oberst called back, more than an element of doubt in his voice.

'Let's go find out.'

Throttling back on the engines, the Oberst steered the launch towards the fishing trawler.

When we were within hailing distance the Oberst called to me again.

'Can you take the wheel? I will talk to them.'

'Sure,' I said moving to relieve him at the helm.

As we neared, I could see three men on the aft deck of the trawler. They had a single jib net crane extended out over the port side and were concentrating on the steel cable hanging from it and disappearing below the surface of the sea into the depths below. The fishermen were obviously engrossed in their operation. Totally unaware of our approach.

I touched the horn to attract their attention, and was amazed to observe the reaction on board the trawler. All three men were taken completely by surprise. They turned in unison to investigate who was approaching their ship. I could clearly make out the expressions on the faces of the men, and was certain I detected, what could only be described as a general look of alarm. I was even more startled and surprised when I observed one of the two younger men reaching down to the deck and straightening up with a rifle in his hands. It looked like an old model M16 to me – not your sporty shot gun that a regular fisherman would hang up on the wall over his fire place. These guys meant business. However, I noticed the older guy was quick to wave down the young man's hasty action. The rifle disappeared from view.

'Ahoy, there.' The Oberst had made his way forward and was leaning over the bow rail, hands cupped to his mouth.

Holding a pacifying palm up to the two young men at his side, the old man moved away from the gantry to the side of the trawler nearest to our approach. I heard him shout back in Norwegian asking if there was something wrong.

' Er det noe galt?'

'Do you speak English?' the Oberst shouted, mainly for my benefit. He could just as well have carried on the conversation in Norwegian.

'A little bit,' the old man called back. 'Do you have trouble?'

'No, we are tourists, just looking for a good spot to do some fishing.'

'You are very far out to do sport fishing.'

'Yes. We thought we might have a chance to catch something really big,' the Oberst explained. Still maintaining the pretence.

'Well you will not find any big fish in this area. You need to sail much further south.'

The Oberst nodded his head, and then conveniently changed the subject.

'What are all those floating things over there?' he asked pointing towards the ring of coloured buoys encircling the *Highlander* exclusion zone. 'Are they fishing nets?'

'Marine hazard. Big oil rig sank there. You must keep well clear.'

'Right, we'll do that.' Still not letting the matter rest, the Oberst added, 'Do you fish this area often?'

'That's what we are doing now,' the old man tried to maintain a level of politeness in his voice, but I could see his other two companions moving about restlessly behind him. 'Much grateful if you let us continue,' the old man called across.

'Of course. Thanks for your help. South you say? OK.'

'Good luck with your fishing,' the old man waved as the Oberst stepped back into the bridge housing.

'Swing her round, Steve and head south.'

I turned the wheel and opened up the throttles. We began to pull away from the trawler.

After a minute or so had lapsed the Oberst said, 'What did you make of that?'

'From what I could hear, not much. From what I could see, plenty. They certainly were not fishing. Not for fish anyway.'

'No,' the Oberst agreed. 'Did you notice the hoist? No big net or trawl equipment attached. Just a single lifting cable.'

'And the one guy in the wet-suit,' I said. 'Did you see, he was kitted-out for diving and surrounded with some very fancy deep diving scuba equipment? They're definitely working the *Torvald* wreck alright.'

The Oberst nodded in agreement and said, 'The old fellow appeared very nervous as well.' Then after another moment of silence added, 'Mind you they could just be legitimate treasure hunters. That's always an activity shrouded in secrecy nowadays.'

'Do you need to carry an M16 automatic weapon for that job?' I questioned.

'You're right. They are working that wreck, and for all the wrong reasons.'

'So, what now?' I asked.

'South for a while, then back to base and wait for the return of our mysterious fishermen. The trawler is registered in Aldvik.'

'Yes,' I agreed. 'I caught her registration markings on the stern as well. The *'Adrea'* out of Aldvik.'

I swung the helm and pointed us on a course a few degrees south of due east.

CHAPTER 43

'You idiot, Egil. What were you thinking? Taking up the gun like that. I don't even know why they gave us that damn thing anyway. None of us knows how to use it properly.' Leif Strand fiercely admonished his youngest son as they watched the launch heading south and away from their boat - the *Andrea*.

'They were only stupid tourists,' Egil responded sullenly.

'We don't know who they were.' Strand shook his head. 'What sort of tourists come out this far from the coast in a flashy high speed cruiser, just to catch big fish? This is not the Caribbean you know.'

'Father is right, Egil,' Strand's older boy Gunnar cut in. 'Sometimes you can be very stupid.'

'Okay, okay. I didn't think. Besides there's no harm done. There was nothing to show we were lifting from the wreck. For all they know we have got nets out.'

'Alright, that's enough.' Olav Strand held up a hand to halt the argument. 'Let's just get on with it,' he said, turning and reaching for the painter line connected to the wire hoist cable hanging over the side of the boat. 'If we work quickly we can be out of here for good in just a couple of hours.'

'I don't know about that. Looks like we've got more company,' Gunner said grimly, motioning behind the other two, off to the aft port side of the trawler.

Strand and his younger son turned and all three watched silently as the black structure of the approaching ship loomed towards them.

'It's the *Panther*,' young Egil said but the other two didn't need telling. There was no fear of them mistaking the vessel, nor its purpose.

'She's arrived early,' Leif Strand muttered, checking the time on his wristwatch. 'She wasn't due for at least another four hours.'

'Change of plan?' Egil asked.

'I don't know. But we will soon find out, she's coming alongside. Better put the fenders over and get ready to take their lines.'

Strand and his two sons moved to catch the fore and aft mooring ropes heaved across from the *Panther*.

With the two boats tied together, Kapitän Rudolf Brett stepped across from his ship onto the deck of the *Andrea*.

There was no cordial greeting from Olav Strand or either of his two sons. But it made little difference to *Panther's* commander. He had not come to socialise.

'What did the visitors want?' Brett asked indicating the launch, now already some distance away.

'Tourists,' the old man replied. 'Just wanting to fish. No problem.'

Satisfied with the explanation and anxious to get on, Brett turned his attention to the activities on board the trawler. He waved an arm around and asked 'And here - what progress?'

'As well as can be expected, considering,' Strand said coldly.

'Considering?' Brett questioned, a note of irritation in his voice. 'Considering what?'

'The slight interruption,' Strand said, with more than a hint of sarcasm in his voice, 'or didn't you know that a drilling rig was blown to pieces just over there.'

'Don't try to make jokes with me, Strand. What's the status of the salvage?'

'Most of the strong room cargo is already up and stored at the warehouse ashore, according to your instructions,' Strand said, moving across the wooden deck to pull a tarpaulin cover away, revealing the latest salvage items from the ship below.

'What you see here is virtually the last load. Just a few loose ones to come up.'

'And the strong room safe?'

'It took some cutting to get through the ship's steel structure to reach it but we finally managed to get in,' Strand explained. 'But it's pretty solid. It's going to be very difficult to open it. We certainly won't be able to cut it open down there. I am afraid it will have to be brought to the surface for that.'

Brett pointed to the lifting gear and the hoist cable hanging over the side of the *Andrea*. 'Can't you lift it with that?'

'No, we can't. Our hoist is not strong enough. You probably could manage it, though,' Strand replied and waved across the narrow gap between the two vessels indicating the heavy lift crane located on the *Panther's* aft deck.

'Okay, get this stuff loaded across to the *Panther*. Now,' Brett commanded.

'But, we are not finished…' Strand started to protest.

'No argument, Herr Strand.' Brett waved aside the comment. 'We shall take over now. When you have done that, you can return to Aldvik. Your reward shall be settled as agreed. Now if you please, start transferring across to the *Panther*. My men will assist.'

CHAPTER 44

We had cleared a distance of about four or five nautical miles from the *Andrea*, when we were alerted to some trouble they must be having back there.

Still at the helm, I was about to make the heading change, that would point us in the direction back to our base at Aldvik. The Oberst came rushing in to the conning position. He had been out on the aft deck generally surveying the area through his binoculars, but now I could see something was up.

'I think you had better take a look at this,' he said solemnly, pointing back in the direction of the *Andrea* and handing me the binoculars. I exchanged the helm for the glasses and moved outside to get a clearer view.

What I was focusing on, sent a shiver through my body. The *Andrea* was on fire, great clouds of black smoke billowing from her decks. There's nothing quite so daunting as standing on the deck of one ship at sea and watching another ship in trouble. I had experienced it before and it was something I would never forget.

'What the hell…' I started to say; then I spotted the other ship. A much bigger vessel, painted totally black. From this distance it was not easy to judge but it looked as if the black ship was pulling away from the burning *Andrea*.

'We've got to take a look,' I shouted in to the Oberst and, without a word, he immediately swung the boat around and opened up the twin engines to full speed.

Getting back to the Andrea took us another twenty minutes. Coming up astern of her we could see that the trawler was not only ablaze but listing heavily on to her starboard side. It was clear she was only minutes away from capsizing. In the distance, all that could be made out of the black ship was its dim silhouette receding out to sea.

'Let's get out of here,' the Oberst called to me from inside. 'They must all be dead.'

'Hold it,' I shouted. 'There's somebody in the water.'

I made my way down onto the forward main deck as the Oberst began to ease back on the engine throttles. It was then that the Oberst must have had some stronger doubts, because he left the helm to come to the bridge wing, and hailed to me.

'Steve, I think we should get out of here, now! If that bastard spots us,' he called pointing in the direction of the receding black ship, 'she could come back to finish us off as well.'

'Just hold it, Oberst. There's a man in the water.'

The cloud of smoke engulfing the area around the Andrea was blown clear for a few seconds giving me an unobstructed view of the figure floating on the surface.

'Steve, we need to move. There's nothing we can do for anybody here, now.'

'I said hold it, Oberst. Nobody gets left in the water.'

The tone in my voice must have had immediate impact. The Oberst just nodded and returned to the helm, calling out, 'I'll follow your signals. We need to get in closer.'

It was a difficult few minutes, navigating through the dense haze, but the Oberst managed to keep steerage way on the launch, sufficient to manoeuvre us close up to the burning *Andrea*. I knew he was finding it difficult to even see me let alone follow my hand signals.

The smoke continued to billow around me on the fore deck, and I began to cough and splutter. But now I could see the person in the water. It was the old man the captain of the trawler I guessed.

Grabbing the boat hook from the rack on the housing, I put the familiar tool to use for a second time in a few days - pulling somebody out of the sea. It was the least I could do. The other somebody had been me.

I failed at the first attempt to secure the hook into the harness that the old man was wearing. Then to my surprise, I watched him grab for the pole himself. He was alive and conscious. But there was no way I was going to be able to heave him aboard by myself – not under these conditions. So, while maintaining my hold with one hand on the boathook, I waved with my free arm, indicating that the Oberst should back the boat away.

'Just hold on,' I shouted down to the old man, now desperately clinging on to the pole. From the way I could see he was gripping the thing I had no fear he was going to let go.

The smoke was engulfing the launch now. We had to pull away from the burning trawler without further delay.

Reading the situation and my signals accurately, the Oberst put the controls into the reverse position and we gently pulled back from the *Andrea*. She was now listing over, severely. We'd managed to pull clear not a moment too soon.

There was a loud rumbling accompanied by the horrendous screeching of steel and timber and the hiss of rapidly extinguished flames as the *Andrea* finally turned completely over, and disappeared below the surface of the Norwegian Sea.

Within seconds the light breeze quickly dispersed what was left of the hanging smoke cloud as we backed slowly away. All that was left to view were a few bits of flotsam floating now on the calm - as if never disturbed - ocean.

The Oberst stopped the engines and joined me on the fore deck. Together we pulled the old man in alongside the boat. When within reach he held up his arms and we grabbed him and heaved him aboard.

Once we'd got him onboard, the old man recovered quickly. He rose to his feet, and would have headed towards the bow, if both the Oberst and I had not restrained him.

He struggled to pull away from us and cried out, 'My sons, my sons. We must save my sons.'

The Oberst and I turned to look out across the sea to where the *Andrea* had gone down. There was nothing there.

CHAPTER 45

Not unlike many of the modern coastal towns and ports located along the western coast of Norway, Aldvik boasted a small, well maintained private airstrip. When sea and weather conditions precluded the use of seaplanes to get into the port, the airport itself usually remained operational, even under the most gruelling climatic conditions. In addition, the strip at Aldvik boasts a designated landing pad and service facility for practically every type of helicopter that flies regularly out and back to the rigs and offshore support ships.

A twin-prop Partenavia PN68 chopper carrying special agents Faulkner and Thompson landed at 15.25hrs.

Within minutes of landing and immediately after leaving the aircraft, Faulkner was on his mobile to Bruce in Aberdeen.

'We're here. Just arrived.'

'Good. You know what to do. Be discrete. And remember what I told you - don't underestimate him.'

CHAPTER 46

Apart from being pretty badly shaken up, the old boy was unharmed. The anguish he was suffering, rather than from any injuries sustained , was now caused by the loss of his two sons and with them his ship the *Andrea*. His family and livelihood, taken from him in minutes.

The Oberst and I did all we could to detect some sign of the boys. But it was no good. A dozen times we circled around the area, ploughing through what little debris remained on the surface of the sea. But there was no sign of either of the young men.

'I am sorry,' the Oberst eventually said sadly to the old man crouched on the foredeck. 'I am afraid there is nothing more we can do here.'

'Bastards, evil bastards,' the old man shouted dragging himself to his feet and facing out to sea in the direction of the long gone, black ship. Shaking his fist he yelled again. 'May you rot in hell.'

'Who were they?' the Oberst asked easing the old man back down onto one of the gunwale bench seats. He was too exhausted to move back into the accommodation for the moment.

Immediately, and rather surprisingly, the old man decided to move on to the defensive. He turned his back on us.

'Nobody…I don't know,' he mumbled.

'You mean they just attacked you? Came out of nowhere?' I said.

'Yes, like that,' he replied again in a low, defensive murmur.

'Why protect them? They killed your boys,' the Oberst cut in.

At those words, the old man seemed to relent somewhat. His belligerent manner short lived. Eventually he turned to face us.

'Truth spoken, I don't know who they are. Me and my sons have just been carrying out a contract.'

'What sort of contract?' the Oberst asked.

I was happy to leave the questioning to the Oberst, but I could see by the grim expression on the old man's face and the light shake of the head that at this stage, he would not willingly want to talk to us.

After a further moment of silence, the Oberst decided to continue the questioning, but this time on a different tack.

'Look, I think you should know. We are not tourists.'

That appeared to come as no surprise to the old man. He just shrugged and grunted something inaudible under his breath, and then in a louder, harsher voice said, 'Of course not. Nobody fishes in the Norwegian Sea for sport in a boat like this and so far out. Not even dumb tourists.'

'My colleague and I are investigating the sinking of the oil rig - the *Highlander*. The one that got blown up and sunk out there,' the Oberst continued, gesturing back towards the wreck site. 'We know that what you and your sons were doing was somehow connected with the attack on the rig.'

'I swear on the souls of my two sons,' the old man said quietly but with a firm resolve, and at the same time lifting a hand to cover his heart. 'I had no idea what they intended to do. After the rig sank, they just ordered us to stop working the wreck for a few days. So we did. They told us it was terrorists. But it was too much to believe that. It was clear that the presence of the rig would interfere with our work on the *Torvald*. It would have to be moved. My boys and I just thought they would call off the salvage operation until things were fixed.'

There it was, the first concrete mention of the name *Torvald*. The Oberst and I exchanged satisfied looks. This was confirmation that the ship lying below *Highlander* was indeed the mystery ship that Nils Olsen had named before he'd died - the *Torvald*.

'What exactly were you salvaging from the wreck?' I asked and was more than a little surprised by the frankness of the answer. The old guy seemed to have suddenly decided to tell all.

'Mainly gold.'

'Gold!' the Oberst and I exclaimed together.

'Yes. Bullion. Gold ingots.'

'How much?' I asked, feeling a bit like a prospector just having picked up a handful of nuggets from the bed of a Klondike stream, and about to realise a lifetime dream. It's rather strange how just the mention of the words *gold bullion* seems to conjure up some dormant urge in a man. For me anyway. I guess if I had been around at the time, I would have been one of the first making for the Klondike to join all the other gold diggers.

The answer from the old seaman proved even more tantalising.

'A lot. We have been working this wreck for more than a year.'

'You said mainly gold,' the Oberst cut in, 'what else?'

'I don't know but they seemed very interested in getting to the contents of a safe in a strong room down there.'

'Did they tell you what was in it?'

'No. We had only just reached the safe when those bastards turned up. It is clear they did not want us looking any further. The Captain of the *Panther* told us our job was finished. We could head back and would be paid what was owing to us. And then…' the old man paused and shook his head, '…when they had loaded the last of the gold onto the their ship, they fired on us… and… well you know what happened.'

'The *Panther*,' I said, another piece of the puzzle falling into place. 'The ship that carried out the attack on *Highlander*.' It was a statement and the old man just nodded confirmation.

Then I recalled the view I'd had of the departing black ship through the binoculars, only about an hour ago, as we had headed back towards the burning *Andrea*.

'Of course,' I exclaimed. 'No wonder we couldn't see her on the satellite scan. She's a stealth design. Hard enough to track with normal vision let alone from a satellite. Unless you know what you're looking for.'

'These people certainly know what they're doing, Steve,' the Oberst said.

'And must have a considerable amount of financial resources to do it,' I added. 'What group of people can afford to design, build and run a ship like that?'

'Very rich and very powerful ones,' the Oberst replied, and then turned to address the old man again before I could ask anymore searching questions.

'Right. Now I want you to understand something, Herr...?' The Oberst hesitated, waiting to hear the old man give his name. I realised he was maintaining the dialogue in English solely for my benefit. He could have just as easily carried out the interrogation in Norwegian. But the old man's English was pretty good and speaking it seemed to be keeping him focused.

'Strand. Leif Strand,' the old man answered cautiously, still uncertain who in fact we were. But, I felt by now he must have realised we meant him no harm.

'I don't have to tell you Herr Strand that those who used you and did this to your sons, are fanatical terrorists of the worst kind. There is no doubt in my mind that once your task on the wreck was completed, you would have been of no further use to them. They are neo-Nazis who have established a political foothold in most of Western Europe - particularly here in Norway. There are many members and thousands more signing up every day - willing to follow.'

All this was news to me, but no real surprise. It was common knowledge that there were extreme right wing organisations dotted around the globe. The cranks bent on re-incarnating Adolf Hitler and his regime. But it appeared that the Oberst had no intention of letting me in on everything. He seemed to be happy just to feed me snippets of information, and then allowing me to draw my own conclusions. I knew there was another agenda. I guessed we were slowly working our way towards it. Just sit tight I told myself – it will all come out. But, I desperately hoped I would get all the facts before anything happened to Karen.

The old man was offended by what he obviously believed to be an accusation, and snapped angrily back at the Oberst.

'And you suspect me of being a Nazi? I am one of them?' Strand was genuinely shocked. 'Let me tell you - if these people know I am still alive, they will not hesitate to complete the job. I am not one of them. This was just a diving contract. We thought the secrecy was all about the gold.'

The Oberst held up his hand in a gesture of apology and said, 'I think we need to get back to Aldvik. There is much more I would like to know about the *Torvald* and its cargo. You will be safer with us for the time being and I think, for the moment, the least number of people who know about all this the better.'

We helped Strand up from the deck and into the accommodation.

'Steve, can you start us back to Aldvik. I'll take care of Herr Strand.'

I watched the Oberst guide the old man down the companionway and caught just a few of the comforting phrases that were spoken in Norwegian. Strand muttered something back. He was still in a state of shock.

A few minutes later, I was heading us back to Aldvik at full speed, and beginning to wonder when the Oberst would decide to call in the proper authorities. Surely there was enough evidence to link these people to the *Highlander* massacre. We knew their stealth ship the *Panther* was involved and there was no denying what we had just witnessed happening to the Andrea back there. Plus Strand's story. So why didn't the Oberst take some action now?

CHAPTER 47

'So Karen Olsen is it? You realise you led us quite a merry chase.'

The Fuhrer stood in the doorway, leaning heavily on the frame that she relied on now, almost all the time, to get about, when she wasn't in the wheelchair. Otto Klensch waited obediently a few steps behind, ready as always to provide assistance.

'Is that the ridiculous reason why you are keeping me captive in this place?'

'Don't be foolish girl.' Annelise Raven was beginning to lose her patience. 'Do you still not understand just how important your role is to us?'

'So what more do you expect of me?'

'You know quite well.'

'And you think this is the way you will get my co-operation?'

'Please,' Otto Klensch cut in. ' May I remind you that you are speaking to the Fuhrer.'

'And may I remind you that I am not used to being held a prisoner like this. Have you all gone mad? Have I not done enough for you?'

Annelise Raven, the Fuhrer, moved with difficulty across the room to confront the young woman.

'There is so much more that will be asked of you - for the new Reich, and you know it.'

CHAPTER 48

It was near midnight by the time we secured the boat and drove the short distance back to the apartment and parked the car in the road at the rear of the building. Yet it could just as well have been twelve noon. Twenty-four hour daylight time had arrived and would continue like this until late August. To those people not used to it, the continuous glare of daylight could develop into something of a pressure point on the nervous system. They say most of us are creatures of habit and habitat. We are groomed to feel like sleeping when it gets dark. So, being expected to sleep when it's still broad daylight can, understandably prove to be most disruptive. One needs to adopt the night-shift worker mentality in addition to fitting thick black-out curtains to the windows.

However, with all that was going on, I had not the slightest desire to sleep. It was the same for the Oberst. He showed no signs of fatigue at all.

Olav Strand however, was a different case. He was totally exhausted. Still suffering from the trauma of his ordeal out in the Norwegian Sea and the loss of his two sons. He sat slumped in a chair hanging onto a glass of aquavit, the powerful Norwegian schnapps, distilled from potatoes and maize and running with nearly 50% alcohol content. The Oberst had produced a bottle of the stuff from somewhere. Strand seemed quite content to let the Oberst handle the whole situation. I guessed there was more than a little guilt and self preservation preventing the old man from running straight to the authorities. Besides, he knew it was already too late to do anything for his boys.

I'd returned to my study of the chart, when the Oberst appeared again holding a can of coffee and three mugs which he stood on the table and filled before handing one to Strand and another to me. The coffee was black and hot and tasted good. Even Strand seemed to rally, although I am not sure if it was from the effects of the coffee or the aquavit - probably a bit of both.

'So what is the story of the *Torvald*?' the Oberst asked pulling a chair to the table and sitting down opposite the old man.

'Goes back many years,' Strand answered. 'The war. In those days, the *Torvald* was one of the gold ships.'

'Gold ships!' I exclaimed. This was a new turn of events, and to cap it, the magic word 'gold' had come into the picture once again.

The Oberst nodded, and I could see he knew what Strand was talking about and took a large mouthful of his coffee before starting to explain to me.

'It is a little known fact that when the Germans invaded Norway in April 1940, they received less of a welcome than they expected. We put up quite a fight you know,' he said proudly, almost as if he had been in the front line back then. And for all I knew, he could well have been. He took another drink from the mug before continuing. 'Stopped them in their tracks we did. Gave them a really bloody nose as you guys say. On the very first day of the invasion. We even sank one of their latest cruisers, the *Blücher* on its way up the Oslo Fjord. That provided us with the opportunity to get our Royal Family and the Government Ministers, and more significantly perhaps, our Gold Reserves all safely out of Oslo.'

'Right.' I nodded. 'I remember now. Your King, Haakon and his family, plus practically all the Storting Government Ministers and, of course, the total Bank Gold Reserves, were transferred from Oslo north ahead of the advancing Germans. Eventually all, including the gold, were shipped out of Norway to Britain.'

'That's precisely what happened,' the Oberst confirmed. 'And, a large amount of that gold was shipped out on board the Royal Navy cruiser *HMS Devonshire* along with the King.'

'I suppose the remainder of the bullion found its way on to smaller ships,' I added. 'Like the *Torvald*.'

'Exactly,' the Oberst confirmed. 'Most of them heading out to rendezvous with Royal Naval ships or, like many did, making straight for Britain on their own.'

'And, I suppose, the unfortunate ones, like the *Torvald* that didn't make it, ended up at the bottom of the ocean, along with their cargo,' I added.

'It was not like that with the *Torvald*,' the old man interrupted us. Speaking quietly but now, with an intensity in his voice that immediately commanded our full attention, he continued the story. 'The *Torvald* was carrying a very large amount of gold bars and sailed out to transfer it to one of the destroyers. She never returned.'

'I guess she obviously didn't make the transfer,' I said.

'That's what everybody believed at the time, until the day the *Torvald's* Captain, a local fisherman named Jens Siversen turned up back in Aldvik during the last months of the war. Everybody thought he was dead. Assumed he had gone down with his ship. His story was that the *Torvald* had been torpedoed and sunk by a German S-Boot.'

I recognised Strand was using the German name for the motor torpedo fast attack boats the Schnell-Boot, as the Germans called them - we christened ours the E-Boats.

'What was a loan German torpedo boat doing so far north?' I wanted to know.

'I don't know,' Strand said, shaking his head and taking another slug of the fire water. I had the impression he felt he had imparted more information than he'd intended.

'So this Captain Siversen must have had a good idea of the location where his ship went down. So why didn't he just inform the Norwegian authorities so *they* could recover the gold from it?' I questioned again. 'And what took him so long? Why did he wait until the end of the war to tell his story?'

'I think I can make a good guess at the answer to that question, Steve,' the Oberst intervened. 'Captain Siversen obviously did not want anybody to know where his ship was lying, because he wanted to go back at a more convenient and somewhat safer time to salvage the gold - for himself.'

We both stared at Strand. He deliberately avoided eye contact, positively confirming the Oberst's observation.

'But we still don't know how these Aryans got to know about the *Torvald*. And, more to the point, what else is lying down there that interests them so much?'

'Perhaps Herr Strand can enlighten us a little further,' the Oberst said, not really expecting to get much more out of the old man, who was now showing clear signs of the effects of the day's events, helped on by the glass of almost pure alcohol that he had emptied. But he surprised us.

'Siversen died before he could get back out to the *Torvald*,' Strand began to explain again. Taking up the story from where he'd left off. 'But he told only one man the truth about the sinking of his ship. Of course Siversen did not know the exact location of the wreck, but was able to provide enough information for the position to be narrowed down with some accuracy.'

Strand hesitated for a moment. A glazed, distant look in his eyes; as if he was trying to recall something from way back. The Oberst and I remained silent, and waited for him to focus again on the story. Eventually he did.

'The man he told was his brother - my father, and before you ask why the different family name, I can tell you they were half brothers - same mother, different fathers.'

'And your father started searching for the *Torvald*?' it was a statement more than a question from the Oberst as he reached for the aquavit and refilled Strand's glass.

'My father spent the rest of his life trying to find out where that damned ship lay. It cost him his fortune, as little as that was at the time, and eventually his life.'

'And you continued where he left off?' I said.

'No never,' Strand shook his head vehemently. 'I had watched what it had done to my father and my mother and our family. I would have been happy to let the whole thing rest.'

'But?' I ventured.

Strand, anticipating my question let out a deep sigh of resignation, and continued.

'I'd washed my hands of it all. Then, just over a year ago a man came to Aldvik - a German. His name was Günther Bauer. He was looking for Siversen, and eventually found his way to me.' Strand swallowed a fresh mouthful of aquavit before continuing. 'This Bauer man said he had been in the German Navy, the Krigsmarine, during the war. He was taken by the Russians near Narvik shortly after his boat had been sunk up here. He said he had been on a mission to Norway in the last few months of the fighting. He was in his eighties, but surprisingly fit and active, considering he had survived nearly twenty years in a Russian Gulag.'

'So what did he have to say about the *Torvald*?' I was intrigued.

'He knew exactly where she was.'

CHAPTER 49

The two men were getting kitted out for the hit. They were going to carry it out in broad daylight. No other option. No strange clothing and no face covering until they were inside the building. Just in case some local might be up and about in the early hours, and decided to call the local police. They were going to have to look and act as normal as anyone would expect, even though it was virtually the middle of the night. They could not take a chance on who may or may not be taking a look out of their windows at that time.

Each man carried a PPK hand gun, tucked beneath an anorak, and two spare clips of shells in the pockets of their jeans. Their superior had made it quite clear that no one in the apartment was to survive.

They knew their targets had returned to the apartment. They had watched them secure the launch at the harbour and drive into the town. They also noted that the bastard Craig and his friend had now been joined by a third character. He would have to go too, whoever he was. The instructions were to clean up the whole mess - no mistakes.

It was 3am when the two men left the hotel that they had checked into earlier, posing as tourists. The single man behind the reception desk was fast asleep in a chair. Lucky for him. They had no intention of returning to the hotel. Thus intending to leave no witnesses behind - alive.

The hire car was parked a block away. They walked the short distance without speaking. Each man occupying his own space. Each preparing in his own way for the task ahead.

CHAPTER 50

'If you expect to get some sleep tonight you should draw those blinds,' Strand said changing the subject and pointing towards the main window. He was again drinking from the glass of aquavit that once again had been generously topped up by the Oberst.

The Oberst moved to switch on the lights, before crossing to the window, to draw the heavy black-out curtains. I was surprised and somewhat comforted to feel that we were back in the normal night time mode of things, and even had some trouble stifling a yawn. Of course there was no way I was going to settle down to sleep until I'd heard the conclusion of Strand's tale. If he was still capable of continuing.

'So, this Krigsmarine sailor had returned to claim the gold,' the Oberst put the point bluntly, getting the account back on track, and this time, filling up a glass of the fire water for himself. He held the bottle up to me but I declined. I was now beginning to feel drowsy enough and needed no additional assistance.

The Oberst continued.

'He was obviously one of the crew of the S-Boot.'

'I don't know, but he knew about the gold onboard and he knew where the wreck was.'

'And he hired you and your boys to go out and salvage the gold?'

Strand nodded.

'What about the 'something else' you mentioned?' I asked recalling what Strand had told us shortly after we'd picked him up. 'The 'something of great importance' in the *Torvald's* safe?'

'I don't know any more of the details about that. We had been lifting gold bars from the wreck for about four months, when the *Panther* appeared for the first time at the site. It was then they suggested that as well as the gold, there might be something else of value down there in a safe and we should try recovering that too.'

'When did you discover that these people were neo-Nazis?' I asked.

'From the very first. The way they talked. The way they acted. But this was a very good paying job for me and my boys. As far as I was concerned they wanted the gold. That was all. Until…until the rig…"

'Alright, I think we have heard enough for now,' the Oberst said. 'We all need to get some rest. Herr Strand you can take the bed in there.' He pointed to a door leading to one of the bedrooms.

Without another word, Strand threw back the last drops in his glass, and heaving himself to his feet, tottered off, unsteadily towards the bedroom.

A few seconds after Strand had closed the bedroom door behind him, both the Oberst and I were startled by the course ringing tone of the old fashioned phone standing on a table against the wall.

The Oberst lifted the receiver. He listened for a few seconds, and then said, 'Okay, keep the place covered. Let me know if there's any movement.' Then he hung up, and just stood there deep in thought.

'Trouble?' I asked.

'Could be. We've got company. Some rather unpleasant visitors arrived in town, a short time ago. You could say the usual suspects.'

'Is that bad for us?'

'Could be.'

'So what next?'

I looked up and found myself staring into the barrel of a hand gun. The one that the Oberst was pointing at me.

'This,' the Oberst answered with little emotion in his voice.

CHAPTER 51

At the big house on the high ground outside Aldvik a group of people sat around a large polished oak table in the huge dining room. They had just finished dinner. The members of the household staff were busily clearing away dishes and plates around them. One senior assistant moved around the table offering to pour vintage port into crystal glasses.

At the head of the table Annelise Raven sat - back in her wheelchair. To her right Otto Klensch, to her left Olav Jorgensen. Three other places had been laid but only two were occupied. One by Major Taig the other by Leutnant Bucher. The third had been set for the young woman upstairs. She however, had declined the invitation to join them.

Klensch had been angry that the girl had stubbornly refused to dine with the Fuhrer and the Reich hierarchy and in fact, had gone so far as to suggest sending Taig and Bucher to escort her down from her room. At this point the Fuhrer had intervened, overriding Klensch, and assuring everyone that the young woman would soon come to her senses and start to cooperate. She just needed a little more time. After all, she had only recently experienced some very bad news. The loss of a parent could be devastating.

Turning her attention to Jorgensen, the Fuhrer said, 'So Olav I think we can begin. Would you be so good as to bring us up to date with the preparations offshore?'

Olav Jorgensen took a sip of port and wished he could light up a cigar, but there was no such possibility at this table. The Fuhrer forbade smoking anywhere on any premises that she occupied - home or away, in the long or short term. At least she was not so demanding about alcohol. He wondered what fads the new Fuhrer might have.

'As soon as the funds are in place, the signal will be given to our teams on all the main production oil platforms. Norway's oil will be in our hands.'

The group around the table sat silently waiting for the Fuhrer's response.

'That is very good, Olav,' she said. 'And the Storting?'

'Once again my Fuhrer I can confirm, our people in the Norwegian parliament will act as soon as the promised funds have been deposited in their personal accounts.'

'It still disturbs me that the take over of the oil rigs and the government coup are totally dependent on financial reward? Where is the loyalty to the Party - to the Reich?' Otto Klensch interrupted, a note of angry dissent in his voice.

'Come now, Otto,' Annelise Raven said, 'you know as well as I, that everything in politics is based on financial reward. Money *is* loyalty. What regime in the world today could possibly function or even exist without its funding?'

Then Jorgensen cut in.

'I can guarantee that the Storting coalition will be ousted and the new Aryan party installed. And, with thirty percent of the global oil reserves in our hands, the outside world will have no alternative but to accept the New Aryan regime,' he stated confidently.

'I would still have preferred the party to be supported for its ideals rather than its wealth,' Klensch moaned.

'Otto, please don't forget the network of supporters we now have right across Norway,' Jorgensen reminded Klensch, the fervour in his voice building up. 'Plus growing numbers in Sweden and Denmark. And of course Germany and Great Britain. With Norway established as the home of the New Aryan Reich our followers around the world will act. In addition to all that, please do not forget that we will mobilise the armed forces to quell any unrest.'

'And don't you forget Olav that all this is very much dependent on our retrieving the contents of a safe, in a strong room of a ship, at present, lying at the bottom of the Norwegian Sea,' Klensch growled.

'Gentlemen, please,' the Fuhrer sharply interrupted the discussion that was becoming far too heated for her liking. 'We know it is down there, and it will be in our possession by this time tomorrow. Günther Bauer is onboard the *Panther* with Kapitän Brett at this very moment. They will receive us onboard in Aldvik first thing in the morning. So shall we drink to our success?' The Fuhrer of the reborn Reich raised her glass.

Immediately and together the men around the table rose to their feet, holding their glasses out, ready for the salute.

'To the new Aryan Reich - Heil Quisling. Sieg Heil!'

'Heil Quisling,' the men chorused, 'Sieg Heil.'

One hour later Olav Jorgensen, badly in need of a cigar, excused himself from the group of men remaining at the table. The Fuhrer had already retired to one of the large salon rooms in a side wing of the house, leaving the men to finish their brandy.

Out in the clear air, Jorgensen lit up and tasted the tobacco with something of a look of ecstasy on his face. The initial craving satisfied, he glanced around to ensure no one was about, and retrieved his mobile from an inside pocket. He dialled and waited.

The receiver was lifted at the other end but the person did not speak. They did not have to.

'So do I go ahead?' Jorgensen said.

'Of course.'

CHAPTER 52

For a moment I was tempted to raise my hands but whether it was fatigue or just plain bloody mindedness I just couldn't be bothered.

'Do you know what this is, Steve?' the Oberst asked.

'The piece in your hand, or what you intend to do with it?' I replied, trying to get my battered thoughts into some sort of order. 'The latter…I haven't a clue. The piece however, is a Walther P99 double action, 9mm, 16 round hand-gun. German.'

The Oberst produced that enigmatic smile but still kept the gun levelled straight at me.

'You are quite right, but then one would expect an ex-member of the Royal Marines Special Boat Service, and one with your impressive record, to have some considerable knowledge of these things. Here, catch!'

He tossed the Walther to me. I caught it by the barrel and held it that way round - still pointing towards me.

'You didn't really think I was going to shoot you?'

'Oberst,' I answered him with a deep sigh, 'a lot of unexpected things have befallen me in the last few days. To my mind almost anything is possible, but in any case, I don't find a demand for these things anymore. I won't be needing it,' I told him, as I walked to the table and set the gun down on the polished surface.

The Oberst shook his head. 'It's probably going to get very rough out there,' he said gravely.

'Probably going to?' I could not disguise my frustration. 'Fifty men murdered on a rig offshore. Two guys blasted to death in the mountains. A couple of young Norwegian fishermen killed at sea. Yours truly, thrown over the side of a ship, and my… an innocent girl kidnapped by a bunch of twisted thugs. How much rougher than that is it going to get?'

'A lot. Believe me,' the Oberst replied. 'These people are fanatics, dedicated to re-establishing the mad fascist rule that almost prevailed over half a century ago. They will stop at nothing. And believe me, there is something big going down this time?'

'What?'

'I don't know what. But far too many undesirable characters are descending on Aldvik at the present time.'

'I still don't need a weapon,' I said firmly. Although, only a few seconds were to pass before I realised what a fatuous remark that eventually turned out to be…because…

…at that very moment, the entrance door to the flat was smashed open, and two men, with faces covered in black stocking masks, barged in, and immediately started firing. The silencers on the weapons ensured that the only sounds projected were soft, popping claps as each round was fired.

My instincts must have cut in without me fully realising, and I dived for cover behind a sofa across the far side of the room. But not before seeing the Oberst reaching for the Walther I had placed on the table. He almost made it, when a series of shots from the first intruder's gun hit him, sending him and the gun skidding across the floor. By an odd trick of fate, the gun landed within my reach. I grabbed it, and realising I had no direct line of fire at the two men, I instantly sent off two shots above my head, aiming at the overhead lights and shattering them. The room was thrown into complete darkness.

Scrambling to my feet I ducked my way towards the main windows, trusting my memory of the layout of the room as a guide.

With the place being thrown so rapidly into total blackness, the two hit men were temporarily halted, giving me time to acquire some sort of cover from a pillar near the curtained windows. I could hear the low curses in the dark as the attackers stumbled over furniture.

Then, the bedroom door squeaked open, and a startled Strand appeared, tottering out, now fully succumbed to the effects of the aquavit, and silhouetted by a dim night light emitting rays from the interior of the room behind him. Sufficient illumination for both the men to hit him quickly and cleanly. Which they did. The old man stood no chance, and died instantly under the hail of bullets. He toppled backwards into the bedroom, and hit the floor with a thump. Enough light was emitted from Strand's bedroom for the men to re-establish their bearings. I knew I had no time left. If I was going to survive this, I had to act at once - and I did.

Quickly pulling on the chords of the main window blinds, I was able to drench the room in blinding daylight as the curtains were swept back. The sudden flood of light, and the temporary blindness it caused the two attackers, provided me with sufficient time to fire off six rounds. Three assigned to each of the murdering bastards. The men crumpled silently to the floor. I remember thinking how simple it had been. Whatever phobia I thought I had previously possessed, appeared to have evaporated. On this occasion though, I had got it right. These were the ones who deserved to die.

I could see that Strand was dead too. He lay in the entrance to the bedroom with open but blind, staring eyes and blood, already beginning to congeal, running from a wound in his neck.

The Oberst, to my relief however, was still alive. He had managed to pull himself up into a sitting position, and was propped against the base of one of the armchairs. I went to him. I could see immediately that he had taken just a single shot from the volley fired at him, but that one shot was to the stomach. Not much bleeding. Just a slow trickle running between his clasping fingers. This type of wound, I had witnessed before, on the battlefield. It wasn't good. I knelt down by his side, and he turned to look at me. That familiar but this time, more defiant smile breaking onto his deathly pale face.

'Seems you are cultivating the habit of witnessing the last words of old dying men,' he gasped.

'You're not old and you are not going to die. I'll get help.' I began to rise.

'Stay where you are. Stomach wound. I will not be conscious much longer. So you'd better pay attention.' He coughed and a trickle of blood ran from the corner of his mouth. 'There's something more you need to know, Steve.'

'I thought you'd told me everything.'

'Up to this point my friend, as I informed you earlier, you have been provided with information on a need to know basis. What I have to say now…' he gasped for breath, '…under the present circumstances…you definitely need to know.'

'I'm listening,' I said.

'The people we are chasing are not led by Germans. The hierarchy is Norwegian.'

'No big surprise. All that has taken place so far has been in Norway or in Norwegian waters.'

'Just listen to me, Steve. The key person in all this is just one man. His name is Vidkun Quisling.'

'Quisling? You mean the World War II Norwegian Nazi collaborator?'

'The very same. Quisling, the traitor - he even donated his name as a new word for treachery that the world wasted no time in adding to its vocabulary.'

'He's dead,' I exclaimed. 'Executed in 1945 for war crimes - here in Norway.'

'Hitler is dead too. But still has a massive global following.'

'Are you telling me that there is still a significant number of Norwegians who actively subscribe to Nazism?'

'National Samling that's what they called it here. There were sixty thousand of them by 1943. Just three years into World War two. At the end of the war 23,000 Norwegians were tried and imprisoned.' The Oberst gasped with pain but it just seemed to emphasise the magnitude of what he was telling me. After a moment's pause he took up where he'd left off.

'During the occupation of Norway, the Nazis set up a thing called Lebensborn or 'fountain of life'. German soldiers were virtually ordered to father children with true ethnic Norwegian women. The fruit of the union, a perfect Aryan child, who would become a true member of the master race and the thousand year Reich.'

'I've heard about that as well,' I nodded. But I was still anxious to get the Oberst to some medical aid.

'Even to this day there is a terrible stigma attached to those children. Of course they are all grown up now. The decent ones have kept silent. Just ordinary respectable people; loyal to Norway and the higher values of human behaviour. But many longed for the return of National Socialism and a new Reich. Together, under the manipulation of the true Nazis believers, these people have become extremely well organised.'

'So where does all this take us?'

'As I explained, the Lebensborn scheme was designed principally for participation by German soldiers and Norwegian women. There were a few exceptions, the most significant being between a woman called Helga Raven, a close friend of Eva Braun, Hitler's mistress, and none other than Vidkun Quisling the Norwegian Nazi puppet leader.'

'God. How do you know all this?'

The Oberst waved my irrelevant question aside with a limp hand and continued, his voice becoming noticeably weaker.

'Actually Hitler and Quisling were very close friends. The Fuhrer had great plans for Quisling. They met many times in Berlin and up in Bechtesgarten. It was there, at Bechtesgarten, Hitler's mountain retreat, that Helga Raven came into the picture. Apparently the couple were actually married up there, with Hitler's blessing. There is even evidence. A marriage certificate. What is also known, is that the union produced a daughter. In 1943 Annelise Quisling was born.'

'But Quisling already had a wife.' I said.

'Yes, but she was of Russian descent. Not quite the thing to boast about in those days. That part of the family history was never referred to.'

Suddenly, the Oberst began to cough blood.

'Oberst, you must allow me to get you some help.'

'Hold on, Steve. What I've got to relate to you now is very important. As the prospect of success for the Third Reich and its allies began to rapidly decline in 1944, Quisling decided to get his German wife and daughter out of Norway and into neutral Sweden.'

'Fascinating story, but so what? Look, Oberst you need medical attention - right now!'

'Please hear me out, Steve,' he gripped my arm. 'Nothing more was heard of Helga Raven and her daughter. Quisling covered their tracks.

He was executed in 1945 and that was supposedly the end of that. Nobody heard from them...' He coughed and more blood appeared around his mouth but the Oberst was determined to continue. He did not lessen his grip on my arm. '...that is until 1985 when a woman calling herself Annelise Raven appeared in Munich; claiming to be the daughter of Vidkun Quisling and the rightful heir to the Aryan crown. She also claimed that her father had been nominated by none other than Adolf Hitler to inherit the leadership role of the Third Reich, on the Fuhrer's death. What's more she was prepared to provide evidence to support her claim.'

By now the Oberst was beginning to slur his words. He would not be lucid or even conscious for much longer.

'Please Oberst...' I started to say but he took no notice.

'Let me finish. Annelise Raven reawakened a whole new and massive revival of National Socialism, not only in Germany but, through her links here in Norway.....somehow she managed to influence some of the most important people in politics, industry and finance.'

The Oberst's voice sounded weaker. He was slipping away from me.

'Oberst, please let me get help - the police.'

'No, Steve. We do not know who can be trusted. It's up to you now. Get up to the house. Karl and Andre will help, and I hope by now they have been joined by my second in command... his name is Gabrielsen, Henrik Gabrielsen...he knows all that I have just told you. You must find out what the plan is - there is something very big going to happen...you must..' his words tailed off as he lost consciousness.

Then I heard the sirens outside. Although there had been little noise generated during the attack, barring the crash as the door was knocked in, all the shots from the guns, not counting my six, had been muted by silencers. But I guess that had been enough to disturb the relative quiet of the neighbourhood. Somebody had called the police. They would be in the building at any minute.

I was not going to stick around. The mayhem around me was not going to do my case the least bit of good, and without the Oberst I would present them with the perfect fall guy. But at least I knew the Oberst would get taken to a hospital.

Through the gaping, smashed-in apartment door, I detected the rush of footsteps echoing up the stairs outside. I tucked the Walther in my belt and grabbed the car keys from the table and headed for the window. It opened easily and I could see the road below was empty, for the moment anyway. Our car was parked a short distance down. I wasted no further time and swung myself out through the window. A short balancing act on the broad sill brought me to a down pipe of some sort. One fortunately proving strong enough to take my weight. I was on the ground in seconds and heading for the wheels up the road.

As I reached the car I heard a second siren announcing the arrival of another police vehicle. This one, lights flashing and siren screaming turned into the narrow street at the top end. By a stroke of luck, somebody had badly parked a few car lengths behind me and had virtually blocked the road back there.

I was in the driving seat and away in seconds - exiting the street at the opposite end.

There was no doubting I was now the prime suspect. Whatever they discovered back in the flat would be set squarely on my shoulders. In the rear view mirror I watched two uniformed policemen jump from their car and point to me as I accelerated out and onto the road leading down towards the quay.

I was not too familiar with the layout of Aldvik but I knew the way to the harbour, and a plan of escape began to form as I heard again the wail of a siren behind me. The first police car must have been alerted by the one stuck back there in the side road, because it was now full on my tail. I floored the accelerator pedal.

Fortunately the roads of Aldvik were completely clear. It was after all the middle of the night.

I swung the car onto the quayside and headed in the direction up the jetty, towards the disembarkation point that I had earlier seen Karen use on leaving the coastal ferry. She was upper most in my mind now, as an escape plan began to materialise.

I had traversed more than half the length of the jetty when the flashing lights appeared in my mirror. The police car had followed me onto the quay and was closing fast.

Ahead, I could see a row of cargo sheds with a number of drays and hand carts stacked with goods, lined up outside. Alongside these a pile of crates were piled. A passing nudge with the nearside wing of the car, managed to dislodge the bottom of the pile, and I watched the whole stack tumble across the dock behind me. A temporary diversion, but every second I could gain on the chasing police car was a bonus.

Just before turning off the quay and up onto the main highway link, I caught a glimpse of the police car behind slowing down to negotiate past the boxes strewn across its path. A few precious seconds gained. I put my foot hard down and accelerated up the road that led out of Aldvik. A minute later I joined the highway that would take me up to the big house, where I hoped I would find Karen – safe and well. I was done with the waiting. My intention now, was to get her out of that place as soon as possible.

There wasn't a single vehicle on the road. I had a clear run and took full advantage of it. I pushed the speed up to 150 kilometres per hour and began to pull well away from the chasing police.

Within another kilometre, the road levelled out and I began to traverse the coastal section of the highway. With the high ground rising up and away on my right, I started to catch glimpses, on the opposite side, of the sea and the mouth of the fjord running inland. The section I was looking for soon appeared. It was a clearing at the side of the road that led right to the edge, and I knew, a hundred metre drop down the cliff face to the sea below. I eased my foot off the accelerator and pulled off the road, steering straight for the cliff edge.

CHAPTER 53

Still occupying Broadhurst's office and seated at his desk in the HSE building in Aberdeen, Commander Bruce lifted the phone and dialled. He could hear the ringing at the other end but there was no answer. Irritated, he slammed the phone back onto its cradle. After staring angrily at it for a few seconds he lifted the receiver again and dialled another number.

This time it rang only a couple of times before it was answered.

'Hello?'

'Jorgensen? Where the hell have you been? I've been trying to contact you all day.'

'I am sorry, Commander. Something important cropped up.'

'I haven't heard from Faulkner and Thompson since they arrived in Aldvik. Do you know what's going on? Did they get to Craig?'

'I do not think you should worry about Mr Craig....'

Jorgensen's voice began to break up.

'Jorgensen I can't hear you. Does that mean they've got him?'

The line was dead. Bruce tried redialling the number several times but no contact was made.

'What the hell's going on up there?'

CHAPTER 54

I watched the car disappear over the cliff edge from a concealed position under a group of fir trees that I had scrambled towards after rolling out of the driving seat. I could hear the police car siren screaming closer and ducked down as it flashed past. It would be a few kilometres and some minutes before they realised that I had left the road way behind them. By the time they figured it out and eventually discovered the smashed car at the bottom of the cliff, I hoped I would be finished with what I intended to do next.

I decided that the most sensible plan was for me to get off the main road and head along the wooded fringe skirting the high ground. Slow going, but there was no way I wanted to risk being picked up by the police at this stage of the game. The comforting fact was that the Oberst's men, Karl and Andre, would by now have received some additional support and would be waiting in the bogus hedge trimming van up near the big house.

As I worked my way through the trees, there was time to reflect on the events of the past hours. Of course, I had no idea if the Oberst was dead or alive by now. At least I assured myself, if he was still alive, he would be in relatively safe hands. The authorities would surely be in the process of patching him up.

Then my thoughts turned to the two killers. Who were they? Who'd sent them? How did they know where we were? Back there, in the heat of the moment, I'd had no time to lift their masks to see if I recognised either of them. The plain fact was that these people were on to us.

There was just a remote chance that they were after the Oberst and not me. So it still could be possible for me to maintain my cover - as delicate as it continued to be.

I also had time to reflect on the tale of the rise of the New Aryan order that the Oberst had described to me. I couldn't understand if they were so powerful and entrenched in most of the global political systems, why had no one ever heard of Annelise Raven nee Quisling? The woman had come on the scene in 1988. Why had she sat back out of the political limelight for so long? More questions. Still no answers.

Forty minutes later I reached the point where the stone perimeter wall began to encircle the grounds of the big house. I could see it stretching ahead parallel with the highway, and in the other direction, running at a right angle it disappeared into the thicker trees on the upper slope. The estate was massive.

Still taking advantage of the tree cover, I worked my way along the wall towards the main gate until I spotted the white van of Karl and Andre parked under the trees on the other side, a short distance up the road ahead of me. There was no sign of either of the men. Still, it was four thirty in the morning. A couple of guys still seen cutting hedges at that time would most certainly have raised a few questions. However, I assumed at least one of them would be awake and watching the main gate.

Just about to cross the road to the van, I heard a car approaching - fast. Pulling back into the cover, I waited. The police car that had been chasing me appeared - siren silent now but still travelling at full speed with lights flashing. It was on its way back to Aldvik. The car slowed momentarily as it passed the white van but after a cursory visual inspection it sped off again.

Coast clear, I crossed the road to the van. I guessed either Karl or Andre would be observing the main road and the gate. I would surely be spotted and recognised as I approached. But there was no sign of life, and the rear door of the van was ajar. Reaching the vehicle I pulled the door fully open and was surprised to find neither of the Oberst's men inside. Two dishevelled sleeping bags were strewn out among a variety of agricultural hand tools, and there were signs they had been recently used, both the tools and the sleeping bags.

Then I spotted the red patch on the floor of the van and a smear leading to the door where I stood. It was blood.

Moving back, I immediately spotted the furrowed marks on the soil at my feet. Someone had been dragged to the cliff edge - the route was streaked with blood. I followed the short trail to the overhang and peered over. Lying on a ledge of rock just a few metres below was the body of Andre. He was dead and there was no sign of Karl or the new guy that the Oberst had mentioned, Gabrielsen, or anybody else for that matter. I guessed the same men who had attacked the flat were responsible for this slaughter. Instinctively I touched the Walther still tucked in my belt. It appeared that I may be needing it, and the eight rounds remaining in the magazine, sooner than I'd thought.

It also looked as if I was on my own again.

I now realised that time was running out fast, and I couldn't afford to waste any more of it. The police would soon be back with reinforcements searching the whole area on both sides of the highway. It would not take them long to discover the van and the bodies of the men. And the way things were going it was a hard, cold fact that I was going to be prime suspect, if not public enemy number one.

What I also realised was that this Aryan gang would be in the same boat as me. There was no way that the police would avoid investigating things at the big house behind the wall just across the highway. The people in the house would have to make a move soon. And from what Strand had said about the *something of vital importance* still down there in the *Torvald's* submerged safe, my guess was the next stop for the Aryans was going to be out there in the Norwegian Sea, at the wreck site.

The thought uppermost in my mind now was how to get to Karen. What ever they had planned for her, I had no idea, but I was afraid of what they might do to her when she proved to be of no further use to them. I'd racked my brain for the possible reasons why they might need her. The *Torvald* and its hidden contents was the prime reason, even though Karen seemed to know nothing about the ship and its secrets. I decided I had to get into that estate and see if I could find out what was going on up in the big house and, if possible get her out of there.

Two minutes later I'd crossed back over the road and was working my way around the stone wall perimeter. I soon found a section of the wall that looked easy to climb, and quickly scaled it.

On the other side the trees and shrubs were dense but I managed to find a route through. Moving forward I could see the big house across an expanse of neatly tended lawn. The place was obviously lived in and well taken care of. Could it be the home of one of the senior Aryans?

It was still light of course but getting lighter. My watch said 6.30 a.m. The midnight sun was on its sinusoidal ascent again. The sky was clear and predicted another fine dry day ahead.

I was at once both relieved and puzzled that I'd detected no sign of any guards or security men patrolling the area. A couple of them had obviously carried out the attack on us down in the town, and they were certainly responsible for the slaughter of the Oberst's stake out men across the road. Perhaps they believed they had effectively dealt with all known threats. But surely they would soon find out that their two hit men had not succeeded down in Aldvik. The thoughts tumbled through my mind. Few answers coming back.

However, there was one thing in my favour. They wouldn't know anything about me for some hours yet - not until the morning news broke about the shootings in town. Even then they may not realise that I was the Oberst's companion - the man who had escaped in a car and was now on the run.

At the edge of the tree boarder I had my first real, unobstructed view of the house. I was totally taken by surprise at the size and grandeur of the place. It was a mansion. The last sort of building one would expect to find tucked way up here in the north of Norway. I had seen photographs of the famous 18th century Damsgard Manor near Bergen in the south, but looking at the weather boarded and brick-faced Rococo walls, I had the feeling that this place had been designed and built far more recently than that. Somebody with a lot of cash had produced this masterpiece of architectural magnificence, and I wondered why they had chosen a small town within the Arctic Circle to locate it. Why would anyone want to build such a place up here - so far north? Did this mansion mean something special to this new generation of Nazis? Was there a link to the *Torvald* and its treasures? Another flood of questions. The answers still yet to come.

Satisfied that the coast was clear of any patrolling guards, I moved quickly across the lawns and reached cover in the shade of the house walls. I wasn't sure what I was going to do or how I would locate Karen. She was probably locked up in one of the numerous rooms that this place must have. I moved cautiously along the wall. Except for the early birdsong going on around the place, everything was still and silent - the birds alone were the only ones who seemed to know exactly what time of day it was. I even wondered if cockerels around here also got notice of exactly what was day and what was night. Although, I hadn't heard that familiar wake-up call up here - not once.

It was as I approached a large latticed window that had been left open that I heard the voices. Moving closer, the talking became clearer. I could hear people engaged in an intense discussion. They were speaking German.

CHAPTER 55

In one of the spacious ground floor rooms of the big house the Fuhrer of the New Aryan Reich sat in her wheelchair. There was however little in her demeanour to indicate the level and importance of her authority. She looked pale and the anguish she experienced each time she tried to move position in her seat, was obvious. Even under the massive cocktail of drugs she consumed to control the pain there was little sustained relief for her. She had not slept uninterrupted for more than an hour on any occasion in the past twelve months. Tonight was no different. The disease was rapidly taking over and would soon overwhelm her entire body. Despite all this, she rejected all requests from the likes of Klensch and the other senior members of her staff, to maintain a physician of any kind, in permanent attendance. Or as she put it - she did not want to have a doctor continually fussing around her, thus clearly demonstrating that, although her body may be failing, her mind certainly was not.

Otto Klensch stood near one of the massive bay windows he had pushed open to let some of the fresh morning air into the room. He had been unable to sleep either, but for a different reason - anticipation. His life time dream was achingly close to being realised. The fact that the damn place never got dark at this time of the year did little to help matters, regarding sleep.

Klensch and his Fuhrer had been talking together for some hours. Only censoring the content of their discussion at the regular intervals when a member of the household staff would tap lightly on one of the two huge oak doors to the room, and enter offering some light refreshment and enquiring of any other requirements they might have - otherwise they were left undisturbed.

'I say again we must move today,' Klensch said, speaking in German - the language that he and the Fuhrer most often used when conversing in private. Of course the diversity of languages now spoken by the international spread of the party members usually meant that English was the one in predominant use. Turning from the window, Klensch continued - a certain uncomfortable edge persisting in his voice. 'We must move today, tonight, whatever part of the day or night it is in this godforsaken place.'

'Otto, you must calm yourself,' Annelise Raven's words were almost whispered - her voice wracked with pain. 'Now is not the time to panic. We are almost there.'

'My Fuhrer,' Klensch began to speak - this time with less agitation in his words. He had known the Fuhrer from the time, when to most she was plain Annelise Raven - she would never have dared to use her real name Annelise Quisling. For twenty years now, he had served her, from the beginning but, in all that time had never once addressed her by any other title than Fuhrer. From the very first, Otto Klensch had totally accepted this lady as his true Leader. The final proof of her right to that title was now so close at hand. 'My Fuhrer, I am not panicking. I am just concerned that things are not going according to plan. That trouble last night, yesterday, this morning whatever, confirms they are closing in on us.'

'You worry unnecessarily Otto. Our people will have completed their task by now and tomorrow the *Panther* will arrive in Aldvik and take us out to the *Torvald*.' She hesitated for a second as a sudden jab of pain knifed through her fragile frame but she recovered quickly and continued. 'We will have it in our hands, Otto and the true Aryan Reich will be born.'

There was a sudden loud knocking on the main door to the room - louder and more persistent than the usual gentle announcement made by the house officer.

Klensch crossed the room and pulled one of the massive wooden doors open. Major Taig entered.

'I am afraid there's been trouble. Our men did not complete their mission. There was a counter-attack.'

'And what about the Oberst and the Scotchman?' Klensch asked.

'The Oberst was seriously wounded. It is unlikely he will survive. As for Mr Craig, - apparently he retaliated with a vengeance. Both our men are down - dead.'

'My God,' Klensch growled. 'And where is he now, Craig?'

'He escaped. Drove away. The police chased his car out of Aldvik - up in this direction. Then they lost him. He's gone to ground. He obviously has hidden the car and my guess is, he's probably snooping around up here somewhere, looking for his lady companion. My men are searching the grounds as we speak.'

'If you are right we have to move at once. What time is the *Panther* expected to arrive in Aldvik?'

'Not for another two hours. And then she has to refuel and take on necessary supplies. Brett assures me he can turn her round in a further two hours.'

'Then I think we all need to leave very soon,' Klensch said, turning his attention to his Fuhrer. 'I trust you will agree. We need to prepare to move out now.'

'Of course,' she replied in a low voice wracked with pain. 'I agree, Otto. Please make the necessary arrangements.'

CHAPTER 56

I had seen the black limousine speed up the drive from the main gate and swing to a halt in front of the steps leading up to the entrance of the house. Pulling back into the limited shadow of the building to avoid detection, I watched as a man in a dark suit exited the car and ran up the steps into the building.

What I had heard of the exchange coming from the open window of the room above me had proved to be most informative, but I guessed that in a few seconds I would get to hear a lot more.

I was right, and thankful my command of German had proved a definite advantage. I'd understood enough. And from what I'd overheard, a plan was already forming in my mind.

From the open window where I had listened to most of the discussion taking place inside, I detected the sounds of raised voices. The guy who had pulled up in the car a minute or so before, was now in the room just above my position. I could still hear everything clearly.

So, they knew I was back in the frame. However, I was surprised by the claim that guards were searching the estate looking for me. Because not a soul was in sight. I could only assume they must have started at the perimeter wall. If that was the case, it would not take them long to work their way back in my direction. There was no time to try to get Karen out, but I was sure she would be with these people when they joined the *Panther*. I'd heard more than enough anyway. It was time for me to get out.

Still using the wall of the house with its numerous alcoves as cover, I worked my way to the rear of the building. The coast was clear so I crossed over into the line of perimeter trees and climbed back over the wall.

Retracing my steps to the main highway I picked up the faint sounds of men's voices calling to each other on the other side of the wall. The guards I guessed. The ones probably searching for me.

Except for the occasional passing car, it was quiet when I reached the highway. I emerged some distance up from the main gate. I could see the white van still parked off the road on the other side and a plan of action began to get clearer in my mind. Basically, I had to get on board the *Panther*, and the van was going to be very instrumental in that exercise.

Once aboard the ship I had no definite idea of how I would proceed. I would have to trust my instincts. There was nobody left to call on or whom I felt I could trust. How different things might have been if I'd had Jack and Lee by my side, but they were both dead, and as one of my old Norwegian friends used to say - *There's nothing to be said about that.*

My task was to get Karen out of their hands. Whatever it was they required from her, I still hadn't fathomed out. Of course, I realised it had to have some link with the *Torvald* and her father's involvement and whatever he might have unwittingly passed on to his daughter. But I was more concerned with what they may have planned for her when her role had been fully played out. At the point when she would be considered of no further value to them.

On a more practical and personal note, I knew that Karen Olsen was the only witness to what had really happened up on the Hardangervidda. The only one who could vouch for my innocence in all this.

I still had the Walther and the eight rounds. My options were few. Just play it by ear I told myself. Just like I used to, very often, in the old days.

I reached the van and climbed up into the driver's compartment.

CHAPTER 57

The quayside at Aldvik was a hive of activity when the *Panther* entered the harbour. A lot of the people working the dockside area interrupted what they were doing to stand and stare at the strange, black ship cruising into port. The unusual streamlined contours of her sleek hull and superstructure and her almost totally jet black, painted appearance, raised more than a few eyebrows. Some rich, foreign big-shot indulging his fantasy, was the general consensus.

For a small selected group of men waiting patiently on the quayside, the display of awe was not shared. These were the insiders, specially selected for the job. One of the men nodded to the others and each member of the group moved to take up his position. These men were preparing to handle the ship's mooring lines, about to be heaved ashore.

The *Panther* was quickly tied up at the quay and within minutes, a fuel oil bunker barge cruised up and manoeuvred into position alongside the ship on its far side. The hose connections were quickly made and the process of taking onboard a few thousand litres of diesel oil commenced. At the same time, another signal from one of the men in charge of things on the quay, brought up a small fleet of trucks and commercial vehicles loaded with supplies for the ship. The loading got underway and, while the refuelling was taking place on the other side of the ship, there was soon an ant-like trail of men scurrying back and fore between the ship and the supply vehicles on the quay, transporting boxes and sacks.

A late arriving smaller white van pulled onto the quay and tagged on the end of the line of vehicles servicing the *Panther*. The driver, wearing white coveralls and a flat cap climbed out and moved to the rear of his van. He opened up and began rummaging inside and at the same time, out of the corner of his eye, studied the activities of the gangs carrying supplies up onto the *Panther*. He waited until he observed the two men working the van just ahead of him, each lift a box from the inside and head back towards the ship's gangway. He estimated they would be taking about three minutes to complete the round trip.

Moving quickly to the same van, he lifted a carton containing what appeared to be canned food of some sort out of it, and worked his way through the milling loaders and stepped onto the gangway.

The guard at the top of the gangway paid no attention to just another one of the tradesmen humping victuals aboard. The stowaway was on the ship and after trailing around the outside of the accommodation he eventually worked his way aft to a position from where he would be able to observe the gangway. A small deck, fire fighting equipment locker turned out to be an ideal position. It was just big enough to take him and the box of cans. He slipped inside the locker. He left the steel door slightly ajar, so he was able to observe all the activity taking place on the deck around him.

Steve Craig was onboard and ready to go.

CHAPTER 58

From my cramped position in the fire locker, I watched the last shore tradesman depart the ship, and a few minutes after that, with the decks cleared and the fuel filling line from the bunker barge disconnected, I witnessed the arrival of the big shots.

First up and onto the deck, I observed two men. They were wearing smart dark suits, and looked like a couple of city dealers. Both in their thirties, and both exuding that unmistakable air of arrogant confidence and authority. I recognised one of them as the guy who had brought the news up from the town, during my eavesdropping session at the big house.

Out of the ship's accommodation block, two other men now emerged. The *Panther's* welcoming committee I guessed. In stark contrast to the newcomers, these two men were dressed in smart naval uniform. Outfits, I noticed, bearing a striking resemblance to the Wartime German Krigsmarine uniforms. The younger and taller of the two, I assumed was the captain of the ship, if the four rings on his sleeve were anything to go by. The other uniformed man was quite elderly - he looked to be at least in his eighties but seemed sprightly enough standing erect in the old military fashion when greeting the two young arrivals. After a quick exchange, the four men took up positions on each side of the gangway - forming a sort of mini-guard of honour. All four came to attention as two more men emerged from the gangway carrying a woman in a wheelchair. The wheelchair was carefully set down on to the deck and I had the opportunity, for the first time, to study the occupant. She was elegantly dressed and sat proudly erect despite the fact that she was obviously severely disabled. This was of course the woman whose voice I had listened to last night up at the big house - the one they all seemed to address as Fuhrer.

So this was Annelise Quisling - the one claiming to be the daughter of Vidkun Quisling, and hence, pretender to the throne of the new Reich. How this, so frail a figure, could be chosen to lead the new invincible global Nazi regime, I had some difficulty in understanding.

I continued to view the proceedings, and observed the next person stepping from the gangway onto the deck. He was a heavily built man, in fact, one rapidly approaching obesity. His greying hair was cut close to his scalp and with the classic trace of a scar running down his cheek from the left eye, he reminded me of one of those old Hollywood baddies - the ones of supposedly Germanic origin who made silver screen life tough for the likes of Bogart and Cooper. This one wasted little time with the formalities of exchanging greetings with the Captain and his colleague, and was soon fussing around the woman in the wheelchair. It appeared that the fat guy wanted to transport the Fuhrer into the ship's accommodation immediately. I watched him grab the handles of the wheelchair ready to push her along. But it seemed his Fuhrer was in no hurry to be moved. She indicated that they should wait, and then I saw where they were focusing their attention. The group had turned towards the gangway access and as I watched, I witnessed, with a mixture of relief and anxiety, Karen Olsen appearing and stepping down onto the steel deck. So much had happened since I last saw her and with so many doubts in my mind, I was just relieved to see she was safe and apparently unscathed.

I had not set eyes on Karen since the day she had disembarked from the coastal ferry and was hauled off in the limousine up to the big house outside Aldvik. At the moment, she appeared calm and composed. Understandably however, she did not look all that happy. I noticed the glare in her eyes as she was introduced to the two ship's officers and yet was surprised to see both the men coming to attention. What ever they wanted from her they certainly seemed to be showing her considerable and unusual respect in the effort to get it. I felt better knowing that. But I still wanted to get her released and off that damn ship. Perhaps she was playing along with their wishes until the right moment. She must have come to the conclusion that she was on her own; obviously believing that I was dead, and probably deciding that the best option was to cooperate with her captors.

I was still intrigued by the question of what value the New Aryans had placed on Karen. However, there was no doubt in my mind that these people did not fully trust Olsen's daughter and my thoughts were soon confirmed as two burly men followed up from the gangway and took up positions on either side of her before escorting her into the ship. There was no way they were going to let her make a run for it back down onto the quay. The rest of the hierarchy followed and seconds later I heard the order being given to disconnect the gangway. The *Panther* was preparing to leave port.

The vessel must have already singled up - just one mooring line forward and one aft holding her - when there was a commotion on deck. A gang of crew men appeared at the disembarkation rail and hoisted up a lightweight, ship to shore gangway from the dockside. Seconds after it was anchored in place on the deck, I watched as the old man I'd seen greeting the arrivals earlier, was led off the ship. He was no longer in uniform and appeared to be in some distress as he was guided down the gangway.

Once the old guy was safely ashore, the crew men delivered the gangway back to the shore guys and within another couple of minutes the mooring lines were released and winched aboard. The two short horn blasts operated from the *Panther's* bridge signalled that she was going to turn to port and with the added throb of the ship's engines we began to move away from the quay.

CHAPTER 59

Two of the three young skiers were getting tired. They had all been up on the Hardangervidda skiing since early morning. Hard exercise that had taken them from the south, over the highest level of the plateau, and now onto the long, more gentle slopes leading them down the mountain towards the town of Helmsvik. There, they would spend the night.

Bente Larsen the most talented and least tired skier of the trio was, as she had been most of the day, forging way ahead of her two friends, Arne Mortensen and Marie Berg.

With wisps of attractive copper coloured hair flying out from under her knitted ski-cap and showing no signs whatsoever of fatigue, after the efforts of the gruelling day, Bente Larsen raced away from her two companions.

'Bente,' Arne called out to the girl as she rapidly disappeared down the slope away from them. 'Bente, take it easy. And for goodness sake - wait for us.'

'Oh, just leave her,' Marie tapped the young man on the arm with her ski pole. 'She's in her element. Besides we haven't had a chance to be really alone all day. Thanks to miss high speed mountain skier Bente Larsen.'

The girl moved closer to Arne and leaned over to kiss him on the lips. They kept it simple for a few seconds before things developed into something more intense, and their mouths opened in passion. Surprisingly it was Arne who was first to break free from the embrace.

'Not now Marie, not up here anyway,' he laughed pulling away from his girlfriend's arms. 'Two poles for skiing are plenty. I don't want another one coming into play just yet.'

'Arne! That's disgusting,' Marie exclaimed with mock indignation. 'How dare you utter such a thing to a lady?'

'Sorry, darling,' Arne said contritely, a wicked glint still flashing in his eyes. 'I promise I will make it up to you when we get down to Helmsvik.'

They both laughed and set off again down the slope, following in the track Bente had cut in the snow ahead of them.

Bente was now quite a distance in front. They had lost sight of her through the trees that had gradually begun to thicken as they worked their way down from the plateau. They could not see her - but they heard her scream clearly enough. One sharp, piercing shriek that echoed around the slope.

'My God,' Marie gasped, then shouted into the trees ahead, 'Bente! What is it? Are you alright?'

There was no reply.

'Come on,' Arne called out as he picked up speed and headed down the incline and along the tree lined piste. As he raced down he could make out more than one set of ski tracks in the snow. Although he knew he and the two girls had been skiing off piste for some time, he could now see that they had come upon a route that had been recently skied, and according to the tracks, by more than one or two people. In fact he soon reached an area where it looked as if more than a dozen or more persons on and off skis had churned up the snow across a large area. There were even tracks made by some sort of vehicle. Arne could see that the light dusting of snow over the last few days had failed to cover the ploughed up snow across the whole area.

Still no sight or sound of Bente.

Then, through the fir trees he spotted Bente's bright yellow jacket. At first he was just relieved to see she was still standing. His concern that she may have taken a fall and injured herself while they were still such a long way from any help, was immediately dispelled. He slowed to make his way through the narrow gap in the trees to where Bente stood with her back to him, motionless. She was staring down at something on the ground in front of her.

Arne drew up alongside Bente. The girl did not acknowledge his arrival, she just continued focusing on something at her feet.

'Bente, are you alright? What is it?'

Then Arne saw for himself. A body. A dead body. A girl's dead body.

CHAPTER 60

I waited until we had cleared Aldvik harbour and were well on our way out to sea, before deciding to exit the locker. The *Panther* was running smoothly and at full speed, on course towards the sunken wreck of the *Torvald*. Most of the crew's duties on deck had been completed. Ropes and wires stowed and things generally secured for deep sea operation. I watched the gang of crewmen retire into the accommodation block.

I had no illusions regarding my vulnerability at this stage. With just eight rounds in the Walther and no doubt, up against virtually the whole compliment of the *Panther*, I realised I was in a very precarious situation. The rough plan already formed in my mind, was to somehow get to the Fuhrer. If I could threaten the woman in the wheelchair, the leader, I might be able to bargain for Karen's release. Of course I knew there was no way these people were willingly going to let either me or Karen get off the ship alive. But with Karen safely in my care, I hoped to be able to put the second part of my plan into action. Namely, with Karen's help as a marksman and the acquisition of a couple of the Kalashnikovs that I noticed to be in abundance on the ship, we shoot it out. And, at the same time, use their Fuhrer as cover. Risky, dangerous, crazy? Maybe, but what other option? I had counted about eight crewmen carrying out duties on the deck during the time the *Panther* was alongside the quay at Aldvik. In addition, I knew there was the Captain and the fat guy and then of course the Fuhrer and her entourage. Adding a dozen more deck officers, engineers, cooks, stewards and the like, and discounting the Fuhrer herself, I knew we were going to be two up against at least twenty five. With more than half of them armed and trained killers. Not easy. But what else? I made my move.

The safest route off the open walkway and into the relative protection of the accommodation block, led me around the perimeter of the lower deck. The few access doors on that level led only to more safety equipment storage lockers, entrances into the engine-room space and lower workshops. Nobody was about.

I climbed a steel staircase that took me up onto the first accommodation deck. At this, the lower level of the living quarters, I expected to find more general service rooms - the dining areas for officers and crew, recreation rooms and the ship's offices. This was the area of the ship where, if I was going to run into anybody, it would be here. However, it was surprisingly quiet. I listened at the entrance to the cross alleyway. Nothing. Not a sound. Just the regular purring of the ship's engines way below my feet.

An internal staircase, a few steps in, was deserted and I made my ascent. Before reaching the upper level I heard the faint sound of voices and removed the Walther from my belt.

Ensuring it was all clear, I stepped into the passageway with the gun raised and ready. I moved quietly towards a pair of glass paned doors ahead of me. One of which was open, and through it I detected the sound of voices drifting out. I drew closer and glanced through the panes of the closed side door into the room. I could see that it was a conference room of sorts. An elegant one at that. Displaying much of the ornate grandeur as the rest of the ship. I expected nothing less - I had already seen that expense proved of little concern to these people.

Through the pane I could distinguish a group of people sat around the table. No surprises here. The Fuhrer and her henchmen were in conference. The fat man with the scar sat beside Annelise Quisling who, although still occupying her wheel chair had switched to an impressive change of attire. The classical ladies dress I remembered her wearing on her arrival on the ship, had now been replaced by a more severe and distinctly masculine styled outfit. A dark fitted suit - jacket and trousers - a uniform. I could see only part of the insignia on the armband she displayed on her left upper arm but I knew it was probably the Nazi

Swastika or something very close to it. I realised the Fuhrer was dressed for ceremony.

To her left the two City Gents sat next to each other but now they too had made a significant outfit transformation. In the same, oh so predictable style, they sat in their uniforms - one wearing the black of the old German SS , the other in a more bronzed material, but both, also displaying the feared emblem on their arms. Although, on closer examination, it did appear that the motif was actually not the classic swastika - but something very similar to it.

There was no sign of the *Panther's* Captain. So, was this the hierarchy of the new Aryan Reich? The view I had through the glass door reminded me of a modern day film set – a group of actors dressed up, about to take part in a World War II movie.

'Ah, Mr Craig. Do please come in. We have been expecting you.'

The fat man was looking straight at me through the glass pane of the door. The others all calmly turned to focus in my direction. Not one of them seemed at all surprised to see a stranger peering through the glass. The moment of surprise was just that - a moment- and not for them but for me. I rapidly recovered and moving into the room I aimed the Walther directly at the woman in the wheelchair. Of course I had an eerie feeling, even at that point, where this was all heading.

'Where is she?' I demanded, not taking either my eyes or the snub nose of the barrel for one second off the woman.

'All in good time, Mr Craig,' the fat man said calmly and seemingly unperturbed by the Walther pointing at his leader.

The others sat around the table, appeared equally unruffled. One of the City slickers even had a smirk on his face. It was at that precise moment that the pieces really did begin to drop down into place.

'Where is she?' I snapped the question at them for a second time. 'What have you done with Karen Olsen?'

The fat man shook his head at me, as if I should have known the answer to that question all along. His expression said it all. It was just too obvious.

'Karen Olsen is dead, Mr Craig.'

CHAPTER 61

The phone on the desk in Commander Bruce's office didn't make it halfway through the first ring before it was snatched up.

'Bruce.'

'It's Faulkner, Boss.'

'Where the hell have you been?'

'Bit of a mix up over here Boss. I am afraid the Norwegian police assumed we were the bad guys. Locked us up.'

'Tell me you're joking.'

'No joke, Sir. We traced Craig. He turned out to be holed up here in Aldvik, together with, of all people, the Oberst. But, by the time we arrived on the scene, things had gotten messy.'

'The Oberst? What the hell is he doing up there?'

'At the moment probably dying. He got shot up just before we arrived at the house they were using. Couple of guys, unidentified shot the place to pieces. But it looks like Craig ended their performance - permanently. The local Norwegian law were not too pleased with us rushing onto the scene waving weapons, shortly after the event. Put us in the local nick for a few hours. Took a while to explain. They sprang us about ten minutes ago.'

'And Craig?'

'Lord knows. Off on his one man crusade again, I guess. He survived the attack unscathed. There's something else, Boss. They found another body up on the Hardanger Plateau.'

'Where Mac was shot?'

'Same place. It was a female. Bullet in the head from the same gun that killed Olsen and Mac. The thing is the dead girl has been identified as Karen Olsen.'

'Then who's the woman running around with Craig? It would appear that this so called Mrs Eriksen is turning out to be a very dangerous lady. Any idea where she fits into the big picture?'

'Dead end there, Boss.'

'I don't suppose the Oberst is in any fit state at the present to enlighten us?'

'Afraid not. They are not even sure he will make it, and it seems he was up here on his own. No sign of any backup.'

'OK. I'll get on to The Hague. Try to find out what he was up to. You'd better stick with the Norwegian law. Let me know as soon as anything on Craig and his mysterious girlfriend turns up.'

CHAPTER 62

For a moment I was stunned. I tried to convince myself that the fat guy must be lying - bluffing - but deep down I knew he could only be telling the truth. In fact the whole truth was at last beginning to dawn on me.

'If that is true,' I threatened again, indicating that I was fully prepared to fire the Walther, 'then so is your Fuhrer.'

I watched the two City slickers start to rise at my threat to dispatch their leader and addressed them without taking my eyes off the woman in the wheelchair.

'Another move from either of you two gentlemen and your Fuhrer dies.'

The two men settled back onto their chairs. The tables had been slightly turned. They weren't looking so smug anymore.

I started again.

'Alright, you know who I mean. Where is she? I want to see her now.'

'And indeed you shall, Mr Craig. But first I must ask you to put your weapon down.'

'I don't think so...,Mr?'

'My name is Klensch. Reichsleiter Otto Klensch and these gentlemen are...'

'Hold it Mr Reichsleiter Otto Klensch, you can dispense with the introductions and the crap. I am only going to ask this question one more time. Where is she?

'I am here, Mr Craig.'

I recognised the voice coming from behind me, but the tone was so different now. Far removed from the one she had so convincingly adopted on our journey north together. I felt little consolation that all the pieces had now dropped so neatly into place. The biggest revelation was of my own total and utter gullibility. I had fallen for the oldest trick in the book, and by one of the oldest methods.

I kept the gun trained on the old lady Fuhrer as she spoke for the first time.

'Young man, if you are going to pull the trigger, I suggest you do it now. You see there is a strong possibility that I might die before you even make the decision. My days are numbered. And I am afraid so are yours.' She spoke calmly and clearly and without fear or emotion, although I detected the debilitating effect of her condition in the quivering tone of her voice. 'You see, Mr Craig,' she continued, nodding at some point over my shoulder. 'The gentleman standing behind you will fire his pistol the moment you fire yours. And, unlike me Mr Craig you will die without ever knowing exactly what cause you believed you were fighting for or the one you were fighting against.'

I lowered the gun and felt it snatched immediately from my grasp and replaced by the cold press of steel against the back of my neck.

Why had I given in without a fight? Quite simple really. Firstly, there had never been the slightest chance that I would do anything other than threaten Annelise Quisling's life. I'd had my fill of killing unarmed people, no matter how evil they were. The second reason was even more elementary.

Curiosity.

Yes, Annelise Quisling was right, I just wanted to know what this whole business was all about. I needed to understand what manic dream had led to the deaths of so many people - including my best friend. I wanted to know what was down in that ship besides the gold. And finally, and most of all, I wanted to know what part the girl I had called Karen Olsen played in this mad drama.

Of course, I realised they would eventually want to kill me, and I guessed that the only reason they had not already done so, they'd had ample opportunity, was that they wanted me to know just who they were and what they intended. They had no intention of closing the book until they had forced me to read through to the very last page, and frankly, neither did I.

I turned round to confront the woman who I had believed all along to be Karen Olsen. Except for the outfit she was now wearing she looked much the same. The same natural, long golden hair that seemed to hold its style under any circumstance - never appearing ruffled or unkempt. The same blue eyes that had so captivated and deceived me. The uniform she wore, although stylishly tailored to every curve of her lithe body, served only to present the picture of a hardened female. The suit material was the fine dark grey colour, almost black, that the Fuhrer was wearing. The New Aryans seemed to be as obsessed with the uniform as their political forebears, the Nazis, had been. Even the armband was the same - or was it? For the first time I was presented with a clear view of the sleeve pattern. I could now see it was not the swastika but a very similar emblem. Then I remembered where I had seen such a design before. The intriguing tattoo I had noticed on the upper arm of Karen back on the *North Star,* had been made up of a chain link pattern of this same emblem. I could see now what had eluded me then - the insignia almost resembling the swastika, and the attraction it must have had to these fanatics. They wanted to emulate the Nazi Reich, and yet somehow stand independent. So they introduced their own unique qualities, and of course, an exclusive insignia.

'It's called the Odal Rune, Mr Craig,' said the woman I had thought I'd known so well. The one who'd convinced me she was Karen Olsen. She'd noticed my eyes trained on her armband. 'It is the modern emblem of the New Aryans.'

'So what's new about it all, this time?' I questioned. 'Fuhrers, Reichsleiters, poorly disguised swastika emblems, murder of the innocent. Seems to be following a very familiar pattern.'

'You will not speak to the new Fuhrer in such a manner.' Otto Klensch was on his feet, growling at me while the two heavies behind the girl started to head in my direction, with unmistakable intent. Karen held up her arm to stop the two goons and then waved Klensch to sit back on his chair.

I watched her walk to the table. The whole group, barring the woman in the wheelchair, rose to its feet as she took her position at the head of the table and sat down. So that was it.

'The new Fuhrer,' I said. 'The next in line.' And it wasn't a question. At last my sluggish brain was recognising the clear facts. 'So would that be Fraulein or Frau Fuhrer?'

This time Klensch just nodded to one of the guards standing behind me. The guy quickly responded and moved in to deliver a punch to my kidneys. The force of the blow dropped me to my knees and I could see the guard was not finished. He was preparing for another sortie, using his boot this time. My instincts prodded me to rise and prepare to retaliate, but the new Fuhrer's voice cut in sharply.

'That's enough.'

The goon grudgingly backed off and I slowly rose to my feet.

'Why did you not just stay out of this, Mr Craig?' The Fuhrer to be, asked. It was a stupid question.

'Perhaps you should ask that of the woman back in Aberdeen you just made a widow. The one with a newborn child, now without a father. And the families of the fifty other innocent men you murdered on the *Highlander*.'

'This is war, Mr Craig. Innocent people sometimes get hurt.'

'Let's hope it doesn't turn out to be another six million.'

The tough guy made to come at me again but she waved him away.

Klensch also had again hoisted himself to his feet.

'We should get rid of this man,' Klensch snarled.

'Not yet,' Karen stated calmly although there was no doubting it was a command and Klensch sat back down.

I knew where this was going and said, 'Not before you've explained to me how clever you have been and how justified are your divine plans for the new world order. And, how utterly blind and stupid I have been. By the way what are you going to call it this time the Fourth Reich or is that going to be too mundane?'

'Mr Craig, unfortunately I will have to prevent you jeopardising our cause. A cause which far outweighs the needs of any one individual. We all have to make sacrifices.'

'That was some sacrifice you made to me in the cabin back there on the ferry. My Fuhrer.'

This time she made no attempt to prevent the guard from propelling me to the floor again. But on this occasion, it was she who rose angrily to her feet. Now though, I could see not just anger but a look closer to panic on her face. Could it be nobody in the room was aware what the heir apparent had been up to out on the waters of the Norwegian Sea?

'I will speak to this man alone,' she said.

'But, My Fuhrer,' Klensch, for a third time, was up and protesting.

'I said alone. Leave me with a weapon. When I have finished you may remove him - for good.'

CHAPTER 63

Sigmund Sandved realised that something out of the ordinary had been going on up on the high road for the past few days. He had been making his regular trip on foot out of Aldvik almost every single day since his retirement two years previously. Accompanied by old faithful Rasta, summer and winter, it did not matter, Sandved and his dog could be found walking somewhere along the route from the port up the main highway as far as the *Nyehuset* - the new house.

The rich man from the south had built it only four years previously.

Most of the views looking out to sea from anywhere in Aldvik were pretty magnificent, although nobody in the town ever said so. The locals seemed to take it all much for granted. However, few people would deny that the views from the cliff top on the high road out across the Norwegian Sea were anything but spectacular.

Sigmund Sandved had worked his whole life on the family's farm located a short distance inland. Too far from the bay to appreciate any of the sea views. So, now in his retirement years, Sigmund Sandved was finally catching up with the pleasures to be gained from just standing and looking out to sea from the cliff top. A simple but very satisfying pastime.

Normally, except for the regular passing of the traffic to and from Aldvik, the high road was quiet. Only on the weekends, some town's people and occasionally a few seasonal tourists managed to make their way this far up from the harbour. But this past week the old man had been surprised at the level of activity taking place up on the high road.

First, he could hardly help but notice the small convoy of big, black, expensive cars driving back and fore between the port and the big house. Who and how many were travelling in each vehicle, he never really had a clear enough view through the impenetrable smoked glass windows to tell.

Some sort of gathering was taking place in the mansion - that was obvious. Not that he knew much about such things, but Sandved had the idea that some cult or other was holding one of its meetings up there.

Further more, it was plain that the general public, as in the townspeople of Aldvik, were unwelcome. Confirmed by the almost permanently closed iron gates and the fleeting glimpses the old man had of what appeared to be guards patrolling inside. The second and even stranger activity that had grabbed his interest was the appearance of a white van and two men, strangers, dressed in ill-fitting overalls who, when he'd questioned them had given the weak explanation that they were carrying out tree pruning - under contract. Fifty years in the farming business provides a man with a certain knowledge of most things relating to the natural world. Arboreal science included. And there was no way that this pair had the least idea of how to prune a tree.

Sandved assumed that the two men were part of the security system adopted by the people up in the big house. Still it was none of his business. So Sigmund Sandved just carried on as usual. However, his suspicions were confirmed after a few days, when arriving at the location of the white van, he could see that hardly any of the surrounding trees had been touched. Further, there was no sign of the two men. The van appeared to be abandoned.

Sandved was not the type to get involved with things that did not concern him. He looked to maintain the quiet life. So, apart from the cursory observation, he made a point of avoiding the white van; to the extent that he even crossed to the other side of the road when required to pass it.

This morning Sandved noticed up ahead that the van was no longer there and neither of the men was to be seen. He was about to make his usual detour onto the other side of the road when Rasta, running well ahead of him as usual and skirting the cliff edge about thirty metres further up, started barking. Rasta barked only when something was wrong.

Sandved hurried to where the dog was poised at the edge of the cliff, growling at something just below. Sandved peered over.

'My God,' he whispered to himself.

The area around the cliff top on the road out of Aldvik teemed with men and vehicles. Sigmund Sanved's call on his battered, old fashioned but still fully functional mobile phone, had brought the law and emergency services out in force. Already, he had watched two black plastic body bags being lifted up the cliff face and placed in one of the ambulances. These two unfortunates had been discovered below the cliff edge near to where the van had been parked. The man that Rasta had sniffed out was however, still very much alive.

With the dog now on a leash and sitting obediently at his master's heel, Sandved watched the attempts of the paramedics to stabilise the badly injured man before transferring him to the ambulance. Further up, where a couple of men could be seen sifting about, presumably for evidence, a rescue crew was still working on the cliff face. Sanved guessed they were searching for anyone else who may have been equally unfortunate.

The old man had overheard them saying that they'd already found a car smashed up on the rocks a hundred metres below. All part of the same game, and what a game. It was not every day that this sort of event took place in Aldvik - in fact this sort of thing never took place in Aldvik.

Another car arrived on the scene. This one was unmarked, and after obtaining clearance from one of the local policemen on duty, proceeded to drive onto the site. Parking near the ambulance, Sandved watched as two men exited the vehicle, and flashing their identities, moved to where the paramedics were tending the man they had brought up from the cliff face – the one who was still alive.

'Trust the Brits to turn up at the last moment,' Henrik Gabrielsen said in a weak voice, although still maintaining a touch of humour as he addressed Faulkner and Thompson approaching the stretcher he was propped up on. 'Is the Oberst OK?'

'Sure,' Faulkner replied. 'We just got news. He's going to pull through. What about Craig?'

'Craig?' the man on the stretcher questioned back in surprise through clenched teeth. A spasm of pain shooting through his body. 'I thought he was with the Oberst.'

'He was,' said Faulkner. 'Even managed to despatch the two guys sent to get rid of them both. And, according to the local law, was chased by them as he headed up in this direction, shortly after. From what we hear, he could have been done ten times over for dangerous driving and speeding – and I mean speeding.'

'I don't know anything about that. I've been pretty much out of the picture for the last few hours. I'd only just arrived when the bastards got to us. Gunned down my two men. I got lucky though. They thought they'd finished me off too, when I made the dive over the cliff after taking this bullet.' Gabrielsen indicated the blood stained bandage on his chest. 'But they didn't spend much time looking for me. My guess is they are on the move. My guess also, is we won't see any of them again up here.'

'This man has to be taken to hospital immediately,' one of the paramedics cut in as he and a second man took up positions at each end of the stretcher, while a third swung the ambulance rear door open.

'All I know is that Craig was chasing around with the Oberst,' Gabrielsen said as they began lifting him into the ambulance. 'The last I heard was that they were both going out to the wreck.'

'The Rig?' Faulkner asked.

'No, a ship called the *Torvald*. Been on the bottom for years. The one that was obstructing the *Highlander*. That was yesterday. Nothing since then. Shortly after that the bastards from that house jumped us. My guys didn't stand a chance.'

The paramedics guided the stretcher into the ambulance and began to pull the doors shut.

'One last question,' Faulkner called out. 'Where do you think Craig could be now?'

Gabrielsen's weak voice drifted out from the interior. 'Your guess is as good as mine. But if he's still alive my bet he's going back to that wreck. It certainly seems to hold the key to all this.'

'Thanks Henrik, and good luck,' Faulkner said finally and watched the doors slam shut and the ambulance pull away.

CHAPTER 64

'So, my Fuhrer,' I said, addressing the woman who's real name I did not know for certain, but took a good guess that it was going to turn out to be Raven or even Quisling. That would be if anybody of any political persuasion and in their right mind would nowadays choose to adopt the latter title.

We were alone in the room with the two glass doors firmly shut behind us. She standing, gun in hand. Me standing a few paces in front of her, waiting. Waiting for the right moment.

'My Fuhrer,' I repeated the title again. 'Do you realise just how ridiculous that title actually sounds?'

I noticed her fingers tighten on the gun in her hand but she kept it passively pointing down at her side. However, I didn't doubt for one second that, if needs be, she would not hesitate to aim and fire the thing - at me. Why she or one of her lackeys had not attempted to do so already, still remained something of a mystery.

'It might sound ridiculous to you, but may I remind you it was the exclusive title bestowed on the world's greatest leader and will soon be adopted again.'

I was beginning to suspect that chances of me getting out of this alive were becoming increasingly slim. I guess I had nothing to lose so I said, 'I would not have thought that the macho Nazi doctrine would be particularly enthusiastic about adopting a female Fuhrer.'

She appeared unruffled by the remark.

'If it was not for we, the women, there would be no reborn National Socialist movement. No New Aryan beginning.'

'We, the women?' I questioned. 'Do you mean you and your mother? You are the daughter of Annelise Raven are you not? Is it your intention then, to rule jointly?'

'You obviously do not realise that my mother is dying. She has only weeks if not days to live. I will take her place. I did not ask for this position. I was quite content to serve my Mother and the cause in a lesser capacity. But I am blood and I will take up where she left off. I am the only heir - I am a Quisling.'

I shook my head in disbelief. Who in their right mind would make such a statement - *I am a traitor*?

Disregarding my cynical gesture she continued.

'Take a seat, Steve and I will try to enlighten you,' she said shifting to a more personal form of address; calling me by my Christian name for the first time since we had been so unceremoniously parted on the coastal ferry. Although any hint of affection was long gone.

I shook my head, declining the offer to sit.

'I prefer to stand,' I said.

I wanted to be on my feet when the time came for me to act. However, I took the opportunity to move a couple of paces nearer to her. The key lessons of my early training starting to resurrect from somewhere within. *If unarmed, get as close as you can to the target.*

'As you wish,' she said and lowered herself into a chair, at the same time laying the gun on the table just in front of her. She was still out of my reach but that move would definitely be to my advantage.

'Why explain?' I asked. 'What's stopping you just pulling the trigger and getting rid of me right now?' A risky thing to say – but what the hell?

If I had sensed the slightest intention she may have had or any attempt she might have made to reach again for the gun, I was ready. My whole course of action had now taken on a massive change. Instead of planning for her to join me in getting off the ship alive, I was going to have to take care of that by myself. Frankly, I believed my chances of success had suddenly doubled. I was back on home ground – my fate in my hands alone.

She went on to answer the question.

'Because, for one reason, I think you could provide a valuable service to our cause. A man of your intelligence and martial skills could go a long way in our organisation.'

'Yes. A man with such a high level of intelligence, that he allowed you to completely fool him, Karen.'

'My name is not Karen, it is Freya.'

At that revelation, I smiled and said, 'Of course it would be. Freya - famous Wagnerian heroine and ancient Goddess of Love, Beauty and War. What more appropriate title for the leader of the new Aryan Reich. And what about your surname - Quisling?'

'I shall continue to use the adopted family name of Raven until the new Reich is established. Then, I will become Freya Quisling. I will wipe out the stigma attached to my grandfather's name and re-establish it with honour. You know, Steve, thousands no millions of people, not just here in Norway but around the whole world, admired my grandfather. They still do even to this day. He was a true leader - a great man.'

For the first time I could see just how misguided this woman really was. Like all of her type - just another mindless fanatic.

'So it was you who shot Olsen on the mountain.' I changed the subject. 'And who was the other guy you disposed of up there? Just out of interest.'

'One of yours, I assume Steve. Probably MI something or other. I assume he was supposed to be looking after your interests. Not too efficiently it would appear.'

'And the real Karen Olsen?'

'Up there too,' she said without the slightest hint of remorse. 'I am surprised they haven't found her even though I hid her body. But she was a nobody. Although I must say her orienteering rifle came in very useful.'

'Do you mind if I enquire what the future Fuhrer of the New Aryan Reich was doing up on the Hardangervidda plateau, all on her own, shooting at people?'

Again she chose to ignore the sarcasm.

'Something you should not find too hard to comprehend. You see, as the future leader of any movement, it is always essential to display strength of command, prior to taking office. What better way than by personally disposing of the traitors who most threatened the cause? By my example, others will follow.'

Now I knew for certain - she was crazy.

'Including the murder of an innocent young girl?' I asked.

'As I have already stated, there will always be unavoidable civilian casualties in war. I believe nowadays everybody has heard of collateral damage. Even your great democratic Britain subscribes to that philosophy or do you have some alternative explanation for your country's war game antics in Afghanistan and Iraq to name just two?'

'So what exempted me from the fate of the other unfortunates up on the mountainside?'

'Practical reasons basically. Number one, you offered yourself as my perfect cover and at the same time provided quite a lot of useful inside information, and of course, the added bonus was that you and not I became the prime suspect.'

'God, what an idiot,' I mumbled to myself.

'You served the purpose and the Cause very well, Steve.'

'I seemed to have served it well enough in your bed. It must have come as quite of a shock, me turning up here alive and well, with all the sordid details to hand.'

'A necessary action on my part. I wanted to discover what information that old fool Olsen had passed to you about the *Torvald*.'

'And by a rather well established method. And when you acquired that information, I was of no further use. Especially when one of your lackeys turned up on the ferry – the so called latecomer.'

In retrospect it was all so predictable I thought. I had just been blind from the start.

'So, what now?' I asked and got ready to rush her, the instant she made any attempt to reach for the gun. My chances were slim but I had no intention of going down without putting up some sort of a fight.

'You have three choices,' she answered. 'Join us, die quickly or die slowly.'

'That's easy then. I will join you.' I didn't hesitate, but even I anticipated the obvious response.

'Sorry, Steve. I never really rated that as one of the more plausible options.'

'I thought not,' I said. 'But then I do get to choose quick or slow departure. Bullets or piano wire, I guess, if all Fuhrers are cast in the same mould.' I moved another step closer and added, 'Why not just finish it now - on the spot? You've got the gun.' I was ready to counter.

'Far too messy,' she said smugly, not even attempting to pick up the weapon. I could see she was obviously enjoying the moment. 'No, I will grant you a civilised execution - quick and painless - provided you make no further reference to our...the liaison on the ferry.'

'Agreed,' I said, standing down. It would serve no real purpose and, much more importantly, it would give me just a bit more time to find a way to dig myself out of this mess.

Besides, I believed her and realised she wanted me to witness some more of her powers before she would consider me ready for disposal. For now I was satisfied. I would live to fight another day as they say. I could wait.

'But don't I get to find out what is so important down there on the *Torvald*? In addition to the gold that is.'

'So you know about the gold? I'm very impressed. You seem to have gathered quite a lot of information in such a short time, Steve,' she said. 'And of course, if you remain silent about the ferry, I will give you the opportunity, not just to find out what is so important onboard the *Torvald*, but the chance to see it for yourself.'

'How can I turn down such a generous offer?'

'Ever the joker, Steve.'

CHAPTER 65

The Royal Norwegian Navy frigate *Kong Haakon* anchored in the deep water of the outer harbour at Aldvik just after midday, and awaited the arrival of the two British agents being transferred out from the shore.

Minutes before she dropped anchor, Faulkner and Thompson were already heading on their way out towards the warship in a high speed Coastguard launch.

Since returning to the town from the scene of carnage up on the highway outside Aldvik, both men had been actively engaged in pulling together the resources they were going to need to stop this bunch of fanatics from carrying out any more mayhem. There was now more than sufficient evidence to pull the whole gang in. If they could be found and rounded up in time.

Top Priority Clearance from Bruce in the UK and the permission granted by the Norwegian Government to utilise the full powers of their Navy, soon got everything into full swing.

The nearest armed naval ship was the *Kong Haakon*, commanded by Kommandør Jon Rasmussen. Rasmussen was ordered to break off from routine patrol of the northern sector of the North Sea and head without delay to the port of Aldvik. Once there, the instructions were to take onboard two British agents. The order was classed *High Alert*, and by the time she arrived off Aldvik the crew and the armament of the *Kong Haakon* were in full operational readiness. Prepared for action.

Kommandør Rasmussen had made his way from the bridge down onto the main deck to greet Faulkner and Thompson as they arrived.

'Gentlemen, welcome aboard the *Kong Haakon.*' Rasmussen saluted and then offered each man a firm handshake. 'If you will follow me up to the bridge. I'll get us underway. Then I would appreciate it if you would put me in the picture. I am going to require quite a bit more information before I give the order to engage with another vessel. I am afraid my seniors were unusually reserved with the details of this operation.'

Faulkner and Thompson followed the ship's commander up to the bridge. On the way, Rasmussen began issuing orders. He spoke in Norwegian, addressing the crewmen standing ready at their various stations. By the time the trio reached the bridge the vessel was in full readiness to go.

Rasmussen, wasting no more time, gave the order for full speed ahead and the *Kong Haakon* was on her way.

CHAPTER 66

'We are at the strong room entrance,' the diver's voice crackled over the intercom.

The group around me on the aft deck of the *Panther* instinctively moved to get a closer view of the VDU screen set up on a trestle adjacent to the ship's lifting gear.

I inched my way forward, following the group, but was quickly reminded of my current status as a heavy hand gripped my shoulder and the individual assigned to guard me prodded my neck with the blunt nose of a handgun.

They had taken the precaution of cuffing me shortly after my interview with the Fuhrer elect came to an end. She had summoned her entourage back into the conference room. The fat Otto character was still all for despatching me without further discussion. But one sharp command from Freya Quisling put a stop to his proposal. She ensured there was no doubting who was in charge. She was also determined that I should witness whatever secret was soon to be hauled from the depths of the ocean.

Freya Quisling herself had issued the curt order for me to be handcuffed. Then informed the heavies that I would be joining the party on deck when the last item was ready to be raised from the *Torvald*. However, her guards had made one classic mistake in carrying out her instructions. My hands were manacled in front of me, and I had already run through in my mind, at least half a dozen copy book actions that can be carried out when so restrained. Manoeuvres both defensive and aggressive. As I said, I had no intention of giving up without a fight.

The lead players were all assembled on the well of the *Panther's* aft deck. All except Annelise Raven. Being manhandled down to this level would have proved neither dignified nor practical and had certainly not appealed to the outgoing Fuhrer. I noticed she seemed to have become even more frail looking and much weaker since her arrival on the ship. Eventually she had been guided to a position on a sort of flying bridge - a railed walkway running across the back of the main accommodation block. From there, she was awarded a bird's eye view of the events that were about to take place on the deck below.

The Captain of the *Panther*, I had heard them addressing him as Brett, was directing the operation.

'Can you see the safe?' Brett asked, speaking into a hand microphone, more than a note of irritation in his tone. 'Because our monitor up here is showing nothing.'

I could see for myself that they were getting a rather poor signal from the divers moving about down on the wreck. All the VDU displayed was a misty image.

'Affirmative, Sir,' came the response from the depths. 'We are at the location of the strong room safe. The camera is following right behind. We should have a picture for you soon.

At those encouraging words the group inched forward. I noted the expressions on the faces of the people around me. Somewhere between expectation and awe.

A path had been made for the new Fuhrer and I watched Freya Quisling lean over and position herself to ensure she had a better view of the monitor screen.

'Still cannot see anything,' Brett snapped.

Then the picture transmitted from the sub-sea camera stabilised, and slowly the image on the screen began to take shape. There was a sharp intake of breath from some of the members standing around me as the picture of a large, rusted but still pretty solid looking steel box filled the screen.

'That's it,' exclaimed Klensch. 'They've located the safe.'

I watched Freya, who had been quietly observing the operation, now reaching to relieve Brett of the hand microphone he was holding.

'Is it possible to open it?' she asked the man working seventy meters below the surface.

The diver made no mistake in recognising the voice as the tone of his reply reflected.

'Doubtful my Fuhrer. Not down at this depth without keys. We need to get it up to the surface. Up there we should have no trouble gas axing through the locks.'

'Gas axing?' Freya Quisling turned to Brett with a puzzled look. That was one expression in English that she had obviously never come across.

'He means, to cut through the steel using an oxy-acetylene torch,' Brett explained. 'May we proceed?'

She nodded assent and handed the microphone back to him.

'Standby below. We are getting the lifting gear rigged up,' Brett announced into the microphone.

Twenty minutes passed, while a great deal of activity took place both on the deck of the *Panther* and in the strong-room of the ship deep down there. *Panther's* crane was rigged with 150 metres of heavy gauge lifting cable and four wire slings designed to be shackled around the safe.

Eventually the response came back from the divers.

'Everything in place. Wires secured. Ready when you are, to lift.'

The words from the deep echoed from the PA speakers dotted around the ship - everybody on board could hear what was going on.

Brett waved his arm to the man sat at the hydraulic controls of the lifting winch.

'Hoist away - easy.'

On the VDU, those of us standing on the well-deck could see clearly the huge steel box, now secured by four wire lifting cables. We watched the cables tighten and then slowly the massive weight beginning to move from the position it had rested in for over 60 years. A murmur of satisfaction came from the Fuhrer's entourage. The expression on Freya's face was approaching ecstasy. I remembered witnessing that look before but under quite different circumstances. I was getting closer by the minute to finding out what the big deal was with the contents of this safe, and I must admit, I was becoming more intrigued by the minute.

'It's on its way up,' the voice of one of the divers crackled over the speakers and the VDU screen displayed the safe swinging free in the deep water below. Then the screen went blank. Obviously, the cameraman had ceased filming and was probably on his way back up to the surface. Now all attention was focused over the side of the ship, and the steel cable hanging down from the crane hoist.

In just a short while, the safe from the strong-room of the *Torvald* would break the surface.

CHAPTER 67

The frigate *Kong Haakon* was running at its full operational speed of 26 knots, on course for Block 6204 in the Norwegian Sea.

Agents Faulkner and Thompson stood inside the bridge house alongside Kommandør Rasmussen. They had explained the situation to the frigate's commander and were filling in the details. Rasmussen relayed the relevant information to his First officer, who in turn issued instructions to the bridge crew and by PA throughout the rest of the vessel.

When Faulkner had completed the story of the sequence of events of the past few days, Rasmussen put a very pertinent question to him.

'Is this *Panther* vessel armed?'

'Difficult question to answer,' Faulkner replied.

'We have very little information on that. Of course we know they are carrying explosives and small arms. Heavier fixed armament, we just don't know.'

'I'm surprised from the reports that such a ship has been able to avoid detection for so long,' Rasmussen said.

'As I explained,' Faulkner replied. 'The vessel is of a very sophisticated design. An extremely effective stealth construction. We have not been able to spot her on our conventional satellite scanning. That's why she was not identified on the *Highlander* attack.'

'Well sophisticated or not, the *Panther* seems to have shown little of that quality in displaying herself to all by sailing into Aldvik harbour.'

Rasmussen said with raised eyebrows. 'I suspect she could be planning to leave the area as soon as she gets what she wants from the wreck?'

'More than likely,' Faulkner replied. Then asked, 'How much longer?'

'An hour, not more.'

'Do you expect them to put up a fight, Commander?'

Rasmussen shook his head and then indicating down in the direction of the foredeck said. 'Lord knows what these fanatics are capable of. But if they do try fighting it out, we shall be more than ready for them.'

Faulkner followed Rasmussen's pointing finger through the bridge window to the fore deck below. A team of sailors were removing the canvass cover from the ship's 76mm Melara Super Rapid deck gun.

'We are prepared to give them a run for their money as you gentlemen would say.'

CHAPTER 68

The group of New Aryans gathered around the solid mass of metal were mesmerised. Even the guard assigned to me was paying more attention to the events unfolding around the *Torvald's* rust stained safe, than he was to his prisoner. Under different circumstances, it would have been the ideal moment to make a move. But the events being played out on the deck in front of me, frankly, proved just as compelling for me to witness as it did my captors. My time would come, but first, the safe and its long awaited contents. I conjured up visions of untold wealth in the form of priceless artefacts and the like, or maps identifying the locations of some of the stolen treasures and arts buried around the world by the Nazis during World War II.

The oxy-acetylene torch had been throwing up a continuous stream of sparks and molten metal for some minutes as its flame cut through the rust stained steel. The diver, who had earlier been running things underwater, after having safely and quickly decompressed, had now taken charge of the task of getting into the safe. Divested of his breathing equipment but still dressed in the diving suit, he was personally operating the oxy-acetylene torch to cut through the metal.

After a few minutes of burning, two chunks of steel that had made up the hinges of the safe, fell to the deck with a resounding clatter. With the hinge brackets gone, the door started to sag inwards - the accumulated rust and sea growth unable to support the massive weight. Only the locking tumblers on the opposite side still held the door in place.

'Pass me a lever,' Brett commanded, shouldering the diver with the cutting torch out of the way.

A crewman was quick to provide a steel crowbar. Brett inserted the end into one of the gaping holes cut into the door, and levered downwards on it. Slowly the massive plate started to move and the edge, breaking free from its corroded seating, began to rise. Anticipating the next command the crewman dragged into position a shearleg portable hoisting frame on which a chain block and shackle had been mounted. The hook was secured into the edge of the door.

'Lift,' Brett commanded and the crewman began to pull on the chain. All eyes watched as the huge slab slowly began to rise.

From what I could see from my position at the back of the group, it looked just like a pile of muddy, decomposed paper lying inside the safe. Originally probably watertight, the seals, over time, had slowly corroded away letting the sea water penetrate into the safe. What documents of any importance had been placed in there, were now almost totally destroyed. I couldn't see what else of any possible value could have remained intact. But I was soon to find out.

It surprised me to see Brett himself rolling up his sleeve and plunging his hand into the black slime. He struck me as one who would prefer to delegate this sort of dirty work to a lesser mortal. In this case however, it seemed he was intent on being the one to retrieve the treasure - whatever it was going to turn out to be.

All attention was focused on Brett as he swirled his arm around the clinging sludge, searching through the confined space. Then, everybody recognised the change of expression on Brett's face as his hand must have come into contact with something solid beneath the water.

The item he pulled out certainly proved somewhat of a disappointment to me. It looked just like a soggy rag wrapped around something the size of a twenty millimetre cannon shell. But the gasps of awe and admiration from those around me dispelled any doubts about the significance of this object. They all seemed to know exactly what it was.

Brett started to unwrap what was left of the original, covering material. It looked as if it once might have been a velvet fabric of some kind - most of it now falling to shreds as he stripped it away from the solid object within.

The first glimpse of what was inside the wrapping, created a further murmur of awe from the New Aryans around me. They obviously knew what to expect. Peeling away the last shreds of the velvet material, Brett raised the item up for all to see.

It was a metal baton. Not just an ordinary baton, like the kind you see twirled in the hands of a drum majorette. No, this was something far more special.

As Brett started to wipe the film of muddy deposit from around the baton, I began to realise just what a fabulous item it really was.

About half a metre in length and six centimetres diameter, my guess was that it was probably made of pure gold. It had a red ceramic coating along its length into which had been embedded more than a dozen solid gold eagle swastika mouldings, surrounded by silver and jet black ceramic knights' crosses. At each end was a raised, ornate, gold and silver crown piece with a large moulding of an eagle and swastika cast into each face.

It was the classic Nazi, Field Marshall's baton. Every top military man in the Reich at one time or another had possessed one of these. The higher the rank, the more ornate and priceless the baton awarded to the individual. Most of these batons were personally presented by Adolf Hitler himself.

Brett handed the baton to the girl Fuhrer.

It was ornate and probably extremely valuable as an article of World War II memorabilia but this baton now in the hands of Freya Quisling obviously was something of far greater significance, not only to her but to all those assembled on the main deck of the *Panther*.

She raised the baton proudly above her head like an Olympic athlete and turned to face her mother who had, all the time, been closely following what was taking place on the deck below her position.

We all watched in astonishment as Annelise Raven grasped the ship's rail with both hands and slowly pulled herself into an upright position. A guard, standing just behind, moved to assist her but was waved away as she straightened up unaided. I watched with less enthusiasm than those around me as the outgoing Fuhrer of the New Aryan order steadied herself with one frail hand clasped around the steel rail, and proudly raised her free arm in the historic yet still chilling Nazi salute.

'Heil, Quisling!' she proclaimed.

Freya Quisling and her entourage down on the deck below, responded in the same manner, each elevating an arm outward and upward as they drew themselves to erect attention.

'Heil, Quisling!' was the unanimous chorous.

'So is that what all this is about? A bloody truncheon,' I called out from my position at the back of the bunch, rudely breaking the air of mesmerized, fascist adoration. They all turned to look at me. The expected payment punch came from the gorilla behind me and the effect of being hammered repeatedly in the kidneys was beginning to tell on me. I barely managed to stay on my feet. But it was worth it. Freya and her retinue now directed their attention towards me.

She waved the punch happy bastard to back off. He did, but not before landing a parting shot into the small of my back - at least it wasn't the kidney this time.

'This, Mr Craig,' Freya Quisling said, holding aloft the baton. 'Is the true emblem of authority, bequeathed to the true Leader of the new Thousand Year Aryan Reich. Whoever holds this is the rightful successor to the great Adolf Hitler, and I claim that right as the sole descendent of the man the Fuhrer chose to inherit his position - my Grandfather Vidkun Quisling.

'And the price for that antiquated chunk of memorabilia was the mindless slaughter of some fifty people and that's only the ones I know about. And, I suspect only just the beginning.'

The pulverising blow from behind, this time ensured I met the steel deck with a crash.

Yet again, the Fuhrer waved the thug to back off.

'You know, Mr Craig,' she said, something of a note of humour in her voice. She could afford the jocularity; it wasn't her lower body being pummelled. 'If you bothered to choose your words more carefully, perhaps you would spend less time on your knees in front of me.' She raised the baton in both hands. 'It is not just the baton itself - not just the power of authority that it signifies. It means much more to all of us than that.'

As she spoke she commenced twisting one of the golden carved ends of the baton. It began to unscrew and after a few turns the crown end was released completely from the main body and she pulled it clear. Passing the solid gold head to Brett to hold, she reached with her fingers into the hollow, tubular internal of the baton and withdrew what appeared to be a watertight, oilskin wrapper. It was almost as if the sender had anticipated the thing might end up at the bottom of the ocean; and in such an event, had made more than adequate arrangements to keep it dry. Including the fitting of what looked like heavy watertight seals set into the body of the baton. Although he would have been quite optimistic expecting it to stand the test of sea and time - but it certainly appeared to have done so. The whole thing was in pretty good condition considering the decades it had spent at the bottom of the ocean. Some sixty years.

Freya soon had the waterproof protection carefully cut away by one of the crewmen, exposing a large rolled document. In fact, it turned out to be two documents, one furled inside the other.

Another one of those, now becoming increasingly irritating, sycophantic eruptions of awe and wonderment was emitted by the gang of Aryan elitists, who were beginning to sound to me more like a gang of school kids on a day's outing rather than the vicious fanatics that they really were.

Freya unravelled the top document and after a quick scan turned to Otto Klensch with a nod and a smile of satisfaction.

'That's it,' she said, handing the sheet to him. 'You know what to do with that. He will be waiting.'

Klensch accepted the document from her and, without a word turned and headed for the accommodation steps.

Freya now focused her attention on the second sheet and, unrolling it, glanced quickly through the content and then, just as she had done with the baton itself, raised it up for all to see - displaying it to the gathering around her and finally ending up, once more, facing her mother on the upper deck.

'The last will and testament of Adolf Hitler, and his personal authority bequeathed to the true holder,' she proclaimed loudly and this time received a round of applause and even a few cheers from some of the *Panther's* crew who had now also moved in and were gathered around the group of leaders on the aft deck.

Then turning to me she said, 'So Mr. Craig, now you know everything. We may dispense with your services.'

'Not quite everything, my Fuhrer,' I said, not trying too hard to moderate the sarcasm.

'Oh?' she feigned surprise at the fact that I might have something further to ask.

'Just two final questions,' I said, and at that same instant, I noticed something rather interesting taking place over the shoulder of the new Fuhrer. Way out to sea off the aft port quarter of the *Panther* I spied another ship. Not just any old, ordinary ship but a warship. And there was no mistaking the fact that she was running at full speed directly towards us.

'Ask,' Freya ordered.

'Firstly,' I began, putting the oncoming vessel out of my mind for a second. 'How did the baton get onboard the *Torvald* in the first place?'

'A fascinating but too long a story. You'll just have to use your imagination. And the second question?'

'What was the other document? The one you handed to the Reichsleiter a minute ago?'

'Ah,' she said. 'Another even longer story I am afraid. But in a word, Mr Craig - finance. I am truly sorry that I just do not have the time to elaborate.'

'For once, my Fuhrer I fully agree with you,' I said, recognising the flash, followed a second later by a cloud of smoke issuing from the deck of the approaching frigate. I was down on my knees again but this time it was of my own volition.

The first shell whistled above our heads and over the superstructure of the *Panther* and exploded barely twenty meters in the water over the starboard side. Not exactly a shot across the bows but pretty damn close, and the intention was unmistakably clear.

At that point, decorum, pomp and vanity evaporated, all rapidly replaced by pandemonium, confusion and panic as all hell broke loose around us.

'Sound the alarm! All personnel to action stations! Prepare to return fire,' Brett issued the orders to the ship's crew gathered around. All moved off immediately and at high speed to execute the commands.

Brett then focused his attention on the upper cross walkway, waving to the guard up there to move Annelise Raven back into the cover of the accommodation. As he did so, another shell exploded in the water close by. This time on the port side but much closer to the ship. It looked like they had found the range.

I glanced up and immediately noticed that the woman in the wheelchair was now awkwardly slumped forward - her head resting down on her chest. I knew that Annelise Raven was out of the game for good. The Fuhrer was dead! Long live the Fuhrer! Some might say.

Already the two Officer types had begun herding their new Fuhrer and Otto Klensch back towards the accommodation.

'Get rid of him,' Brett snarled at my guard, before turning to follow the others.

I half expected the bastard to literally obey his captain's order immediately and try to put a bullet in my head then and there. But the guy just jammed the gun up against the back of my neck, and twisting his hand into the collar of my jacket turned me round and hustled me towards a steel door on the lower deck. I didn't resist because I was more than happy to be getting out of the direct line of fire. We reached the door and the goon released the dog levers and pulled it open. Just as the guard was shoving me through the doorway, I heard the distinct whining sound of hydraulic machinery being operated and turned to see a section of the aft deck opening up and a gun turret rising up into position.

CHAPTER 69

On the *Kong Haakon,* agents Faulkner and Thompson were positioned out on the flying bridge alongside the Commander of the frigate. Rasmussen was focusing on the *Panther* using a large electronic pair of binoculars.

'Is she taking any notice of your warning shots, Commander?' Thompson enquired.

'Oh, she's taking notice alright,' Rasmussen replied calmly and then turned to address his executive officer stationed behind him at the control panel inside the bridge. He spoke in Norwegian although neither Faulkner nor Thompson failed to understand the command. In an instant the *Kong Haakon's* main heavy guns had opened fire again. No warning shots on this occasion.

'Gentlemen,' Rasmussen raised his voice against the roar of the guns, addressing the two Englishmen at his elbow, 'It appears that the *Panther* has decided to shoot it out with us. She's uncovered some heavy deck armament!'

The Norwegian frigate was soon close enough to the *Panther* for Faulkner and Thompson to view the action without the aid of binoculars. They had a clear view of the jet black ship and the two turrets that had appeared on her fore and aft decks. Converting her in an instant, from an ordinary merchant vessel to a man of war. Once in position, both guns had immediately commenced firing at the *Kong Haakon.*

'Might be very sensible Gentlemen,' Rasmussen said calmly as the first shells hit the water about fifty metres from the ship, 'if we stepped inside.'

The two British agents required no second bidding and smartly followed the Frigate Commander back to the relative cover of the bridge.

CHAPTER 70

Inside the accommodation, the goon with the pistol still jammed up against the back of my neck, suddenly appeared to be uncertain of exactly what was expected of him. These guys are great at obeying specific commands, but like this one, they generally had no idea how to think strategically for themselves. This, of course, was turning out to be very much in my favour.

With the panic and disarray that had taken place up on the main deck a few minutes earlier, the priorities had initially been to respond immediately to the attack from the approaching warship, and at the same time to get the big wigs out of the line of fire, without further delay. Thankfully, on this occasion, I had been placed way down the pecking order on that list of duties.

I could see by the confused expression on my guard's face that he hadn't the faintest idea what to do next. If I gave him much longer, he might just come to the conclusion that he should finish the job here and now? I had no intention of waiting to find out.

As it turned out, two separate yet closely related events solved the dilemma for both of us - me and the rattled guard - once and for all.

The first was initiated by the direct hit the *Panther* took somewhere behind us on the aft deck. The explosion was deafening and the whole ship shook and lurched over to her port side. The second was the resulting, instant release of pressure of the snub-nose against my neck as the guard was hurled across the companionway; crashing with some force into the steel bulkhead with sufficient momentum to stun him. That was more than enough for me.

Never one to lag behind in making the best of any advantage, particularly in a case of a life or death scenario, I set to.

Just as the guard was starting to straighten up, I moved in on him. I decided on the most deadly method of attack. This was serious business. This character had to be put out of the game – for good. I raised my cuffed hands above my head and, taking full advantage of one of the metal locking cylinders protruding from the handcuffs, I slammed my hands into the space between his jaw bone and shoulder. I heard the crack of the bone on impact and was satisfied. No further effort would be required from me. I stood back as the body slumped to the deck – lifeless.

A quick rummage through the pockets produced the key to the cuffs. I was out of them in a second, and stopping only to retrieve the dead guy's weapon from the deck, I retraced the route along the alleyway to the door that would take me back out onto the aft section of the main deck.

CHAPTER 71

The direct hit on the *Kong Haakon* came as a complete surprise to the men occupying the frigate's bridge.

Having delivered two significant strikes on the *Panther,* Rasmussen naturally thought that would be pretty much the end of it for the black ship.

The *Panther* was now ablaze both fore and aft and it was clear, by the way she was awkwardly slewing through the water, that her steering system had been rendered totally out of action.

The Commander of the Norwegian frigate had been about to give the order for his gunners to cease fire on the forward 76mm gun, and change roles from attacker to rescuer.

Like the men around him on the bridge, including Faulkner and Thompson, Rasmussen had assumed the worst was over. The attack successfully completed and the life saving plan ready to take priority.

What Rasmussen had not expected was one last devastating response from the stricken ship.

The aft gun turret of the *Panther* had been knocked out of action completely before they had hardly time to get off a single shell. The gun on the fore deck however, had fared somewhat better. Despite the severe damage to the ship the forward turret had managed to keep firing and the next salvo had achieved the desired result.

The shell from the *Panther* hit the *Kong Haakon* just forward of amidships, penetrating the Frigate's hull just below the waterline. The high explosive warhead on the missile ripped a massive hole in the side structure of the ship and immediately tons of sea water began to flood into the vessel.

Rasmussen could see that the *Panther's* forward gun was still in action as another missile hit the water, this time just short of the *Kong Haakon's* hull. He quickly gave the order for his ship to turn hard to port and at the same time increase to full speed.

The commands were fired back in acknowledgement and the Frigate began to swing away from the field of action; rapidly widening the distance between the two vessels.

Faulkner and Thompson dodged smartly back out of Rasmussen's way as he moved to the ship's PA mike and scooped it up.

'Skade-rapporten?' Rasmussen requested the damage report.

The answer came back immediately from the Damage Control officer. The frigate had taken the direct hit on its starboard side, between frames 48 and 52. Watertight doors had been closed, but the bulkhead between the two compartments was breached. They were pumping out at maximum rate.

Rasmussen turned to the two Brits.

'Gentlemen, I am afraid it is necessary for us cease our engagement. We are in no condition to continue. However, I do not think that the *Panther* will pose us much harm once we move out of range.' Rasmussen indicated out of the bridge window to the expanse of water on the starboard side where already the *Panther's* missiles were dropping harmlessly short of the frigate.

'I have radioed for assistance,' Rasmussen said as he moved back out onto the bridge wing, lifting the binoculars to his eyes. 'But, as I said, I don't think the *Panther* will be going very far. In fact it looks as if they have stopped firing and have already decided to abandon ship. At least I can see they are preparing to lower lifeboats.'

CHAPTER 72

I was shocked at the extent of the carnage on the *Panther's* aft deck when I climbed back out on to it over the coaming of the alleyway door.

The gun turret that had emerged from below decks so menacingly only a few minutes earlier, now lay smashed almost beyond recognition. It had taken a direct hit. I could just make out the shapes of two mangled bodies wrapped in the twisted metal. All that was left of the gun and the gun crew.

Another mound of contorted steel just aft of the turret position looked as if a second direct hit had pierced the deck plating and exploded below; destroying the whole steering flat and probably the rudder itself. My conclusion undeniably confirmed by the zigzagging wake tailing away behind the ship. The *Panther*, with engines still running at full speed ahead, was going nowhere fast.

Turning forward, I also recognised that the main accommodation block had faired little better. It too was ablaze, and the deluge of black smoke billowing high into the air in the region of the bridge, signalled the end of any real control that the officers and crew of the ship may have had.

A few more bodies were strewn about the deck and I stepped over the feet of another mutilated individual slumped half way across the ladder leading up to the boat deck. The sights were all too familiar and with them the terror of the Gulf experience came flooding back to me.

I soon noticed that the firing had ceased from both ships. I guessed the *Panther* no longer had the ability to retaliate, and that the Frigate had silenced its own guns believing the outcome of the battle was already decided. My guess was they would soon be sending small boats across to the *Panther,* to save what souls were left and to salvage whatever they could.

There was however, little sign of defeat on the *Panther's* boat deck.

Captain Brett, very much alive and still trying to maintain control of the mayhem taking place around him, was organising the abandoning of the ship. One of the large, twin engine, powered launches was already swung out on its davits. It looked as if they had opted to use the faster open topped launch rather than one of the bulkier and much slower enclosed lifeboats. So I was not surprised to see that in the absence of any children travelling on board the *Panther*, the principal of women Fuhrers and high rankers appeared to be the order of the day. As it became obvious that the fast getaway boat was being hoisted out exclusively for them.

Freya Quisling sat calmly in the centre of the boat, looking pale but quite composed, and apparently ignoring the chaos around her. I noticed also that in a somewhat ridiculous fashion she was clutching the Baton. Sitting there almost like some kind of royal personage on a throne. Did she think that thing was going to save her?

The fat Otto guy, looking almost paralysed with fear, crouched on a seat just ahead of her. One goon was already in position in the stem of the boat, ready to release the hook on the forward line and then probably take over the helm position. A second crewman was ordered in at the stern to handle the ropes there, and I noticed he had been joined by one of the Nazi officers.

Plans for anyone else to join those in the boat were quickly terminated as the sound of a muffled explosion from somewhere deep in the bowels of the ship was followed by a severe and shuddering list of the *Panther* further over onto her starboard side. At the same time the main engines stopped and the speed began to fall off the vessel.

'Lower away!' Brett commanded. He was in a hurry now.

A crewman at the hydraulic winch controls immediately released the brake and set the launch on its way down to the water.

Whatever survival plan Brett had in mind for himself and what was left of his crew, now that the Fuhrer was safely on her way, was unclear. He struck me as quite likely being the type who would prefer to go down with his ship. He certainly was in no position to put up much more of a fight. Unless it was going to be hand to hand stuff on the decks, and there was going to be little time for that. The *Panther* was certainly destined for the bottom, and pretty soon.

I heard the roar of the launch engines as they kicked into life a few seconds before the boat hit the water. From my position on the deck I had a perfect shot of the events taking place. Nobody was taking the slightest bit of notice of me.

By now the angle of list of the ship had increased and the dense cloud of smoke smothering the fore part had intensified. It was obvious that the launch would have to turn and head in a direction towards the stern of the ship, if it was to avoid the choking and blinding fumes.

If I was going to get on board that launch I would have to move with all haste. I needed to be in a position at the stern rail when the boat passed underneath. I certainly had no intention of just letting Fuhrer Freya slip away. Besides there was nothing to keep me on board the doomed *Panther*. I was going to have to leave it sometime soon, whatever. My score to settle now was solely with the woman occupying a seat in that lifeboat. Vengeance was the one single thought uppermost in my mind. Hell could also have no fury, like a guy fucked about like this.

The boat had already commenced its sweeping turn under the transom of the *Panther*. I kept my fingers crossed that the helmsman would swing in real close to the ship's stern. Close enough for me to carry out my planned jump. What I was going to do if and when I managed to achieve that feat, I had only the vaguest idea. But what the hell? If Jack was alongside me now, there would be no debate. *Go for it Mac-limey!*

Skidding down the starboard ladder, back onto the aft deck, I started to make my way towards the stern rail. The deck looked like a scrap yard. Bits of mangled metal and machinery littered the whole area and obstructed my path. I picked my way through the chaos, once nearly loosing my footing as I slid through a pool of congealing blood.

Apart from a few wisps floating up from the cavernous openings torn and ploughed open by the shells from the attacking naval ship, the aft area was virtually smoke free.

I was in luck. I could see that the man at the helm had already straightened the boat up and intended to cut tightly across the stern of the *Panther*. His orders had obviously been to waste no time in making directly for the mainland.

Both the crewmen were armed; the one in the stern with a machine pistol, the guy at the helm with what looked like a Glock. The aid-de-camp fellow or whatever he was, had a buckled holster on his belt - I guessed it wasn't just for show. I was certainly going to have my work cut out.

The launch started to make its pass under the overhanging transom of the *Panther* and I climbed over the deck rail, ready for the jump. Thankfully, the group in the lifeboat were more concerned with what lay ahead of them. All thought of the fate of those left behind, furthermost from their minds. It meant I had a good chance of making my jump without being seen, and more to the point, without getting shot in the process.

Then, at not the very best of moments, I had second thoughts. I could see that, with the Nazi Officer guy occupying the aft most seat alongside the goon with the machine pistol, there was going to be very little landing area for me. At the best I would crash onto the two men, maybe putting them out of action but not doing myself much good either. There was also the certainty of alerting Freya, Klensch and the helmsman none of whom would hesitate in dealing with a stunned intruder. Especially yours truly. My hesitation sealed the decision for me. The boat was already passing under my position. I had no choice; I was compelled to act quickly. Then, in a flash, I caught sight of something on the boat below that decided the whole issue for me. Without further deliberation, I dived off the *Panther*.

The water was cold - not exactly freezing but cold enough to force the air out of my lungs. No big deal however, I had been in colder water than this, many a time. Twice in the last few days in fact - once in the Aberdeen training tank and then again in the North Sea. You could say I'd trained sufficiently for the job in hand.

Surfacing from the dive I immediately struck out to reach the launch that had now straightened up and was moving away from the *Panther* at a rate of knots. Although only just a couple of metres away from me, it would soon be well out of range.

What had made me change my game plan so late, was what I had observed hanging over the stern of the launch and trailing in the water behind it. A painter, a rope - carelessly unnoticed by the crew and left to whip freely in the foaming wake.

Four strokes propelled me within reach of the end of the line. I grabbed it firmly in both hands, and managing to coil a length around my arm, hung on for dear life. I was only going to get one chance at this. As the boat picked up speed I felt the rope bite into the flesh of my hands and arm as it went taught, and suddenly I found myself being dragged through the thrashing water. In my mind I ticked it off. Stage one accomplished.

I managed to hold on through the dragging slipstream of icy water and began to pull myself, hand over hand, slowly towards the stern of the launch. As I drew nearer, I made dead sure I kept my legs and feet well up and away from the twin propellers slicing through the water, only a metre or so below me. Those rotating blades would make short work of slicing me into small pieces and in double quick time at that.

One more bit of luck, as I reached the transom. Fortunately for me, the launch had at one time been fitted with a removable access ladder on the flat stern board facia. Probably a left-over from more leisurely days when the *Panther* had been used as a pleasure boat for the Aryan elite. The ladder itself was no longer a fixture but fortunately for me, the brackets used to fix it in place were still intact. That was all I needed. I grabbed for the metal extensions and pulled myself upwards. I was quickly able to get my feet up onto the lower ladder bracket, well clear of the props, now churning the water at full revolutions.

As the launch turned south, the doomed *Panther,* now fully ablaze, came into view on the starboard side.

Having secured a more stable position, as temporary as it was, I could nevertheless afford to take a breather and regain some of my strength. Second stage completed. But, there was no doubt, the real challenge was yet to come.

CHAPTER 73

The *Panther* had only minutes remaining. She was listing heavily over onto her starboard side. Her superstructure now fully ablaze. The ship was about to capsize.

Brett had carried out his duties to the full. All the *Panther's* lifeboats and rafts were safely away. Most of the ships crew, the ones still alive, had wasted little time in scrambling into the lifeboats. The *Panther's* Aryan senior officers had beaten most of them to it. The elite were the first ones to commandeer the remaining boats. What was left of Brett's crew, the stragglers, soon followed. Those that couldn't get to a boat, had grabbed lifebelts, and anything else that would float, and took the high dive into the sea.

Kapitan Brett himself would stay to the end. Satisfied that he had carried out his duty to the full. The Fuhrer was safely off the ship. There was only one last task for him to carry out.

Brett, stood for a moment, amid the ruins of the aft deck. The remnants of the *Torvald's* steel safe, gloriously recovered and opened so ceremoniously but a short while ago, lay almost indistinguishable amid the wreckage of the bombardment, like some piece of modern art.

From his belt Brett unclipped the heavy, mobile ship to shore radio phone and keyed in a number.

Brett listened as the signal was transmitted. He heard the ringing of the land line at the other end.

'Yes?' a voice answered.

'We have been attacked. The Fuhrer has left the ship. You received the scanned document?'

'Yes.'

'You know what to do?'

'I know what to do.' The voice was calm and flat and impassive.

The line went dead.

Kapitän Rudolf Brett dropped the hand phone over the side of the ship and watched it spin down into the waves below. Then, grasping the handrail, he prepared himself as the *Panther* began to slide. The ship was about to follow the hand phone into the depths of the Norwegian Sea.

CHAPTER 74

Fortunately, none of the occupants had spotted me clinging on to the ladder brackets on the stern of the launch. They were all totally preoccupied; forced to pay stark witness to the final throes of the *Panther*. The fleeing launch had already commenced its turn on a course towards the coast. The line now steered was going to take us down along the starboard side of the ship, past what little remained of the structure. The once elegant vessel was now just a burning wreck. Listing severely over onto her starboard side, the fore part was completely engulfed in a billowing inferno. I could feel the heat being generated across the water

I would have to move now if I was going take advantage of the moment. The spectators in the launch were preoccupied and unprepared.

My decision to act was made not a second too soon. I coiled myself into a crouching position on the tail plate, ready to spring. But the stern goon, sensing something happening behind him, turned to investigate. His surprise proved short lived. His delay proved fatal. Entwining my hands into the shoulder straps of his lifejacket, I yanked him towards me and down, guiding his head on to one of the protruding brackets of the steel ladder that I'd seconds before, used to haul myself up. His face smashed into the steel column. His forward momentum assisted me in ejecting his body straight into the churning water tailing away behind the launch. One down, four to go.

Unsurprisingly, that bit of commotion drew the immediate attention of the young fascist Officer. But his reaction also turned out to be seconds too slow and far too late. By now the gun I had relieved from my goon guard back on the *Panther* was in my hand and ready to use. It had taken me less time than I ever imagined; bringing into play all those old instincts that I thought had long been put to rest. Not that I spent much time dwelling on it at that particular moment.

I still had enough sense not to fire the gun at that stage. A shot would easily be heard over and above the roar of the conflagration taking place on the burning ship. I had to contend with the young Nazi first. I did use the weapon, not as a firearm but as a club. The swinging arc terminated at the side of the man's head - his temple. He would have felt very little. He was already gone and soon joined his colleague in the Norwegian Sea. I had no sympathy for either of them, and there was still work to be done.

The next stage was not going to be so easy. I had to get past both Freya and Otto Klensch if I was going to effectively deal with the armed goon up front, the one steering the launch. By yet another stroke of good fortune, all three of them remained preoccupied - Freya and Klensch, their backs to me, still engrossed in viewing the final throes of the sinking *Panther*. The guy at the helm was also fully occupied in laying a course towards the mainland. He'd obviously seen enough of the condition of the *Panther*, and was expecting no further surprises from that quarter. Unfortunately for him, his surprise would materialise from a totally different source - me!

Still unnoticed by Freya and her Reichsleiter, I scrambled behind them, along the deck towards the conning position, stopping only for an instant to pick up an item from a side ledge.

Coming up behind the man at the wheel, I jammed the cold steel barrel of the pistol against the nape of his neck. He did turn his head slightly to get me in his vision, but he was aware immediately of the position he'd suddenly found himself in. I could have pulled the trigger then and there, but if I was going to apprehend Freya and Klensch, I needed someone to maintain control of the boat. Keeping this goon alive and steering was the only solution.

I relieved him of his Glock, transferring the weapon from its place tucked in his belt to the back of mine. I indicated he maintain his position at the helm. My expression said the rest. I would not hesitate to blow his brains out if there was any problem.

However, my unspoken threat was short lived, and to my cost, obviously did not have the desired effect. I was too slow to realise that fact. The guy did not seem to have any concern about getting himself killed for his new Fuhrer. Perhaps he'd just had enough of it all. Whatever the reason, he turned, and leaving the helm wheel to spin freely, snatched at my gun with one hand and threw a punch with the other; one that caught me squarely on the jaw.

I was stunned, both mentally and physically. For a second, I think I even blacked out. Only my instincts rallied and cut back in to save me. I was able to recover my senses enough to respond to the attack. To my dismay however, I realised that the gun that had been in my hand prior to the goon's onslaught was no longer there, and neither was there time nor opportunity to retrieve the other Glock from my belt. It was a case of back to basics, again.

The tussle that followed is rather hazy in my mind. I believed I was only going to come out of this alive if I stuck to my inbred instincts. Fortunately the raw animal residing in me, having been dormant for so long, had now reawakened, and was in full fighting mode.

One of the most important lessons of close combat engagement that had been drilled into us, was the negative resistance method. Use the enemy's attacking momentum to your advantage. Use it to counterattack. I did just that. Deliberately forcing myself to step one pace backward would have a triple effect. One, it would take me beyond effective reach. Two, it would fool the opponent into thinking I was retreating. And three, it would reverse the result of the oncoming forward momentum of the assailant. The ex-helmsman submitted to all three. One retaliatory blow, at the conclusion of the sequence that had propelled him at speed towards me, clinched the whole deal. I tipped the unconscious fellow overboard. And turned inboard, to find myself looking down the barrel of yet another Glock.

CHAPTER 75

'She's about to go,' Rasmussen said quietly holding the binoculars steady on the sinking *Panther,* now barely more than a couple of kilometres away. The ship had drifted in an uncontrolled circle from her position when the steering gear was hit and put out of action.

The once elegant *Panther,* with smoke billowing out from almost every sector of its hull, had barely seconds to remain on the surface.

'There's not much we can do to stop her going down.' It was a statement of fact from Rasmussen. 'We can, however get our boats out to pick up survivors,' Rasmussen added, while still scanning the area around the stricken *Panther* through his high power binoculars.

The Damage Control Team of the *Kong Haakon* had managed to stem the flow of sea water rushing into the two breached, forward compartments. The frigate was damaged but still operational. She would soon start rounding up the small fleet of lifeboats and rafts dotted across the sea around the doomed *Panther.* It was all over for the men huddled in the small craft.

Rasmussen gave the order to launch the frigate's rescue boats and commence the recovery mission.

Faulkner and Thompson watched the rescue craft being lowered into the sea.

'Looks like they're not taking any chances,' Thompson said, indicating the two sailors in each of the boats, carrying automatic weapons.

CHAPTER 76

'I think it is high time you finally departed the scene, Mr Craig. You've caused more than enough trouble.'

Freya Quisling was levelling the Glock at my chest and was about to fire. But, at that same instant, the launch slewed violently to port. With nobody at the helm and the twin engines racing full ahead the rudder had become locked hard over and the boat was virtually attempting to spin on its own axis.

'Get the wheel, Otto!' Freya Quisling screamed the command at Klensch. He scrambled awkwardly to obey and glared at me as he moved past, but made sure he stayed well out of my reach en-route. Grabbing the steering wheel, he spun it round, and slowly the launch began to straighten up.

In the few seconds that Freya Quisling had taken her eyes off me to check on Klensch, I had acted. When she returned her attention back in my direction she froze as she recognised what I was holding in my hand. Not the gun. I'd had no time to retrieve the one tucked into my belt. What I held up, was going to prove to be, by far, a more effective weapon.

Her eyes widened in disbelief.

'Where did you...?' she started to question looking around her at the side bench seat where she knew she had last set the Baton down, and from where I had retrieved it on my way forward.

She was wondering how it could be possible that I was standing in front of her waving the thing. For a second I could see she was still intent on shooting me. But, she quickly changed her mind as I swung my arm, the one holding the baton, out over the side of the boat. My intention quite obvious.

'Kill him,' Klensch shouted out, straining round from his position at the helm. He had managed to steer the launch back on something of a level course. Well at least the boat was no longer spinning around in circles.

'I can't,' Freya called back, 'he's got the Baton.'

'And, if you don't drop the gun, I promise you I certainly will return this thing to its most recent resting place, at the bottom of the ocean,' I warned.

She knew I meant what I said, but I could see in her eyes that she was beginning to weigh up just how valuable the Fuhrer's Baton would be to her, if it meant that her reign as Fuhrer was going to be prematurely terminated. With her most certainly spending the rest of her days behind bars. On further analysis, she probably came to the quick conclusion, that saving Adolf Hitler's sceptre may just turn out to be too high a price to pay. So, if it meant getting rid of me...

There was no such doubt in Klensch's mind.

'Shoot him!' he shouted again, releasing the steering wheel this time and swinging round to face Freya. Klensch never intended it to be a command to his Fuhrer but it had to be said. If they were to survive and walk away from this, Freya Quisling was going to have to pull the trigger. She knew it and I knew it.

I witnessed the instant she made up her mind to shoot me and acted instantaneously. Hand still locked firmly around the Baton I heaved myself over the side of the launch, and hitting the surface, immediately pulled myself down as deep as I could into the water. I knew I had to remain submerged and as far down as possible in the first moments after going under. I also had no doubt that Freya Quisling and her Reichsleiter would already be spraying the surface of the water above me with gunfire. The longer I could stay under, the further away the launch carrying them would travel. In just a few seconds I would be out of their effective range. And as good a marksman as Freya Quisling had shown herself to be with a rifle up on the Hardangervidda, I knew she would be unlikely to match such shooting skills with a handgun, while at the same time trying to balance upright on the deck of a swaying boat that was also rapidly opening up the range between her and the target.

I was right. When I eventually broke the surface, I could see the launch speeding well out of range, about forty meters into the distance. I could also make out Freya Quisling and Otto Klensch standing in the stern of the boat - still firing off shots in my direction.

The view of the sea beyond the bow of the speeding boat, told me they should have been paying more attention to steering the thing, rather than continuing with the extremely remote chance of putting a bullet in me.

They were heading directly for the marker buoys of the *Highlander* wreck site. Nobody was at the helm of the boat and now it was running true and straight. Towards disaster.

I believe that when the pair finally gave up in their attempts to eliminate me, and finally turned back to the business of handling the launch, it was already too late. In fact I don't even think they realised themselves that they had cut clean through the marker buoy lines and were soon deep in very dangerous waters.

The *Highlander* was resting in an almost upright position on the seabed. The height from the pontoon bottom to the top of the drilling mast was some 70 metres. The water depth there was not much more than that. If not already protruding above the water, the top of the rig's gigantic drilling mast could only be hidden just below the surface.

Whether or not Otto Klensch managed to get back to the conning position in time to take the wheel again, in a last minute attempt to steer away and avoid the collision, no one will ever know. Whether Freya Raven nee Quisling, the second Fuhrer of the New Reich, realised exactly what was happening in those last moments, is also in doubt. I for one didn't care either way. The Quisling dynasty would be, once and for all, terminated.

The explosion and subsequent inferno from the launch was witnessed, as I found out later, over six nautical miles away across the ocean. One of the squadron of small Royal Norwegian naval ships assisting the damaged *Kong Haakon* at the scene of the *Panther* sinking, broke away to investigate. That ship pulled me from the water twenty minutes later. I still had the Fuhrer's Baton in my hand.

As we sailed away from the mangled and still smoking wreck of the launch, I could not resist raising the golden cylinder and waving it high...

'Sieg Heil!'

CHAPTER 77

The last Swiss Air scheduled flight of the day touched down at Zurich International Airport close to midnight. All the passengers and crew were cleared through immigration and customs less than thirty-five minutes after landing.

One of the passengers, carrying just a compact piece of hand luggage, exited from the arrivals hall, and beating the rest of the crowd waiting to retrieve their baggage from the carousel, joined the queue of travellers lined up for taxis. If he had been able to catch an earlier flight he would have requested the taxi driver to take him directly to his destination in the City. The delay in getting to the airport at the other end had cost him another sixteen hours. The earliest he could make the appointment at the United Kreditbank now, was not going to be before 8am the next day.

'Hotel Seiden,' he ordered the taxi driver and settled back for the twenty minute drive into Zurich.

At least the bank was within walking distance from the hotel he had chosen to overnight in. With luck he would be finished and on his way to pick up the hire car, and on the road before mid-day. He had, of course, to give himself sufficient time to purchase the boxes of chocolates and do the necessary. But, at least, he would not have any of those idiots getting in his way. He smiled and was more than pleased how everything was working out far better than planned or expected. Well almost. He had not planned for the intervention of Steve Craig but he was satisfied he would not be further bothered by that gentleman. As persistent as the Scotsman had proved to be, he was now, no longer a threat to anyone. The man congratulated himself. He had succeeded in accomplishing the greater part of his mission in no uncertain manner. The troublemakers all suitably dealt with. No one left to bother him now. Those of the grand New Aryans not dead, were already in custody and he would be long gone by the time any of them showed their faces again outside of a prison wall. And tomorrow? Well, he had been planning for that coming day for a very long time. It was a pity though about his share of the gold they'd pulled up from the *Torvald*. Still, no real loss of sleep over that. In any case he would hardly have been able to hide a 5 kg gold ingot in a box of chocolates. From now on it was going to be plain sailing.

At the Hotel Seidenhof he registered and signed in, and as usual, handed his passport over to the concierge. He was issued with the electronic key to his room - 411, located on the fourth floor, and directed to the lifts.

The concierge watched until the lift doors closed shut, then inspected the passport in his hand in more detail. It was issued in Norway and the holder's name, next to his photo on the page of the document, identified him as one Herr Olav Jorgensen.

CHAPTER 78

Twenty four hours just seemed to slip by from the time I was picked up by the Norwegian Navy and brought ashore, until I was eventually given clearance to leave Aldvik. A quick physical check over at the local hospital had given me the all clear. Apart from a few bruises particularly around the kidney area, there was no serious damage. I was pretty much in good shape.

All the charges that had been piling up against me were dropped, and I was declared free to leave the country by the local authorities. There was just enough time for me to see how the Oberst was getting on before I took off.

'What's the situation regarding the Oberst?' I asked the doctor who had been assigned to me. His name was Kolsaker, a tall, quietly spoken man in his late fifties.

He looked at me blankly for a moment and then said, 'The Oberst? The Colonel? I am afraid I don't know of anybody from the military of that rank in the hospital. In fact there are, to my knowledge, no military personnel here, at all.'

'He was one of the men injured while working on this case,' I explained. 'He must have been brought to this hospital three days ago. He had been wounded in the stomach - seriously.'

The Doctor just shook his head again.

'This *is* the only hospital in Aldvik?' I queried.

'Yes. The nearest other hospital is in Trondheim. If your Colonel friend was seriously injured he may have been taken straight there.'

'Would you not have been able to treat a gun shot wound to the stomach, here?'

'That depends if there were any complications. Normally, I would say yes, but there may have been problems requiring specialist attention. The nearest place then would, as I said, have been Trondheim.'

'Dr. Kolsaker, would it be too much trouble for you to find out if a gentleman answering to the name of …of…the Oberst…not Colonel but just Oberst, was admitted to the hospital in Trondheim in the last few days, for treatment to a stomach wound?'

Five minutes later Dr. Kolsaker returned, again shaking his head.

'There has been no person of that rank or title, admitted to the General Hospital in Trondheim for any sort of treatment at all. No one with a stomach problem of any kind and certainly no one with a gun-shot wound. I am sorry Mr Craig.'

So, I concluded that, having survived the stomach trauma and with the job successfully completed, the Oberst had simply slipped back under-cover. I guessed he must have been taken again under the protective wing of the organisation that had sent him. Like most similar institutions, they would surely look after their own. It was probably most unlikely that I would ever hear from him again. But, as long as he had survived the shot to the gut, I was happy for him. He certainly had faired better than his two men, Andre and Karl.

With the few personal belongings I had salvaged from the apartment in the safe house, which incidentally had proved not to have lived up very well to its name, I was ready to leave the hospital and head back south to Stavanger. From there, homeward bound to Aberdeen. I hoped my old job would still be waiting for me and of course I was anxious to see how Jeannie and little Jack were getting along.

Everything was over up in Norway. Or so I thought.

CHAPTER 79

'Mr Craig could you just hold for a few minutes. There's someone in the hospital who would like to speak to you?'

I was standing in the main foyer of the Aldvik General Hospital waiting for the taxi that would take me to the local airstrip to catch a coast hopping flight down to Stavanger.

I turned to confront Dr. Kolsaker again.

'There is a patient - a gentleman who wishes to speak with you. He's one of the officers from the ship that was in the skirmish with our Navy. I think his vessel was called the *Panther*. He is one of the survivors and apparently the only officer to make it. Although still in police custody, he refuses to talk to anybody else. He's requested to speak to you. He asked for you by name.'

'Why me?' I queried.

'Because he's under arrest and refuses to talk to us.' The man who'd just answered my question was standing in the doorway behind the doctor. He was wearing the uniform of a senior Norwegian police officer.

'My name is Inspector Paulsen. I am in charge of the clean up operation here in Aldvik. You led my people quite a chase Mr. Craig. But I am glad it has all turned out good for you.' He held his hand out.

'Nice to meet you, Inspector,' I said taking his hand. 'But I don't know what further assistance I can possibly be. From what I understand you have pulled in all the key people involved. Those that are still alive.'

'We did indeed Mr. Craig. And most of them are now on their way to Oslo for detailed screening, and then I guess, for many of them, on to the international courts in The Hague. It's more or less out of our hands now.'

'So? What's with the one wanting to talk to me?'

'Two of them were far too badly injured to join the group being transferred. One, a low ranking crewman, is very seriously injured. He's still in a coma and is not expected to last the day. The other person is also in a severe condition - badly injured - third degree burns over most of his body. But he is conscious and wants to talk to you.'

'Once again, why me? How does he know I am even still around?'

'I don't know how,' Paulsen answered. 'But, as I said he asked for you personally.'

Now I *was* intrigued.

'Does this guy have a name?' I asked.

'He calls himself Heinrich Bucher.'

'Okay,' I agreed and followed Paulsen and the doctor back into the hospital.

Encased from head to foot in what looked like a tight fitting body shroud, the man calling himself Heinrich Bucher was stretched out on a hospital gurney. I guessed he must have not long been wheeled in from an operating theatre. His face was covered in much the same material encasing his body. I had no idea who he was although I had a vague recollection of somebody in Annelise Raven's retinue referred to as Leutnant Bucher. Probably one of the young guys always on hand around her.

'Mr. Craig,' the man in the bed croaked as he slowly turned his bandaged face towards me and peered through the narrow slit running across his eye line. 'I am Leutnant Bucher. I would like to speak to you alone. Please ask them to leave.'

I turned to Paulsen and the Doctor and raised my eyebrows. I had no authority here. It was up to them.

Obviously they must have concluded that the man lying there was of no real threat to me or anyone. They turned and left me alone in the room with Leutnant Bucher.

'Thank you Mr. Craig,' Bucher said, his voice faint and muffled by the heavy dressing almost completely covering his whole face, except for the small openings around his mouth and eyes. I guessed he was probably pumped full of morphine. How else would he be able to endure the agony of the horrific injuries he had sustained in the inferno on board the *Panther*.

'I am truly sorry for what happened on the *Highlander*,' he said, trying to hold his arm up in some kind of acknowledgement. 'What we permitted to take place on the rig was wrong. From the beginning, I truly believed that the New Aryan Reich was going to be so different.'

So that was it. Perhaps a little cynical on my part, but I felt this young guy was about to make some sort of last, dying statement. A cry for forgiveness from this world before passing into the next. But I was wrong.

'Mr Craig, there is still time to stop it.'

Something in his tone, this time told me that maybe this was not going to be a last cry seeking redemption after all.

'To stop what, Leutnant Bucher?' I questioned.

'The total destruction of Ekofisk, Troll and Brent to name only three.'

'You mean three of the biggest oil and gas fields in the North Sea?' I was tempted to add that he was hallucinating. But although probably a correct assumption on my part, that would have been cruel, even for me, considering his condition. I decided to spend a few more minutes humouring him and then get out of there as soon as I could.

'Not only those Mr. Craig,' he said, 'but also twenty other major offshore oil and gas fields in the USA, Canada, Russia and Brazil. Excluding Saudi Arabia and most of the Middle East.'

'Why the special exemption terms for Saudi and the Middle East?' I asked. Now I was somewhat intrigued again. I had, at least, to hear the explanation to that particular point of my query.

'Quite simple,' Bucher said. 'Those countries hate the Jews and the Jew lovers and protectors as much as the New Aryans.'

'Good bye, Bucher,' I said, and turned to leave. He had hit the wrong nerve with me this time. Despite his horrific injuries, he was still just a twisted fanatic. The rest of the short time he had to live he could spend it without me having to listen to his anti-Semitic, fascist garbage.

'Please wait Mr. Craig. Those are not my personal views - not any longer.'

'Being on the receiving end of the slaughter has quenched your desires, has it Leutnant?' This time I meant it to hurt. The memory of the broadcast scenes of the sinking *Highlander,* and my own personal, on the spot witnessing of the *Andrea* capsizing, came flooding back.

'You could be right but I have had a different attitude towards the New Aryans for some time. I served Annelise Raven and believed in what she dreamed the new Reich could become. Then, she was suddenly no longer strong enough to control the mad rampage of Klensch and her deranged daughter. We moved from becoming a serious political movement to a masquerade displaying the worst of the old Third Reich.'

'I am sorry, but I have heard enough,' I said and turned towards the door for a second time.

'If you leave now, Sir, hundreds maybe thousands more innocent people will perish.'

Even on his death bed, the young man remained persistent. Could it just be he was telling the truth?

'Leutnant Bucher, from what I understand your New Aryan movement is finished. Your leaders have all perished. There's nobody left.'

'Wrong Mr Craig, you are very wrong. There are still thousands of New Aryans out there - waiting.'

'Waiting?' I asked. 'Waiting for what?'

'For the signal to mobilise.'

The man was out of his mind - and yet? There was something in his persistence that I just couldn't ignore. Dignity? Honour? Or just plain illusion. I had to find out which.

'There is one man ready to lead,' Bucher continued in a weakening voice. 'And, he is still out there. Prepared to strike. The mastermind. You must listen to me Mr Craig. There is a world network of New

Aryans just waiting for the signal. The signal to commence taking over some of the offshore platforms and destroying the rest - and that's just a beginning. The release of the funds from the *Torvald* will be sufficient to reward the people ordered to carry this out. Governments, already infiltrated, will follow'

'My dear fellow,' I said,' shaking my head sadly. 'There are no funds to be released from the *Torvald*. All the bullion from that ship is now locked safely away in Norwegian banks. Except the load that went plunging back to the bottom of the sea on the *Panther*. And I don't expect the authorities will waste much time in retrieving most of that. It is Norwegian national gold and after more than 60 years it will be returned to the rightful owners.'

'I am not talking about the salvaged gold bullion, Mr Craig. I am talking about a treasure worth far more than that. I am talking more than a billion dollars.'

I dragged a stool across the room and sat down at the side of Leutnant Bucher's bed. This boy was either one of two things - deadly serious or stark raving mad. One way or another, I was going to find out which.

CHAPTER 80

Special Agents Faulkner and Thompson arrived back in London on an early flight from Oslo. They had remained in the Norwegian capital with the international security branch guys just long enough to gather sufficient details to clear their reports. For them, it was *Case closed*.

They pulled the car that they had left at Heathrow and drove back into central London.

The head office of the International Security Division, the ISD, is located in a two hundred year old building in Kensington. The two agents logged in and passed through internal security before heading up to their offices on the third floor. Most of the rooms on this level were designed as individual units. Each agent allotted his own private work space. Strip blinds covering the windows maintained a level of privacy, both inside and out. Only the secretarial and administrative staff sat out in the open plan central section. The doors to all the offices were shut and, apart from an occasional nod of acknowledgement from one or two of the girls, the usual air of silent activity prevailed. The two men headed for their offices.

'Better write the 'wrap-up' and get it filed.' Faulkner said to Thompson, while unlocking the door to his office. 'If you take care of the Oslo screenings, I'll fill in the background details of the rest.'

'Sure,' Thompson said over his shoulder, while fiddling with the stubborn lock on his own office door. 'But, shouldn't we at least touch base with the Boss?'

'Commander Bruce is on leave.' It was Gloria Cummings Bruce's PA, on her way in from the lift lobby. 'He said when you got in you were both to report to Collin Hubbard, now that everything is wrapped up.'

'That's a surprise,' Thompson said. 'I didn't realise he had any leave planned.'

'He hadn't,' Gloria replied. 'Some personal matter came up. He left in quite a hurry.'

'Did he say when he would be getting back?' Faulkner asked.

'Said he wasn't sure, but as I already mentioned, you two are supposed to work through Colin upstairs.' Gloria added before heading on her way back out. 'Oh, by the way,' she stopped and turned for a second. 'He said well-done, both of you.'

CHAPTER 81

'So who is this new Leader? What's his name?' I questioned Leutnant Bucher.

'I don't really know his name. But I am sure a Norwegian named Olav Jorgensen knows who he is.'

'Jorgensen!' I exclaimed. 'You mean, the Jorgensen from the Norwegian Maritime Authority? Olsen's boss?'

'Yes, that's him.'

This *was* a new and surprising turn of events. I clearly remembered the encounter I'd had with Jorgensen in the Stavanger Maritime Directorate offices, and how bluntly he had cold shouldered me. I also recalled it was Commander Bruce who had tipped Jorgensen off about my pending visit.

'So how does Jorgensen fit into all this?'

'He has been very active in the movement for some time now. He fixes things on the financial side.'

'I'll bet he does,' I said. Some more pieces of the puzzle falling into place. 'Why couldn't you have told all this to Inspector Paulsen? He would have been able to help.'

'I could not trust him. I think he could be one of them.'

So that was it. Could it be that this young fascist was maybe not so mad after all? How true could his claim be, that Paulsen was involved? And, it was more than a surprise to discover that the aloof Herr Jorgensen from the Maritime Authority was wrapped up in the whole scheme of things, and in a big way, so it appeared. But then again, on reflection, not that much of a surprise. There had to have been quite a complex system in operation back there in Stavanger. It was unlikely that Nils Olsen could have been running things from that end on his own.

Now, if I was going to do something about all this, I had to find out who that other mysterious character was; and therefore I needed to know where I was going to be able to catch up with Jorgensen.

'Bucher lad,' I said leaning in closer. 'I need to know where I can find Jorgensen and his Leader fellow.'

There was no reply from the young man on the bed, his body lying encased in the layers of stained bandage. There was no further movement either.

'Bucher, can you hear me?'

'I am afraid he can't hear anything, Mr. Craig. Not anymore. He's dead.'

I turned to see Paulsen standing in the doorway. The Inspector was pointing at the portable monitor panel with the leads disappearing into Blucher's bandages. The heart monitor screen was running with a dead straight, horizontal line.

'Did the Leutnant have anything interesting to say?' Paulsen asked.

'Just wanted to tell me he was sorry for the *Highlander* attack. A sort of final confession - a touch of remorse,' I lied.

CHAPTER 82

So that was it. Leutnant Bucher was gone. Taking with him whatever else he may have had to tell. I was left in something of a quandary. How much of what he said was true? How much of it was just some form of deluded speculation? Could there really be such a Nazi network extending around the world from offshore installations to national governments and to the extent that Bucher had claimed? And, even if I did believe him, who was going to listen to me? I remembered the struggle I'd had just to get past Commander Bruce at the beginning of all this. No one was going to assign any more credit to the dying Leutnant's ramblings than I first had. But, what if he was right?

Then, something occurred to me. My thoughts flashed back to the deck of the *Panther*, just before the first warning salvo was fired from the Norwegian navy ship. I pictured Freya Quisling holding the Fuhrer's Baton above her head and then recalled, quite clearly, her unscrewing the end of it and pulling out the encased documents. She'd handed one of the scrolled sheets to Klensch - not the will thing - the other rolled up piece.

'You know what to do with that. He will be waiting.'

I remembered that Klensch had wasted little time in heading up to the bridge with the document in his hand. He was going to relay whatever was on it to somebody, probably on the shore. Jorgensen? Or his mystery Boss man?

So after despatching the information, what had they done with the scroll? Had it gone down with the ship or did it by some chance, get put back in the Baton before Freya Quisling fled the sinking *Panther*? My guess was the latter; because if it was that important the new Fuhrer would have wanted to ensure it remained in her possession.

I'd handed the Baton over to one of the senior officers on the navy ship that had picked me up.

Question now? Where was the thing?

'You are in luck, Mr Craig. I know exactly where the famous Baton is.' Inspector Paulsen answered my question a short time later.

Although maybe a long shot, I thought it worth asking the Inspector. He was in the process of wrapping up the case. So, he might just know where the Baton was now.

'If you follow me,' Paulsen said turning and heading for the hospital administration block, where he had set up a temporary case office, 'you can see for yourself.'

Minutes later the Fuhrer's Baton was on display right there in front of me.

'It was left in my care,' Paulsen explained, weighing the Baton in his hand as if it were a dumbbell. 'I'm supposed to make sure it gets to Oslo. I expect it will find a place in some World War II museum. Beautiful piece of craftsmanship though, I expect it is quite valuable.' The Inspector turned the Baton around in his hands, admiring the design and engraved motifs along its length. Then he handed it to me.

'What do you think?'

So, even if Paulsen was one of them, he obviously had no idea what the Baton may actually contain. I guessed there was nobody of any senior rank around to relate the full details of what had happened on the *Panther's* maindeck when the Baton had been recovered from the safe. The significance of the classic documents hidden within it would have been shared on a *need to know* basis only. It was, after all, the real reason for the salvage operation on the *Torvald*. But I was not about to enlighten him. Apart from the fact that he may be a member of the New Aryans, I could easily imagine the response I could expect from the Inspector when I tried to explain Bucher's deathbed claims. Not good. I would probably be tagged as being as mad as the young Nazi officer. The documents inside would be transferred into the hands of the historians and probably take months before the mulling over them would be completed. Maybe they wouldn't even get around to opening the thing. I did not have the time to wait for all that. If I was going to do anything I had to get into that Baton and study its contents. I felt certain from what I'd seen and overheard on the *Panther,* the document removed from the Baton must have been passed on to Jorgensen and almost certainly to the man he was reporting to. I was certain that getting my hands on that piece of paper would provide me with enough information to lead me to these men. I also knew, that if I was going to get anywhere with this, I would have to go it alone. So what was new?

'Inspector Paulsen,' I said, after putting on a show of enthusiastic interest by closely examining the Baton, 'I wonder if you would mind me making a quick sketch of it? I am very interested in this sort of antiquity. Oh, I realise it's not your real ancient stuff but the World Wars have always held something of an historical fascination for me. I would like to make some sort of personal record of this Baton. Apparently it belonged to Hitler himself.'

'I can go one better than that for you Mr Craig. I've got a Polaroid camera out in my car. Allow me to run and get it for you.'

I couldn't believe my luck. I had desperately been trying to figure out a way to get Paulsen out of the way, so I could open the thing up. He obviously had no idea there may be something of value inside it. How could he? All the people who knew anything about the contents were either dead, in jail or already someplace about to make use of that very same information. If they hadn't done so already.

Paulsen left the room to fetch the camera.

I quickly started twisting the end of the baton, exactly as I had seen Freya Quisling do a day or so previously. It rotated easily and smoothly in my hands and I lifted it free. With the end crown off, I probed inside the cylinder with my fingers and at once felt the scrolls tucked down inside. My heart leapt as I carefully withdrew them. Sure enough both documents were intact, one inside the other. I unravelled them to check. Both were in almost perfect condition, considering they had been submerged at the bottom of the Norwegian Sea for the best part of sixty five years. A quick scrutiny confirmed that although handwritten in the classical German Fraktur script, very popular back in the nineteen forties, one was certainly the will. In fact I could see that it was signed, and I knew I had come across copies of that scribbled name before. There was no doubt it was Adolf Hitler's signature. The other document appeared to be some sort of coded listing of numbers. But, it was the printed name heading the top of the sheet that captured my attention. It read - United Kreditbank - Bahnhofstrasse, Zurich. What followed, beneath the title, was a series of numbers, letters and notes handwritten in German. One item read Gewölbe K-88, I knew that stood for Vault K-88.

At the very bottom of the sheet there was another scrawled note. Same hand as on the other document – Adolf Hitler's. There was no time to try to decipher the stuff. Paulsen would be back any minute.

I slipped both documents back into the Baton and screwed the top firmly into place. Not a second too soon. Paulsen entered and handed me the Polaroid camera.

Acting out the role of keen WW2 memorabilia collector, and taking shots of the Baton from just about every angle, I collected the prints that were quickly processed and ejected from the camera. I thanked Paulsen for his help - and made to leave.

'By the way, Mr Craig,' Paulsen halted my departure. Had he noticed something? Detected some irregularity in my behaviour? 'I was just wondering about this mysterious Oberst person you asked Dr. Kolsaker about.'

I disguised my relief well enough.

'One of the Interpol undercover agents. I only knew him as the Oberst. I guess that was a code name he used. He took a bullet when things got bad. I don't suppose you know anything about him?'

'I am afraid not,' Paulsen said. 'I was brought in at the last minute, to clear things up. Besides these Interpol people play their cards very close to their chests - as you Brits would say.' Paulsen held out his hand. 'Good luck Mr. Craig.'

The flight from Aldvik down the Norwegian West Coast took just over an hour. I recognised I was retracing, in the air, the coastline route that I had partly covered with Freya Quisling onboard the *North Star*. From this height I was able to appreciate the magnificent landscape drifting by below, but now the main thing on my mind was the next step in this still unfolding saga, not the aerial view.

I knew I had to get to Zurich - that was going to be the easy part. Finding the United Kreditbank also should prove to be not so much of a problem. It was what to do from then on in.

If Jorgensen and his Boss Man had already accessed the vault and its contents worth more than a billion dollars, then they could well be long gone by the time I arrived on the scene. I would be too late. I was frustrated that there was nobody I could contact to help me. With the Oberst gone to ground and the problems I knew I would most certainly encounter in trying to explain the situation to the likes of Commander Bruce, for example, there was no one to turn to for help. Or was there?

CHAPTER 83

The lift door of the elevator slid noiselessly open on the 4th floor of the Hotel Seiden in Zurich. The sole passenger, carrying a bottle of champagne, stepped out onto the deep piled carpet that spread away in three directions along the corridors. One to the North, one to the East and one to the West. Each to a separate wing of the floor. He selected the East wing. Not by chance. He knew exactly where he was heading.

He stopped, just once, only to scoop a bouquet of flowers from a vase sitting on a polished table top in front of an ornately embellished gold framed mirror.

At the door to Room 411, he hesitated for a second, leaning forward, listening for any sounds from within. There was nothing. He tapped the door firmly and waited. A second or so passed and then he heard the shuffling as the guest on the other side made his way to see who it was. He raised the bunch of flowers to obscure his face and thrust the Champagne bottle at the door in line with the peephole.

'Who is it?' the voice from the other side enquired.

'Room service, Sir. With a small gift from the management.'

Jorgensen opened the door.

'That's very kind of you... My God!'

The blow from the concave bottom of the Champagne bottle smashed squarely into Jorgensen's face. The crack of breaking nose cartilage was unmistakeable. Jorgensen careered backwards and hit the floor with a yelp. The visitor quickly entered the room and kicked the door shut behind him. Stepping over the moaning man on the carpet, he threw the flowers and the still intact Champagne bottle onto a sofa. A brief check around the room and the adjoining bathroom confirmed that the occupant had no surprise guests waiting in the wings. He walked slowly to position himself over Jorgensen and then landed another toecap into the man's exposed stomach. He quite enjoyed Jorgensen's second yelp of pain.

'Did you really think you could lose me so easily, Olav?'

Gasping for air, Jorgensen shrank away. He was shocked to see this man hovering over him. How could it be? How had his attacker found out where he was? And where did this man draw the energy to overpower him with such force? But, more importantly, how could he have survived? The man should be dead or at least locked up in a Norwegian jail.

'Please, I did not intend to exclude you,' Jorgensen whimpered. 'I was going to get the stuff and then contact you - so we could meet.'

'Of course you were.' The words were uttered as if he were addressing a misbehaving child. 'You are not just a liar, Jorgensen. You are a fool. I am not sure which is worse. Never mind that. What's the number and the pass code?'

'Yes of course - the number,' Jorgensen said, wiping the trickle of blood from his broken nose and struggling to sit up. 'I was going to tell you.'

'Well tell me now.'

'I'll write it down for you, if you will pass me that writing pad. It's over there on the table.' He pointed and watched the Boss walk across the room to pick up the jotter, and at the same time scoop up a pile of loose papers strewn across the mahogany surface of a period piece. It took him just a few seconds to scan the documents. He saw what he wanted and threw the notepad back onto the table.

'Olav,' he said shaking his head in disappointment. 'why couldn't you just have told me? All I needed to know was here on one of these sheets.'

'I just wanted to write it out clearly for you. Anyway, that's it,' Jorgensen said. 'That's all we need. The Box Number, the Cache number and the combination. I swear.'

'No need to swear Olav. I believe you. And I can see quite plainly for myself that what I am looking for is indeed here. But my friend, please be assured there is not going to be any *we* in this. Not any more.'

'I did not intend to…' Jorgensen words tailed off as he saw the gun. Jorgensen wasn't into guns. So the fact that it was a Walther P99 fitted with a silencer would have meant little to him. It was a gun – that's all that mattered.

Anybody passing in the corridor outside would have only heard the popping sound of a Champagne bottle being opened.

CHAPTER 84

'Who in heaven's name is calling at four o'clock in the morning?' Arthur Broadhurst croaked.

'Arthur. It's Steve…Steve Craig. I need to talk to you - urgently.'

I waited anxiously for a response. Waking the head of the HSE Marine and Offshore Division with a phone call in the early hours of the morning, was not the best timing. I half expected him to hang up on me.

'Craig! What the hell's going on?'

At least he hadn't hung up.

'Arthur, I know this is very bad timing, but I am in desperate need of your help.'

'Don't tell me you have landed yourself in another load of trouble. God man, you've only just dug yourself out of the last mess.'

'That's just it, Arthur. The last mess isn't over. In fact it's got a lot more messy.'

'Look Steve, what ever it is it can surely wait until sunrise. Get yourself into the office tomorrow and we can sort things out then.'

'I can't do that, Arthur. I am not in Aberdeen. I'm still in Norway. I won't be back in the UK for some days. But I need your help now.'

The urgency in my voice must have paid off. After another short silence, and a sigh of resignation, Broadhurst decided to hear me out.

'Go ahead, Steve.'

CHAPTER 85

He sat impatiently in a large leather upholstered chair in a columned alcove of the massive reception area of the United Kreditbank and cursed his stupidity. He should have extracted more information from Jorgensen before he'd sent him on his way with a bullet to the brain.

It was already 10 am and he had just been informed that his arrival at the bank was two hours later than the appointed time. He was further notified that his name was not the name of the gentleman they were expecting to meet. And that, although he had produced the correct codes and account number, he had, unfortunately not been able to provide the agreed identification password of one Herr Fredrik Lingstrom - the man who had set up the original appointment.

Before he had released his anger on Jorgensen, he should have ensured he had extracted *all* the details from the bastard. Where the hell had Jorgensen come up with the name Fredrik Lingstrom? Oh, he'd managed to get the additional, critical information alright. Although, the main security and account numbers had already been in his possession long before arriving in Zurich. But he needed the final data. It hadn't taken much effort to read Jorgensen's notes. The ones left spread on the hotel room table. The ones displaying, quite clearly, all the account details, codes and passwords.

He had been quite amused to read Jorgensen's ingenious scribbling on how he intended to hide some of the stuff inside confectionary - chocolates of all things. Quite clever for somebody intending to pass through a number of border check points. He was, however, convinced that his own plan was much safer. He would avoid any similar risk. Simply by offloading the stuff in Switzerland, here in Zurich in fact. The arrangements had already been made.

However, what wasn't among all that paraphernalia was the name of the damned contact person at the bank - the one that Jorgenson had agreed to meet. Neither was the time of the meeting nor the damned introductory password. It was the latter that appeared to be causing the greatest problem.

It should have come as no great surprise to him that the United Kreditbank of Switzerland may want to be quite sure, exactly who was going to access one of their very secure safety deposit vaults. Particularly one that was classified DC 'Dormant Account' and had not been accessed since 1945. Even though he had confirmed without hesitation that he was in possession of the very significant sum of cash that was owing to the United Kreditbank as security bond. The, not so paltry, amount of 5 million US dollars.

So, now he was waiting while the matter was under review; the issue being debated behind closed doors. Why was it taking so long? He had no idea. He had explained, that as Herr Fredrik Lingstrom, his junior partner, had been unexpectedly called away on important business, he had been requested by his Board of Directors to take the matter personally in hand. There was nothing more he could do. Just sit and wait.

CHAPTER 86

I managed to get a seat on an internal flight from Stavanger to Oslo, a one hour west to east trip across the country; then onward from there to Switzerland.

I was satisfied that I had eventually managed to persuade Arthur Broadhurst to investigate, verify and of course endeavour to put a stop to the terrorist activities claimed by Leutnant Bucher.

'Are you serious, Steve?' Broadhurst had said. Then asked, 'Why me?'

'Because there's no one else I can trust, Arthur. I know you're probably going to suggest that I contact Commander Bruce,' I added, 'but the fact is I just don't trust him either.'

The silence on the other end of the phone made me think that I had blown any chance of getting Broadhurst involved. I had no idea how close the working relationship between him and Bruce may have developed. Arthur Broadhurst had certainly seemed to be very pro-Bruce during my own early battles with the policeman.

'No point,' Broadhurst finally said.

Was he saying no to me? For a second, I thought so. Then he went on.

'Commander Bruce just happens to be unavailable at the present time. I've been trying to get hold of him for the last few days. They tell me in London he's unavailable, and may be for some time yet. Oh, and I am advised, when I try calling his mobile, that the number is discontinued. I guess like me, he assumed that this particular case was done and dusted.'

From then on in, Arthur Broadhurst was onboard. In fact he proved to show more enthusiasm for the task than I'd first expected. Through his numerous and, in many cases personal contacts throughout the oil, gas and marine industries, he promised to follow up. What's more, I knew the man had also established a number of very close relationships with influential people within the governments of a number of European countries. What he could do about the targeted offshore installations located further afield, like for example, those up in Russia and over on the other side of the pond, in the Gulf and Brazil, I wasn't so sure. But I knew he would certainly make every effort.

I was even less sure what to make of Commander Bruce's sudden disappearance from the scene. But in fact, I felt happier with him out of it. Maybe I'd been wrong about him. After all he had got his two guys in to help clean things up in Aldvik. I'd learned that the two agents had been more than instrumental in bringing the Norwegian Coastguard and Navy into the picture. If Bruce was one of the baddies he would hardly have sent troops in to disrupt the salvage operation.

Still, with things somewhat under control back home, I felt clear to concentrate on the matters in hand here in Switzerland. Namely, getting to the United Kreditbank and stopping Jorgensen and his overlord from lifting whatever fortune was hidden in its vaults. Exactly how the hell I was going to achieve that, I hadn't the faintest idea. I guess I would just have to adopt the procedure that I had been applying to the situation right from the very start of this whole business. Suck it and see!

CHAPTER 87

'I am afraid you are going to have to return later, Sir.'

He had watched as the group of men dressed in smart dark pin-striped suits exited from one of the private conference rooms. A member of the group had broken off from participation in the ongoing, heated discussion and walking briskly over, was now addressing him directly.

'May I ask why? Surely the details and personal information I have provided are quite legitimate. Not to mention the immediate transfer of the holding bond. I am able to authorise and complete the payment from my lap-top at this very moment.'

'Sir. Of course we can accept the bond payment and we are more than satisfied with your credentials.'

'Then, why can't we proceed with the full transaction?'

'Quite simply, because of the size of your safety deposit box and its top-index priority rating. Which means it is secured in a K-vault.'

'And?'

'All the K-vault units are individually timer protected. By pre-arrangement, that is. When security data is confirmed, an access time is agreed and set. Normally this covers the ability for us to open the particular K-vault unit for a time window of exactly one hour. I am afraid your late arrival and the necessary follow up of your credentials have run well over the stipulated time.'

'So when is the next opportunity going to be?'

'Not for another three hours I am afraid. It will take that time for us to reset access time on the locks for them to activate.'

Both men checked their watches.

The bank executive said, 'You are welcome to wait here. We can offer some light refreshment.'

'That will not be necessary. I need something more substantial. I will return at 4 o'clock. The bond payment transfer will be carried out then. Please ensure everything is ready for me.

'All will be arranged. On your return, Sir, please ask for me personally. My name is Sonberg.' The banker held out his card.

The Boss rose from his leather chair, accepted the business card, picked up his briefcase and without another word marched to the exit.

CHAPTER 88

The cab from the airport pulled up at a vacant rank space in Bahnhofstrasse, just across the way from the main entrance of the United Kreditbank.

I was in the process of counting out a number of crisp Swiss Franc notes from my wallet to pay the cabby when I saw him. All I could do was just halt what I was doing and stare in utter disbelief out of the cab passenger window. I froze.

'Is their something wrong, Mister?' The cab driver asked in a heavily accented voice; turning around to look at me with more of an expression of suspicion than concern. I think he thought I was going to jump out without paying.

'No, nothing's wrong,' I said handing him the cash. 'I just thought I recognised an old acquaintance.' I told him to keep the change. Then, focusing again out of the cab window, I added, 'Do you think I could just sit here for a minute or two?'

The driver took the money. Counted it quickly and then turned in his seat again. This time with a satisfied smile on his face.

'Of course you can stay. Are you OK, mister? What is a quaitince?'

I kept my eyes on the man standing beneath the stone columns framing the entrance to the United Kreditbank. There was no mistaking who it was.

'It's what we call someone we think we know. But don't worry I'm fine - just a bit surprised that's all.'

The man across the road began to descend the few steps to the pavement and turned north on Bahnhofstrasse. I noticed he was limping. It would not take much effort for me to catch him up.

I thanked the driver and got out of the cab.

'Thank you, Mister,' the cabby called out. 'Hope you have good time with your friend.'

'Oh, don't worry yourself about that - I plan on having a very interesting time with my friend.'

Dodging the traffic I crossed Bahnhofstrasse, and on reaching the kerb outside the entrance to the bank, I picked up pace. I didn't want to lose track of the Oberst.

CHAPTER 89

Between the main course and dessert he must have consulted his pocket watch more than a dozen times. He had tried to slow the meal down, but there was still a lot of time to kill. Another hour and a half at least. However, he had discovered he was very hungry. Ravenous in fact. On reflection he realised he had not eaten for twenty-four hours.

So here he was waiting for a coffee and brandy barely twenty minutes after arriving at the restaurant, and being seated at the table. He usually had firm control over most things, but on this occasion his hunger had overruled. He had attacked each course with unbridled vigour.

After leaving the bank he had decided to find an eating place, one within easy walking distance. Piazza Del Monte was a small Ristorante conveniently located nearby. He was not keen to walk any great distance. The pain was troubling him again.

He would have stuck to the main thoroughfare, where there were plenty of suitable restaurants and cafes to choose from, but he had a strange feeling he may have been followed.

Neither the time nor place to be dropping one's guard. He had quickly turned into a side street. Almost a narrow passageway. And stopped to look at the front display of a gentleman's clothing shop. He stood at the window for a few minutes scanning the entrance to the alleyway out of the corner of his eye. A girl turned in. She was tall and attractive and he guessed, in her early twenties, and in a hurry. He kept his focus on the store window as her reflection rushed by. She'd traipsed thirty metres down the lane when he turned to look at her. Standing outside the Piazza Del Monte was a young man, about her age. They greeted each other warmly.

He waited another minute at the shop window, then, having observed no one else turning into the lane, decided to follow in the direction the young lady had chosen. He would eat in the same restaurant. Why not? At least he could keep an eye on the couple - just in case, and at the same time be in a good position to check out any other visitors.

So, here he was. Well fed and watered. The young couple, if they were watching him, then they were superb operators. They had not taken their eyes, and for most of the time, their hands off each other since he had occupied his seat. Apart from two smartly dressed women, carrying expensive and bulging shopping bags, no one else had come through the doors.

It was already well past lunch opening hours. The next flow of diners would not begin to appear until early evening. Nothing to raise his concern had occurred out in the lane either.

He sat quietly enjoying an aromatic brandy and a powerful espresso. The next inspection of the gold pocket watch signalled ten minutes to go. He would move soon.

CHAPTER 90

I couldn't believe it. I'd lost track of the Oberst. After recovering from the mental shock of discovering him up to his neck in all this, I thought at least I would be able to confront him, and with a bit of luck put a stop to his game.

One minute I'd had him clearly in my sights, only fifty metres ahead of me. Then - he was gone!

I knew he couldn't have run very far. The dragging limp he displayed was the obvious result of the gun shot wound he had taken in the gut.

The question was - had he spotted me? Was he already making his escape?

I walked briskly to the intersection where I had last seen him and looked about in all directions. Trying to work out what route he would have chosen. Especially if he had spotted me. But I had no chance of guessing where he'd gone. There were numerous possibilities of course. The conglomeration of shops, offices, cafes and the like scattered along Bahnhofstrasse, presented a dozen possibilities.

My overriding thought at that point was that he had spotted me and had decided to get out of there as quickly as he could.

Then, I remembered! The Oberst had been travelling light. He wasn't carrying a large bag or a suitcase. Most unusual if he was supposed to have made any sort of collection at the United Kreditbank. Particularly, if the treasure in question happened to be gold ingots. So what had he been up to in the bank?

Then it struck me. Of course, he must have been in there with Jorgensen. It would have been Jorgensen with all the details for accessing the vault. All the information he required, that had been relayed to him from the *Panther*.

So that was it. It was over for me. It was Jorgensen, and probably by now, well on his way with the stuff. Or was there just a chance that, if the treasure in the vault was heavy or bulky, then they may have had to make arrangements to ship it out as a consignment. There were a few possibilities. Whatever the answer I decided the only option left for me was to return to the United Kreditbank and see what I could find out about the recent transaction of Jorgensen and his Boss – the Oberst. Perhaps with some co-operation from the bank officials I might just be able to convince the authorities to take me seriously. It was worth a try.

Maybe this wasn't such a long shot. I did have in my possession the details of the Deposit Box and the security codes that I had noted down from the Baton document. Somebody in the bank would surely listen to me. As I said, it was a long shot, but I had to do something if I was going to prevent the funds being released to the maniacs about to attempt to blow up most of the largest oil platforms in the civilised world.

I had to convince somebody that this was a real threat.

CHAPTER 91

He arrived back at the United Kreditbank dead on 4 o'clock. The Executive Manger, Sonberg, was waiting for him.

'There are just a few papers to sign and then I will take you down to the vaults. Oh, and of course we shall need to clear the electronic transfer.'

'I will be ready when you are, Herr Sonberg,' He said.

'Shall we proceed then?'

'By all means.'

'Then if you don't mind,' Sonberg said, pointing across the open floor. 'My office is just over there.'

It took fifteen minutes for him to clear the funds. He used his laptop connected by wireless to the Bank's Broad Band system, to log into an offshore account in the Cayman Islands. They had been notified over there and were expecting the transfer. Jorgensen had set the whole financial thing up. At least he had proved to be efficient if not loyal.

The quiet purring of the telephone on Sonberg's desk heralded the confirmation call.

Sonberg replaced the receiver and said 'It's in place. Thank you very much, Sir. We may now proceed to the vault elevator.'

He followed the Bank Executive across the polished floor to a rank of lifts, in front of which stood a group of uniformed Security Guards. An X-ray screening machine for hand pieces and a walkthrough frame similar to airport security systems was already switched on and running.

He was invited to place his bag on the short conveyor belt and then walk through the screener.

'All cleared, Sir,' One of the Security men announced. 'Pass Code is Alpha Romeo 9266.'

Sonberg nodded and led the way to the lifts.

'Only one elevator accesses the K-Vaults,' Sonberg explained. 'Security reasons. We prefer one way in and one way out.'

He pressed the button and the lift doors opened.

CHAPTER 92

'This data appears to be in order Mr Craig, but I am afraid there is nobody to my knowledge associated with this account, answering to the name of Oberst.'

The Bank Executive named Sonberg explained to me, when he had finished studying the papers containing the data of the vault account and my passport. He seemed to be more amused than unduly alarmed at my claim to be an official of the organisation that now held ownership of the vault contents.

'I quite understand that, Herr Sonberg,' I said. 'But, for strict security reasons our organisation requires that senior personnel have to use independent, coded data. The title Oberst happening to be just one of many.'

I knew I was skating on very thin ice.

'That's most interesting, Mr Craig. But we would require more information before permitting access to this type of account. Contemporary as well as long standing passwords and codes would be expected.'

'As I have already explained, my roll is support only. I have been sent to assist,' I said, realising that this approach was just not going to work. In fact I believed that it would not be long before Herr Sonberg's patience ran out and my next explanation would be to the Swiss police.

So, you can imagine my total surprise when Herr Sonberg said 'Well, Mr Craig, I think it would be best if you spoke to your superior personally.'

I wasn't sure what exactly he meant, but it soon became apparent when Sonberg moved to one of the alcoves and lifted a telephone hand piece from a wall cabinet.

He keyed in a few numbers and spoke.

'Sir, I have a Mr Craig up here.'

So that was it. The Oberst must already be down in the vaults! I was making plans to get out of the bank as soon as I could.

'Yes, Craig,' Sonberg said, and then continued with 'that's correct, from your organisation. Very good, I will send him down.'

So the Oberst wanted me down there. He probably thought it better to have me where he could see me. And I wasn't going to miss that opportunity for the world.

Sonberg replaced the phone and said, 'Your colleague would like you to join him. Apparently he has been expecting you.'

A quick but thorough run through security gave me clearance to proceed down to the vaults. The search and screening proved to be very thorough. So at least I was assured that he would be down there without a weapon.

'Press K-4 in the elevator. At that level, you may proceed to Vault K-4-88. You are expected Mr Craig.

The flashing orange light in the lift indicated I had reached level K-4. The doors opened on to a surprisingly dark alleyway. Compared to the light and airy classical main floor above, this was a dingy, dark and a somewhat depressing network of tunnels. It appeared to have been dug out of the rock below the bank. Parts of the walls were thickly lined with a grey cement screed, but most of the structure was plain poured concrete with outcrops of the indigenous rock protruding at intervals along its length. The dim overhead lights were linked together by exposed cable lines that ran in all directions down the series of tunnels. Each branch disappeared into the poorly lit distance for at least fifty metres. It was eerily silent.

The arrow painted onto a wall mounted sign, indicated the route to Vaults K-80 through K-90. I set off down the tunnel that disappeared into the gloom.

As I passed the numbered steel doors, I could see this was not a regularly used area. In many places the paint covering the metal of the doors was blistered with the corrosion of dampness and age. But obviously thick enough to stand solid for another hundred years. Every steel door I passed, I noticed was firmly shut, until I reached the one identified as K-88. That steel door was partly open. The hinges squealed as I pushed it further inwards and stepped into the vault.

The man had his back to me and was concentrating on the contents of a metal box that lay open on a bench-table in front of him. I could see another door standing open in a recess at the back of the room. He could not have missed the screeching hinge accompaniment of my arrival, but continued undisturbed with whatever was captivating him in the box on the table.

'So Oberst,' I said, 'We have come a long way for this.'

He hesitated for a moment, then straightened up and, turning to face me, with a gun in his hand said, 'And who may I ask is the Oberst?'

The man standing in front of me was holding what looked like a WW2 P218 Luger. I knew he couldn't have brought it down with him. So I guessed he must have retrieved it from the vault. Whether by chance or design, I would never know. Whatever the explanation there was no doubt now that he was pointing it in my direction, and I certainly had no doubt he would use it if necessary. I recalled a similar situation back in Aldvik just a few days ago when the Oberst had put me through the same routine. Only this time the man holding it had quite a different intention, and as it turned out, I knew who he was and what he was capable of.

Oh, I knew him alright. Well, let's say I had seen him before and had heard plenty about him.

Only a few days ago, I recalled watching this man being helped down the gangway of the *Panther*. The poor old guy, the friend of the

Kapitän, the one who had appeared to have been taken ill and put ashore in Aldvik before sailing.

'So, you are Mr Steven Craig,' he said quietly in a low, rather gentle voice. 'I have heard so much about you. And, I understand, you turned out to be quite a troublesome fellow. Although your interference and antics onboard the *Panther* proved to have been more of a help than a hindrance to me personally. Saved me a lot of time, trouble and energy.' He articulated well, with very little sign of an accent, but there was the unmistakable guttural hint of the German.

I studied him as he spoke. He was no young chicken as they say. Far from it. Closer to ninety than eighty and yet sporting a full head of silver grey hair; he could easily have passed for a man in his early sixties. And there was certainly no doubting he was sharp and very much on the ball. His actions were quick and fluid and steady even as he levelled the gun at me. His face bore the signs and more than one scar proclaiming a history of a long and tough life. I already had some idea what this man had been through over the last sixty odd years. Because now I knew exactly who he had to be.

'I am afraid I can't honestly say I would like to take the credit for having been of service to you Herr Bauer. Or should I say Leutnant Günther Bauer, Commander of S-Boot 397.'

'Very good, Mr Craig. I'm impressed. They said you were dangerously smart. Although I must admit you displayed quite a shortfall of rationale when it came to Freya Quisling or as you knew her more intimately, I'm sure, as Karen Olsen.'

'You don't sound very respectful talking about your Fuhrer in that manner.'

'My Fuhrer?' he scoffed. 'You don't honestly think I was really a part of all that New Aryan lunacy? They were all mad. Disillusioned. Every single one of them. Particularly the one calling herself Freya Quisling. Believe it or not she was a damn sight crazier than the original madman she intended to emmulate. Oh! Don't look so surprised Mr. Craig. Adolf Hitler was the bastard responsible for sending me to spend the best part of my life in a Russian gulag. Do you think I would seriously want to get involved with a gang of criminal lunatics like that again?'

'So it was just this stuff you were interested in?' I said, waving at the box on the table.

'My dear friend, if you knew exactly what *this stuff* actually is. What the box you see here on the table and the two identical ones in the vault contain, then I'm sure you would certainly understand what may have captured my interest.'

'So why don't you tell me?'

'I will do better than that my boy. I will show you. You can see for yourself what you are going to help me transport out of here. Quite a lot for one person to handle alone, wouldn't you say? You know your persistent interference always seems to benefit me in one way or another.'

'I can't deny I am more than interested to find out what value can be put on the lives of more than fifty people. The ones I know of that is. And God knows how many more there may have been along the way.'

'Collateral damage Mr. Craig. Collateral damage. About the only New Aryan philosophy I agreed with. That and fate of course. Your friend and his oil rig colleagues just happened to be on the wrong rig, in the wrong place at the wrong time.'

Bauer watched me tense. He realised he had touched a tender nerve and was beginning to get to me.

'Let's be careful now, Mr Craig,' he said levelling the Luger at me and stepping back a safe pace or two. 'I wouldn't wish to be forced to dispense with your services too prematurely. So if you are still interested, perhaps you would like to come and take a closer look. Carefully now,' he said, taking a few safe paces back.

I walked to the table and looked down into the opened container. Even under these conditions and my present predicament I could not disguise the awe that welled up inside me. I was looking down on the most incredible array of immensely valuable treasures. The chest was jam packed and almost filled to the top with jewellery and precious stones of almost every type, shape and design imaginable. Rubies, emeralds, pearls but most of all diamonds. Diamonds of all sizes. The majority of precious stones were inlaid into equally precious metals, forming necklaces, broaches and bracelets and at least three tiaras. I could make out more than a few single stones, once again mainly diamonds, protruding from the sea of gems. And that was just the top surface layer of the chest.

I estimated that the dimensions of the box had to provide a storage volume of at least half a cubic meter. You can get an awful lot of treasure of that kind in a space of that size. The dying Leutnant Bucher had said *a treasure worth 1 billion dollars.* If there were two other casks, containing anything like this lot, then he had certainly not been exaggerating.

'Impressive, don't you think?' Bauer said.

'Very,' I agreed. 'But how are you going to get rid of it, once it's out of this vault I mean?'

'All taken care of,' Bauer answered. 'And in fact your unexpected appearance here has made things a lot easier for me. You see, I had intended to remove just a small quantity at a time. I am in pretty good shape for my age but hauling three boxes of this size out of the bank would have proved somewhat difficult for me. To have attempted that, may also have proved rather risky. You see, my dealer for handling the stones here in Zurich, may become more than interested in by-passing me, if the source were to be revealed. Some of these thieves have no honour, you know. In fact I had even contemplated making this my one and only visit to the vault.'

'What about your man Jorgensen?' I asked 'From what I remember, he appeared to be fit and strong enough to make a few lifts from this place. Surely you could have managed, between the two of you. At least made the effort.'

'Otherwise indisposed. My man Jorgensen, as you call him.' Bauer shrugged.

Disposed of, I thought, probably being the more appropriate description.

'So, I stand in and help you carry all this stuff out of the bank. Then what?'

'Ah, Mr Craig let's not dwell on the details just yet.'

CHAPTER 93

Broadhurst had not slept for thirty-six hours. Not since his middle of the night phone call from Steve Craig. For most of that time he had been glued to the telephone lines. After over fifty inter-European calls and almost as many trans-Atlantic ones, he had got absolutely nowhere.

Most of the people he had approached with Craig's claim of imminent attacks on more than half the world's major offshore oilfields had listened politely and had gently humoured him. The majority of his contacts in the big oil companies were also his good friends. Tried and trusted. But now, he was on their doorsteps asking for these same good friends to take action on what to date, appeared to be based on nothing but unsupported rumour. Of course, almost all of his contacts promised diligently to look into the matter. The majority had prior dealings with Broadhurst. They knew if he said there was a threat *he* truly believed there to be one.

There was no denying that he had a further hard time in explaining why he had not gone through the official channels - the police, the ISD, the government?

If the people on the other side of the pond, the Americans, were generally sympathetic, on the European side, with the Norwegians for example, his reception had not been good at all. Most of what Broadhurst claimed, was sitting right on the doorstep of the Norwegian Storting Parliament. And, not only were a number of their major fields implicated in Broadhurst's terrorist attack theories, but by inference, he had been unable to cover the fact that much of the planning for the pending attacks was being instrumented within Norway. Some very influential people appeared to be involved - and that did not exclude Politicians.

The majority of his contacts promised to take immediate action or at least as much action as they could, without starting a stampede throughout the industry. Broadhurst was promised that security checks would be made and screening of crews, visitors and service suppliers to and from the platforms would be stepped up.

However, the political thing was a completely different story. Not a single politician wanted to hear about getting a thick brown envelope to sanction the destruction of one oil platform let alone a list of some of the biggest oil fields in the world.

Things were not going as Broadhurst had anticipated. He also knew that more than one of the executives and a number of the politicians he had approached would, by now have contacted their good friends further up the line - namely the UK authorities. So it was no surprise to him when his secretary rang through to his office.

'Mr Broadhurst, I have a gentleman on the line who says he wishes to speak to you regarding the latest offshore oil platform issues.'

'Put him through, Alice.'

The line went dead for a second then Broadhurst immediately recognised the voice of the caller.

'What's going on, Arthur?' Commander Bruce asked.

CHAPTER 94

I realised that there were two reasons why Günter Bauer had decided not to shoot me.

The first, and probably the one of least importance to him, was for me to assist him in getting all three vault boxes out in one lift. The second, and by far the greater reason, was to prevent me from drawing the wrong sort of attention to what he was up to. Which is exactly what I'd intended to do as soon as we stepped out of the lift on to the United Kreditbank upper floor.

Once I'd turned up in the bank and started asking questions, he realised he couldn't take the risk of letting me raise the alarm. My helping with the transport of the stones out of the building was just going to be an incidental convenience for him.

There was no doubting his intention to get rid of me. I could see he was still debating whether to do it sooner rather than later.

I guessed he'd come down to the vault with the sole intention of moving as much of the cache as he could carry in a single trip. The rest left locked away for some rainy day. Not forgetting, he now had permanent and unrestricted access to the vault. My arrival on the scene had somewhat changed things for him.

Bauer had been silent for some minutes now. He was probably deciding what to do next. He knew he had to exit the vaults with me in tow. The people up top had seen me come down and would expect to see me return back up. So, for the moment, I guessed I was safe enough.

'Mr Craig,' Bauer said finally. 'I have a proposition for you.'

Now what was coming?

'And that would be?'

'For your assistance in helping me to move the boxes from this vault, I am prepared to reward you handsomely, as they say. Whatever you can carry you can have. You let me do what I have to do and I let you go on your way a very wealthy man.'

I guess Bauer must have been somewhat disappointed with my silence and the cynical expression on my face.

'Oh, come now Mr. Craig,' Bauer pleaded. 'I know you have some personal grievances relating to the *Highlander* Rig. But I can assure you what happened out there was the last thing I wanted.'

'So you think a handful of stones can buy back a life?'

'Maybe not a life but it can buy a far better life for your friend's wife and child.'

I felt the anger welling up inside me. Bauer saw it too as I took a pace towards him, fists clenched.

He lifted the Luger.

'If you'd rather, we can put an end to it, right here and now. Your choice.'

I knew that although he would prefer to keep me alive for as long as possible, at least until he had made it out of the bank, he would not be averse, if pushed, to shoot me and leave me down here.

I had no alternative and said, 'Okay, Bauer. I accept your offer. I'll help you transport this stuff from here, and when I've done that, I'll get out of your hair,' I lied.

'Very wise Mr. Craig. Perhaps you can start by bringing the other two boxes out of the vault.

CHAPTER 95

'How long has it been since Mr. Craig went down to the vaults?' The Oberst questioned Sonberg.

The Oberst had been interrogating the Bank Executive for the past ten minutes. Ever since he and eight members of the Swiss Anti-Terrorist Police had arrived in the main foyer, and hustled thirty bank employees and a similar number of bewildered customers out of the building. With just a few senior staff remaining inside, the main doors were closed and locked shut.

'About an hour ago,' Sonberg replied to the Oberst's question.

'And that would have been around half an hour after Herr Bauer?'

Sonberg nodded and then seemed to stiffen up as he caught sight of three men emerging from an office across the floor and headed towards the intruders. They were senior bank officials one of whom was the man in charge

'My name is Leopold. I am the Bank Director and I require to know what this is all about. On what authority do you have the right to close the doors of this institution?'

'You may inspect my credentials, Herr Leopold,' the Oberst said, displaying his identification. 'But, at this particular time I am fully authorised by the Swiss Security Service,' he said, indicating the armed men in uniform around him.

'I understand that this has something to do with one of our vault account holders.'

'It most certainly has, Herr Leopold. I was just in the process of questioning Herr Sonberg here about that very matter. We need to know what the two gentlemen down in your vault K-4-88 are planning.'

'Are you suggesting a bank robbery is taking place?'

'Actually the robbery took place more than sixty years ago, Herr Leopold,' The Oberst said and watched the roll of the Bank Director's eyes and his glance of irritation directed at Sonberg. Director Leopold knew exactly where this was heading.

'Not another of those misappropriated, wartime wealth claims?'

'I think an appropriate description would be the recovery of the stolen property of millions of murdered Jewish people,' the Oberst said coldly. 'But on this occasion we are looking not only at grand theft on a monumental scale, but more contemporary crimes, including murder and terrorism. So, I suggest, Herr Leopold, if you and your bank wish to come out of this only partly scathed, then you will please award us all the co-operation and assistance at your disposal.'

'Sonberg, deal with this,' the Bank Director ordered, and turning on his heel, headed back to the administration block, the junior managers trailing dutifully behind him.

'What do you require, Sir?' Sonberg asked the Oberst.

The Oberst said, 'I assume that there is only one way out from the vaults. Through the lifts over there?'

Sonberg nodded.

'Good. Then we just wait.'

CHAPTER 96

'The Norwegians are not very happy about all this, Arthur,' Commander Bruce said entering Arthur Broadhurst's office and walking to take up a position that he seemed to have laid claim to over the previous weeks; standing at the window and taking in the view of the city of Aberdeen below. 'Mainly because, from what the people I have spoken to say, nobody seems to know just who may or may not be involved with these damned New Aryans. A number of them even denied ever having heard of them. Who would admit to it at this stage of the game anyway? Most of the key players are dead or have already been pulled.'

'I'm afraid it's a similar story with the offshore operators,' Broadhurst said. 'Everybody promising they are going to follow up but nobody coming back with anything concrete. Of course most of them are running security checks out on the rigs. At least I believe we can assume they are checking for any explosive devices or bomb making equipment carried on board. But of course, there's always the suicide bomber to take into consideration.'

'You could be right. About the suicide bomber I mean,' Bruce said. 'But somehow I don't think so. This is not a fatwa. These are fascist sympathisers, and ones that want to get paid before they perform, if what Steve Craig informed you is correct. So we've got to make sure that isn't going to happen. In short, we ensure that the collaborators *don't* get paid.'

'Let's hope Steve Craig knows what he's doing then,' Arthur Broadhurst said.

CHAPTER 97

From a position against the concrete wall I watched Bauer open each of the other two boxes. The ones that I had carried out from the inner vault. Once I'd set the containers on the table, Bauer again ordered me to back off as far as the concrete wall behind me. He was no fool. He knew I wouldn't miss the first opportunity to take him out.

From where I stood, the contents of the boxes, each of which Bauer opened in turn, looked almost identical to the first. Both were filled almost to the brim with loose precious stones and inset jewellery. I guessed that the gold and silver mountings, themselves would also be worth a fortune.

'We will need a trolley or something to move them altogether,' I commented.

'On the contrary Mr. Craig,' Bauer said. 'As I said, you will carry each one out of here.'

'That means three trips up to the Bank hall.'

'In principle, Mr. Craig, correct,' Bauer said smiling. 'In practice, three trips, yes. Up to the Bank hall? I'm afraid not.'

Bauer dropped and secured the lids of each of the three chests and looked across at me. He still maintained the same fixed smile on his face.

'Did you really think I was going to try and get all this stuff out of the United Kreditbank by using the front door?' he paused. 'Yes, I can see by the look on your face, that you probably did.'

Already I was up with him. I realised that, if he had not planned to take the treasure up and out in the normal way, then he must have a plan to leave from down here somehow.

'So where's the tunnel opening?' I asked.

Showing no surprise, Bauer said, 'Just across the road or should I say under the road. Less than forty metres if you take into account the distance from this position to the front door of the United Kreditbank. You might say as the crow flies.' Bauer was understandably proud of his achievement.

'This is quite a set up,' I said, with genuine interest. 'You must have been preparing this whole thing for some time.'

'Longer than you can imagine, Mr.Craig.'

So that was it. My appearance on the scene had become a temporary inconvenience that the old boy was going to turn to good use. He knew he couldn't let me go, and I guess he wasn't going to risk raising the alarm by firing that old gun he had picked up, down here.

Conclusion? He didn't plan to shoot me just yet.

Game Plan? Engage at the first opportunity.

CHAPTER 98

'They've been down there for almost two hours,' the Oberst said, limping up and down in front of the vault lift doors. You'd better call them. Tell them you are enquiring if they need any assistance, and you would like to know how long they intend to stay down there.' The Oberst consulted his watch. 'Say it's coming up to six o'clock. That you are already closed to the public for normal business, and wish to make arrangements to shut things down for the day.

Sonberg crossed to the lifts, opened the phone box cover, lifted out the receiver and stabbed the buttons on the wall panel. He waited with the phone held to his ear. Half a minute passed.

'They are not answering.' Sonberg shook his head.

'Ring off and try again,' the Oberst ordered.

'Still no reply,' Sonberg said after the second attempt.

'That's it,' the Oberst said and turned to the Squad Leader. 'We are going in!'

The Squad Leader assembled his team.

'Please get the lift back up here, Herr Sonberg. Then I would appreciate if you withdrew. You and your colleagues will need to leave immediately.'

Twice, Sonberg pressed the lift call button. But the floor indicator did not move. The light remained fast, showing that the lift was still down on the vault floor level.

Sonberg said, 'It's not responding,' and he pressed the call button again, a number of times in fact. 'The doors are probably jammed open. They must realise something is wrong.

'Herr Sonberg,' the Oberst said. 'I am afraid the alert was given as soon as Mr Craig made his presence known and was invited down there.'

Sonberg didn't seem unduly surprised. The Oberst had a feeling that Herr Sonberg may have had some previous experience of this sort of thing. Although, probably with less complication.

'Is there another way to get down there?' the Oberst asked. 'Stairs, fire escape or something?'

'It's a secure level,' Sonberg replied, shaking his head. 'Access can only be made to the vaults by the lift itself or through the lift shaft, and if we want to go down the shaft, we will have to winch up the cab first.'

The Oberst shook his head. He wasn't about to go into the safety aspects of the bank's one way in, one way out philosophy. 'No time for that. We cannot delay any longer. What about ventilation down there? Trunking? Piping?'

'There is a system, but I am afraid I am not too familiar with the layout. Although, I do know the fan room is located at the rear of the Bank in the service facility annex.'

It took the best part of another hour for the Security men, aided by a bank maintenance engineer to dismantle the air trunk from the ventilation fan. They removed a bolted flange attached to the wall and exposed the main ventilation distribution shaft. They soon identified the section running down to the vault chambers.

No one seemed to know the exact route of the ventilation system and where it would exit into the vault space beneath the bank. Sonberg explained that, as far as he remembered, there were a number of smaller sections branching over the whole underground area and a few grills supplying air into the main passageways. But, he had no idea exactly where these were located.

'No time to find out,' the Oberst concluded. 'We make one more attempt to call the lift up and check the phone again. Then we go down this way.'

There was a loud clatter as the ventilation grill crashed onto the concrete floor of the vault passageway. A couple of seconds later, the lead Anti-Terrorist Police Guard, the one who had kicked it out, followed. He hit firm ground, and with gun in hand, swept the tunnel passage in both directions.

'All clear,' he called up. And the second man dropped down to join him.

The two men immediately split up, setting off in opposite directions. Each following his instruction. The Oberst had told them they should first determine their exact location. They knew they would find directional signs on the tunnel walls.

'Follow the wall signs. You want K-4-80 to 90.' Sonberg had explained. 'You are looking for Vault 88 each one is individually marked.'

It took no time at all for the two men to establish their location. The signs were numerous and clear. However, after the clatter made in landing from the ventilation trunk, they realised they had sacrificed any element of surprise. The two men in the vault would be waiting for them and, despite the high security screening up top; these guys could well have found a way to arm themselves.

The two men moved quickly along the stone passageway towards vault K-88. At K-87 the lead man waved a halt and both men stood and listened. No sound at all from the open steel door of the next vault up, K-88.

They exchanged hand signals; already having agreed to use standard procedure for this type of entry; into a single exit risk zone.

The lead man passed quickly across the open doorway - checking for signs of any occupancy in the vault, with his gun levelled into the space. The room was empty. In position on the other side of the door opening, he gave the *no detection of enemy*, signal.

On the signed count of three the two men moved into the vault together, weapons raised and ready to fire.

The wall phone from the vault level rang loudly in the main foyer. The Oberst snatched it up and listened.

'No surprise,' he said after receiving the report from one of the Policemen below. 'Don't waste anymore time down there. Bring the lift back up. And don't forget the note.'

A few minutes later the Oberst read the scribbled message on the scrap of paper that the two Guards had found lying on the table top in the vault.

Go buy a hat - just 1 in reception, it read.

'Where's the nearest shop selling hats?' the Oberst called to Sonberg as he marshalled the Security team and headed towards the doors.

'There was a place called Le Chapeau in St. Peterstrasse on the other side. But it's been closed down for some time now,' Sonberg replied and watched the Oberst and the men immediately exit the bank.

CHAPTER 99

I was hoping that the Oberst would be making a grand entry pretty soon. I knew he could not be far behind me. Even though my conclusion for the reason he was hanging around the bank had proved to be totally wrong. My mistake was moving in ahead of him. I knew he must be following up, and would appear soon. At least I hoped that was going to be the case.

My options however had now become somewhat limited. Being handcuffed to a cast iron radiator in the cellar storeroom of a hat boutique was not the most favourable retaliatory position to find oneself in. I guessed the shop must be called Le Chapeau - that was the name printed on most of the dusty stacked cardboard boxes around me.

If the Oberst had got my note he must surely be on his way here.

I'd made my initial trip from the vault, struggling with the first of the three boxes, to the place where the tunnel concrete wall had been breached. There I discovered that Bauer, and I assumed Jorgensen, had broken into the underground tunnel from the basement premises of a hat shop located, in my calculation, a little more than 50 metres away from the bank itself. The opening in the tunnel had been cleverly disguised. Short of hitting the fake stone camouflaged insert with a hammer, it would have been impossible to detect. It was an ingenious plan that Bauer had hatched, but it could have only proved successful if he had the means to get into the vaults in the first place. All the bank security was centred on the security of the individual vaults themselves.

Entry codes, laser alarms and the like. Hence, Bauer's tunnel had not been designed to get into the bank, but to get out of the place – with the booty.

Having set the first box down, and followed closely by Bauer, I had run through the same routine. Tracking back to the vault for the second pick up. On the return trip through the tunnel, it wasn't too difficult for me to extract a slip of paper from an inside pocket in my jacket. Then, on the next and final trip to the vault, to pick up the last remaining chest, I managed to jot a few words onto the paper, and placed it on the table top before I picked up the box. With the box in my arms, and making sure I kept my body between the table and Bauer, blocking his line of sight to the note lying there, I headed back along the tunnel.

We passed the lift, still stuck on this level. Not surprisingly, Bauer had jammed the doors open using a chair from the vault. It was going nowhere, and nobody was coming down or going up that way.

The intercom phone on the wall rang again, but like the time before, Bauer ignored it and motioned that I continue on, retracing our steps back the way we'd come.

No matter how quickly the Oberst would find a way to get down to the vaults and respond to my note, I knew it would not be soon enough to prevent Bauer putting a bullet into me. In fact, I was pretty sure he would not waste much more time, once we'd made our way back into the hat shop basement.

As it turned out, instead of pulling the trigger, Bauer decided to handcuff me to an old cast iron radiator. Well, actually I'd handcuffed myself to it. Bauer wisely continued with his practice of staying well out of my reach when he threw the cuffs across and told me to hook up. He just made sure he kept the Luger on me all the while.

I thought perhaps he may have had some more carrying for me to do. Or, perhaps he didn't want to attract attention by letting off a shot so close to the bustling city streets above.

Then it struck me. Of course! The Luger must be empty - no bullets in it! If it had, surely I would certainly not still be alive at this moment. And, like it or not, I had to face the grim fact that I'd made another serious blunder. I should have realised that, and attempted some retaliation before getting myself cuffed to the damn radiator.

Mistakes like that would almost certainly cost lives in the field. This time it could well be my own life on the line. Maybe I had just lost the touch. But instead of sitting there feeling sorry for myself, I decided to do something about it.

Without another word to me, Bauer had left the cellar. For what purpose and for how long I had no idea. But I realised I had to do something pretty soon. He might just have gone to find ammunition for the Luger or, even more likely, to get another gun - a loaded one this time.

A few hefty tugs on the radiator pipe failed to move the thing even a millimetre. I had already ruled out trying to get the cuffs off. It was solid and clamped tightly around my left wrist. No chance.

I looked around the space. Mostly filled with a variety of old hatboxes. The nearest ones were just within reach of my free hand. But what was I going to do with a cardboard box? There was a two wheel hand trolley propped against a stone pillar but well out of reach. Or was it?

If I could tip it over towards me, I might have a chance of reaching it with my feet.

First I had to get the cardboard boxes lined up. Working with my legs stretched out, I managed to manoeuvre the nearest ones so they lined up with the trolley. My idea was to shunt the train of boxes up against the trolley and push it over. It took a while guiding the line in the right direction. I was able to add a new box each time to the end of the line. I persevered as the furthest boxes began to pile up adjacent to the pillar supporting the trolley. Slowly the weight came on to the frame and it began to tip. A few extra kicks saw the whole thing tipping. Finally it tumbled over, hitting the concrete floor with a clatter.

If Bauer was nearby, he couldn't have missed it. I waited. No sign of him. Wherever he was and whatever he was up to, I had to assume it was not going to prove to be to my advantage.

The trolley was now within reach. I was able to hook my foot into the handle and then drag the thing across the floor to grab with my free hand. I pulled it to me.

So, I'd got it. Now what was I going to do with the damned thing. Turn it into a weapon? Hopefully, yes. One of lethal capability? Not quite so easy.

There would be little point in trying to lift the trolley and throw it as a weapon. Too heavy to lift with one arm shackled to the radiator. I turned the thing over and noticed that there was a steel spine attached to the rear section - a device obviously designed to support a central weight, when the trolley was used in a horizontal position. The interesting thing was that the strip of steel, about half a metre long and 5cm wide, was detachable. I had it disconnected in seconds. So, now what? A sword? Very possible at close quarters, but I knew that was never going to happen. Bauer, up to now hadn't stepped within two metres of me. A spear maybe? I weighed it in my hand. Strong but too light. It would be difficult to throw accurately, and could easily be deflected by someone expecting a retaliation from the man he was about to shoot. No, it had to be in the form of some kind of knife - a throwing knife.

However, there were two major drawbacks. For one, the bar was far too long. Secondly, it had no point. I knew I might be able to shorten it, but getting a point on it? Virtually impossible. I decided to tend to the first problem first.

Jamming a good length of the steel bar in between the radiator cast iron fins, and using all my strength, I levered the bar downwards. The metal was not so thick. It yielded more easily than I'd expected. I pulled it to form a right-angle, and then turning it 180 degrees, I jammed it back into the radiator gap. Forcing down again, I bent the steel back in the opposite direction.

It took longer than I'd anticipated and absorbed far more strength than I thought I was capable of providing. But, each time I turned it and heaved down on the bar, it got easier. Eventually I began to feel the steel starting to fail. First a minute rupture appeared in the metal at the edge of the bar, then with the effort becoming easier on each stroke, I could see the formation of a crack beginning to run across the surface. Encouraged by this success, I swiftly swung the bar back and forth until the reward came. It snapped into two pieces.

Keeping the longer of the two sections by my side, thinking it might come in handy as a reserve - I concentrated on the shorter piece. It was just over 25 centimetres long, with a slight curved lip along the line of the fracture. No choice there, that would have to be the handle end. The other end was square and blunt. There was no way it could pierce the cloth of say a suit for example, like the one Bauer was wearing. It would never reach the vital organs. Therefore, the choice of target proved to be no difficult a decision. If I was going to take Bauer out with the homemade throwing knife, then there was only one point to aim for. In short, the bastard's head.

CHAPTER 100

'The place is all shut up. It looks deserted,' the Senior Police Guard reported to the Oberst over the hand radio phone.

The Oberst, had decided to stay in the vicinity of the Union Kreditbank, giving himself the option of safest route into the Boutique. He had a feeling that the vault tunnel might prove the better. By now, whoever was holed up in the hat shop would have noticed the activity taking place on the road outside, and would realise they were cut off.

It had taken them some time for the Police to get the road closed off to traffic, and even longer to get rid of the curious melee of pedestrians, some still milling around and rubbernecking behind the temporary road barriers set up. The aim had been not to alarm whoever was inside the boutique. But they would only have to look out through the partly boarded-up front window to see nobody inside the place was going anywhere.

'Could they have already left?' the Oberst asked.

'Possible,' came the reply. 'But according to the proprietor of a market stall directly opposite, nobody has gone in or come out of the hat boutique for some time and certainly not today. The guy has been attending his sidewalk stall since early morning. When he left it for a few minutes his assistant took over. Both report definitely no activity of any kind across the road.'

'Any exit at the rear?'

'Negative - building backs on to shops on the adjoining street. No way out on that side. We checked.'

'Then I guess they are still inside,' the Oberst said. 'I wonder why.'

'Counting the cash from the vault,' the Security Guard suggested.

'If it was cash, which I very much doubt, considering the vault has been shut up for about sixty-five years. Any cash in there would have long passed its use-by date.'

'Gold then? That's the stuff that just goes on forever and gets more valuable in the process and is usually stored in bank vaults.'

'If you're right, then nobody is going anywhere in a hurry. The next phase is going to have to be some form of heavy transport.'

'So, what happens to Mr. Craig?' the Security Guard sounded genuinely concerned.

The Oberst was about to reply that Steve Craig was quite capable of looking after himself, but he knew that Steve was in a very tight spot this time. The inactivity coming from the boutique was cause for concern.

'Keep cover here,' the Oberst ordered. 'I am going back into the bank.'

CHAPTER 101

Günther Bauer stirred and slowly regained full consciousness. He was lying stretched out on the floor of the hat boutique, where he had fallen.

Struggling into an upright position he came to his senses and looked at the time on a wall clock opposite. He had been out for nearly half an hour. The attacks were coming more frequently now and lasting longer. He promised himself he would seek proper medical attention when he was finished with all this. He certainly would be able to afford the very best.

As his head cleared he rose to his feet. Apart from a slight headache he felt fine again. In any case, this was no time to start feeling sorry for himself.

The attack had hit him just as he was transferring some of the stones from the cask into a holdall. His plan was to head for Alexander's place and start negotiations with the fence. If that went without trouble, he would give it a few days and return here to collect another load.

Bauer had planned all this in advance. He had taken out a one year lease on the hat boutique, after conveniently arranging for the business to fail and finally close its doors. He had also made sure that Jorgensen was kept in the dark about that arrangement. Bauer wasn't surprised at Jorgensen's treachery, although it was an inconvenience. He had been relying on Jorgensen to do most of the leg work. Then, like the others, he would be dispensed with at the right moment. Fortunately, the lad now chained to the radiator in the cellar, had taken over. But he too had outlived his value.

Bauer decided he now needed to do what he'd planned when the blackout overtook him. He picked the Luger up off the floor, checked the clip and headed for the cellar.

CHAPTER 102

The blunt end throwing knife was ready. I'd practiced rotating it a few times to get the feel and weight. If I could draw Bauer close enough, I stood a chance, although I knew I was going to need a lot of strength and faultless accuracy.

I adjusted my position on the floor. Stance and balance vital. I tried to concentrate on preparing myself but I was now becoming distracted by a foul odour seeping into the room. Unfortunately, it was a stench I recognised and had experienced on numerous occasions before. Definitely the miasma of human putrefaction.

It came as no real surprise to me that there could be a corpse rotting down here somewhere. My suspicions grew, and together with the increasing strength of the foul smell, were soon confirmed. Across the floor, I could see where I had been shunting the cardboard hat boxes, that I had displaced a large black plastic cover. Through a tear I must have made in the end, I could see a pair of boots poking through. In fact two pairs protruded. Not just the boots alone. These were still attached to the wearers' feet. What I could smell permeating through the cellar was coming from the bag containing two corpses. I guessed Bauer had not knocked the hole into the vault on his own. I also guessed that when the job had been accomplished he'd had no further use for the diggers.

'Mr. Craig, will you ever give up?' Bauer's voice echoed around the stinking space. 'It would appear that I can't leave you on your own for even a few minutes.'

He still had the Luger, and from the intent registered on his face, I could tell it was loaded and that he was ready to use it.

Bauer kicked a few of the boxes out of the way and moved closer. I noticed that he seemed to be having some difficulty in moving. Now much slower and stiffer. The gun also wavered in his veined hand. He was going to have to come nearer to me, to be sure of a lethal shot. All to my advantage. Not much, but better than nothing.

'I see you were planning to defend yourself with these,' Bauer said, kicking a couple of the boxes out of his path and at the same time trying unsuccessfully to disguise his sudden physical limitations. 'Not providing much stopping power for a Luger bullet, or were you just going to cower behind them out of sight?' He didn't expect an answer and added, 'Also, I notice you have managed to retrieve a hand trolley. What scheme did you have in mind to employ that contraption? Were you going to throw it at me, perhaps?'

Bauer turned his head towards the black plastic bag and the protruding boots.

'I see you have uncovered some ex-colleagues of mine. They don't smell so sweet anymore. Not that they exuded any better fragrance when they were alive and digging through that wall for me,' Bauer said holding his nose. The stench was even getting to him. But, I could see he had already decided it was time for him to put an end to the jokes, and me. So consequently, it was time for me to do my bit.

I moved into the crouch position I had practiced, and steadying my body, I lifted the steel bar. Bauer's hand was still shaking when he started to raise the gun to aim at me, but he was too late. I raised the bar above my head, and holding myself as steady as I could, I threw it across the room, at Bauer. The target – his head.

In slow motion, I watched the missile on its way through the air. And, I saw it hit home. As the blunt end smashed into Bauer's left eye, he instinctively fired off a round from the Luger. The bullet ricocheted harmlessly off the wall behind me as Bauer, groaning with pain, fell backward across the stacked pile of boxes.

I realised that the chances of killing him outright like that were remote and I could see by his writhing on the floor that I had not succeeded. He had stopped groaning but continued to thrash about. The steel bar had fallen from his face when he'd hit the ground. I could see the damage it had done. There was a bloody gaping hole where his left eye used to be. But now, there was nothing more I could do. Bauer was lying well out of reach. I contemplated trying to throw the trolley, but I knew that would not achieve the desired effect, even if I could reach him with it.

Slowly the agitated movements stopped and I watched Bauer pulling himself up into a sitting position. He lifted a hand to feel the damaged eye and then, with blood running through his fingers, he reached into a trouser pocket and pulled out a handkerchief. Amazed, I watched the old man actually stuffing the handkerchief into the gapping hole that once had been the socket holding his left eye. I had to give it to him, the man was tough. I guess he must have to have been.

'A good effort, Mr Craig,' Bauer croaked, and struggled to his feet. 'But, not quite good enough.'

There were only seconds left now. Bauer started to kick the cardboard boxes clear as he searched for the Luger that he'd released and sent flying to the floor on the way down. My options had completely run out. In a desperate last attempt, I grab one of the handles of the steel trolley and pulled it towards me. It was far too heavy for me to lift, let alone throw it as a missile. Instinctively, I manoeuvred it in front of me. Perhaps a lucky ricochet off it? Well maybe not. The only sure thing I remember was that there was certainly no life time experience passing through my mind and no bright light showing at the end of a tunnel. If anything it was a catalogue of my recent blunders. I guessed at the end, when it counted most, the combat skills I had built up over twenty years in action, seemed to have departed and this time it was going to be for good.

'So, Mr Craig,' Bauer said in a tone that told me he had retrieved the gun, 'time for us to finally part company. For real this time.'

I held the trolley in front of me like a piece of armour, more as a temptation to draw Bauer closer. I was literally clasping at straws.

In fact, Bauer did shuffle a little closer. I heard the nearest boxes being skidded to one side. Then, I waited - not for the shot - I knew I probably wouldn't even hear that - I guess I was just waiting for the end.

CHAPTER 103

The shot came.

And I did hear it.

But I didn't feel a thing.

For a second, I thought Bauer had missed and would most certainly try again. I decided to keep the shield up.

The second shot never did come. Just a dull thud and then a recognisable voice.

'How many more times am I going to have to pull you out of the deep?'

I dropped the trolley to look across the room at the Oberst standing there holding a Walther PPK; a huge grin on his face.

'We have to stop meeting like this,' I said.

'I can go along with that. Provided you promise to avoid getting into any more messes like this,' the Oberst said, kicking his way through the scattered boxes to where Bauer was stretched out on the ground, lying on his back, motionless. I watched as the Oberst bent down at Bauer's side and felt for a pulse in the neck.

'Is he dead?' I asked.

'No,' the Oberst replied as he started to rummage in Bauer's jacket pockets. 'But he's just how I prefer him to be at the moment. Out of action. Nasty hole in the eye, though. I suppose you had something to do with that,' he said, kicking the home made throwing knife to one side.

'A man's gotta do, what a man's gotta do,' I said as I watched the Oberst pulling the key to my handcuffs out of one of Bauer's pockets. He threw it over and I released the cuffs and rose to my feet.

Stepping over the boxes I joined the Oberst who was still crouched down by Bauer's motionless body. I was surprised to see how frail Bauer appeared. He looked all of his eighty odd years; wizened and somewhat grotesque with the blood soaked handkerchief protruding from his eye socket.

'We'd better get him out of here. If only to escape the stink,' the Oberst said nodding at the plastic body bag. 'Is that what I think it is, a dead body?'

'Two actually,' I said. 'Redundant tunnel diggers.'

The Oberst shook his head, and reached for his walkie-talkie.

'It's all clear in the boutique. Target is down. We need medics and ambulance immediately.'

The message was answered and the orders confirmed and passed on over the airways. Almost immediately, we heard the front door of the boutique upstairs being broken in and the clatter of boots as the Swiss Security Guards descended the cellar steps.

It was bedlam for half an hour as the various services entered and exited the building. The medics arrived and checked on Bauer. In addition to the missing eyeball, Bauer had sustained a gunshot wound to the shoulder. The one delivered by the Oberst's PPK. The bullet had passed clean through, front to back, but the impact had been enough to knock him out cold. Satisfied he was stabilised, the medics stretchered him up the stairs and out of the hat shop.

At the same time a second group of men had uncovered the rotting bodies from under the plastic. After a quick examination by a couple of Swiss crime scene investigators, the two corpses were bagged and carried up out of the cellar. Most of the stench followed them out.

'So what's in the steel boxes?' the Oberst enquired after the contingent had departed and the atmosphere in the cellar started to become a little less grisly.

I told him, 'Take a look for yourself. The other two are identical. Inside and out.'

He walked across the room and released the clips and raised the lid of one of the rusted containers.

'Now that's what I call treasure!' He dug his hand in among the stones, grabbing a handful. After studying them in his palm for a minute or so, he let them spill back down into the chest. Even the ripple of precious stones hitting precious stones sounded lavish. 'No wonder these guys were more interested in the contents here than the gold bars buried on the *Torvald.*'

'Yes,' I agreed with the Oberst, 'but you can see now why they wanted so desperately to get their hands on the Baton.'

'If there are two more casks filled like this one,' the Oberst said, 'then there must be a fortune far exceeding the bullion value, and at a tiny fraction of the weight. Bauer and Jorgensen certainly had their priorities right. All they needed was a few suitcases and not a fleet of trucks.'

'Speaking of Jorgensen, what's happened to him?'

'Up until an hour ago, I wouldn't have been able to throw any light on his whereabouts,' the Oberst replied. 'Then I got the report that came in from the Swiss Police, that Jorgensen's body had been discovered in a room at a Zurich hotel called the Seiden. He had been knocked about a bit and finished off with a bullet in his head. I guess Bauer got to him first. Strange thing too, they tell me that Jorgensen was lying on the floor with a dozen or so boxes of Swiss chocolates scattered around him. He must have had a mighty sweet tooth as you Brits would say.

'So Bauer decided to go solo,' I said.

'Probably his plan all along. Until you arrived on the scene and upended things. Obviously forcing him to change his plan. He must have guessed you had probably alerted others. Like me, for example.'

'Why didn't you come in through the tunnel in the first place?' I asked.

'Too risky at the time. That hole in the concrete back there is far too small. Easily defended from this side. I didn't want any of the Swiss Security guys or me for that matter, getting it as soon as they poked their head through. Also, I wasn't sure exactly what condition you were in. No, I had decided early on that whatever was in the bank vault, would have to be brought out, at some time, through the front of the shop. After reading your note telling us you had only one contender, I decided to chance coming in from the tunnel.'

'OK, that all makes sense, and I am most grateful,' I said, 'but how did you come to be here in Zurich in the first place? I thought you'd gone to ground when I discovered nobody up in Aldvik seemed to have any idea of your existence even.'

'Very simple really,' the Oberst smiled. 'My people were able to intercept the signal sent from the *Panther*. I probably got the message that there was something of value in the vaults of the United Kreditbank, around about the same time as you. However, I was still recovering from the gut wound, which, luckily turned out not to be as serious as we first thought. Painful, of course, but I was soon fit enough to follow this up.'

'How did you find out about me?' I asked.

'Old friend of yours.' The Oberst grinned. 'Commander Bruce said he'd been in touch with Broadhurst.'

'So you followed on.'

'And the rest, as they say, is history.'

CHAPTER 104

It had taken forty eight hours for the Swiss doctors to patch up Günther Bauer. They'd repaired the bullet wound in his shoulder but nothing could be done about his eye. The eyeball had been totally destroyed. The handkerchief had held what was left of it in the socket but it was beyond repair.

Despite the injuries Bauer had sustained, he still appeared to be displaying a relentless strength and determination to survive. Both the Oberst and I were amazed to witness the recovery of a man who had appeared to be on death's door the last time we had seen him being carried from the cellar on a stretcher. Although, as they say, appearances can sometimes deceive.

Apart from the patch over a wad of dressing covering his left eye, and his arm hung up in a sling across his chest, he didn't look too bad at all. What's more he displayed no animosity whatsoever to the two visitors who had played the major roles in his downfall. Not to mention the loss of around a billion dollars in fine gemstones, and of course, an eye.

'Ah! My two assailants!' he laughed as we entered. 'I have been waiting for you.'

'So you've been expecting us?' the Oberst said. 'What made you think we would want to *see* you?

'Oh, come now Herr Oberst, you know as well as I do that there are a lot of unanswered questions. And no one left but me to provide the answers. You had no choice, you had to come.'

Ignoring Bauer's standard German choice of address, the Oberst said, 'Since you are in this accommodating frame of mind Herr Bauer, perhaps you would care to tell us how to ensure that one or more of your mad band isn't standing by at this very moment awaiting an instruction to detonate a bomb on one or more offshore installations?'

'Surely you must have found out by now that the arrangement was, that nothing goes ahead until the hard cash is deposited in the perpetrators' private bank accounts. And, with you having relieved me of the source of funding for that cash, surely it would be simply a case of 'no money, no honey.' Let's all go home.'

'You seem to be taking it all rather lightly, Leutnant Bauer,' I said.

'Ah. The inimitable Mr Steven Craig without whom I may have been sitting now on my own desert island in the sun, drinking the finest champagne. Not a bad ending for a lowly German Krigsmarine Leutnant.'

'As I said. You appear to be taking it lightly. Although I must admit I didn't expect to witness any significant sign of remorse from you.'

'Remorse? Never!' Bauer snarled. It was the first time since we'd entered, that the smile had disappeared from his face, and the anger in his voice seemed more deadly than I'd ever heard. 'Remorse?' it was a question again. 'Regret perhaps, but never remorse.'

'So the regret you feel. Is for your actions?' the Oberst enquired. 'For the innocent lives you've taken?'

'The regret is not for what I did, but for what I did not do.'

'And that is?'

The Oberst's question hung in the air.

'Succeed Herr Oberst, succeed,' Bauer said finally.

'Then, getting back to my question. How can we be sure that your fanatics won't continue to act for their cause? The New Aryan cause.'

At that point, Bauer began to laugh. Loud, almost hysterically. For a moment I thought he might have suddenly snapped. Then, he stopped and just lay on the bed shaking his head. When he did speak, something of the anger had resurfaced in his voice.

'The New Aryans, the neo-Nazis,' he sneered. 'Do you think I give a damn about that herd of lunatic fanatics? They were nothing compared to the true German Reich. And Quisling? What did he bequeath to the great, new order? I'll tell you. Nothing. Nothing but a tainted title and a generation of misfits.'

I could see by the expression on the Oberst's face that he was as surprised as I was at Bauer's outburst.

But Bauer wasn't finished.

'The real Fuhrer, the only Fuhrer, Adolf Hitler put his misguided faith in Vidkun Quisling. If things hand gone differently - according to plan, Quisling would have inherited the new Reich and would have had the financial resources and support to re-establish it. Instead of that it was bequeathed to this mad bunch, led by his disillusioned offspring jumping on the band wagon.'

'Then, your aim was not to regenerate a new Reich?' I said.

'Young man,' Bauer turned his head and focused his one good eye on me. 'As I have already said, there was only one Reich and only one Fuhrer, and neither did much for me. I lost my faith in both a very long time ago. My interest in the New Aryans went only as far as they could assist me in getting my hands on the Fuhrer's Baton, from the *Torvald*. I knew what was inside that Baton and I don't mean the Fuhrer's last will and testament. That was going to prove to be something of value for the historians to mull over. It meant nothing to me. I wanted those bank details.'

'So you didn't mind breaking your Fuhrer's trust by opening the Baton and stealing the access data?' I questioned, and not waiting for a response, I carried on. 'So you read the Bank stuff and even wrote it all down, I suspect. But then you hadn't counted on S-Boot 397 itself taking a hit.'

'Clever deduction, Mr Craig,' Bauer said, pulling himself up in the bed. 'But you are only partly right. I did read the bank stuff, as you call it, and I did write it all down. The details had all been recorded in my log book. But after unexpectedly closing action with a British E-Boat as you called them, I was forced to abandon S-397. Needless to say I lost the battle. My ship went down. It was then I carried the logs and the Fuhrer's Baton into the sea with me.'

'And, at that point the *Torvald* came to the rescue,' I said.

'Spot on again, Mr Craig,' Bauer smiled at me, before continuing. 'Captain Siverson pulled me and what was left of my crew out of the sea. We had been in the water for ten hours. Of course I did not realise at the time that his ship was loaded with gold bullion or that he had no intention of delivering any of it to the United Kingdom. I still had the Baton safe and sound but my log books had suffered badly, being immersed for so many hours in seawater. Only part of the original bank data was legible.'

'But…' I began.

Bauer raised his uninjured arm to stop me, and said, 'I know I still had all the details rolled up in the Baton. But, I was in pretty bad shape, after so long in the water. In fact, I was close to dying. So while I was recovering, the Baton was locked safely away in the *Torvald's* safe.'

There was a long pause as Bauer stared silently into space. I guess he was thinking of what might have been. Finally he took up the tale again.

'By the time I was fit enough the *Torvald* had moved well back into Norwegian waters. Not far off the coast from Aldvik. And, then fate struck again with a vengeance. The *Torvald* hit a mine - one of ours this time. We managed to get a lifeboat away and made it to the shore just North of Aldvik. I headed back to join our occupation forces but, in a few months it was all over. Unfortunately for me, it was the Russians who got to me first. The rest you know.'

'Just one more thing,' I said. 'When, you returned to Norway after so many years, how were you able to pinpoint the exact location of the *Torvald*?'

'Fascinating question,' Bauer said, enthusiastically pulling himself further up on the bed. The question had fired his memory. 'And a fascinating answer. You see, as fortune would have it, on the day the *Torvald* hit the mine, I was up on the bridge with Siversen, the Captain. He had an old sextant up there. Never bothered to use it. Always running close enough to the coast to navigate by 'dead reckoning'. As it was coming up to midday and the sky was crystal blue, I thought it might be interesting to take a sight. I did just that and pinpointed our position exactly. A few seconds later we hit the mine. Those longitude and latitude co-ordinates were fixed in my mind, and stayed with me for 60 years.'

Nobody said a word for a few minutes. Then the Oberst spoke.

'A very interesting tale, but no happy ending for you Bauer.' The Oberst spoke without even a hint of sympathy. 'I am not looking for remorse but I would like you to make up for the innocent lives you have destroyed. You are going to spend a long time in prison.'

'On the contrary,' Bauer replied, 'I am going to spend a very short time in prison, if I even get there at all.'

I looked across at the Oberst and raised my eyebrows. What was coming now?

'You obviously have not been talking to the right doctors here, Gentlemen. You see I have been diagnosed with terminal brain cancer. They give me just weeks; not months even. So I am afraid I will hardly experience a trial let alone incarceration.'

'Then what about helping us to clear this up? What have you got to lose?' the Oberst said.

'In what way?' Bauer threw the question back.

'By providing us with information on the New Aryan network. Who they are, where they are. I know the front line leaders are out of it, but what about the politicians, the business people, the offshore operators?'

Another long silence. Then ex-Leutnant Günther Bauer made a final decision and spoke.

'I have nothing more to say to you on this matter, gentlemen.'

AUTHOR'S NOTE

The Quisling Legacy is a work of fiction. The only real characters referred to in the book are Vidkun Quisling himself, Adolf Hitler and Eva Braun. Whether or not they were close friends, or that Quisling ever took part in a secret marriage is pure fantasy.

However, there are a number of very true and significant events that actually took place.

The Germans did invade Norway on 9th April 1940, and things certainly didn't go according to plan. One of Germany's newest heavy cruisers the *Blücher*, was sunk in the Oslo Fjord by a Norwegian shore battery.

The German attack was delayed long enough by the defending forces, for the Norwegian Royal Family, the Government Ministers, and the country's total Gold Reserves to be transported out of Oslo, to the north of Norway.

Eventually all, including the gold, were shipped across the North Sea to Britain.

Most of the Norwegian Gold bullion, about 50 tons, was carried across by British Royal Navy ships, but some was transported in smaller Norwegian vessels, similar to the book's fictional *Torvald*.

Very much a reality, are the coastal express ships, like the *North Star* of the story. These vessels carry tourists from all over the world. They sail from Bergen, up the Norwegian coast, viewing the spectacular sights along the route and way up into the Arctic Circle.

Finally, Major Vidkun Quisling, as he was known then, took control of the Norwegian Government in 1940. He had established the nationalist party, National Samling, years before, and was appointed by Hitler as Minister President after the German invasion. He was tried as a traitor in 1945 and executed by firing squad.

Lightning Source UK Ltd.
Milton Keynes UK
03 April 2010

152315UK00001B/206/P